WHEN ALL SEEMS LOST

WHEN ALL
SEEMS LOST

WILLIAM C. DIETZ

THE BERKLEY PUBLISHING GROUP
Published by the Penguin Group
Penguin Group (USA) Inc.
375 Hudson Street, New York, New York 10014, USA
Penguin Group (Canada), 90 Eglinton Avenue East, Suite 700, Toronto, Ontario M4P 2Y3, Canada
(a division of Pearson Penguin Canada Inc.)
Penguin Books Ltd., 80 Strand, London WC2R 0RL, England
Penguin Group Ireland, 25 St. Stephen's Green, Dublin 2, Ireland (a division of Penguin Books Ltd.)
Penguin Group (Australia), 250 Camberwell Road, Camberwell, Victoria 3124, Australia
(a division of Pearson Australia Group Pty. Ltd.)
Penguin Books India Pvt. Ltd., 11 Community Centre, Panchsheel Park, New Delhi—110 017, India
Penguin Group (NZ), 67 Apollo Drive, Rosedale, North Shore 0632, New Zealand
(a division of Pearson New Zealand Ltd.)
Penguin Books (South Africa) (Pty.) Ltd., 24 Sturdee Avenue, Rosebank, Johannesburg 2196,
South Africa

Penguin Books Ltd., Registered Offices: 80 Strand, London WC2R 0RL, England

This is an original publication of The Berkley Publishing Group.

Copyright © 2007 by William C. Dietz.
Text design by Kristin del Rosario.

First edition: October 2007

Library of Congress Cataloging-in-Publication Data

Dietz, William C.
    When all seems lost / William C. Dietz—1st ed.
        p.   cm.
    ISBN 978-0-441-01524-5
    1. Space warfare—Fiction.   I. Title.
    PS3554.I388W45   2007
    813'.54—dc22   2007012756

PRINTED IN THE UNITED STATES OF AMERICA

10   9   8   7   6   5   4   3   2   1

For Ensign Jessica Anne Dietz USN.
With love and respect. You are truly amazing.

ACKNOWLEDGMENT

Many thanks to Jeffrey T. Slotstad for his expert advice concerning the creation, maintenance, and destruction of space elevators. Technical errors, if any, are the exclusive property of the author.

1

Surprise, the pith and marrow of war.

—*Admiral of the Fleet Lord Fisher*
Standard year 1906

ABOARD THE CONFEDERACY DESTROYER ESCORT DE-11201, THE *LANCE*, IN HYPERSPACE

An almost palpable sense of tension filled the control room as the *Lance* prepared to exit hyperspace and enter a solar system where anything could be waiting. As with all Spear-Class ships, the Executive Officer and the navigator sat to either side of the captain within a semicircular enclosure. The rest of the bridge crew were seated one level below in what was often referred to as "the tub." All wore space suits, with their helmets racked beside them. "Five minutes and counting," Lieutenant j.g. "Tink" Ross reported as he eyed the data that scrolled down the screen in front of him.

"Roger that," Lieutenant Commander Hol Tanaka acknowledged calmly, as he stared at the viewscreen and the blank nothingness of hyperspace beyond. The naval officer had thick black hair, almond-shaped eyes, and a compact body. The *Lance* was his first command, and even though the DE was older than he was, Tanaka was proud of both the ship and his crew. "Sound battle stations. . . . Bring primary and secondary weapons systems online. . . . And activate the defensive screens. All Daggers will stand by for immediate launch. Give me a quick scan as we exit hyperspace, followed by a full-spectrum sweep, and a priority-alpha target analysis."

The ship's Executive Officer, Lieutenant K.T. Balcom, responded with a pro forma "Aye, aye, sir," but there was no need to actually do anything, because the orders had been anticipated, and the crew was ready. What *couldn't* be anticipated, however, was what the DE would run into as it entered normal space off Nav Beacon CSM-1802. Because even though it was statistically unlikely, there was always the possibility that the *Lance* would exit hyperspace within missile range of a Ramanthian warship. *Which, come to think of it, is exactly what we're supposed to do,* Tanaka thought to himself. *So that the rest of the battle group will have time to drop hyper and respond while the bugs clobber us!* The thought brought no sense of resentment. Just a determination to succeed. Not just for the Confederacy, but for Tanaka's parents, who had been among thousands killed when the bugs glassed Port Foro on Zena II.

Then the time for reflection was past as the last few seconds ticked away, and DE-11201 entered the Nebor system, which was only a hop-skip-and-a-hyperspace-jump away from the battle group's final destination inside the sector of space controlled by the Clone Hegemony. Stomachs lurched as the ship's NAVCOMP shut the hyperdrive down, and the *Lance* entered normal space.

What followed took place so quickly that Tanaka, his crew, and the ship's computers were just beginning to process what was waiting for them when ten torpedoes scored direct hits on the destroyer escort and blew the ship to smithereens. All that remained to mark the point where the ambush had taken place was a steadily expanding constellation of debris and bursts of stray static.

There was no jubilation aboard the Sheen vessels that had been positioned around the nav beacon for more than one standard month. Because the formerly free-ranging computer-controlled ships were entirely automated and therefore incapable of emotion.

But crewed or not, the remote-controlled ships made excellent weapons platforms, a fact that was central to Commodore Ru Lorko's plan. And, as luck would have it, the stern if somewhat eccentric naval officer was not only awake at the precise moment when the *Lance* was destroyed, but present in the *Star Reaper*'s small control room as well. Like all Ramanthians the naval officer had big compound eyes, a pair of antennae that projected from the top of his head, a hooked flesh-tearing beak, and a somewhat elongated body. It stood on two legs, and was held erect by a hard exoskeleton. Which in Lorko's case had been holed in battle and patched with a metal plate. A shiny rectangle that had given rise to the nickname, "Old Iron Back."

There was a burst of joyful pincer clacking that could be heard throughout the ship as the destroyer's crew celebrated an easy victory. But that came to an end when Lorko spoke over the ship's intercom system. "Do not be fooled!" the officer cautioned. "That was the easy part," he reminded the crew. "It's possible that the destroyer escort was on a solo mission. But, if this is the moment we have been waiting for, then the DE was little more than the tip of a very long spear. Prepare yourselves and know this: He who fails to do his best will feel the full weight of my pincer!"

And every member of the crew knew that Lorko was not only serious, but *fanatically* serious, since the commodore, like approximately 20 percent of the Ramanthian officer corps, was a member of the rigid, some said inflexible *Nira* (Spirit) cult. A semireligious group determined to live their lives in accordance with the *Hath*, or true path, which required each adherent to follow a very strict code of behavior. One that equated surrender with cowardice, mercy with treachery, and love for anything other than the Ramanthian race as weakness. Which explained why Lorko, like so many other members of the *Nira*, had severed his relationships with his mates.

But what *wasn't* apparent to the crew was what the straightbacked officer felt deep inside. Which was a tremendous sense of relief and anticipation. Because in order to gain command of the Sheen ships, the carrier *Swarm*, and half a dozen smaller vessels, Lorko had been forced to go straight to Grand Admiral Imba for approval. Thereby offending a number of superiors as well as risking what had been a successful career on what many considered to be a stupid idea. Because the whole notion of waiting for an enemy convoy to drop out of hyperspace struck many as not only a tremendous waste of time but a poor use of scarce resources. Which was why Lorko had been given exactly thirty standard days in which to try his plan before returning to fleet HQ for reassignment. Now, three full days *past* the end of his allotted time, Lorko had what he had gambled on: *a victory*. Not a major victory, but a victory nonetheless, which might be sufficient to forestall a court of inquiry. Or, as Lorko had just explained to the crew, the Confederacy DE could be the precursor of a much larger force. Which, were he to destroy it, would not only vindicate the naval officer but quite possibly result in a promotion. But with the seconds ticking away, it was time to take action. "You know what to do," the commodore said to the *Star Reaper*'s captain. "Do it."

A good deal of time and computer analysis had been spent coming up with what Lorko and his subordinate officers believed to be the standard intervals employed by Confederacy battle groups as they entered potentially hostile systems. And that number was five standard minutes give or take thirty seconds. So, given the fact that one minute twenty-six seconds had already elapsed, it was time for the Sheen vessels to open fire. Not on a specific target, but on the exact point where the ill-fated DE had left hyperspace. Because according to Lorko's analysis, that was where the *next* ship would most likely exit as well. And the *next*, and the *next*, until the entire formation lay before him. An assemblage of ships that might be less than, equal to, or larger than Lorko's modest fleet. A threat but only if the enemy vessels were allowed to respond.

So the remotely operated Sheen vessels opened fire with their extremely powerful energy cannons, and where their pulses of bright blue light converged, an artificial sun was born. Lorko was committed at that point, because while the Sheen ships could maintain a sustained fire for up to eight minutes, their accumulators would have to recharge after that. And while the machine-ships were armed with missiles, they carried a finite number. All of this meant that if the theoretical force arrived later than expected, it might break out of the trap and attack not only the *Star Reaper* but the more vulnerable *Swarm*, thereby turning what could have been a magnificent victory into one of the worst naval disasters in Ramanthian history. Lorko would commit suicide, of course, assuming he survived long enough to do so, but it would be humiliating to arrive in the next world carrying such a heavy burden of shame.

Nav Point CSM-1802 shimmered within a cocoon of lethal energy as the seconds ticked away.

ABOARD THE CONFEDERACY BATTLESHIP *GLADIATOR*, IN HYPERSPACE

The battleship's primary Command & Control (C&C) computer was generally referred to as "Big Momma" mostly because she had a soft female voice. It echoed through miles of corridors, hundreds of weapons stations, and even found its way into the spacious cabin normally reserved for admirals but presently occupied by the Confederacy's extremely competent but slightly pudgy President and Chief Executive Officer Marcott Nankool. Who, being confronted with the plateful of pastries that had been brought in for the enjoyment of his staff, was struggling to ignore the calorie-laden treats as the computer spoke via the ship's ubiquitous PA system. "The ship will drop hyper in five, repeat five, minutes. Secure all gear, check space armor, and strap in. Primary weapons systems, secondary weapons systems, and tertiary weapons systems have been armed. All fighter aircraft are prepared for immediate launch. . . . Marine boarding parties are on standby at locks one through thirty-six. All supernumerary personnel will don space armor and remain where they are until the ship secures from battle stations. I repeat . . ."

But none of the six men and women who had been sent along to assist the chief executive during high-level talks with the Clone Hegemony were interested in hearing Big Momma's spiel all over again. And, having already struggled into their ill-fitting "P" for passenger space suits some fifteen minutes earlier, the staffers were content to let the C&C computer drone on as their discussion continued.

"That's utter bullshit," Secretary for Foreign Affairs Roland Hooks said contemptuously. "There's no goddamned way that the clones are going to agree to an alliance with us. I mean, why should they? We're getting our asses royally kicked while they sit around and congratulate each other on how superior their DNA is!"

The slender Dweller required a mechanical exoskeleton in order to deal with the Earth-normal gravity maintained aboard the *Gladiator*. One of his servos whined as the diplomat shifted his weight. "Maybe," Ambassador Omi Ochi countered cautiously. "But consider this . . . Regardless of the way the manner in which they mate, or *don't* mate as the case may be, the clones are still human. That means they think, see, hear, feel, and taste things just as *you* do. So, who are they going to side with? The bugs? Or beings similar to themselves?"

Foreign Service Officer (FSO)-3 Christine Vanderveen had shoulder-length blond hair, very blue eyes, and full red lips. Though not senior enough to participate in the increasingly heated discussion, she thought the serious-faced Dweller was essentially correct. After dithering around for a shamefully long time, the famously insular clones would eventually be forced to align themselves with the Confederacy, which, while not exclusively human, was certainly humanistic insofar as its laws, culture, and traditions were concerned. "That makes sense, Ambassador," Secretary Hooks allowed stolidly. "Or would, if the clones had a brain between them! How do you explain their continuing dalliance with the Thrakies? The furballs don't look human to me."

The discussion might have gone on indefinitely, but having given both sides an opportunity to express their opinions, Nankool wanted to move the meeting forward. "Both of you make good points," the moonfaced chief executive said soothingly. "But the fact remains. . . . We're on the way to the Hegemony in an effort to gain support from the clones. And, based on the fact that *they* invited us to come, there's the possibility that Omi is correct. So, let's plan for success. Assuming the Alpha Clones are open to a military alliance, they're going to want some say where command decisions are concerned. General Koba-Sa . . . How much input could you and your peers tolerate before your heads explode?"

All of Nankool's advisors knew that General Booly and the rest of his staff wouldn't want to surrender *any* authority, so everyone chuckled as the Hudathan worked his massive jaw as if preparing it for battle. The officer had a large humanoid head and weighed 252 pounds. He wasn't wearing a kepi, so the half-inch-high dorsal fin that ran front to back along the top of his skull was visible, as were his funnel-shaped ears and a thin-lipped mouth. Though white at the moment, the officer's skin would automatically darken when exposed to cold temperatures. The Hudathans had once been the sworn enemies of nearly every sentient species; but rather than remain imprisoned on the dying planet of Hudatha, Koba-Sa's people agreed to join the Confederacy. And a good thing, too, since the big aliens were fearsome warriors, and many of the Confederacy's other members were not. Koba-Sa's voice was reminiscent of a rock crusher stuck in low gear. "The clone army was bred to fight," Koba-Sa said approvingly. "And gave a good account of themselves during the rebellion on LaNor. But their senior officers lack initiative at times—and spend too much time on the defensive. My people have a saying. 'He who waits for the enemy should dig his own grave first.'"

Vanderveen didn't like Undersecretary of Defense Corley Calisco for any number of reasons. Because Calisco was a man who could typically be found on every side of an issue. But what bothered her most was the way he would stare at her breasts, and then lick his lips, as if he were able to taste them. So, when the undersecretary opened his mouth, the foreign service officer fully expected Calisco to slime the Hudathan. But that was the moment when the four-mile-long *Gladiator* exited hyperspace, passed through the remains of the three warships that had gone before it, and came under immediate attack. The ship shuddered as a volley of missiles exploded against her shields, Big Momma began a rhythmic chant, and the conversation was over.

ABOARD THE RAMANTHIAN DESTROYER *STAR REAPER*, OFF NAV BEACON CSM-1802

The third ship to emerge from hyperspace managed to kill one of the Sheen vessels with her weapons and destroyed a second by ramming it! A display of courage and determination very much in keeping with the code of the *Hath* and therefore to be admired by Commodore Lorko and his senior officers.

And now, as the other Sheen ships expended the last of their ordinance, and the *Swarm*'s fighters began to die by the dozens, the Ramanthians had to wonder if they were about to become victims of their own trap. But the fanatical Lorko wouldn't back down, *couldn't* back down, were he to face his peers again. So, despite of the fact that his flagship was only a quarter of the Confederacy ship's size, the commodore ordered the *Star Reaper* to attack. And waited to die.

But Lorko *didn't* die, nor did anyone else aboard the Ramanthian destroyer. Because as the battle continued a flight officer named Bami was pursuing a zigzag course through a matrix of defensive fire when he saw a quarter-mile-wide swath of the battleship's metal skin suddenly appear in front of him as a shield generator went down. Fortunately, Bami had the presence of mind to fire all four of his Avenger missiles before pulling up and corkscrewing through a storm of defensive fire.

There was a huge explosion as one of the Ramanthian's weapons struck a heat stack and sent a jet of molten plasma down the ship's number three exhaust vent into the decks below. *That* vaporized 120 crew beings, cut the fiber-optic pathway that connected the NAVCOMP with Big Momma, and forced the computer to hand over 64.7 percent of the *Gladiator*'s weapons to local control. And, without centralized fire control, it was only a matter of time before the Ramanthian fighters found *another* weak point and put the Confed vessel out of her misery. Of course Bami didn't know that, but the explosion spoke for itself, and the flight officer was thinking about the medal he was going to get when his fighter ran into a chunk of debris and exploded.

ABOARD THE CONFEDERACY BATTLESHIP *GLADIATOR*

The front of Captain Marina Flerko's uniform was red with the blood of a rating who had expired in her arms fifteen minutes earlier as she entered Nankool's cabin and stood across the table from him. "I'm sorry, Mr. President, but the *Gladiator* is dying."

Nankool's face was pale. "And the rest of the battle group?"

Flerko's voice cracked under the strain. "Destroyed, sir. The moment they left hyperspace. The bugs were waiting for us."

"Your advice?"

"Surrender, sir," the officer answered grimly. "There is no other choice."

Calisco swore, and Vanderveen felt something cold trickle into the pit of her stomach. Only a small handful of beings had been able to escape from Ramanthian prisoner-of-war (POW) camps, or been fortunate enough to be rescued, and the stories they told were universally horrible. In fact, many of the tales of torture, starvation, and abuse were so awful that many citizens assumed they were Confederacy propaganda. But the diplomat had read the reports, had even spoken with some of the survivors, and *knew* the stories of privation were true. And now, if Nankool accepted Flerko's recommendation, Vanderveen would learn about life in the POW camps firsthand.

Nankool's normally unlined face looked as if it had aged ten years during the last few minutes. His eyes flitted from face to face. His voice was even but filled with pain. "You heard the captain. . . . What do you think?"

"We should fight to the death!" Koba-Sa maintained fiercely. "Give me a weapon. I will meet the Ramanthians at the main lock."

"They won't have to board," Flerko said dispiritedly. "Eventually, after they fire enough Avengers at us, the ship will blow."

"Which is why we must surrender immediately!" Calisco said urgently. "Why provoke them? The faster we surrender, the more lives will be saved!"

"Much as I hate to agree with the undersecretary of defense, I fear that he's correct this time," Ambassador Ochi put in wearily. "There's very little to be gained by delay."

"I think there *is* something to be gained," Vanderveen said firmly, causing all of the senior officials to look at her in surprise. "Losing the battle group, plus thousands of lives is bad enough," the diplomat added. "But there's something more at stake. . . . If we allow the Ramanthians to capture the president, and the bugs become aware of who they have, they can use him for leverage."

"Not if they *don't* capture me," Nankool said grimly. "Captain, hand me your sidearm."

"Not so fast," Vanderveen insisted. "I admire your courage, Mr. President. I'm sure we all do—but what if there's another way?"

"Such as?" Ochi inquired skeptically, as the deck shook beneath their feet.

"We need to find a dead crew member with at least a superficial resemblance to the president and jettison his body," the diplomat replied earnestly. "Once that's accomplished, we can replace him."

"Damn! I think she's onto something," Secretary Hooks said approvingly as he made eye contact with Vanderveen. "Your father would be proud!"

The FSO's father, Charles Winther Vanderveen, was a well-known government official who had long been one of Nankool's principal advisors. And while the elder Vanderveen *would* have been proud, he would have also been beside himself with worry had he been aware of what was taking place millions of light-years away. "We must act quickly," the young woman said urgently. "And swear the crew to secrecy."

"I'll offer to surrender," Flerko put in. "Then, assuming that the bugs accept, we'll stall. That should give us as much as half an hour to find a match, put the word out, and implement the plan."

"What about the hypercom?" Koba-Sa growled. "Can we notify LEGOM on Algeron?"

Having lost the converted battleship *Friendship*, on

which it usually met, the Senate had been forced to convene on the planet Algeron. Until recently it would have been impossible to send a message across such a vast distance unless it was sealed inside a message torp or carried aboard a ship. But, thanks to the breakthrough technology that had been stolen from the Ramanthians on the planet Savas, crude but effective hypercom sets had already been installed on major vessels like the *Gladiator*. "Yes," Vanderveen said decisively. "They need to know about the trap—so the navy can find a way to prevent the bugs from laying another one just like it. Plus, they need to know about the rest of our plan as well, or the whole thing will fall apart."

Under normal circumstances any sort of suggestion from such a junior foreign service officer would most likely have been quashed. But the circumstances were anything but normal, so there was clearly no time for formalities, and Nankool nodded. "Agreed. Make it happen."

ABOARD THE RAMANTHIAN DESTROYER *STAR REAPER*

Commodore Lorko was still in the destroyer's control room when the vessel's com officer entered with the appalling, not to mention somewhat repugnant, news. The extent of the junior officer's disgust could be seen in the way he held his head and the position of his rarely used wings. "I'm sorry to interrupt, Commodore, but the enemy offered to surrender."

"They *what*?" Lorko demanded incredulously.

"They offered to surrender," the com officer reiterated.

It was all Lorko could do to maintain his composure. Because by dishonoring themselves, the humans and their allies had effectively dishonored *him*, and reduced what could have been a glorious victory to something less. It didn't seem fair. Not after the risks Lorko had taken, the resistance he had overcome, and the blow that had been dealt to the enemy.

But such was Lorko's pride and internal strength that none of that could be seen in the way he held his body or heard in the tenor of his voice. "I see," the commodore replied evenly. "All right, if slavery is what the animals want, then slavery is what they shall have. Order the enemy to cease fire, and once they do, tell our forces to do likewise. Send a heavily armed boarding party to the battleship, remove the prisoners who are fit for heavy labor, and set charges in all the usual places. Once the animals have been removed, I want that vessel destroyed. Captain Nuyo will take it from here. . . . I'll be in my cabin." And with that, Lorko left.

Though Nuyo wasn't especially fond of the flinty officer, he understood the significance of the blow dealt to Old Iron Back's honor, and felt a rising sense of anger as Lorko departed the control room. "You heard the commodore," Nuyo said sternly as he turned to look at the com officer. "And tell the battle group *this* as well . . . Mercy equates to weakness—and weakness will be punished. Execute."

ABOARD THE CONFEDERACY BATTLESHIP *GLADIATOR*

Fires burned unabated at various points throughout the ship's four-mile-long hull, the deck shook in sympathy with minor explosions, and gunfire could be heard as Ramanthian soldiers shot wounded crew members, people who were slow to obey their commands, or any officer foolish enough to identify him or herself as such. An excess for which they were unlikely to be punished. Klaxons, beepers, and horns sounded as streams of smoke-blackened, often-wounded crew beings stumbled out of hatches and were herded out into the center of the *Gladiator*'s enormous hangar deck.

The fact that the bay was pressurized rather than open to space spoke volumes, as did the fact that rank after rank of battle-ready CF-184 Daggers were sitting unused. The simple truth was that the ship had come under attack so quickly that Captain Flerko had never been able to drop the *Gladiator*'s energy screens long enough to launch fighters.

But there was no time to consider what could have been as Vanderveen and a group of ratings were ordered to make their way out toward the middle of the launch bay, where large metal boxes were situated. One of the prisoners, a gunner, judging from the insignia on her space black uniform, was wounded and had been able to hide the fact until then. But the sailor left a trail of blood droplets as she crossed the deck, and it wasn't long before one of the sharp-eyed troopers noticed them.

Vanderveen shouted, "No!" but fell as a rifle butt struck her left shoulder. The diplomat heard two shots and knew the gunner was dead.

It was Nankool who pulled the FSO to her feet before one of the troopers could become annoyed and put a bullet into her head as well. "Get going," the president said gruffly. "There's nothing you can do."

Vanderveen had to step over the rating's dead body in order to proceed, and realized how lucky she'd been, as a burst of automatic weapons fire brought down an entire rank of marines.

The Ramanthian troopers were largely invisible inside their brown-dappled space armor. Their helmets had side-mounted portals through which their compound eyes could see the outside environment, hook-shaped protuberances designed to accommodate parrotlike beaks, and chin-flares to deflect energy bolts away from their vulnerable neck seals.

The vast majority of the alien soldiers wore standard armor; but the noncoms were equipped with power-assisted suits, which meant the highly leveraged warriors could rip enemy combatants apart with their grabber-style pincers. So that, plus the fact that the bugs carried Negar IV assault rifles capable of firing up to six hundred rounds per minute, meant the aliens had more than enough firepower to keep the *Gladiator*'s crew under control. Something they accomplished with brutal efficiency.

Some of the Ramanthians could speak standard, while others wore chest-mounted translation devices, and the rest made use of their rifle butts in order to communicate. "Place all personal items in the bins!" one of the power-suited noncoms ordered via a speaker clamped to his right shoulder. "Anyone who is found wearing or carrying contraband will be executed!"

The so-called bins were actually empty cargo modules, and it wasn't long before the waist-high containers began to fill with pocketknives, wrist coms, pocket comps, multi-tools, glow rods, and all manner of jewelry. Vanderveen wasn't carrying anything beyond the watch her parents had given her, a belt-wallet containing her ID, and a small amount of currency. All of it went into the cargo container, and Vanderveen wondered if the Ramanthians were making a mistake. A *good* mistake from her perspective, since it would be difficult for the bugs to sort out who was who once the military personnel surrendered their dog tags. A factor that would help protect Nankool's new identity. Which, were anyone to ask him, was that of Chief Petty Officer Milo Kruse. A portly noncom who had reportedly been incinerated when molten plasma spilled out of the number three exhaust vent into the *Gladiator*'s main corridor.

Now, as various lines snaked past the bins, a series of half-coherent orders were used to herd the crew beings into groups of one hundred. Vanderveen thought she saw Ochi's exoskeleton in the distance, but couldn't be sure, as a Ramanthian trooper shouted orders. "Form ten ranks! Strip off your clothing! Failure to comply will result in death."

Similar orders were being given all around, and at least a dozen gunshots were heard as the Ramanthians executed prisoners foolish enough to object or perceived to be excessively slow. Meanwhile, Undersecretary of Defense Calisco hurried to rid himself of his pants, but was momentarily distracted when he looked up to see that one of his fantasies had come true! Christine Vanderveen had removed her top and unhooked her bra! She had firm upthrust breasts, just as he had imagined that she would, and the official was in the process of licking his lips when Nankool's left elbow dug into his side. "Put your eyeballs back in your head," the president growled menacingly, "or I'll kick your ass!" So Calisco looked down but continued to eye the diplomat via his peripheral vision, which was quite good.

Vanderveen stood with her arms folded over her breasts as a Ramanthian officer mounted a roll-around maintenance platform. Meanwhile a cadre of naked crew beings, all picked at random from the crowd, hurried to collect the discarded clothing and carry it away. "You are disgusting," the officer began, as his much-amplified voice boomed through the hangar deck. "Look at the bulkhead behind me. Read the words written there. *'For glory and honor.'* That was the motto you chose! Yet you possess neither one of them."

The deck shuddered, as if in response to the alien's words, and a dull *thump* was transmitted through many layers of durasteel. Some of the *Gladiator*'s computer-controlled firefighting equipment remained in operation, and the ship's maintenance bots were doing what they could to stabilize the systems they were responsible for, but without help from her crew, the ship was dying.

"Why are you *alive*?" the Ramanthian demanded through the loudspeaker on his shoulder. "When any self-respecting warrior would be dead? The answer is simple. You aren't warriors. You're animals! As such your purpose is to serve higher life-forms. From here you will be taken to a Ramanthian planet, where you will work until you can work no longer. Or, perhaps some of you who would prefer to die *now*, thereby demonstrating that you are something more than beasts of burden."

The officer's words were punctuated by a bellow of rage as General Wian Koba-Sa charged through the ranks in front of him. A Negar IV assault rifle began to bark rhythmically as a Ramanthian soldier opened fire—and Vanderveen saw the Hudathan stumble as he took two rounds in the back. But that wasn't enough to bring the huge alien down—and there was a cheer, as Koba-Sa jumped up onto the maintenance platform. The formerly arrogant Ramanthian had started to backpedal by that time, but it was too late as the Hudathan shouted the traditional war cry, and a hundred voices answered, "Blood!"

And there *was* blood as Koba-Sa wrapped one gigantic hand around the Ramanthian's throat and brought the other up under the flared chin guard. The helmet didn't come off the way the Hudathan had hoped it would, but the blow *was* sufficient to snap the bug's neck, even as Koba-Sa fell to a hail of bullets.

Then *all* of the prisoners were forced to hit the deck as the Ramanthians opened fire on the helpless crowd, and didn't stop until an officer repeatedly ordered them to do so, but only after many of the soldiers had emptied their clips.

Dozens of bodies lay sprawled on the deck by that time, but there was something different about the crew beings still able to stand, and the emotion that pervaded the hangar. Because rather than the feeling of hopelessness that filled the bay before—Vanderveen sensed a strange sort of pride. As if Koba-Sa's valiant death had somehow infused the prisoners with some of the Hudathan's headstrong courage.

And, rather than attempt to humiliate the POWs as the

previous officer had, Vanderveen noticed that his replacement was content to line the survivors up and march them past tables loaded with blue ship suits and hundreds of boots. All taken from the *Gladiator*'s own storerooms. But there was no opportunity to check sizes, or to try anything on, as the prisoners were herded past. The best strategy was to grab what was available and trade that for something better later on.

And it was during that process that one of ship's main magazines blew, people struggled to keep their feet, and the entire operation went into high gear. The Ramanthians were afraid now, afraid that the ship would disintegrate with them still aboard. So Vanderveen and all of the rest were herded into the waiting shuttles. The air was warm, thanks to the heat from their engines, and heavily tainted with the stench of ozone.

It didn't take a genius to figure out that there were more prisoners than the twenty shuttles could hold. And Vanderveen knew that meant that some of the *Gladiator*'s crew would be left behind. Other people began to realize the same thing, and there was a mad rush to board the spaceships. Guards fired over the crowd in a futile attempt to stem the flood, but suddenly realized that *they* could be left behind and hurried to join the fear-crazed mob.

Vanderveen wasn't sure she wanted to board one of the shuttles, especially if there was an opportunity to enter one of the *Gladiator*'s many escape pods instead; but she never got the chance to do more than think about the alternative as the people behind her pushed the FSO forward. Naked bodies collided with hers, an elbow jabbed her ribs, and the man directly in front of the diplomat went down.

Vanderveen attempted to step *over* the body but couldn't, and felt the crewman's back give as she was forced to put her weight on it, and tried to shout an apology as the river of flesh carried her up a ramp and into one of the shuttles.

There were bench-style seats along both bulkheads, but no one got the opportunity to sit on them, as the lead POWs were pushed forward and smashed against the bulkhead. Fortunately, Nankool was there, ordering people to be calm, and somehow convincing them to do so.

Then the ramp was retracted, Vanderveen felt the shuttle lift off and start to move. There were lights, but not very many, and only a few viewports. However, the diplomat was close enough to see dozens of screaming, kicking prisoners sucked out of the launch bay into the airless abyss of space as massive doors parted.

The shuttle jerked back and forth as the Ramanthian pilot was forced to thread his way through a maze of floating debris before finally clearing the battle zone. Then, as the spaceship began to turn away, there was a massive explosion. Bright light strobed the inside the of the shuttle, but there was no sound, as the *Gladiator* came apart. Someone began to pray, and even though Vanderveen had never been very religious, she bowed her head. The journey to hell had begun.

2

For those who would rule, the greatest threat can often be found standing right next to them, with a well-honed blade and a ready smile.

—Lin Po Lee
Philosopher Emeritus, The League of Planets
Standard year 2169

FORT CAMERONE, PLANET ALGERON, THE CONFEDERACY OF SENTIENT BEINGS

As a stream of formally attired dignitaries shuffled in through the double doors, Legion General William "Bill" Booly III, and his wife, Maylo Chien-Chu, were forced to pause while the colorfully plumed Prithian ambassador was announced to the crowd beyond. That gave the couple a moment in which to look at what normally functioned as the fort's mess hall but, having been commandeered for the vice president's first annual military ball, had magically been transformed into a ballroom.

All of the grim posters cautioning legionnaires about the dangers of land mines, unsecured weapons, and sexually transmitted diseases had been replaced by yard upon yard of colorful bunting that hung in carefully measured scallops along the walls. The previously green support columns had been painted white, detailed to look like marble, and hung with pots of artificial flowers. The normally bare mess tables wore crisp white bedsheets. And the Legion's best silver, which had been brought up out of the vaults for the occasion, sparkled with reflected candlelight.

Additional color was provided by dress uniforms and the clothing worn by civilians, senators, and other government officials. It was quite a transformation, but Booly had never been one for parties and frowned accordingly. "It looks like a rim world whorehouse," the officer observed in a voice so low that only his wife could hear it.

Besides being Booly's wife, Maylo Chien-Chu was president of a vast business empire founded by her uncle, Sergi Chien-Chu, *and* a natural beauty. She had raven black hair, large almond-shaped eyes, and the high cheekbones of a model. The stiff-collared red sheath dress clung to her long lean body like a second skin and had already begun to attract attention from both men and women alike. She smiled and gave her husband's arm an affectionate squeeze. "Don't be such a grump. People need to relax once in a while. Besides, when did *you* become an expert on rim world whorehouses?"

Booly might have made a response but never got the chance, since that was the moment when the formally attired sergeant major announced both their names and brought his intricately carved staff down with a decisive *thump*. "General William Booly—and Ms. Maylo Chien-Chu."

As the senior officer on Algeron, or anywhere else, for that matter, Booly was a someone in the small, highly charged world of the Confederacy's wartime government. And given the fact that there were always plenty of people who wanted to curry favor with the officer's billionaire wife, the two of them were soon hard at work maintaining important relationships, resisting tidal waves of flattery, and listening for the nuggets of information that are accidentally or intentionally shared at such affairs. Tidbits that can be stored, used, or traded according to need.

Meanwhile, the Legion's band continued to play, there was a stir as the by now red-faced sergeant major announced,

"Vice President Leo Jakov, and Assistant Undersecretary for Foreign Affairs Kay Wilmot." The words were punctuated with another *thump* of his heavy staff. The vice president was theoretically the number two person in the government, but actually had very little power, so long as the president was capable of performing his or her duties. Jakov had thick black hair, a vid-star-handsome face, and a full, some said sensual, mouth. His body, which was thick without being fat, seemed to radiate physical power. This fact was not lost on what were said to be dozens of lovers, some of whom were not only well-known, but willing to testify regarding his sexual prowess.

Less known to those outside the realm of government was Jakov's companion of late. An extremely ambitious diplomat named Kay Wilmot. Those who kept track of such things agreed that the assistant undersecretary had shed at least ten pounds since accepting a temporary position on Jakov's staff, where, according to certain wags, the "under" secretary took her title quite literally. But even the harshest of critics would have been forced to admit that Wilmot was a match for any of the vice president's previous consorts on that particular evening. Though not a beautiful woman, the foreign service officer was attractive, and she knew how to emphasize what she had through the use of carefully applied makeup. That, plus a green dress cut to emphasize her large breasts, drew plenty of attention from the human males in attendance.

All conversations came to a halt, and there was light-but-sustained applause as the couple entered the huge room, both because Jakov was well liked, and because the military ball was not only the vice president's idea, but had been funded out of *his* pockets. Booly and Maylo watched with amusement as at least half of their fickle admirers left to join the throng of beings now gathered around Jakov and Wilmot.

But such defections were to be expected, and without

President Nankool being there to claim the spotlight, it was Jakov's night to be at the center of attention. A role he clearly enjoyed, as senators, ambassadors, and senior military officers lined up to claim their smile, pat on the back, or well-honed joke.

Hors d'oeuvres were served fifteen minutes later. In spite of the fact that the Legion's cooks spent most of their time churning out thousands of meals for both the troops and the large contingent of civilians who had been forced to take up residence on Algeron, they could still produce something approaching haute cuisine when the occasion demanded, a fact that quickly became apparent as trays of beautifully prepared appetizers made the rounds. Included were a variety of creations that not only melted in the mouth, beak, or siphon tube, but represented the full spectrum of culinary traditions found within the boundaries of the Confederacy. Never mind the fact that some of the offerings were difficult to look at, had a tendency to crawl about, or produced what some guests considered to be unappetizing odors.

Thanks to the hors d'oeuvres, and the free-flowing drinks from the bar, most of the guests were in a good mood by the time they were instructed to take their places at the carefully arranged tables. Because who sat next to whom, and how close they were to the vice president's table, was not only an indication of status but a matter of practical importance as well. Since it would never do to put potential antagonists right next to each other—or to unintentionally promote alliances that might prove to be strategically counterproductive later on.

That meant "reliable" people such as Booly and Maylo had been paired with individuals like the recently named Senator Nodoubt Truespeak, who not only lacked some of the social graces expected of top-echelon politicians, but had a tendency to get crosswise with any Hudathan he encountered. Because, while others might have put the horrors of the Hudathan wars aside in the interest of political expediency, both Truespeak and his constituents were slow to forgive.

And as if the sometimes cantankerous Truespeak wasn't a sufficient challenge, Booly and Maylo had been saddled with the treacherous Thraki representative as well. In fact the short, somewhat paunchy Senator Obduro had recently been part of a conspiracy to help the Ramanthians recondition some of the Sheen warships they had stolen. An offense for which he was anything but contrite.

The evening's entertainment had begun by then, which, in keeping with the military nature of the ball, involved various displays of skill by well-practiced legionnaires, sailors, and marines. A group of naval ratings had just begun a spirited stick dance, when Booly noticed that a contingent of noncoms were delivering notes to guests who, having read them, immediately got up to leave. Jakov and Wilmot the first to do so.

That was not only unusual, but cause for concern, since any news that was so important that the duty officer felt compelled to notify the vice president was probably bad. Maylo had noticed the messengers as well, and the two of them exchanged glances as a staff sergeant approached their table. "For you, sir," the legionnaire said, as he handed a note to Booly.

The officer thanked the soldier, read the note, and hurried to excuse himself. Though careful to hide her emotions, Maylo felt something heavy settle into the pit of her stomach as her husband walked away, and knew her appetite wasn't likely to return.

Fort Camerone's com center was a windowless cluster of rooms buried below ground level, where it would be safe from anything short of a direct hit by multiple nuclear bombs. It had always been important, but now that the government was in residence on Algeron, the complex was at the very center of the vast web of communications that held the Confederacy together.

Most of the intersystem messages that came into the center arrived via FTL courier ships—or hyperdrive-equipped message torps. However, thanks to a new technology stolen from the Ramanthians, the old ways would soon be obsolete. Because once all of the Confederacy's ships had been equipped with hypercoms, it would be possible to communicate with each vessel in real time from any point in space. Of course it would be a while before the big clunky contraptions could be miniaturized and mass-produced—but battleships like the *Gladiator* already had them. Which was why the ship's commanding officer had been able to notify Algeron of the Ramanthian trap, the loss of her entire battle group, and the resulting surrender.

The vice president was reading the message for the second time when Booly arrived in the dimly lit com center. A single glance at the miserable faces all around him was sufficient to confirm the officer's worst fears. "Here, General," the grim-faced duty officer said, as he gave Booly a copy of the decoded text. "This arrived about fifteen minutes ago."

Booly read the short, matter-of-fact sentences, saw Captain Flerko's long angular face in his mind's eye, and swore softly. She was good, *very* good, so it was unlikely that the loss of the battleship and its escorts had been the result of human error. No, it looked like the Ramanthians had come up with a new strategy, and it was one that Confederacy military forces would have to find a way to counter. In the meantime there was the last part of the message to consider. One that left the officer feeling sick to his stomach. "Have no choice but to surrender . . . The president is alive and will blend with the other prisoners. Do not, repeat do not, announce his capture. Pray for us. . . . Captain Marina Flerko."

Booly wasn't the only one who was moved, because when he looked up, it was to see Vice President Jakov comforting a com tech. "There, there," the official said, as the woman sobbed on his shoulder. "It's a tough break, but we'll get the bastards."

Many, perhaps most, onlookers would have been impressed by the vice president's composure and his willingness to provide comfort to a lowly technician. But there was something about the scene that troubled Booly. Was it the look of barely contained avarice in Jakov's eyes? The cold, somewhat calculating look on Assistant Undersecretary Wilmot's face? Or a combination of both?

But there was no opportunity to consider the matter, as everyone followed Vice President Jakov into the adjoining conference room, and the group that Nankool liked to refer to as his "brain trust" took their seats.

Six people were present besides Jakov and herself, and while Wilmot didn't know any of the group intimately, she was familiar with their reputations. First there was General Booly, who, had it not been for the fact that he was married to the formidable Maylo Chien-Chu, would have been worth a roll in the hay. He was part Naa, and if the rumors were true, had a strip of fur that ran down his spine.

Also present, and looming large in one of the enormous chairs provided for his kind, was Triad Hiween Doma-Sa, who functioned as both his race's representative to the Senate *and* head of state. Which made the craggy hard-eyed alien a very important person indeed. And one that Wilmot wasn't all that fond of given the manner in which the Hudathan had recently gone around her to form a back-channel relationship with a low-level subordinate named Christine Vanderveen. Still, if Nankool was sitting in a Ramanthian prisoner-of-war camp, then so was Vanderveen! A bonus if there ever was one.

Not to be taken so lightly, however, was the woman

generally referred to in high-level government circles as Madame X. Her real name was Margaret Xanith. She had a head of carefully styled salt-and-pepper hair and a surprisingly youthful face, which wore a seemingly perpetual frown. Perhaps that was a reflection of her personality, or the fact that as the head of Confed Intelligence she knew about all of the things that were going wrong and rarely had much to smile about. She whispered something to one of her aides, who nodded, and left the room.

Seated next to Xanith was an extremely powerful man who though no longer president of the Confederacy, or head of the huge company that still bore his name, continued to hold the rank of reserve navy admiral and was Maylo Chien-Chu's uncle. A cyborg who, in spite of the fact that he looked to be about twenty-five years old, was actually more than a hundred.

The final participant was a relative newcomer to Nankool's inner circle. A female Dweller named Yuro Osavi. Her frail sticklike body was protected by a formfitting cage controlled by a microcomputer that was connected to the alien's nervous system through a neural interface. The academic had been living on a Ramanthian planet and studying their culture until the war forced her to flee. Osavi had been drafted by Nankool to provide the president with what he called ". . . an enemy's-eye view of the conflict." Just one of the many reasons why the wily politician had weathered so many storms and remained in the Confederacy's top job for so long.

"Okay," Jakov said somberly, "I suppose we could be on the receiving end of even worse news, but it's damned hard to think what that would be. And, like you, I am absolutely devastated by the tragic loss of an entire battle group plus thousands of lives. That having been said, you can be sure that our absence will be noted, and unless we return to the ball soon, all sorts of rumors will begin to fly. So, unless there are immediate steps we can take to strike back, or free our personnel, I suggest we adjourn until 0900 hours tomorrow morning. By that time I'm sure that Margaret, Bill, and Yuro will have prepared some options for us." At that point Jakov scanned the faces all around him, and having heard no objections, rose from the table. Wilmot hurried to do likewise. "All right," the vice president said cheerfully, "I'll see you in the morning." And with that he was gone.

There was a long moment of silence once Jakov and his companion had left the room. The people still at the table stared at each other in utter disbelief. Because although rumor control was important, surely the vice president could have remained long enough to hammer out some sort of initial plan. Unless the politician wasn't interested in a speedy response that is? A possibility all of them had considered—but only Doma-Sa was willing to give voice to. "So Jakov wants to be president," the triad rumbled cynically. "This reminds me of home."

Hudathan politics had been extremely bloody until very recently, so the others understood the reference, even if some were reluctant to agree. "It does seem as if we could go around the table," Booly agreed. "How 'bout you Margaret? Assuming our people are still alive, where would the bugs take them?"

"We're working on that," the intelligence chief replied gravely. "Although we're pretty sure they wouldn't be taken to Hive."

"I agree," Osavi put in. "The Ramanthian home world serves as the residence of the Queen and is therefore sacred. To land aliens on the surface of Hive would be unthinkable."

"Well, they'd better get used to the idea because it's going to happen," Doma-Sa responded grimly. "And when it does, a whole lot of bugs are going to die."

"Sounds good to me," Booly replied. "But it's going to be a while before we can penetrate their home system, much less drop troops onto Hive. In the meantime, let's put every intelligence asset we have on finding out where our people are. Margaret's staff is working on it, but maybe there's something more we can do. How about Chien-Chu Enterprises, Admiral? Can your people give us a hand?"

The possibility had already occurred to Sergi Chien-Chu. The family business was a huge enterprise, with operations on dozens of planets, some of which were no longer accessible due to the war. But the vast fleet of spaceships that belonged to Chien-Chu Enterprises had access to those that were—and there was always the chance that one or more of his employees would see or hear something. The problem was time, because while all of his vessels would eventually have hypercoms, none was equipped with the new technology as yet. "Maylo and I will put out the word," the businessman promised. "And report anything we hear."

"Thank you," Booly replied gratefully. "In the meantime I will tell the public affairs people to work up a release concerning the loss of the *Gladiator* but with no mention of Nankool or his staff."

"It's imperative that we keep the lid on," Xanith agreed earnestly. "Because if the Ramanthians realize they have the president, they will use him for leverage. I'm sure he would tell us to refuse their demands, but who knows how much pressure Earth's government will bring to bear? Or what the Senate may decide? The Thrakies might lead a 'Save our president' movement actually intended to aid the Ramanthians."

"And there's something else to consider," the frail-looking Dweller added gloomily. "Very few people within the Confederacy are aware of the *Spirit* cult that has grown increasingly popular within the Ramanthian military. They believe true warriors always fight to the death. That means they have no respect for prisoners and tend to treat them like animals. So, if Nankool and the rest of the survivors fall into the pincers of those who believe in what they call 'The True Path,' life will be very hard indeed. So hard that one of his fellow prisoners may be tempted to reveal the president's identity in hopes of receiving favorable treatment." It was a sobering thought, and even though all of them had to return to the party, it was difficult to think of anything else.

THE VILLAGE OF WATERSONG, PLANET ALGERON, THE CONFEDERACY OF SENTIENT BEINGS

As the sun started to rise somewhere beyond the cold gray haze, daylight began to fade in, as if emanating from within the planet itself. And gradually, as the mist started to clear, the jagged Towers of Algeron appeared more than a thousand miles to the south. Some of the peaks soared eighty thousand feet into the sky, making the mountains so heavy that if they were somehow transported to Earth, their weight would crack the planet's crust.

But the two worlds were different. Very different. Because while it took Terra twenty-four standard hours to execute a full rotation, Algeron completed a full 360-degree turn every two hours and forty-two minutes. The cycle was so fast that centrifugal force had created a globe-spanning mountain range, which thanks to the gravity differential between the poles and the equator, weighed only half what it would have on Earth.

None of which was of the slightest interest to the one-armed bandit chieftain named Nofear Throatcut except to the extent that most of those in the village below him had been asleep for two local days and would remain so for two additional planetary rotations. There would be sentries, of course, because no self-respecting Naa village would be so foolish as to rest without posting some, but having been on duty for a while, and with the gradual return of daylight, the watch keepers would not only be a little sleepy, but slightly overconfident.

But Throatcut and his mixed band of deserters, rene-
gades, and thieves were anything but typical. A fact that
quickly became apparent as Nightrun Fargo pulled the
trigger on his homemade crossbow and sent a metal bolt
speeding through the early-morning mist. The razor-sharp
point ripped a hole through a sentry's unprotected throat.
Which was no small feat since it had been necessary for the
bandit to crawl within 150 yards of his target without
generating noise or being detected by the villager's acute
sense of smell.

The target, a youngster of only seventeen, made a gur-
gling sound as he attempted to shout a warning, tugged at
the now slippery shaft, and was already in the process of
falling as Nosay Slowspeak loosed *another* bolt. This one
was directed at an older sentry. There was a dull *thump* as
the bolt hit the warrior's chest, penetrated his leather armor, and knocked the oldster off his feet.

But the more senior watch keeper was a clever old coot
who, having tied a lanyard to the cast-iron alarm bell
mounted next to him, managed to ring the device even as
he fell. Throatcut swore as a loud metallic *clang* was heard,
and a third sentry fired into the mist. "Okay," the chieftain
said, as he brought a Legion-issue hand com to his lips.
"Lindo, you know what to do. Don't kill all of the females,
though. Some of the boys are horny!"

That got a laugh, plus some ribald commentary that
would never have been tolerated by the noncoms Throatcut had served under in the Legion. "You got that right!"
Longride Doothman put in.

"Save one of those whores for me!" Salwa Obobwa
added eagerly, as more shots were fired from within the
village.

But Throatcut put forward no objection because he
knew how important it was to maintain just enough discipline to get the job done and not one iota more if he
wanted to remain in command.

The villagers were beginning to emerge from their underground homes by then. The locals were only half-dressed in many cases but armed to the teeth with a mix of locally produced rifles, Legion-issue weapons of every possible description, and oversized Hudathan hand-me-downs. And, given the rough-and-ready nature of the Naa tribespeople, the villagers would have been able to give a good account of themselves had it not been for Throatcut's secret weapon.

Like many of his kind, Cady Lindo had been executed for murder back on Earth, given an opportunity to trade oblivion for a place in the Legion of the Damned, and downloaded into a succession of increasingly complex electromechanical bodies until he was qualified to occupy the very latest version of the battle-tested Trooper II (T-2) combat vehicle. A ten-foot-tall machine that stood on two armored legs and could carry a single bio bod into a variety of combat environments while employing a truly devastating array of weapons ranging from an arm-mounted air-cooled .50-caliber machine gun, to an arm-mounted fast-recovery laser cannon and two shoulder-mounted missile launchers, both of which were safely stored up on the mesa that Throatcut and his gang used as a base.

But Lindo had no need for missile launchers as he emerged from hiding to enter the north end of the village. Bullets began to *ping* against his armor, and a poorly thrown grenade went off about fifteen feet away, as the cyborg opened fire. The outgunned defenders never had a chance as they were snatched off their feet, cut to shreds, or incinerated as they attempted to flee.

Seeing that the head-on assault had failed, some of the local warriors sought to outflank the mechanical monster by turning west into the protection of the rocks that backed the ravine-hugging village. But Throatcut had anticipated such a move and a force of bio bods were there to cut them down. The human named Obobwa, along with

Musicplay, Fargo, and Slowspeak opened fire with fully automatic weapons as a dozen half-seen warriors charged into a hail of lead.

Throatcut, who had been watching the slaughter from the top of the rock-strewn slope, began to issue new orders before the last body hit the ground. "Cease fire! Save your ammo! And make sure all of them are dead."

The bandits rose from their various hiding places, and a series of shots rang out, as Throatcut followed a steep switchbacking trail down into the now-devastated village. A comely female, armed with an old muzzle loader, popped up out of a hole. But the long-barreled rifle was too heavy for her, and she was still trying to aim it when Throatcut struck the side of her head with his pistol. She collapsed at his feet.

Though no longer engaged in combat, Lindo was standing guard. Though unlikely, there was always the chance that warriors from another village would happen by, or a group of locals would return from the hunt. If so, the T-2's sensors should pick them up, thereby giving the rest of the gang time to flee or prepare themselves for combat.

There were screams, interspersed by *more* gunfire, as the bandits fought their way down into the subterranean dwellings, where loot in the form of food, booze, and ammo was theirs for the taking. The older females were generally murdered, as were many of the younger ones, unless they were pretty enough to catch someone's eye. Then they were hauled up to the surface and loaded onto one of the woolly dooths that were waiting to haul the plunder back to the mesa. Most were crying, some continued to struggle, and one committed suicide by attacking Musicplay with a kitchen knife.

There were cubs of course. Which were typically left to fend for themselves unless they got in the way, as one youngster did when he threw a rock at Lindo. That impertinence earned the cub an energy bolt.

Finally, having obtained what they had come for, and led by Throatcut, who rode high on the T-2's back, the bandits followed a meandering course back toward the mesa they called home. A trip that exposed them to one of Madame X's spy sats as it passed overhead. Back in the days when Algeron had been classified as a protectorate, a fly-form would have been dispatched to inspect the group. Especially in the wake of other attacks by a renegade T-2. But the planet was independent now, and theoretically responsible for protecting its own citizens, even if the new government lacked the means to do so. So no action was taken by Xanith's analysts other than to generate a report that was copied to Senator Nodoubt Truespeak and that individual's overworked staff.

Seven Algeron-length days had passed by the time Throatcut and his band arrived at the base of the massive stone pillar and began the long arduous journey to the top. The sun had risen once again as the cyborg and the heavily laden dooths made their way up past an extremely treacherous rockslide to the plateau's windswept top. A rocky spire marked the entrance to their subsurface habitation, and once there, the bandits began to dismount. Cybertech Wylie Rin came out to greet the freebooters, as did three forlorn-looking females, all of whom were put to work unloading the dooths.

In the meantime the latest captives were taken down into a warren of underground rooms to be raped, and in one case tortured, because that was Slowspeak's notion of sex. Some, those deemed worthy, would be kept, but the others would be put to death a few days later. Because enjoyable though the females might be, slaves require food, and the bandits had no desire to venture out more frequently than they had to.

As night fell, and the relentless fingers of the wind began to probe the ruins, a sad, keening noise was heard. It was as if the cries of those who had suffered on the mesa in the past had somehow been blended with the screams of those held there in the present to produce a time-spanning cry of anguish. But now, as in the past, no help was forthcoming.

FORT CAMERONE, PLANET ALGERON, THE CONFEDERACY OF SENTIENT BEINGS

It was easy to lose track of time on a planet where the days were so short, buried under a fortress where there was no natural light, immersed in a flow of work that never stopped. Which was why Booly was surprised to find that after working through the artificial eight-hour "night," it was suddenly time to attend Jakov's strategy session. A meeting in which some sort of plan would no doubt be hashed out even if doing so proved to be frustrating. The part of his job that Booly hated most.

The officer was running about five minutes late, so when Booly entered the conference room, he expected to find the other participants present. But in spite of the fact that Chien-Chu, Xanith, Doma-Sa, and Osavi were seated around the table, neither Jakov nor Wilmot was anywhere to be seen. Of course with the entire weight of the Confederacy resting upon his shoulders, it would be quite understandable if the vice president was delayed. So Booly took some food from a side table, poured himself a cup of caf, and listened as Xanith gave an informal report.

"Bottom line, we don't have the foggiest idea where the prisoners were taken," the intel chief said grimly. "So, no progress there. The *good* news, if that's the right word for it, is that when the *Samurai* and her battle group dropped into the Nebor system to investigate, they were able to recover a life pod containing a junior officer from one the *Gladiator*'s escorts. She was able to confirm the essence of Captain Flerko's hypercom message. Not the part about Nankool—but the way the trap was set. The *Sam* found lots of debris, but no Ramanthians, or anyone else for that matter."

The naval command structure would be eager to get any details they could concerning the trap, but the information wasn't going to help locate the POWs and rescue them.

"I haven't got anything, either," Chien-Chu confessed glumly. "Nor would I expect to at this early date."

There was more conversation, all of which was trivial, until Jakov and Wilmot arrived twenty minutes later. Rather than offer some sort of pro forma apology, as Booly expected he would, the vice president simply took a seat. And if the politician was feeling the weight of the additional responsibilities that had been thrust upon him, there was no sign of it on his freshly shaven face. "So," Jakov began blandly, "what have you got for us?"

Wilmot, who made it a habit to monitor Jakov's words for indictors of where she stood, heard the word "us" and felt an immediate surge of pleasure. By including her in the sentence, the vice president had elevated her to a status higher than that of the other beings in the room! Even Triad Doma-Sa, who qualified as a visiting head of state! Clearly her official, as well as unofficial, efforts to keep Jakov happy were working, including the rather rigorous bout of sex that had delayed them.

"So," Xanith concluded, as she finished her report, "we don't know where they are."

Jakov nodded soberly. "That's regrettable—but understandable. I'm sure you'll keep me informed. By the way, I'd like to hold these meetings on a regular basis. . . . Although I don't see any need for all of you to attend. I know Triad Doma-Sa, Admiral Chien-Chu, and Professor Osavi are all very busy. With that in mind I will designate members of my personal staff to fill in for them. Then we can convene the larger group when circumstances warrant. Perhaps Assistant Undersecretary Wilmot would be so kind as to make the necessary arrangements."

Chien-Chu, who had once been president himself, couldn't help but feel a sense of grudging admiration for the skillful manner in which he and the other Nankool loyalists had been removed from the inner circle to make room for some of the vice president's political protégés. And there wasn't a damned thing any of them could do about it.

"So, unless there's something else, I'd better get back to work," Jakov announced lightly. "It seems that the Prithians are upset over the way Thraki freighters have started to appear in the small, out-of-the-way systems that *they* have traditionally served. Even though such routes couldn't possibly be profitable for our diminutive friends. And that raises the question of why? Both sides are waiting in my office."

"Sir, yes, sir," Booly acknowledged. "But I would appreciate it if you could find time to take a look at the rescue plan that my staff and I hammered out."

"Later perhaps," Jakov said dismissively as he came to his feet. "It saddens me to say it, but there isn't much point in working on a rescue plan until we know where the POWs are. Even then, the realities of war, combined with other priorities, may make it difficult to implement such a plan. So keep it handy, but let's focus on our most important objective, which is winning the war." And with that, both Jakov and Wilmot departed.

A long silence followed the moment when the door closed. "Damn," Xanith said finally. "He doesn't *want* to find the POWs."

"No, I think it's President Nankool that he doesn't want to find," Doma-Sa said cynically. "A strategy I can easily understand since it's the sort of thing that my people are known for!"

All of those present knew how dangerous Hudathan politics could be, so no one chose to debate the point. "I fear you are correct old friend," Chien-Chu said grimly. "But I'd like to be wrong."

"Well," Booly replied thoughtfully, "let's continue to refine the rescue plan. Then, once we know where the POWs are, it will be ready to go."

"And if Jakov refuses to authorize a rescue mission?" Chien-Chu wanted to know.

"We'll cross that bridge when we come to it," the officer answered stolidly.

"Any attempt to send a rescue party without the vice president's approval could be interpreted as treason," Xanith warned.

"And failure to try and rescue them could be regarded as treason as well," the general replied grimly. "So let's hope that we're never forced to choose."

3

Any officer or trooper who surrenders will be executed.

—*Ramanthian Fleet Admiral Niko Himbu*
Standard year 2846

ABOARD THE RAMANTHIAN FREIGHTER *ABUNDANT HARVEST,* IN HYPERSPACE

More than a thousand prisoners stood at the bottom of the long, narrow hull and stared up through the metal grating located a few feet above their heads. They could see lights, and the soles of their tormentor's feet, but very little else. Christine Vanderveen was among them and, like all the rest, was extremely thirsty. Although the diplomat had been forced to surrender her watch back on the *Gladiator*, she figured that the POWs had been aboard the freighter for about three miserable days. And like those around her, Vanderveen's body was so conditioned to the daily schedule that it somehow *knew* when the rain was about to fall. That's what the prisoners called the water, in spite of the fact that the substance that gushed out of the Ramanthian hoses had already been swallowed, processed, and pissed many times before.

Even so, the brackish stuff tasted good, *real* good, to people who were desperately thirsty. Which was why Vanderveen, Nankool, and all the rest of the POWs stood with their heads thrown back and their mouths wide open.

Many, Vanderveen included, were naked. Having willingly traded their modesty for the opportunity to take a shower. And, even though the diplomat's body was well worth staring at, such was the condition of their dry, cottony mouths, that none of the neighboring men were looking at the diplomat lest their heads be in the wrong position when the precious liquid started to fall. All of which stemmed from the fact that the Ramanthian command structure hadn't expected to take prisoners in the Nebor system—and had been forced to put the animals on an H class freighter. A ship so inadequate that even the most beneficent of captors would have been hard-pressed to treat the POWs well, never mind Captain Dorlu Vomin, who regarded empathy as a sign of a weakness.

But Vomin *was* resourceful. So, rather than sit around and complain about the burden he'd been given, the veteran freighter captain employed both his recalcitrant crew and the prisoners themselves to shift all of the cargo from Hull 2, through the connecting cross section to Hull 1, thereby making half of the H-shaped ship available to house the mostly human cargo. Then, rather than attempt to rig some sort of temporary plumbing for the undeserving POWs, Vomin came up with a more efficient plan. By turning hoses on the animals twice each day, the crew could not only provide the prisoners with an opportunity to drink but flush their waste products into the bilges at the same time! Then, having been pumped out and purified, the water could be used again. The only problem was that the freighter's recycling equipment was working overtime and might eventually fail under the strain.

The sound of footsteps echoed between the metal bulkheads as Vomin began to pace back and forth. The Ramanthian was toying with them, and the prisoners knew it, because they'd been through the routine before. It was tempting to lower their heads until the coming diatribe ended, but they knew better than to do so. Because the wily Ramanthian had been known to start the rain halfway through one of his harangues. And once the water began to flow, there would be only fifteen seconds in which to take advantage of it. So as Vomin began to talk, the prisoners kept their eyes focused on the grating above.

"Good morning," the freighter captain began evenly. "I see that you stare up at me, like flowers following the sun, knowing that *I* am the source of all life."

The first time Vomin had delivered one of this strange speeches, there had been jeers, catcalls, and all manner of rude noises from the prisoners standing below. But having had their "rain" shortened by ten seconds, the POWs never made that mistake again. So they stood, jaws achingly open, while Vomin strutted above them. "You will lose the war," the Ramanthian informed the prisoners. "And for a very simple reason. Because as you gathered various cultures under a single government each polluted the rest. Weakness was piled upon weakness, and flaw was piled upon flaw, until the center of the obscenity you call the Confederacy began to rot. A process that is well under way and will inevitably lead to a series of poor decisions. Decisions that my race will take advantage of.

"Fortunately, the rest of your lives will be spent working on something worthwhile. Because there are jungles on Jericho. . . . Jungles that must be cleared for the benefit of our newly hatched nymphs. So as the Ramanthian rain begins to fall, I suggest that you savor each drop, knowing the full glory of the task that awaits you! That will be all."

As usual the hoses came on without warning as Vomin's crew began to spray the gratings. The water cascaded down through thousands of openings to splatter grimy faces, fill dry mouths, and run in gray rivulets down along necks, torsos, and legs.

Like those around her, Vanderveen took advantage of the "rain" in her own unique way. The key was to keep her head back, thereby gulping as much of the heavenly liquid as possible, while the jumpsuit that hung capelike down her back absorbed additional water. Water that she would suck out of the fabric once the hoses were turned off. Some people liked to use their boots to collect water, but that involved taking them off and risking a cut. A rather dangerous thing to do given all the nasty bacteria that lived on the bilge grating.

So Vanderveen was content to swallow what she could, take a shower, and suck water out of her overalls before pulling them on again. Something the diplomat hurried to do so that the surrounding men had only a limited amount of time to stare at her.

Then, their thirsts momentarily quenched, the prisoners were ordered to line up against both bulkheads facing inwards. *Not* by the bugs, who didn't care how the animals positioned themselves, but by their own officers and noncoms. Who, with support from Nankool, were determined to maintain discipline. Especially at mealtime—which took place once each day.

A section of grating rattled loudly as it was removed, and Vanderveen heard a sustained series of *thumps*, as exactly sixty cases of MSMREs (MultiSpecies Meals Ready to Eat) were dropped through the hole. The food had been scavenged from one of the *Gladiator*'s support ships subsequent to the battle and transferred to the freighter. Each case held twenty meals, which meant that twelve hundred meals were available, in spite of the fact that there were only 1,146 prisoners. That meant there was an overage of fifty-four MSMREs per day, which allowed the tightly supervised food committee to provide the Hudathan prisoners with extra calories, and to dole out additional meal components to everyone else on a rotating basis. And, since each meal consisted of a main dish along with six other items, such distributions were followed by a frenzy of trading as everyone sought to get rid of things they didn't care for and secure those they liked.

Food could even be bartered for sex, or that's what Vanderveen had heard, although she made it a point to avoid the aft end of the hold, where such transactions were said to take place. But one meal a day wasn't enough, so even though the FSO looked forward to eating whatever was in her ration box, the human knew she was losing both weight and strength.

An hour later, the diplomat had finished the tiny cup of fruit that she had traded a candy bar and some crackers for, and was about to take the empty packaging forward, when one of the so-called word-walkers stopped by. He was a small man with narrow-set eyes, a twice-broken nose, and a three-day beard. "There's gonna be a leadership meeting," the messenger whispered. "Ten minutes."

Vanderveen thanked the man and took the trash forward to the "workshop," where a team of prisoners was busy converting the MSMRE boxes into sandals for those who lacked boots, and multilayered body armor for the all-Hudathan assault team that would probably never have an opportunity to use it. Not unless the bugs made some sort of really stupid mistake. "But, it's good to be prepared," as Nankool liked to say. And work, any kind of work, was a morale booster.

From there, Vanderveen made her way back to the point where a small group of people were assembled around Nankool. The filtered light threw dark bars across the president and those crouched around him. Sentries had been posted in an effort to maintain security, but the FSO knew that there was no way to protect the most important piece of information that the prisoners had, and that was Nankool's true identity. *Everyone* knew that, and because they did, were in a position to betray not only the president but the rest of the leadership team as well.

Not that the bugs would have been surprised to learn that Commander Peet Schell, the *Gladiator*'s XO had assumed command of all military forces. But the rest of the leadership group (LG) wasn't so obvious, starting with the president himself, who was posing as petty officer Milo Kruse, the square-jawed Roland Hooks, and the slimy Corley Calisco. Unfortunately, General Koba-Sa, Ambassador Ochi, and Captain Flerko had been killed. Nankool, who seldom if ever lost his sense of humor, smiled as the FSO joined the group. "Welcome, Ms. Vanderveen. May I be the first to say how lovely you look today?"

Vanderveen, who was well aware of the fact that her skin was peeling and her hair was matted, made a face. "Thank you, Chief Petty Officer Kruse. And please let me be the first to congratulate you on the size and density of the furry thing that is in the process of eating your face."

Everyone laughed, Calisco loudest of all, as he imagined what the diplomat would look like without any clothes. Maybe, if he moved in closer just prior to the next rain, he could score a look.

"So," Nankool began. "For the first time since they put us aboard this tub, Vomin had something useful to say. It sounds like we're headed for Jericho—which, if my memory serves me correctly, was one of the worlds that the Senate granted the Ramanthians as partial restitution for damage suffered during the Hudathan wars."

"That's correct," Hooks confirmed. "You may recall that Ramanthian Senator Alway Orno was quite skillful in arguing his case."

"*Before* he blew the *Friendship* to smithereens," Schell added bitterly.

"Not that we can *prove* that," Calisco interposed primly.

"It was a diversion," Schell replied hotly. "The bugs stole thousands of Sheen ships while we were busy searching for survivors! How much goddamned proof do you need?"

"It doesn't matter *who* triggered the bomb," Nankool said soothingly. "Not anymore. The point is that the Ramanthians snookered us out of some prime planets—and now they want us to make improvements on one of them."

"For their newborns," Hooks added darkly. "Some five

billion of them if our intelligence estimates are accurate."

"Which is why the bugs started this war," Schell reminded them. "To obtain more real estate."

"Precisely," Nankool agreed, as he scanned their faces. "So, how 'bout it? Has anyone been to Jericho?"

Being the most junior person present, Vanderveen waited to see if any of her superiors would respond before raising a tentative hand. "I haven't been there. . . . But I remember reading the survey report that was filed immediately after the second Hudathan War."

Nankool smiled indulgently. "Well, don't keep us in suspense child. Share your knowledge!"

Vanderveen's blue eyes seemed to go slightly out of focus as she worked to summon the data acquired more than two years previously. "Jericho is an Earth-normal planet," she began. "Which means it is Hive-normal, too. And, judging from the ruins that cover much of the planet's surface, it was once home to an advanced civilization. Based on studies carried out by archeologists prior to the first Hudathan war, there are notable similarities between ancient structures and artifacts present on Jericho and those cataloged on planets like Long Jump, Zaster, and Earth."

"All of which is consistent with the possibility of a forerunner race," Hooks observed. "Or races . . . Which might account for some of the physiological similarities between certain species."

"Many of whom would rather slice off a nose or beak than admit to any sort of common ancestry," Nankool observed. "Go ahead, Christina. . . . You were saying?"

"I don't remember all the details," the diplomat confessed. "But I believe Jericho has a middle-aged sun, a stable orbit, and plenty of natural resources. Which is why the Hudathans sought to grab the planet during their expansionist phase—and the Ramanthians lobbied to take it away from them. A great deal of the surface is covered with jungle, however, which implies what could be a nasty food chain, not to mention some very uncomfortable conditions."

"*How* nasty?" Calisco wanted to know.

"*Real* nasty," Schell replied pessimistically.

"Which means it's going to be tough," Nankool said thoughtfully. "And we have an obligation to prepare our people for that. Christine, once this meeting is over, round up our doctors. What have we got? Two of them? Good. Tell them we need to build strength, but conserve calories, and see what sort of exercises they suggest. Then, once we have a regimen ready, pass it to Commander Schell. He'll make it mandatory. Okay?"

What the president said made sense, and, as always, the FSO was impressed by the quality of Nankool's leadership. "Yes, sir," Vanderveen replied. "I'll take care of it."

PLANET JERICHO, THE RAMANTHIAN EMPIRE

As the yellow-orange ball of fire began to appear over the eastern horizon, the usual cacophony of sounds began as thousands of arboreal life-forms hooted, screamed, and squawked their morning greetings. But, strange though some of the native species were by human standards, none could compare to the camo-covered alloy sphere that rested high in the branches of a towering sun tracker tree. Which, having a very flexible trunk, was already turning its huge heat-absorbing leaves toward Jericho's sun.

The construct, which was home to a human brain named Oliver Batkin, was very similar to the so-called recon balls employed by Confederacy military forces, in that the sphere was about four feet in diameter, and equipped with repellers that allowed it to fly at altitudes of up to three hundred feet.

The similarities ended there, however, since recon balls have tactical applications, and Batkin's mission was to gather raw intelligence, upload it to one of the message torps in orbit around the planet, and send the vehicle back to Algeron. But not very often, since the number of reports the cyborg could make was limited by the number of torpedoes at his disposal.

Now, as the more vocal members of the local biosphere combined their multitudinous voices to wake the spy from his slumbers, Batkin activated one of the four high-resolution vid cams that had been built into his technology-packed body. He had a good view thanks to the fact that the sun tracker tree stood head and shoulders above all the rest. The top layer of the forest looked deceptively soft and inviting even though Batkin knew that all sorts of dangers lurked below. But the view was beautiful, which was why the spy ball preferred to nest in the tallest of trees, standing like lonely sentinels over the jungle.

That, at least, was consistent with how the onetime banker had imagined his new job, back in the hospital, when the recruiter dropped in to make her pitch. Six years working for the government. That's what Batkin had agreed to in exchange for a Class IV cyber body, the kind that only the wealthiest humans could afford. Of course that was back just *before* the war, when the Ramanthians were members of the Confederacy, and he had been in intensive care. Since that time, Batkin been through a grueling training course, the bugs had precipitated a war, and the newly graduated spy had been sent to Jericho "to find out why the Ramanthians want it so badly."

That, at least, had been accomplished, because about three months after the cyborg plummeted through Jericho's atmosphere, the egg-ships began to arrive. That's what Batkin called them, because that's what the freighters carried, lots and lots of eggs. Thousands upon thousands of the big ten-pound monsters that crews of specially trained Ramanthians "planted" in the jungle and left to hatch on their own.

It didn't take a genius to figure out what was in the eggs, of course, but Batkin knew better than to make assumptions, and was therefore obliged to break one of the hard-shelled containers open and dissect its contents. A rather disgusting process that confirmed the spy's hypothesis. A Ramanthian population explosion was under way, Jericho was being used as a gigantic nursery, and all of known space would soon be crawling with voracious bugs. All this had been documented, uploaded to a message torp, and sent to HQ, along with enough electronic intercepts to keep Madame Xanith's analysts busy for a couple of weeks. The accomplishment provided the cyborg with a momentary sense of satisfaction.

But that was yesterday's news, Batkin hadn't uncovered anything since, and he was convinced he wasn't going to. Not unless one counted the ugly-looking second-stage nymphs that had started to hatch and crawl around the jungle floor. A biologically interesting process, no doubt, and one that Batkin was duty-bound to document, but hardly the sort of intelligence coup that the spy dreamed of. Because even if the ex-banker's physical body had been reduced to little more than raw hamburger during the high-speed train crash—the ambition that drove him remained undiminished. Something which, unbeknownst to him, was among the personality traits that Madame X's recruiters had been looking for. Because complacent, self-satisfied intelligence agents had a very low success rate, especially when working alone.

And so it was that the only spy on Jericho was resting among the branches of a very tall tree when artificial thunder rolled across the land, six white contrails clawed the clear blue sky, and a flock of red wings burst out of the jungle below. All of which caused Batkin to feel a sudden surge of hope. Because something was about to happen.

The cargo compartment stank, or certainly should have, given the big globules of tan-colored vomit that floated in the air. But Vanderveen couldn't smell them, the stink of excreta, or her own rank body odor anymore. In fact, it was as if nothing had the capacity to offend her nose as Jericho's gravity reached up to take hold of the Ramanthian shuttle and pull it down. Not just the ship, but the solar systems of vomit as well, which fell like a putrid rain.

The POWs were standing cheek to jowl, front to back, dozens deep in the musty cargo compartment as the entire shuttle began to shake violently, a horrible creaking sound was heard, and somebody began to pray.

Vanderveen no longer cared by that time, and would have been content to die in a fiery explosion if that meant freedom from the sick feeling in her gut, the panicky claustrophobia that made the diplomat want to strike out at the people around her, and the man behind her, who in spite of the disgusting conditions, was determined to rub his erection against her bottom.

There wasn't much room, but by lifting her right foot and stomping on the marine's toes, the FSO forced the man to back off. Then the shuttle began to buck as it hit successive layers of air, fittings rattled as if the entire ship might come apart, and the pilot said something over the intercom. Unfortunately, it was in Ramanthian, so Vanderveen couldn't understand it. A warning perhaps? There was no way to know as the shuttle continued to lose altitude, and the ride stabilized.

What seemed like a month, but was actually only about twenty minutes, passed as the shuttle completed its descent. Then, after a tight turn to starboard, the ship came in for what even the Confederacy pilots had to admit was a very smooth landing. As the spaceship slowed, a human watched the shuttle turn off the main runway and taxi toward the apron where five similar craft were parked. Their passengers were already streaming out onto the hot tarmac. Both the airstrip and the long, low terminal building that adjoined it were temporary. Later, after the Ramanthians finished the Class I spaceport that was being constructed some thirty miles to the east, the whole facility would be torn down. Not that Maximillian Tragg cared what the bugs did with it so long as they paid him. Which, having accidentally acquired a thousand POWs, the Ramanthians had agreed to do. And the renegade had huge gambling debts that would have to be paid before he could return to the Confederacy.

Tragg was an imposing man, who stood six-four even without his combat boots and looked like a weight lifter. Both a sleeveless shirt and the custom-made body armor that molded itself to Tragg's wedge-shaped torso served to emphasize his muscularity. The fact that the human wore two low-riding handguns, and was backed by four heavily armed Sheen robots, made him look even more impressive. And now, as the POWs began to spill out of the final shuttle, the renegade's *real* work was about to begin.

Vanderveen felt a tremendous sense of relief as the shuttle finally came to a stop, the back ramp was deployed, and a wave of thick humid air pushed its way into the cargo compartment. Orders were shouted from outside, and boots clattered on metal as the first wave of prisoners stumbled out into the bright sunlight, where two dozen helmeted Ramanthian troopers waited to take charge of them.

Once the bodies immediately in front of her began to move, the diplomat followed. Her head swiveled back and forth as she made her way down the bouncing ramp and onto the heat-fused soil beyond. But there wasn't much to see beyond the thick vegetation that threatened to roll out onto the tarmac, a row of neatly parked Ramanthian shuttles, and the crowd of POWs, who were being systematically herded toward a slightly raised platform. Five figures stood on top of the riser, but they didn't appear to be Ramanthian. And as the distance closed, that impression was confirmed. Hooks had taken up a position next to Vanderveen by that time and was the first to comment on the individual who stood out in front of the others. "What the hell is going on?" the official demanded. "That guy is human!"

"That's the way it looks," the FSO agreed. "But his friends certainly aren't."

Hooks might have commented on the robots but was prevented from doing so as Commander Schell shouted a series of orders, officers and noncoms responded, and began to circulate through the crowd. It took about five minutes to sort everyone out, but when the process was over, the POWs were standing in orderly ranks. Vanderveen found herself toward the front of the assemblage and less than thirty feet from the raised platform. President Nankool was standing a couple of ranks behind her.

From her position in the second row, Vanderveen found she could assess the man in front of them. The first thing she noticed was his height. Of more interest, however, was the man's bald skull, dark wraparound goggles, and horribly ravaged face. It had, judging from appearances, been badly burned. The man's eyes were effectively hidden, but his nose was missing, as were his ears. The ridges of scar tissue that covered his face were interrupted by the horizontal slash of his mouth.

And it was then, while Vanderveen was searching the man's face, that his eyes came into contact with hers. The FSO *felt* the momentary connection as the black goggles came into alignment with her gaze and something passed between them. The diplomat felt something cold trickle into her bloodstream as the creature on the platform came to some sort of decision and went on to scan the crowd.

Having chosen the POW he was going to kill, Tragg spoke for the first time. "Welcome to Jericho." The renegade had a voice that would have done justice to a regimental sergeant major, and it was amplified as well. Not by a standard PA system, but by the four robots arrayed around him, all of whom had external speakers.

"The Ramanthians see you as little more than domesticated animals," the mercenary continued. "So, rather than force one of their officers to supervise your activities, they hired me to handle the task for them. My name is Tragg. *Overseer* Tragg. And you will call me, '*sir*.'"

Tragg paused to let the words sink in before starting up again. "Because I am a paid contractor, and *you* are my work force, I need you in order to succeed. But by no means do I need *all* of you. Of course you may not believe that. So in order to prove that I'm serious it will be necessary to kill someone. Not because the person in question has done anything wrong, but because I believe their death will make a lasting impression, and ensure compliance with my orders."

Calisco stood on the opposite side of Vanderveen from Hooks. "The bastard is *crazy*," the undersecretary said sotto voce, but Vanderveen wasn't so sure. Because everything the man named Tragg said was logical if amoral. And, based on the contact experienced only minutes before, the diplomat was pretty sure that she *knew* which person had been chosen to die. Something heavy settled into the pit of her stomach. The diplomat felt light-headed and struggled to keep her feet. Vanderveen saw a mental picture of her parents, followed by one of Legion Captain Antonio Santana, and felt a wave of guilt. The two of them had agreed to meet on Earth, but she'd been called away to become part of Nankool's staff, and there was no way to tell him. If only there had been an opportunity to *see* Santana, to let the legionnaire know how she felt, but now it seemed as though that opportunity was gone forever.

"So," Tragg continued conversationally, "while you consider the very real possibility that *your* life is about to end, let's go over what everyone else will be doing for the next few days. Given the fact that our hosts are a bit strapped for ground transportation, most of you will be required to walk the 146 miles to Jericho Prime, where you will take part in a rather interesting construction project. More on that later. . . . Now that you know *where* you're going, and *why*, it's time to shoot one of you in the head, something I prefer to do personally rather than delegate the task to one of my robots."

A murmur ran through the ranks, and the assemblage started to shift, as some of the POWs made as if to attack, and others considered making a run for it. But the robots had raised their energy projectors by that time, and the Ramanthian troopers were at the ready, which meant neither strategy stood any chance of success. Seeing that, and hoping to avoid a bloodbath, Schell shouted an order. "As you were!" Surprisingly, the prisoners obeyed, as Tragg drew a chromed pistol, and aimed the weapon at the crowd.

Some people flinched as the gun panned from left to right and finally came to rest. Vanderveen found herself looking right into the renegade's gun barrel, knew her intuition had been correct, and closed her eyes. The diplomat heard a loud *bang*, followed by a communal groan, and opened her eyes to discover that she was still alive. But the young woman who had been standing not three feet away wasn't. Her body lay in a rapidly expanding pool of blood.

The first thing Vanderveen felt was a sense of relief, quickly followed by a wave of shame, as the victim's name echoed through the crowd. "Moya, Moya, Moya, Moya, Moya, Moya." The sound of it continued, like the soft rustle of wind that sometimes precedes a rainstorm, and eventually died away as the name was repeated by the last rank of POWs. "Lieutenant Moya," Hooks demanded incredulously. *"Why?"*

More than a thousand beings were assembled on the tarmac, and while Vanderveen knew very few of them, she had been aware of Moya. Partly because the officer had been assigned to serve as liaison with Nankool's staff, and partly because the young woman was so beautiful that she seemed to glow, which attracted attention from males and females alike. Because for better or worse, human beings were wired to pay attention to the most attractive members of the species and find ways to please them, a reality the diplomat occasionally took advantage of herself.

And suddenly, as *that* thought crossed Vanderveen's mind, the diplomat realized that she knew the answer to the question Hooks had posed. Moya had been murdered because of the way she looked. Had Tragg been rejected because of his face? Yes, the FSO decided, chances were that he had. So to kill Moya was to kill *all* of the women who had refused him. Or was that too facile? No, the diplomat concluded, it wasn't. Because deep down Vanderveen knew that *she* had been considered, found wanting, and dismissed in favor of Moya.

"Good," Tragg said as he holstered the recently fired pistol. "*Very* good. I'm glad to see that we have been able to establish a good working relationship in such short order. Now, if you would be so kind as to follow the red remote, it will lead you to a pile of packs. Each pack contains a basic issue of food and other items that you will need during the next few days. You can leave your pack behind, consume all of your food on the first day, or ration it out. That's up to you. . . . But it's all you're going to get until we arrive at Jericho Prime. And remember, the Ramanthian guards don't like you, so don't piss them off! That will be all."

As if on cue, a dozen Ramanthian sphere-shaped remotes sailed into the area from the direction of the low-lying terminal and immediately took up positions above the POWs. Each robot was armed with a stun gun, a spotlight, and a speaker, but only one of them was red. It led Schell, and therefore the rest of the prisoners, out across the tarmac and toward the jungle on the far side. Lieutenant Moya lay where she had fallen, the first POW to die on Jericho, but certainly not the last.

4

Peace is very apoplexy, lethargy: mulled, deaf, sleepy, insensible: a getter of more bastard children, than war is a destroyer of men.

—*William Shakespeare*
Coriolanus
Standard year 1607

PLANET EARTH, THE CONFEDERACY OF SENTIENT BEINGS

Having landed at Vandenberg Spaceport, and rented a ground car, Captain Antonio Santana drove north toward the metroplex that now encompassed what had once been the separate cities of San Francisco, Vallejo, Berkeley, Oakland, Hayward, Sunnyvale, and San Jose.

It had been a long time since the legionnaire had been on what some still referred to as "Mother Earth." Having spent extended periods of time on primitive worlds like LaNor and Savas, it was difficult to adjust to the flood of high-intensity sensory input, as the skyscraper "skins" that lined both sides of the elevated expressway morphed into a single panoramic advertisement, and sleek sports cars passed him at 130 miles per hour. Meanwhile the onboard computer fed him an unending stream of unsolicited advice, which the soldier managed to escape by switching to autopilot and allowing the Vehicle Traffic Control System (VTCS) to drive the car for him.

A not-altogether-comfortable experience since the computers that controlled the system were primarily interested in moving Santana through the metroplex as quickly as possible. He felt the car accelerate and gave in to the urge to look back over his left shoulder as the VTCS steered his vehicle into the fast lane. It was a scary moment since a single electronic glitch could cause a massive pileup and cost hundreds of lives. But there hadn't been one of those in *years*, or so the onboard computer claimed, not that the assertion made Santana feel any better.

What *did* make the officer feel good, however, was the knowledge that the Ramanthians wouldn't be shooting at him anytime soon and that he was about to be reunited with Christine Vanderveen, the beautiful diplomat he had met on LaNor.

There was a downside, however, and that was the fact that Santana was on his way to see both Vanderveen *and* her parents, wealthy upper-crust types with whom a junior officer from humble beginnings was unlikely to be comfortable. Of course, the fact that Vanderveen wanted him to meet her family was a good sign and suggested that the diplomat wanted to continue the relationship that had begun within the Imperial City of Polwa and eventually been consummated in the hills off to the west. And that, from his perspective, was nothing short of an out-and-out miracle.

So as the enclosed highway dove under San Francisco Bay and made a beeline for the community of Napa, Santana felt a sense of anticipation mixed with concern. He'd been through a lot since LaNor, and so had she, so would the chemistry be intact? And what about her folks? They couldn't possibly be looking forward to his arrival. Not given his working-class origins. But would they give him a chance? And assuming they did—would he be able to take advantage of it? Or wind up making a fool of himself?

Those questions and more were still on Santana's mind

as what had mysteriously turned into Highway 80 surfaced just north of the hundred-foot-tall seawall that kept the bay from flooding the burbs and the traffic control system shunted the rental car onto a secondary road that led to the gated community known as "Napa Estates," a huge area that included all of what had once been called "wine country," and was protected by a twelve-foot-high steel-reinforced duracrete blastproof "riot wall." Which was designed to keep people like him out.

There was a backup, and Santana had to wait fifteen minutes before he finally pulled up to one of four inbound security gates. That was where an ex-legionnaire with a face so lined that it looked like one of the Legion's topo maps scrutinized the officer's military ID and shook his head sadly. "Sorry, sir, but I'll have to put you through the wringer. No exceptions."

Santana nodded. The fact that the legionnaire had fought for the Confederacy on distant worlds, and been separated from the military with a retirement so small that he had to work, was just plain wrong—a problem only partially addressed in the wake of the great mutiny. "What regiment?" the officer inquired, as the veteran scanned his retinas.

"The 13th Demi-Brigade de Legion Etrangere, sir," the guard answered proudly. "We fought the Hudathans on Algeron and whipped 'em good!"

"You sure as hell did," Santana agreed soberly. "I've seen the graves."

"And if the frigging bugs make it to Earth, you'll see some more," the legionnaire predicted grimly. "There's plenty like me—and we still know how to fight."

The comment raised still another issue, and that was the fact that with the exception of people like the elderly security guard, no one seemed to be worried about the war with the Ramanthians. In fact, based on what the officer had seen so far, it was as if the citizens of Earth were only marginally aware that a war was being fought. A rather sad state of affairs given all the sentients who had died in order to protect their planet.

"Your invitation cleared," the old soldier announced, and delivered a textbook-perfect salute. *"Vive la Légion!"*

"Vive la Légion," Santana agreed, and returned the gesture of respect. Thirty seconds later he was inside Napa Estates and driving north along a four-lane road that took him past all manner of formal entries, gently curving driveways, and mansions set back among the vineyards the area was so famous for. Many of the estates included their own wineries, which in the case of the larger operations, were allowed to produce a few thousand bottles for sale. But those were the exception, since most of the residents made their money in other ways and preferred to consume the wine they produced rather than sell it.

All of which seemed fine on the one hand, since Santana believed in free enterprise, yet bothered him as well since there were those like the security guard who had risked everything to protect Earth and been denied a respectable retirement. It was a fate that might very well befall *him* if he wasn't careful.

The common areas, like the broad swatches of irrigated grass that fronted the streets, were groomed to perfection. So each estate was like an individual element within a larger work of art. Nothing like the military housing in which Santana had spent his youth, prior to being accepted into the academy, where experts turned him into a gentleman.

But *acting* like the people who lived in the mansions to the left and right of him was one thing—and being like them was something else. Just one of the reasons why Santana slowed the car as he topped a rise, spotted the house that Vanderveen had described to him, and looked for a spot where he could safely pull off the road.

Then, having accessed his luggage, the officer did what any sensible legionnaire would do prior to launching an assault on an enemy-held objective. He took a small but powerful set of binos, waited for a break in traffic, and crossed the road. A camera mounted high atop the nearest streetlamp tracked his movements.

The grassy verge sloped up to a waist-high stone wall that served to define the estate's boundaries. And, judging from appearances, the Vanderveen property was quite large. As Santana brought the glasses up to his eyes and panned from left to right, he saw rows of meticulously pruned vines that were the ultimate source of the Riesling that the Vanderveen family was so proud of. He could also see some pasture beyond, a white horse that might have been the one the diplomat liked to ride, and a cluster of immaculate outbuildings. The house itself was a straightforward three-story Tudor, and Santana knew that it was within that structure that the woman he loved had been raised, prior to being sent off to a series of expensive boarding schools.

But rather than pursue a career in science or business as she easily could have—Vanderveen had chosen to follow her father into the world of politics and diplomacy. A not especially profitable career path, but one that Charles Winther Vanderveen could well afford, thanks to his inherited wealth.

Santana heard a whirring sound, felt a puff of displaced air hit the back of his neck, and was already in the process of turning and reaching for a nonexistent sidearm when the airborne robot spoke. "Raise your hands and stay where you are," the globe-shaped device advised sternly. "Or I will be forced to stun you consistent with Community S-reg Covenant 456.7."

Santana raised his hands, and was forced to answer a series of security-related questions before the robot finally offered a pro forma apology and sailed away. The incident was humiliating, and if it hadn't been for the opportunity to spend time with Vanderveen, the soldier would have left Napa there and then.

Having guided his rental car in between the stylized stone lions that stood guard to either side of the steel gate, Santana was forced to pause while a scanner checked his retinas. Only then was he allowed to proceed up the gently curving driveway that passed between an ornate fountain and the front of the house. Strangely, the mixture of emotions that Santana felt was reminiscent of going into combat.

The well-packed gravel made a subtle crunching sound as the tires passed over it, and by the time the vehicle rolled to a stop, a woman dressed in riding clothes was already exiting the front door followed by two human servants and a domestic robot. She had carefully coiffed gray hair, a slim athletic build, and covered the distance to the car in a series of leggy strides.

But what Santana found most striking of all was the woman's face, which though older, was so similar to her daughter's that there was absolutely no doubt as to who she was. "Captain Santana!" Margaret Vanderveen said enthusiastically. "We're so glad you're here! I hope the trip up from Vandenberg was comfortable."

Prior to making the journey, Santana had been careful to brush up on proper etiquette, and therefore waited for his hostess to extend her hand before reaching out to shake it. The grip was strong and firm, as was to be expected of someone who worked side by side with the people who tended her vines. "It's a pleasure to meet you, ma'am," Santana said formally. "I can see where Christina got her looks."

"Please call me Margaret," the woman replied easily. "And I can see how *you* managed to turn my daughter's head! Please, come in. Thomas, Mary, and John will take care of your car and luggage."

Santana wondered which name applied to the robot, as he turned to retrieve a professionally wrapped package from the backseat, before allowing himself to be led inside. A formal entranceway emptied into a spacious great room that looked out over verdant pasture toward a turreted home perched on a distant hill. Though large, the home seemed smaller than it was because of all the artwork that Charles Vanderveen had not only inherited but brought home from a dozen different worlds. All of which had been integrated into an interior that was both eclectic and warm. A tribute to Margaret Vanderveen's eye—or that of a professional decorator.

"Please," Margaret Vanderveen said. "Have a seat. What can I get for you? A drink perhaps? I'd offer something to eat, but dinner is only an hour away, and Maria would be most unhappy if I were to spoil your appetite."

"A drink sounds good," Santana allowed. "A gin and tonic if that's convenient."

"It certainly is," the matron replied as she rang a little bell. "And I think I'll join you."

There was the soft *whir* of servos as the robot appeared, took their orders, and left the room. Santana took that as his opportunity to present Mrs. Vanderveen with the carefully wrapped box. "Here," he said awkwardly. "I had this made on LaNor."

As Margaret Vanderveen accepted the present, she discovered that it was surprisingly heavy. Although hostess gifts weren't important to her, the fact that the young officer had gone to the trouble of bringing one spoke to his manners, and a desire to make a good impression. Both of which were promising signs. Especially given his rough-and-tumble beginnings. "Why, thank you, Antonio! That was unnecessary, but the Vanderveen women love presents, so I therefore refuse to give it back."

Mrs. Vanderveen was clearly attempting to be nice to him, so Santana allowed himself to relax slightly and wondered where Christine was. Out for a ride perhaps? Or gone shopping? There was no way to know, and he was afraid to ask lest the question seem rude.

The wrapping paper rattled as Margaret Vanderveen

took it off to reveal a highly polished wooden box. Intricate relief carvings covered the top and all four sides. Later, when the matron had time to examine them more closely, she would discover that they were battle scenes in which her daughter had played a role.

But given the weight of the object, Margaret Vanderveen knew that the box had been designed to contain something more important. Something which, judging from Santana's expression, he hoped she would like. Having found all of the little brass hooks that held the lid in place, Mrs. Vanderveen pushed each of them out of the way and removed the top. A sculpture nestled within.

"There are some truly remarkable artisans on LaNor," Santana explained. "The locals refer to the carvers as 'wood poets,' and for good reason."

As Margaret Vanderveen removed the wood sculpture from its case she found herself looking at a likeness of her daughter's face that was so lifelike that it took her breath away. And then, before she could clamp down on what *her* mother would have regarded as an inappropriate display of emotion, tears began to flow down her cheeks. "It's very beautiful," the matron said feelingly. "And, outside of Christina herself, perhaps the nicest gift that I have ever received. Thank you."

The reaction was much stronger than anything Santana might have hoped for, but he wasn't sure how to handle it, and he felt a tremendous sense of relief when the robot arrived with their drinks. That gave Mrs. Vanderveen an opportunity to excuse herself for a moment. Her eyes were dry when she returned. "Sorry about that," she said. "But the likeness is *so* good that it took me off guard. Antonio—"

"Please," Santana interrupted. "My friends call me Tony."

Margaret Vanderveen smiled and nodded. "Tony, the truth is that I have some bad news to share with you, and I've been stalling. A few weeks after Christine came home on vacation, she was asked to join President Nankool's personal staff and felt that she had no choice but to do so."

The older woman's eyes seemed to beseech Santana at that point as if begging for understanding. "She knew you were on the way here," Mrs. Vanderveen said. "And she knew there was no way to reach you in time. Believe me, Christine was absolutely beside herself with concern about how you would feel, and many tears were shed right here in this room. But there's a letter," the matron added. "*This* letter, which she left for you."

The letter had been there all along, sitting between them, concealed in a beautiful marble box. The lid made a soft *thump* as she put it down. "If you'll excuse me, I'm going to change for dinner," the hostess said tactfully. "Ring the bell when you're ready, and one of the servants will show you to your room."

The soldier said, "Thank you," and stood as his hostess got up to leave. Once she was gone, he sat on the couch. The drink was still there, so he took a pull and returned the glass to its coaster. Then, with hands that shook slightly, Santana opened the envelope. As a faint whiff of perfume found his nostrils, the legionnaire was reminded of what it felt like to bury his face in Vanderveen's hair.

"My dearest Tony," the letter began. "By now you know that I was called away by the one thing that can take precedence over you—and that is my duty to the Confederacy. And if we were not at war, even that would be put aside so that I could be with you!

"But these are troubled times, my dearest. Times when bombs fall on innocent cities, when missiles destroy unarmed ships, and when all that we both hold dear is at risk. So I beg your forgiveness, trust that you of all people will understand, and look forward to the moment when your arms will embrace me once again.

"With love and affection, Christine."

The name was a little blurry, as if a tear might have fallen on it before the ink could dry, and Santana felt something rise to block the back of his throat. He wanted to run, to get as far away from the house that she had grown up in as he could, but it was too late for that. So the officer finished his drink, slipped the letter into the inside pocket of his new sports coat, and rang the little bell. The robot, whatever his name was, had clearly been waiting.

PLANET ALGERON, THE CONFEDERACY OF SENTIENT BEINGS

By the time Booly received the summons and arrived at what had once been Nankool's private conference room, there was standing room only. The members of Vice President Jakov's inner circle, including Assistant Undersecretary for Foreign Affairs Kay Wilmot, were seated around the long oval table, leaving everyone else to stand along the walls. Doma-Sa had been given a huge Hudathan-sized chair consistent with his status as a head of state. But others, Madame X and Chien-Chu included, weren't so lucky. Booly, who found himself crammed in next to his wife's uncle, whispered into the cyborg's plastiflesh ear. "What the hell is going on, Sergi? This wasn't on the schedule."

"No," the entrepreneur, politician, and reserve admiral agreed. "It wasn't. And that was no accident! I used to pull the same stunt myself. . . . There's nothing like a surprise meeting to catch the opposition off guard."

Booly looked at the room and back again. "The opposition being?"

"Anyone who was close to Nankool," Chien-Chu answered matter-of-factly. "And that includes *you*."

Booly had never seen his relationship with the president that way, since he was a soldier, and sworn to serve whatever person held the office. Including Jakov, were he to succeed Nankool. But it looked like the vice president had other ideas and intended to marginalize the Military Chief of Staff. Preliminary to replacing him? Yes, Booly decided, and wondered which one of his subordinates would be put in charge of the Confederacy's military forces.

There was a stir as Jakov entered the room from what had been Nankool's office. The politician nodded and waved in response to a variety of greetings before stepping up to the table and looking around. "Hello, everybody—and thanks for coming on such short notice. But, as all of you know, we face something of a crises. President Nankool is dead or missing. And, absent information to the contrary, the first possibility seems to be the more likely of the two."

Jakov paused at that point and his staff, led by Kay Wilmot, nodded in unison. "It's been my hope that our intelligence people would be able to figure out what happened to the president," Jakov continued. "And I know they've done their best. But time has passed, and there are those who feel we should activate the succession plan before word of what happened in the Nebor system leaks out. Because if we fail to stay out in front of this thing, the news could result in panic."

Booly had to give Jakov credit. Rather than call for the activation of the plan himself—the politician had arranged for some of his cronies to do it for him. And one of them, the senator from Worber's World, was quick to come to his feet. "The vice president is correct," the bland-faced politician said fervently. "All of us feel badly about President Nankool, but we're at war, and it's absolutely imperative that we have strong leadership!" Wilmot had written those words and was pleased with the way they sounded as she added her voice to the chorus of agreement from those seated around her.

"The first step," Jakov continued, "is to issue a carefully worded press release. A confirmation vote will be held soon thereafter. With that out of the way, we'll be free to tackle some new initiatives, which could trim years off the conflict and save millions of lives. More on that soon."

Doma-Sa's hard flinty eyes made contact with Chien-Chu's artificial orbs at that point, and even though they were from very different cultures, each knew what the other was thinking. There was only one way that Jakov and his sycophants could shorten the war—and that was to give the bugs a large portion of what they wanted. A period of relative peace might follow such an agreement. But at what price? Because ultimately the bugs would settle for nothing less than *everything*. A servo whined as the businessman's hand went up. "May I say something?"

It had been Jakov's hope, and Wilmot's as well, that neither Chien-Chu nor Doma-Sa would hear about the meeting quickly enough to attend. But both were present, and given the past president's undiminished popularity, there was little the vice president could do but acquiesce. "Of course!" Jakov said heartily. "What's on your mind?"

"Simply this," the cyborg said bleakly. "We know the president was planning to assume a false identity in order to blend in with the other POWs. So, if you announce that Nankool is missing, the bugs may very well take another look at the prisoners and quite possibly identify him. At that point the Ramanthians will almost certainly make some very public demands. What will happen *then*? Especially if it looks like you were in a hurry to succeed him?"

Nankool was popular, *very* popular, so Jakov knew what would happen. A lot of voters would be unhappy with him. So much so that they might seek to block or even reverse his confirmation. Especially if ex-president Chien-Chu stood ready to oppose him. But the facts were the facts, and like it or not, the cyborg would have to bow to reality. "You make an excellent point," Jakov replied smoothly. "But surely you don't believe we can wait indefinitely. . . . How would we explain the president's continued absence?"

Jakov had a point, and Chien-Chu knew it, so the entrepreneur went for the best deal he thought he could get. The
key was to buy time and hope that word of Nankool's fate
would somehow filter in. Then, if the president was dead,
the cyborg would throw his support behind Jakov and try
to exert influence on whatever decisions the politician
made. "Thirty days," Chien-Chu said soberly. "Let's give the
intelligence-gathering process thirty days. Then, if there's
no word of the president's fate, I will support your plan."

The vice president would have preferred fifteen days, or
no days, but didn't want to dicker in front of his staff. That
would not only appear unseemly but smack of desperation.
Besides, assuming that Chien-Chu kept his word, the ex-
president's support would virtually guarantee a speedy
confirmation process. "Thirty days it is then," Jakov allowed. "In the meantime, it's absolutely imperative to
keep the lid on. Is everyone agreed?"

There was a chorus of assent, but Wilmot knew her
sponsor was likely to blame her for the way the meeting
had gone, since she was the one who had put the idea forward. But Nankool was dead, Wilmot felt sure of that, and
the day of succession *would* come. And when it did, Chien-
Chu, his stuck-up niece, and the rest of Nankool's toadies
were going to pay. The thought pleased the assistant undersecretary so much that she was smiling as the meeting
came to an end.

PLANET EARTH, THE CONFEDERACY OF SENTIENT BEINGS

Having surrendered the rental car to the traffic control system, Santana took his hands off the steering wheel and
pushed the seat away from the dashboard. It was early afternoon, the Vanderveen estate was behind him, and he
was happy to be free of it. Not that Charles and Margaret
Vanderveen hadn't been kind to him. They had. But what
all of them had in common was Christine, and without her

there to bind the three of them together, dinner had been stiff and awkward.

Diplomat Charles Vanderveen had taken the opportunity to tell his wife about the importance of the hypercom, Santana's role in capturing the all-important prototype, and his recent promotion, all intended to build the officer up. A kindness Santana wouldn't forget.

But when dessert was served, and Santana announced his intention to leave the following morning, neither one of the Vanderveens objected. And now, as the car carried the legionnaire south into the San Diego–Tijuana metroplex, Santana was looking for a way to kill some time. Fortunately, there was a ship lifting for Adobe in two days. That would allow him to save some leave and rejoin the 1st Cavalry Regiment (1st REC) earlier than planned. Now that he was a captain, Colonel Kobbi would almost certainly give him a company to command. And, after the casualties suffered on Savas, it would be necessary to create it from scratch. It was a task the officer looked forward to and dreaded at the same time.

The vehicle's interior lights came on as the sprawling city blocked the sun, and the car entered the maze of subsurface highways and roads that fed the teeming beast above. A hab so large that the westernmost portion of it floated on the surface of the Pacific Ocean.

But Santana couldn't afford the pleasures available to people like the Vanderveens, not on a captain's salary, and felt his ears pop as the car spiraled down toward the Military Entertainment Zone (MEZ), where his credits would stretch further.

An hour later Santana had checked into a clean but no-frills hotel, stashed his luggage in his room, and was out on the street. Not a normal street, since the "sky" consisted of a video mosaic, but a long passageway lined by garish casinos, sex emporiums, tattoo parlors, cheap eateries, discount stores, and recruiting offices.

Nor was Santana alone. Because hundreds of sailors, marines, and legionnaires flowed around him as they searched the subterranean environment for something new to see, taste, or feel. Most were bio bods, but there were cyborgs, too, all of whom wore utilitarian spiderlike bodies rather than war forms. Ex-criminals for the most part, who had chosen a sort of half-life over no life, and served a very real need. Especially during a period when the Confederacy was literally fighting for its life. Even if people on planets like Earth seemed unaware of that fact as they continued to lead their comfortable lives.

The legionnaire was dressed in nondescript civvies, but the denizens of the MEZ knew Santana for what he was, and it wasn't long before hustlers, whores, and con men began to call out from doorways, sidle up to tug at his sleeve, and pitch him via holos that exploded into a million motes of light as he passed through them.

Most were little more than human sediment who, lacking the initiative to do something better with their lives, lived at the bottom of the MEZ cesspool. But there were some, like the one-armed wretch who sat with her back to a wall and had a brain box clutched between her bony knees, who fell into a different category. Men, women, and borgs who had been used by society only to be tossed away when their bodies refused to accept a transplant, or they became addicted to painkillers, or their minds crumbled under the strain of what they had seen and done.

Santana paused in front of the emaciated woman, saw the 2nd REP's triangular insignia that had been tattooed onto her stump, and nodded politely. "When were you discharged?"

The ex-legionnaire knew an officer when she saw one, even if he was in civvies, and sat up straighter. "They put me dirtside three years ago, sir. . . . As for Quimby here," the vet said, as she tapped the brain box with a broken fingernail. "Well, he's been out for the better part of five years. Ever since his quad took a direct hit, his life support went down, and he suffered some brain damage. A civvie was using him as a shoeshine stand when I came along. So I saved the money to buy him. He's overdue for a tune-up though—so a credit or two would help."

Santana knew she could be lying but gave her a fifty-credit debit card anyway. "Take Quimby in now. *Before* you buy any booze."

The woman grinned toothlessly as she accepted the piece of plastic. "Sir, yes, sir!"

Santana nodded, and was just about to leave, when a raspy voice issued forth from the beat-up brain box. Though not normally equipped with any sort of speaking apparatus, Quimby's brain box had been modified for that purpose. And while far from functional, the creature within could still think and feel. "I'm sorry, sir," Quimby said apologetically. "But there were just too many of them—and we lost Norley."

Santana felt a lump form in the back of his throat. "That's okay, soldier," he said kindly. "You did what you could. That's all any of us can do."

The crowd swallowed the officer after that, the woman stood, and lifted Quimby off the sidewalk. "Come on, old buddy," she said. "Once we get those toxins flushed out of your system, we'll charge your power supply and go out for a beer."

"There were just too many of them," Quimby insisted plaintively. "I ran out of ammunition."

"Yeah," the woman said soothingly, as she carried the cyborg down the hall. "But it's like the man said. . . . You did everything you could."

It was hunger, rather than a desire to see a fight, that drew Santana to the Blue Moon Bar and Fight Club. A well-known dive in which the patrons were free to eat, drink, and beat each other senseless. The interior of the club was about a third full when Santana entered. That meant there were plenty of seats to choose from. Especially among the outer ring of tables that circled the blood-splattered platform at the center of the room. It squatted below a crescent-shaped neon moon that threw a bluish glare down onto a pair of medics as they tugged an unconscious body out from under the lowest side-rope. That left the twelve-foot-by-twelve-foot square temporarily empty as those fortunate enough to survive the previous round took a much-deserved break.

Santana chose a table well back from the platform, eyed the menu on the tabletop screen, and ordered a steak by placing an index finger on top of the cut he wanted. A waitress appeared a few moments later. She was naked with the exception of a thong and a pair of high-heeled shoes. Most of her income came from tips generated by allowing patrons to paw her body. And even though the waitress did the best she could produce a pouty come-hither smile, there was no hiding the weariness that she felt. "So, soldier," the woman said for what might have been the millionth time. "What will it be? A beer? A drink? Or *me*?" Her saline-filled breasts rose slightly as her hands came up to cup them.

"Those look nice," Santana allowed, as he eyed the giant orbs. "But I'll take the beer."

The waitress looked relieved as she wound her way between the tables and headed for the bar. She had a nice and presumably natural rear end, which Santana was in the process of ogling, when a commotion at the center of the room diverted his attention. "Ladies and gentlemen!" the short man in the loud shirt said importantly. "The battle began with six brave sailors, and five legionnaires, who gave a good account of themselves until the last round, when all but one was eliminated. So, with a total of three sailors left to contend with, our remaining legionnaire is badly outnumbered. Of course you know the rules. . . . New recruits can join the combatants up to a maximum of six people per team, one Hudathan being equivalent to two humans."

The short man raised a hand to shade his eyes from the glare. "So who is going to join this brave legionnaire? Or would three additional sailors like to come up and help their comrades beat the crap out of her? She could surrender, of course. . . . Which might be a very good idea!"

The sailors, all male, had climbed up onto the platform by that time and were in the process of slipping between the ropes. The legionnaire, who was quite obviously female, was already there. She wore her hair short flattop style, and a black eye marred an otherwise attractive face. The woman stood about five-eight, and judging from the look of her arms and legs, was a part-time bodybuilder. Her olive drab singlet was dark with sweat, and a pair of black trunks completed the outfit. Her hands and feet were wrapped with tape, but the only other protective gear the legionnaire had was a mouthpiece that made her cheeks bulge. If the soldier was worried, there was certainly no sign of it as she threw punches at an imaginary opponent.

There were loud catcalls from the naval contingent, plus laughter from a sizable group of marines, but no one appeared ready to join the woman in the ring. That struck Santana as surprising, because in keeping with their motto *Legio Patria Nostra* (The Legion Is Our Country), legionnaires were notoriously loyal to each other. But by some stroke of bad luck it appeared the young woman and he were the only members of their branch present. And the *last* thing the officer wanted to do was be part of a stupid brawl.

"Uh-oh," the short man said, as his voice boomed over the bar's PA system. "It looks like the odds are about to change!"

Santana saw that two additional sailors were climbing into the ring, both confident of an easy victory. Suddenly the odds against the lone legionnaire had changed from three to one to five to one. But rather than leave the ring as she logically should have—the woman continued to jab the air in front of her.

Santana sensed movement and turned to find that the waitress with the large breasts had arrived with his steak. The huge slab of meat was still sizzling, and the smell made his stomach growl. "That looks good," the officer said as he got up from the table. "Keep it hot for me."

The waitress glanced toward the ring and back again. "Okay, hon, but you'll have to pay now. Because if those sailors send you to the hospital, then the boss will take your dinner out of my pay."

Santana sighed, paid for the steak, and threw in a substantial tip. "Like I said, keep my food warm."

The waitress wondered why such a good-looking man would want to get his face messed up and gave him a kiss on the cheek. "Good luck, honey," she said kindly. "Your steak will be waiting in the kitchen."

"Wait a minute!" the short man proclaimed, as Santana began to make his way down the aisle. "What have we here? A legionnaire perhaps? A knight in shining armor? Let's hear it for our latest contestant!"

Everyone, the sailors included, wanted a *real* contest, so a cheer went up as the officer removed his shirt and shucked his shoes. The MC gave Santana a mouthpiece and pointed to the lengths of tape that hung from one of the side-ropes. "Help yourself, bud, and good luck to ya. . . ."

As Santana began to wrap his hands, his brain kicked into high gear. The latest sailors to enter the ring were clearly inebriated. Would it make more sense to take them out first? Assuming that such a thing was possible. Or leave the drunks in, hoping they would get in the way? And what plans if any did his new ally have in mind?

As Santana climbed into the ring the naval contingent

handed a bottle of booze up to their team, who continued to trash-talk the Legion, while passing the bottle around. That gave the legionnaire a chance to get acquainted with his teammate. "My name's Santana. . . . And you are?"

Before the young woman could answer, it was first necessary to remove the protective device from her mouth. Her left eye was swollen shut by that time—and Santana could see that her upper lip was puffy as well. "Gomez," the woman said thickly. "Corporal Maria Gomez."

"Glad to meet you, Corporal," the officer said. "Although I wish the circumstances were different."

The eye that Santana could see was brown and filled with hostile intelligence. "You're an officer," she said accusingly. The statement was tinged with disappointment.

Santana raised an eyebrow. "Yes, I am. Is that a problem?"

"It could be," the noncom said flatly. "No offense, sir, but when was the last time you were in a barroom brawl?"

Santana had been fighting for his life only two months before, but he knew what the soldier meant, and he answered in kind. "Ten, maybe twelve years ago."

"Then I'd say you're a bit rusty," Gomez replied. *"Sir."*

The honorific had been added as an obvious afterthought, and Santana couldn't help but grin. "You don't like officers much, do you?"

"I wouldn't go to a meeting without one," Gomez replied disrespectfully. "But when it comes to a fistfight, then no sir, I don't have much use for 'em."

"Fair enough," Santana replied gravely. "So, given your obvious expertise, how should we proceed?"

"We'll take a corner and defend it," the noncom replied confidently. "And, since at least two of the swabbies are drunk, they'll get in the way as their buddies try to rush us."

"I like it," Santana said agreeably. "What sort of intel can you provide?"

"None of them use their feet well," Gomez answered

clinically. "But the big bastard has plenty of power—which is why I was standing here all by myself until you showed up."

"No," Santana objected. "That's why you were *alone*, not why you were standing here. Maybe you would be kind enough to explain that to me."

Something flickered deep within the noncom's good eye. "I'm here because I like a good fight, no fucking asshole has been able to put me down so far, and the Legion don't run."

Santana might have answered, but the gong sounded, a cheer went up, and the battle was on. There wasn't any ceremony. Just a loud *bong*, followed by a reedy cheer, as Gomez and Santana bit their mouthpieces. They stood side by side, with their backs to a corner, a strategy that made it difficult if not impossible to attack them from behind.

Like Gomez, Santana had been taught the fine art of kickboxing by the Legion, which considered the sport to be the martial art of choice for everyone other than special ops. They were expected to master other disciplines as well. But, as both of them assumed the correct stance, Santana could see that his teammate's form was superior to his. So the legionnaire brought his eyes up, tucked his elbows in against his ribs, and reduced the distance between his legs. The officer knew the key was to put about 50-percent of his weight on each leg, with his right foot slightly forward and fists held shoulder high. Gomez saw the adjustments, nodded approvingly, and made a minute adjustment where her attitude toward officers was concerned.

In the meantime, the sailors were closing in. Given their recent successes against the legionnaires, plus the advantage that went with numerical superiority, the navy team expected an easy victory. Because of that, plus the scrutiny of those in the audience, the entire group wanted in on the kill. So the sailors charged in, but given the way the space narrowed, only three were able to make direct contact. That improved the odds as the first blows were struck.

The main reason that Gomez was still on her feet was the legionnaire's ability to kick. Because most men had more upper-body strength than she did, the noncom knew the battle would be over if they got their hands on her. So now, as a drunk shuffled forward, Gomez brought her right leg up in the bent position and struck with the ball of her foot. The sailor saw the kick coming, made a clumsy attempt to block it, but was way too slow. The blow struck his sternum, forced the air out of his lungs, and sent him reeling backwards.

That was when the rating collided with one of the two men who had been forced to wait and knocked the unfortunate sailor off his feet. Both went down in a flurry of uncoordinated arms and legs. The marines in the audience thought that was funny and laughed uproariously.

Meanwhile, Santana was fighting to hold his own against the man Gomez had warned him about. The sailor wasn't a kickboxer, and didn't need to be, given powerful shoulders and a quick pair of hands. Worse yet was the fact that the big noncom was taller and heavier than the legionnaire was.

The officer managed to deflect another blow with raised hands, flicked his head to one side, and felt a searing pain as a bony fist grazed the left side of his head. His ear was on fire, and Santana resisted the temptation to reach back and touch it. The gunner's mate grinned happily and shuffled his size-fourteen feet.

The legionnaire could smell the other man's foul breath as he took a step backwards and readied a front-leg round-kick. With his leg cocked, the officer turned sideways and put everything he had into the kick. Santana heard a satisfying *grunt* as his shin made contact with the other man's groin. But the noncom was wearing a protective cup, so other than being forced to take a couple of involuntary steps backwards, the sailor was largely unaffected.

The momentary respite gave Santana the opportunity to pummel the second drunk with a series of quick jabs, the last of which brought a torrent of blood gushing out of his nose. Then, as the unfortunate rating sought to stem the flow with his fingers, a blow from Gomez put the drunk down for good. But four opponents were still on their feet—and they were pissed.

Having been bested once, and chided for it by the audience, the first drunk was determined to teach the Legion bitch a lesson. And, foggy though his thinking was, he knew her feet were the key. In an act that was part inspiration and part desperation, the rating made a diving grab for the woman's legs.

Gomez saw the move coming, tried to leap up out of the way, but was a hair too slow. A pair of powerful arms wrapped themselves around her calves, the noncom came crashing down, and a loud cheer went up. "Stomp her!" someone shouted, and two of the sailors were quick to seize upon the opportunity.

Unable to rise, and therefore unable to protect herself, all Gomez could do was curl up in the fetal position and try to protect her head as dozens of blows connected with her body. The sailors weren't wearing boots, thank God. . . . But each kick hurt like hell.

Santana wanted to help, and would have, had it not been for the big sailor with the ham-sized fists. The two of them had traded at least a dozen blows by that time, but in spite of the new cut over the noncom's right eye, the swabbie showed no signs of tiring. If anything, the gunner's mate appeared to be enjoying himself.

Finally, Santana locked both hands together, brought them down over the other man's head, and jerked him in close. Then, having shifted his weight to his front leg, the legionnaire brought the other leg up in a classic side-knee strike. He felt the blow connect with the petty officer's solar plexus, knew he had scored, and heard a shrill whistle. Somebody shouted, "Freeze! Military Police!"

Santana would have been happy to obey the order, except one of the men who had formerly been stomping Gomez, chose that particular moment to take a roundhouse swing at his head. The blow connected, the lights went out, and it felt as if someone had snatched the platform out from under the legionnaire's feet. There was a long fall into darkness followed by a wonderful feeling of peace. The fight was over.

5

There can be no greater battle than that fought within the heart and mind of a prisoner of war.

—Grand Marshal Nimu Worla-Ka (ret.)
Instructor, Hudathan War College
Standard year 1957

PLANET JERICHO, THE RAMANTHIAN EMPIRE

Had it not been for the way in which Overseer Tragg murdered Lieutenant Moya, and left her body to rot on the spaceport's tarmac, the first few hours of the 146-mile hike might have been somewhat enjoyable. Especially since it was a sunny day, the terrain was relatively flat, and they were no longer aboard Captain Vomin's claustrophobic freighter.

However, most of the prisoners could still *feel* the fear, *hear* the gunshot, and *see* the young woman's dead body as it lay on the pavement. And that, Vanderveen knew, was no accident. Tragg had a powerful ally, and it was fear. So there was very little conversation as the long column of Confederacy prisoners followed a crude trail though the triple-canopy forest. There wasn't much ground vegetation because very little sunlight could reach the ground. What there was fell in patches and bathed each prisoner in liquid gold as he or she passed through it.

A cacophony of bird sounds rang through the jungle,

and Vanderveen heard mysterious rustlings as small animals hurried to escape the alien invaders, and brightly colored insects darted back and forth. There was a brief rainstorm about an hour into the journey, and the raindrops made a gentle rattling sound as they exploded against thousands of waxy leaves. The diplomat felt refreshed once the rain stopped, but not for long, as both the temperature and humidity continued to increase.

Meanwhile what had begun as a relatively easy march gradually became more arduous as the trail trended upwards. The column slowed as those in the lead struggled up a long, slippery hillside, topped a gently rounded hill, and slip-slid down into a ravine. The only way out was to climb a stairway of intertwined tree roots. It was a treacherous business at best since some of the cablelike structures were unexpectedly brittle, others had the ability to pull themselves up out of reach, and at least one sturdy-looking tuber morphed into an angry snake when a naval rating wrapped his fingers around it.

Fortunately Vanderveen, Nankool, Hooks, and Calisco were among those at the head of the column. Because once two or three hundred sets of boots passed through an area, solid ground was quickly transformed into mud, which forced those following behind to work even harder.

Adding to the difficulty of the march was the fact that with the exception of the marines, very few of the prisoners were physically prepared for that sort of journey. President Nankool was an excellent example. While the chief executive was able to hold his own during the first few hours of the journey, he soon began to pant and was forced to pause every few minutes. Then, when it came to clambering up over the ridge, he needed assistance from Vanderveen and others, which placed even more stress on them.

Fortunately, a marine named Cassidy was among their group, and in a blatant attempt to impress Vanderveen, devoted what seemed like an inexhaustible supply of energy to helping the president over the rocky summit, for which the FSO was very grateful. Nankool never gave up, though, and never complained, as he forced his ungainly body to continue the struggle. Others were less resolute, however, and at least two dozen of them fell by the wayside. Some were simply in need of a rest, but others were too exhausted to go on, and simply collapsed.

Because the Ramanthian guards were not only in good shape themselves but members of a jungle-evolved species, they had no patience with what they perceived as slackers. So when troopers came across a prisoner lying next to the trail, the first thing they did was to kick the unfortunate individual and order them to stand. Those who managed to obey were allowed to live. Those who couldn't get up were executed. Some of them willingly, glad to end the torture, even if that meant death.

The general effect of the gunshots was to send a shiver of fear along the entire length of the column. But that didn't stop the first prisoners to come upon the scene from scavenging the dead person's pack, clothing, and boots. Because on Jericho, survival took priority over squeamishness.

Meanwhile, back at the tail end of the column, where a half dozen prisoners stumbled along under the combined weight of Tragg's food, shelter, and other equipment, the overseer welcomed the summary executions, knowing it was all part of a logical process. After all, the mercenary reasoned, those who were weak would die anyway, so the sooner the better. Because that was the way of things on any planet—and would make the overall group stronger.

But nothing lasts forever, so what had been a climb was transformed into a rapid descent as the head of the column snaked up over the rocky ridge and started down the other side. A moment that came as a considerable relief to Nankool, who was happy to let Jericho's gravity do some of the work, as he skidded down a scree-covered slope.

From there the prisoners made their way down through an ancient rockslide, reentered the triple-canopy forest, and followed the trail along the side of a hill. Vanderveen thought things were going to get better at that point but soon learned how wrong she could be as the vegetation began to change and the ground softened. The sun was hanging low in the western sky by the time the diplomat was forced to wade out into the murky waters of a swamp. As the cold water closed around her legs, Vanderveen wondered if the column would be able to reach solid ground before darkness settled in around them.

An hour later the answer was clear as the red monitor led the prisoners out of a forest of frothy celery-like trees and into shallow water. The sky had turned a light shade of lavender by then, and stars had begun to appear, as the exhausted POWs followed a line of vertical poles out toward the low-lying island at the center of the lake. "Look!" Hooks said as he splashed through the water at Vanderveen's side. "I see ruins."

The diplomat knew there were forerunner ruins on Jericho, *lots* of them, so she wasn't surprised as the bottom shelved upwards, and their boots found firm footing. *So* firm it was quite possible that they were walking on a submerged road.

Nankool was exhausted by the time he arrived on dry land, but rather than collapse when a guard announced that the prisoners would be staying the night, he took charge instead. "We need firewood," the chief executive announced firmly. "Enough to fuel at least six fires. *We* had a relatively easy time of it today," the president added, "so the least we can do is have everything ready when the rest of the column arrives. Secretary Hooks, please find Commander Schell and tell him to come see me. The people who led today should follow tomorrow.

"FSO Vanderveen," Nankool continued, "find the doctors. Tell them to open a clinic. I hope they know something about feet—because they're going to see a lot of them. Once that's accomplished, we'll need some latrines. And pass the word for people to boil the lake water before they drink it. Lord knows what sort of bugs are swimming around in that stuff."

Vanderveen figured that few if any of the local microorganisms would be able to exploit alien life-forms on such short biological notice, but it made sense to be careful, so she nodded.

By the time darkness fell, fires illuminated parts of the mysterious half-buried building, and most of the prisoners were clustered around what little bit of warmth there was. Meanwhile, the night creatures had begun to grunt, hoot, and gibber out in the swamp. And just in case the night sounds weren't sufficient to intimidate any would-be escapees, Tragg's monitors floated through the ruins like silvery ghosts, bathing everything below in the harsh glare of their floodlights. The overseer was camped on a smaller island, where his robots could better protect him, but it soon became apparent that the mercenary could see what the monitors saw. Because as the airborne machines continued to patrol the area, the overseer made occasional comments intended to let the POWs know how omniscient he was.

But intimidating though such measures were, some of the prisoners managed to ignore them. Once such individual was Private First Class Cassidy, who, having devoured all his food during the day's march, went looking for more, a practice very much in keeping with the survival training the Marine Corps had given him.

So neither Vanderveen nor the rest of the people gathered around Nankool's fire were alarmed when Cassidy disappeared, or especially surprised when the torch-bearing marine reappeared forty-five minutes later, with a rather remarkable prize cradled in his arms. The egg, which had a yellowish hue, was at least twelve inches in circumference.

And, as Hooks put it, "A sure sign that something big and ugly lives in the area."

Cassidy, who was clearly pleased with himself, grinned happily and immediately went to work preparing his find for a late dinner. No small task, given the shortage of tools and cooking implements. But finally, after painstaking experimentation, the marine managed to remove one end of the oval-shaped egg with repeated taps from a triangular piece of rock. Then, having seen how thick the shell was, Cassidy placed the container on a carefully arranged bed of coals. It was slow going at first, since there were solids within the yellowish goo, but the process of stirring became considerably easier as the now-scrambled yolk began to heave and bubble.

A tantalizing odor had begun to waft through the smoky air as the marine bent to remove the protein-packed shell from the fire—and Vanderveen felt a moment of temptation as Cassidy offered her both a grin and a spoon. "Here, ma'am. Dig in!"

But for reasons Vanderveen wasn't entirely sure of, she shook her head and smiled. "I'm full at the moment. But thanks."

Cassidy shrugged good-naturedly, ate a spoonful, and rolled his eyes in obvious pleasure. That spurred a sailor to try some—followed by a greedy Calisco. All three were busy chewing when the Ramanthian guard shuffled into the circle of light and eyeballed them. All conversation came to a sudden stop, and firelight danced in the alien's coal black eyes. He couldn't speak standard, but when the trooper spotted the fire-blackened egg, his electronic translator did the job for him. "What-is-*that*?"

The rifle made an excellent pointer, and, being a marine, Cassidy had plenty of respect for it. "That's an egg," the young man said proudly. "A big honking egg that I found out in the swamp. You want some?"

The question was followed by a moment of profound

silence, during which Vanderveen began to feel a strange emptiness take over her stomach. Because as the Ramanthian processed Cassidy's words, the diplomat remembered something important. Rather than give birth to *live* offspring, the way many species did, the Ramanthians produced eggs, some of which were allowed to hatch naturally.

The diplomat wanted to say something, to find a way to forestall what she feared would happen next, but it was too late. There was a loud *bang* as the Ramanthian shot Cassidy in the left knee. The marine uttered a cry of pain as he grabbed hold of the bloody mess and began to rock back and forth. "Why, God damn it, *why?*" the soldier wanted to know.

Half a dozen prisoners had come to their feet by then, Nankool among them, and the Ramanthian might have been in trouble had it not been for the sudden shaft of light that washed over the entire area. "Hold it right there," Tragg said grimly. "Or pay the price."

More Ramanthians arrived after that. There was a brief burst of conversation as the first guard made his report, followed by an obvious expression of anger from a heavily armed noncom. "Who else?" the trooper demanded. "Who else eat our young?"

Cassidy screamed as *another* shot rang out. His good knee had been transformed into a ball of bloody hamburger, and he brought both wounds up against his chest where he could cradle them with his arms. "Nobody!" the marine insisted stoutly. "Just me."

There was a long moment of silence as the noncom surveyed the beings around him. Tragg, who was watching the episode from afar, spotted at least two guilty-looking faces. But the Ramanthian noncom had no experience at reading alien facial expressions, and the overseer had no reason to intervene. Especially since the POWs were unlikely to make that particular mistake again.

Nankool made as if to step forward, but Hooks held the president back. And, with nothing else to go on, the Ramanthian was forced to accept the marine's confession. Orders were given, Cassidy was borne away, and Calisco threw up.

Tragg, who was still watching via the monitor, nodded knowingly and turned his attention to another face. A *beautiful* face second only to the one he had destroyed back at the spaceport. There was something about the blond woman that reminded him of Marci. He had spared her once. But for how long?

Vanderveen felt a sense of relief as the spotlight clicked off, but the feeling was short-lived as the Ramanthians began to cook Cassidy over a fire, and the screaming began.

PLANET HIVE, THE RAMANTHIAN EMPIRE

Having only recently been elevated to the post of Chief Chancellor, Itnor Ubatha was still rather conscious of the perks associated with his position and took pleasure in the fact that a government vehicle was waiting for him as he left his home. The driver opened the rear door. Ubatha slipped inside and reveled in the cell-powered car's luxurious interior as it carried him along busy streets, through one of the enormous chambers in which the citizens of the city lived, and past a bustling shopping center. The Chancellor and his mates could purchase almost anything now. But that was a recent development. The path from junior civil servant to a position second only to the Queen had been perilous but well worth the effort. Now, having arrived, the bureaucrat faced a *new* challenge. And that was to hold on to what he had. Because one could never rest within the labyrinthinal world of Ramanthian politics.

The key to survival was to not only anticipate what the Queen would want next, but to take action if such a thing was possible, which in this case it was. Because after a long series of brilliantly executed schemes, the Egg Orno's single surviving mate had not only failed to deliver on his most extravagant promise, but gone into hiding somewhere off-planet. But *where?* That's what the Queen might very well ask Ubatha when he met with her later in the day. She wouldn't really expect him to know the answer, of course, since the intelligence functionaries had been unable to locate the missing diplomat, but what if he were able to develop a lead? The official had nothing to lose other than some time, so the decision was easy. Especially since he would be in control of the interview and everything else that happened, too. Which, come to think of it, was the way things should always be.

Having been notified of the Chancellor's visit the day before, the Egg Orno's emotions had initially been buried beneath the weight of the preparations necessary to receive someone of Ubatha's high rank, but everything was finally ready. And, with no means to distract herself, the female was nearly paralyzed with fear. Because Ambassador Alway Orno had been missing for a long time by then, the government was trying to find him, and she had been interrogated five times.

And that, the Egg Orno feared, was the purpose of Chancellor Ubatha's visit. To interrogate her in a way that lower-ranking officials couldn't. And, if successful, to find out where Alway was hiding. So when her sole remaining servant entered the carefully screened reception alcove to announce Ubatha's presence, the Egg Orno was painfully aware of how much was at stake, and determined to perform well. Because it was her duty to protect both her mates and her progeny. A responsibility that she, like the Queen, took very seriously indeed. Except that she had produced only three eggs, while the monarch was in the process of laying *billions*, a reality that was fundamental to Ramanthian foreign policy. Because billions of additional lives implied more planets. And more planets implied more ships to serve them, which her mate had successfully stolen from the Confederacy. A fact that both the Queen and her advisors seemed to have forgotten. The anger she felt acted to neutralize the Egg Orno's Fear.

Like all his kind, Ubatha was equipped with two antenna-shaped olfactory organs that protruded from his forehead and provided the official with all sorts of information as he entered the Orno family's abode. The air was redolent with the odor of expensive incense, but it wasn't sufficient to conceal the smell of spicy grub sauce that wafted from the kitchen, or the lingering tang of recently applied cleaning agents.

And, while the Chancellor's compound eyes wouldn't allow him to focus on anything more than a yard away, he saw the sandals next to the front door, the carefully arranged rock garden beyond, and the exquisite layering of fabrics that had been hung in front of the earthen walls. Farther back a glistening water-walk carried the official into the reception room, where the Egg Orno was required to sit behind an opaque screen rather than confront him directly.

A well-placed light served to project the Egg Orno's carefully groomed profile onto the paper-thin partition, thereby protecting both Ubatha and herself from any possibility of scandal. But, even though the bureaucrat couldn't *see* the female directly, he could smell the heady combination of perfume, wing wax, and chitin polish that identified the Egg Orno as a member of the upper class. "Welcome," the Egg Orno said, as her pincers went through a highly stylized series of movements. "The Orno clan is honored to have such a distinguished visitor. Please sit down."

"As I am honored to be here," Ubatha said, as he straddled an ornately carved chair. "Ambassador Orno is fortunate to have such a skillful mate and charming home. If only he were here to enjoy both."

Now it begins, the Egg Orno thought to herself. *And*

rather quickly, too. "Yes," the female agreed out loud. "Nothing would please me more."

"I'm glad to hear that," the Chancellor replied smoothly. "Because if you were to offer your assistance, I suspect the government would be able to locate Ambassador Orno and bring him home."

For what? The Egg Orno thought scornfully. *So you can kill him? Never!* But to actually say something like that would be to reveal the way she actually felt and thereby foreclose any possibility of joining her mate on Starfall. So the Egg Orno lied with the same elegance she brought to everything else. "Having already lost the War Orno in service to the empire, I fear that the ambassador is dead as well," she said sadly. "Nothing else could explain his prolonged absence. However, lacking proof of such a calamity, I continue to hope for a miracle."

Though almost certainly false, it was the right thing to say, and Ubatha was impressed by the Egg Orno's cool unflappable persona. "Perhaps you are correct," the bureaucrat allowed politely. "But I would be less than forthright if I were to ignore a second, and to some minds, more plausible possibility. And that is that having bungled his latest assignment, and fearing the Queen's wrath, your mate has gone into hiding. An understandable, if not-altogether-honorable strategy, that seems beneath a person of Ambassador Orno's accomplishments.

"So," Ubatha continued gravely, as he continued to eye the now-motionless silhouette, "should you somehow learn of Ambassador Orno's whereabouts, I urge you to contact *me*, so that we can take steps to ensure a safe return. I think such a course would be best for both of us."

He wants the credit, the Egg Orno thought dully. *And he's offering to protect me if I go along.* "I understand," the female replied coolly. "It was kind of you to come."

Ubatha knew a dismissal when he heard one and, lacking a way to force a response, had no choice but to go. "Thank

you for your hospitality," the official said smoothly, and
the visit was over.

The Queen, who had once been the same size as her female
subjects, was *huge*. It was a transformation that continued
to bother the monarch, because her body was so large that
a special cradle was required to support her swollen abdomen, and she could no longer move around on her own.
Which, when combined with the nonstop production of
eggs, made her feel like a factory. A cranky, increasingly
paranoid factory, that was very hard to please. Especially in
the wake of the Confederacy's suicidal attack on the subsurface city of First Birth, in which 1.7 million Ramanthian lives had summarily been snuffed out of existence.
The disaster was referred to as "a tragic seismic event" on
Hive but was heralded as a tremendous victory within the
Confederacy.

But, while not equal in magnitude, the recent annihila-
tion of an enemy battle group in the Nebor system had
done a great deal to restore the Queen's previously flag-
ging spirits. This meant the monarch was in a relatively
good mood as Chief Chancellor Itnor Ubatha arrived on
the platform in front of and directly below her normal-
sized head.

For his part, the bureaucrat was well aware of not only
the Queen's hard-eyed scrutiny, but the colorful drape intended to hide most of her swollen body, and the rich pungent odor of recently laid eggs that wafted up from the
chamber below. The smell caused certain chemicals to be
secreted into the Ubatha's bloodstream and flow to his
brain. As a result, the official suddenly felt simultaneously
protective, receptive, and subservient. Just one of the
many reasons why the monarch's clan was still in power after thousands of years. "So," the Queen said, without pre-
amble, "how did the meeting with the Egg Orno go?"

Ubatha bent a leg as his mind raced. It seemed that the

Queen had him under surveillance. A perfectly logical move from her perspective. But why signal that fact to him? Because the Queen wanted him to know that even though she had been immobilized, very little escaped her notice. And to seize control of the conversation—a technique she was famous for. None of what Ubatha was thinking could be seen in the movement of his antennae or the set of his narrow wings, however. One of many skills the bureaucrat had mastered over the years. "I failed, Majesty. Of which I am greatly ashamed."

Ubatha *hadn't* failed, not really, but his willingness to portray himself in a negative light amounted to an oblique compliment. Because by opening himself to the possibility of punishment, the Chancellor was demonstrating complete faith in the Queen's judgment. It was the sort of political finesse for which the official was known. "Come now," the Queen said indulgently. "I fear you are too hard on yourself. Especially since the failure, if any, should accrue to the head of my so-called intelligence service."

Ubatha knew, as the monarch did, that the official in question was standing not fifty feet away, talking to a group of royal advisors. And, because the Queen's voice was amplified, there was little doubt that he was intended to hear the comment. "Your Majesty is too kind," the Chancellor replied. "When asked about her mate's whereabouts, the Egg Orno continues to maintain that Ambassador Orno is dead."

"But you don't believe that."

"No, Majesty. I do not."

"Nor do I," the monarch replied thoughtfully. "I have *my* reasons. What are yours?"

Rather than address the fact that there was no body, or other physical evidence of Orno's death, Ubatha chose to pursue another strategy instead. "As I entered the Egg Orno's home," the Chancellor said, "I noticed that a single pair of sandals had been left in the vestibule."

There was a moment of silence while the Queen absorbed the news. Ramanthian culture was rich in traditions. One of which compelled females to leave clean sandals by the front door to welcome her mates home. But when a male died, the sandals were ceremoniously burned. So if *both* of the Egg Orno's mates were dead, as she steadfastly maintained, then there wouldn't be any sandals in the vestibule.

Yes, the whole thing could be explained away, and no doubt would be had the Egg Orno been given a chance to do so. But above all else the Queen was female, and possessed of female instincts, which meant that the presence of sandals next to the door carried a great deal of weight where she was concerned. "You have a keen eye," the Queen said quietly. "And a keen mind as well. . . . I know you're busy Chancellor, *very* busy, but please lend your intelligence to the hunt for citizen Orno. He made a promise. It was broken. And he must pay."

Ubatha bent a knee. "Yes, Majesty. Your wish is my command."

PLANET JERICHO, THE RAMANTHIAN EMPIRE

It was raining, and had been for hours, as Oliver Batkin continued to fly just below the treetops. Having seen the Ramanthian shuttles a day earlier, he'd been looking for the ships ever since. No small task because even though the spy ball knew where the interim spaceport was, he'd been hundreds of miles away when the contrails appeared, and the cyborg's top speed was about thirty miles per hour.

So as water cascaded off the leaves above, Batkin followed a trail of dead bodies from the spaceport toward the future site of Jericho Prime. The corpses had already been victimized by jungle scavengers and were starting to decay. It was a shocking sight, or would have been, except that Batkin had seen it before. Because slave labor had been put to use elsewhere on the planet as well.

What made *these* dead bodies different, however, was the fact that all of them wore identical blue uniforms and were clearly military. The first such POWs the cyborg had seen on Jericho given that the Ramanthians routinely killed any member of the Confederacy's armed forces unfortunate enough to fall into their pincers.

However, judging from appearances, this particular group had been spared. For a particular purpose? That was possible, although the bugs were notoriously unpredictable, and the whole thing could be the result of a whim by some high-ranking official.

Still, Batkin's job was to investigate such anomalies, so the cyborg was determined to follow the trail of corpses wherever it led. Which was why the spy ball topped a ridge and followed the opposite slope down to the point where a vast marsh gave way to a lake. Thousands of interlocking circles radiated outwards as the rain continued to fall, and the alien sphere followed a row of vertical poles out to the island beyond.

The prisoners were gone by the time Batkin arrived, but tendrils of smoke marked the still-smoldering fires. The cyborg had given the ruins a quick once-over, and was about to depart, when he heard a strange keening sound. Which, after further investigation, originated from a fire-blackened lump that was wired to a metal spit. Batkin looked on in horror as two eyes appeared in what he now realized was a badly burned face. The raspy words were almost too faint to hear. "P-l-e-a-s-e," Private Cassidy said. "*Kill me.*"

It was a reasonable request given the circumstances, but the cyborg knew that his main source of protection lay in the fact that the bugs were unaware of his presence. So if he put the poor wretch out of his misery, there was the possibility that one or more Ramanthians would happen along and realize what had taken place. Especially since Batkin lacked the means to dispose of the body.

But the chances of that seemed remote, so the cyborg activated his energy cannon, and there was a *whir* as the barrel appeared. "I will," Batkin promised solemnly. "But first . . . Can you tell me where you were captured?"

Both of Cassidy's startlingly blue eyes had disappeared by then, and there was a long pause, before the pain-filled orbs opened again. The long, drawn-out answer came as a sigh. "*G-l-a-d-i-a-t-o-r.*"

Batkin felt an almost overwhelming sense of despair. He was cut off on Jericho, with no way to receive news, but if the Ramanthians had taken the *Gladiator*, then the Confederacy was in dire straits indeed. "You're sure?" the spy demanded. "You were aboard the *Gladiator*?"

"Y-e-s-s-s," Cassidy hissed. "*Kill m-e-e-e. . . .*"

So Batkin fired the energy cannon, the marine was released from hell, and the rain continued to fall as the cyborg followed the trail east. Even though the spy's top speed was rather limited, it didn't take him long to catch up with the tail end of the column. But what Batkin lacked in speed, he more than made up for where sophisticated detection equipment was concerned, which was fortunate indeed. Because it wasn't long before his sensors detected a substantial amount of electromechanical activity and he made visual contact with four Sheen robots. And, for one brief moment, the machines made contact with *him*.

But Batkin had disengaged by that time, activated all the cloaking technology resident in his highly sophisticated body, and taken refuge in thick foliage. So, having been unable to verify a contact, the robots continued on their way. As did a large heavily armed human whose eyes were concealed by a pair of dark goggles. The only human on Jericho other than Batkin who was wasn't a slave.

Cautious now, lest one of the robots spot him, Batkin propelled himself out and away from the column. Then, having given himself sufficient electronic elbow room, the cyborg sped ahead. After about fifteen minutes, he turned back again, located the trail, and snuggled into a treetop. In spite of the rain and the curtain of leaves that served to screen his hiding place, the spy had a mostly unobstructed view of the point where the POWs would be forced to cross a small clearing. With his cloaking measures on, and most everything else *off*, the agent was confident he could escape detection. And thanks to some truly magnificent optics, Batkin would be able to snap digital photos of each person or thing that crossed the clearing. An important step in verifying whether the bugs had captured the *Gladiator* or not.

A full fifteen minutes passed before the first poor wretch emerged from the dripping trees to splash through a series of puddles directly opposite the spy's position. Batkin took at least one frame of each person's face, and couldn't help but be moved by the misery that he saw there. All of the men wore beards, most of the prisoners were filthy, and some were clearly lame. A woman who was walking with the aid of a homemade crutch tripped on an exposed tree root and fell facedown in a pool of rainwater. And when a man paused to help her up, a Ramanthian trooper subjected both prisoners to a flurry of blows and kicks.

And so it went as the long, ragged line of POWs passed before Batkin's high-mag lens. There were hundreds of them, so the faces began to blur after a while, until the unmistakable countenance of President Marcott Nankool appeared! The chief executive was wearing a beard, but was quite recognizable to a political junkie like Batkin. Still, the cyborg continued to wonder if such a thing was possible, until he spotted Secretary Hooks! A person he had met at a political fund-raiser and was likely to be at the president's side.

The discovery resulted in a heady combination of consternation, fear, and excitement. Because if he was correct, and Nankool was a prisoner, the sighting was a very big deal indeed! But even as the cyborg continued to snap his pictures, one aspect of the situation continued to trouble him. Assuming that the man who had already crossed the clearing and reentered the jungle *was* Nankool—then why was he being treated in such a cavalier fashion? Surely, assuming the Ramanthians knew who they had, the president would be treated in an entirely different manner. He would be more heavily guarded, for one thing, transported via flyer for another, and held separately from the other prisoners. But what if the bugs *didn't* know?

That possibility would have caused Batkin's heart to race had he still been equipped with one. But the sensation was very much the same as the cyborg took pictures of the Sheen robots and the strange-looking human who trailed along behind the main column. Then the POWs were gone, having been consumed by the jungle, as the column continued on its way. That was Batkin's opportunity to depart the area and upload his report to one of the message torps above. *No*, the agent decided, make that *two* message torps, just in case one went astray. Because of all the reports that Batkin might eventually file—this was likely to be the most important.

Confident that it was safe to leave his hiding place, the cyborg fired his repellers, and "felt" the surrounding leaves slip over his alloy skin as he rose up through the thick foliage to emerge into the open area above. And that was when a host of threat alerts began to go off, and the sphere-shaped monitor that Tragg liked to refer to as "Tail-End-Charlie," began its attack.

Tragg was a careful man, so even though the overseer wasn't aware of a specific threat, one of the airborne robots had been ordered to follow along behind the column just in case somebody or something attempted to follow it.

And, had the Ramanthian-manufactured machine been equipped with more potent weaponry, Batkin would have been blown out of the sky. Still, the remote did have a stun gun, which it fired. That was sufficient to partially paralyze the cyborg's nervous system, which caused the spy ball to shoot upwards, as his now-clumsy brain attempted to reassert control over the nav function.

All this was effective in a weird sort of way, because it was impossible for the alien robot to predict what would happen next and plot an intercepting course. But Batkin had entered a death spiral by then, the jungle was coming up quickly, and the remote stood to win the overall battle if the human cyborg crashed into the ground.

In spite of the numbness that threatened to end his life, the spy summoned all of his strength and forced a command through the neural interface that linked what remained of his biological body with its electromechanical counterpart. The response was immediate, if somewhat frightening, as the cyborg suddenly swooped upwards. The monitor pursued Batkin at that point, but the device lacked sufficient speed, and it could do little more than follow the spy as he led the robot away from the trail.

Meanwhile, as the effects of the stun gun began to wear off, Batkin regained more control over his body. Still hoping to conceal his presence on Jericho, the spy chose to activate his energy cannon rather than the noisy .50 gun that was also hidden inside his rotund body. Conscious of the fact that there wouldn't be any second chances, the recon ball dropped into the jungle below.

The robot followed, and for thirty seconds or so, the creatures of the forest were treated to a never-before-seen sight as two alien constructs weaved their way between shadowy tree trunks and flashed through clearings before exploding out into open spaces. Then the chase came to a sudden end as the monitor swept out over the surface of a rain-swollen river where it was forced to hover while its sensors swept the area for signs of electromechanical activity.

Meanwhile, just below the surface of the river, where the cool water screened the heat produced by his power supply and other systems, Batkin took careful aim as he fired a steering jet to counteract the current. Had there been someone present to witness the event, they would have seen a bolt of bright blue energy leap up out of the suddenly steaming water to strike the monitor from below. There was a loud *bang*, followed by a puff of smoke, as the robot fell into the river. The mechanism was light enough to float, and was in the process of drifting downstream, when a large C-shaped grasper broke the surface of the water to pull the monitor under.

Batkin spent the next couple of minutes piling river rocks over and around the robot before firing his repellers and bursting up out of the river. Water sheeted off the construct as it shot straight up into the air, turned toward the protection of the trees, and moved parallel to the ground. Then, having established himself high in the branches of a sun tracker tree, the spy hurried to establish contact with two of the message torps orbiting above. It took less than a minute to upload both the images the spy had captured and a verbal report that would put them into context. Then, having instructed the vehicles to pursue different routes, Batkin sent the torpedoes on their uncertain way.

6

Murder is a tool, which, like all tools, can be used to build something up or to tear it down.

—*Hive Mother Tral Heba*
Ramanthian Book of Guidance
Standard year 1721

ABOARD THE CONFEDERACY VESSEL *EPSILON INDI,* IN HYPERSPACE

The combined effects of the worst headache the officer had ever experienced, plus an urgent need to pee, brought Santana back to consciousness. The legionnaire's eyes felt as if they'd been glued shut, and once he managed to paw them open, the officer found himself looking up into an unfamiliar face. A med tech, judging from the insignia on her uniform, and the injector in her right hand. The name tag over her right breast pocket read "Hiller."

The rating had big brown eyes, mocha-colored skin, and a pretty smile. "Welcome aboard, Captain Santana. You're on the Combat Supply (CS) vessel *Epsilon Indi,* presently en route to Algeron, with a full load of supplies. Roll to your right so I can get at your arm."

Santana winced as the injector made a popping sound, and some sort of liquid was forced in through the pores of his skin. "There," Hiller said as she took a step backwards. "That should help with the pain."

"Algeron?" Santana croaked. "Why *Algeron?* My outfit's on Adobe."

"Beats me, sir," the technician answered blandly. "But maybe Major Lassiter can fill you in. . . . He wants to see you at 0930, so we'd better get cracking."

"I gotta pee," Santana said thickly.

"*And* brush your teeth, *and* shave, *and* take a shower," Hiller added pragmatically. "In fact, you might even want to get dressed. Can you sit up for me?"

So Santana sat up, but the process was painful, as was the act of standing. Not only because of the many contusions suffered during the battle in the Blue Moon Bar and Fight Club—but as a result of whatever drugs had been administered to him thereafter. A subject the legionnaire planned to raise with Major Lassiter. "There was a non-com," Santana said, as Hiller escorted him toward the head. "A corporal named Gomez . . . What happened to her?"

"Gomez has been up and around for quite a while now," the med tech replied. "She comes to check on you every couple of hours. The corporal says that while you have a lousy left hook, you've got some major cojones, and that's rare where officers are concerned. Her opinion—not mine."

One hour later, Santana was shaved, showered, and dressed in one of his own uniforms. Which had clearly been removed from the hotel room in the MEZ and brought aboard the *Indi*. The pain still lingered but was under control by the time Hiller provided the legionnaire a hand wand and sent him out into the ship's labyrinth of corridors.

The *Epsilon Indi* was more than three miles long, could transport five million tons of cargo, and carried a crew of more than two thousand bio bods and robots. The corridor that ran the length of the ship wasn't all that crowded as Santana followed the directional wand toward the stern, but that would change quickly once the watch changed. The overhead glow panels marked off six-foot intervals, the durasteel bulkheads were gray, and brightly colored decals marked maintenance bays, emergency lockers, and escape pods. A steady stream of inflection-free announcements continued to drone through the overhead speakers as the directional wand tugged Santana to the right. What seemed like a seldom-used passageway led to a hatch and a programmable panel that read, "Legion Procurement Officer." The title didn't bode well since Santana had a bias against REMFs (rear echelon motherfuckers).

But orders were orders, so Santana rapped his knuckles against the wooden knock-block mounted next to the hatch and waited for a response. It came in the form of a basso "Come!" pitched to carry over the PA system, the chatter of a nearby power wrench, and the eternal rumble generated by the *Indi* herself.

Santana took three paces forward, executed a sharp left face, and came to rigid attention. "Captain Antonio Santana, reporting as ordered, *sir!*"

In spite of the fact that the legionnaire's eyes were focused on a point over the major's head, he could still see quite a bit. The officer on the opposite side of the fold-down desk had short gray hair, a weather-beaten face, and a lantern-shaped jaw. And, unlike so many of the staff officers that Santana had encountered in the past, this one wore ribbons representing some rather impressive decorations. A good sign indeed. "At ease," Major Lassiter said. "Grab a chair. . . . I got blindsided once, and it still hurts. How do you feel?"

"Better, sir," Santana answered truthfully, as he sat down. "How did you know I was blindsided? If you don't mind my asking."

"Corporal Gomez was kind enough to fill me in," Lassiter replied dryly. "She likes you—but I get the feeling that her affection for officers ends there."

"No offense, sir," Santana ventured cautiously. "But why were Gomez and I put aboard the *Indi*? Are we in some sort of trouble?"

"No," the major said, as he leaned back into his chair. "You aren't. Not that I'm aware of anyway. . . . General Booly sent orders to find you, and my team was busy touring all the dives in the MEZ when we came across the Blue Moon. You were already laying on the mat by then, so we had you removed and put aboard a shuttle. About halfway through liftoff you returned to consciousness, attempted to escape your stretcher, and were put back to sleep."

"*General* Booly?" Santana said incredulously. "The Military Chief of Staff? Why would General Booly send for *me*?"

"Hell, I don't know," Lassiter replied lightly. "But then I rarely do! When the general wants something, it's my job to find it for him. But he rarely tells me why, and I always forget to ask."

"So you're a member of military intelligence," the line officer concluded.

Lassiter smiled and shook his head. "No, of course not! I think of myself as a procurement officer. Just like the sign says."

But there was a lot more to Lassiter's job than procurement, of that Santana was sure, even if the other officer wasn't willing to admit it. "So, what about Corporal Gomez?" Santana wanted to know. "Did General Booly send for her as well?"

"Nope," Lassiter answered. "But given that the order to find you was highly classified, it seemed best to bring her along."

"And you can do that?"

"Of course," the major replied with a grin. "Procurement officers can accomplish just about anything. So," Lassiter continued, "let's move on to the *real* purpose of this meeting. And that's to let you know when you aren't plodding through virtual-reality scenarios—you'll be working out with a company of really gung ho marines."

Santana eyed the major suspiciously. "And that's all you can tell me?"

"That's correct," the other officer confirmed mischievously. "I'm afraid I won't have time to join you—but I hear the marines are looking forward to the opportunity of spending some time with a cavalry officer!"

Both men were well aware of the long-standing animosity between the Legion and the Marine Corps. So when Lassiter said that the jarheads were "looking forward" to the workouts Santana knew he was in trouble. He stood. "Sir, yes sir!"

"One last thought," Lassiter added, as his expression became more serious. "I don't know why the general sent for you, or why he wants to make sure that you'll be in tip-top shape by the time you arrive on Algeron, but there's bound to be a very good reason. So bust your ass. Understood?"

"Sir, yes, sir!"

"Good. Dismissed."

And Santana's leave was over.

THE THRAKI PLANET STARFALL (PREVIOUSLY ZYNIG-47)

What light there was emanated from a small window set high on the earthen wall and a single battery-powered lamp on the makeshift desk. Thrakies might have been comfortable in the underground chamber, thanks to their thick fur, but the Ramanthian was cold. *Very* cold. Which explained why ex-ambassador Alway Orno sat swathed in heavy blankets as he brought the pistol up and placed the barrel against the side of his insectoid head. There was a loud *click* as the firing pin fell on an empty chamber.

Satisfied that the firearm was fully functional, the Ramanthian broke the tubular weapon open and dropped a stubby bullet into the shiny firing chamber. Then, having placed the weapon to one side of his desk, the fugitive returned to work. The letter was addressed to the Egg Orno—and would soon be found next to his body.

Rather than record his voice, or compose his message on a computer, Orno had chosen to write an old-fashioned letter. During the manufacturing process the paper had been flooded with a thin layer of colored wax and left to dry in the sun. Now, as small amounts of the surface material were removed with an antique stylus, clusters of white characters appeared.

"The end has come dearest," the letter began. "And my heart yearns for one last moment with you. But with every pincer turned against me, I cannot return to Hive. So there can be no reunion until we meet in the great beyond. Then, with you between us, the War Orno and I will—"

The fugitive's thoughts were interrupted by a loud *bang* as the trapdoor that led down into the underground chamber was thrown open and Orno felt a sudden stab of fear. His right pincer went to the gun, but rather than the assassins the Ramanthian half expected to see, the intruder was Ula, his host's youngest daughter. She had large light-gathering eyes, pointy ears, and horizontal slits where a nose might otherwise have been. Ula spoke standard, a language that Orno as a diplomat, spoke fluently as well. "I have a message for you!" the youngster said excitedly as she raced down the ramp and into the underground chamber.

Orno was about to chide the youngster for failing to announce herself, but he knew it would be a waste of time, and said "thank you" instead. The message was sealed in a box that immediately popped open, allowing a tiny bipedal robot to climb out. Which wasn't surprising since the Thrakies loved to make robots and use them for tasks that could have been carried out in other ways. Ula squealed in delight at the sight of the electromechanical form, but the Ramanthian was in no mood for frivolity. "If you have a message for me, then deliver it," the fugitive said gruffly.

Even though the robot was small, the voice that issued forth from it was in no way diminished by its size and belonged to Sector 18—one of a small group of individuals who sat on the Committee that governed the Thraki people. "A representative from the Confederacy of Sentient Beings would like to meet with you regarding subjects of mutual interest," the voice said. A time and a place followed, but there were no pleasantries as sparks shot out of the robot's ears, and it toppled off the writing table onto the earthen floor.

"Are you going to go?" Ula wanted to know as she bent to retrieve what remained of the robot.

It was a good question. Because even though the voice *sounded* like that of Sector 18, it could have been synthesized in an effort to draw the fugitive out of hiding. *But so what? While such a death is less dignified than suicide, dead is dead.* Orno thought to himself. "Yes," the Ramanthian answered. "Please notify your father. I will need some ground transportation. Something discreet."

Ula was thrilled by the opportunity to carry such an important message to her father and dashed up the ramp. That left Orno to consider what lay ahead. There was no way to know what such a meeting might portend. . . . Was Nankool hoping to establish back-channel negotiations with the Ramanthian government? If so, Orno might be able to parlay such an opportunity into a promise of clemency, or even full restoration of his previous rank! The mere thought of that was enough to make his spirit soar. Thus emboldened, Orno rose, shuffled over to his travel trunk, and opened the lid. Either redemption was at hand or a group of assassins were about to kill him. Either way it was important to look good.

Orno was too large to ride in a Thraki ground car, so the fugitive was forced to hunker down in the back of a delivery vehicle as it approached the city from the south and swerved onto a downward-sloping ramp. Whatever architectural traditions the Thrakies might have had before they left their home system had been forgotten during the race's long journey through space. And now, as they put down roots on the planet they called Starfall, new cities were rising all around the world. All of which were constructed in a way that forced vehicular traffic underground so pedestrians could have the surface to themselves.

Lights blipped past as the vehicle sped along an arterial, then slowed as the driver turned off and came to a stop in front of a subsurface lobby. The rear doors were opened, and a ramp was deployed so that the Ramanthian could shuffle down onto the pavement, where a Thraki waited to greet him. Not an official but a low-level flunky. Still another sign of how far the Ramanthian's fortunes had fallen. From the pull-through it was a short journey up an incline to a row of freight elevators. Would the lift carry the ex-diplomat higher? Back to respectability? Or deliver him to a team of assassins? *No*, Orno reasoned, *if assassins were waiting, they would take me right here.*

Thus reassured, the fugitive allowed himself to be ushered onto an elevator that lifted him up to the twenty-third floor, where it hissed open. Though scaled to accommodate alien visitors, the ceilings remained oppressively low by Ramanthian standards, something Orno sought to ignore as his guide led him into a hallway. From there it was a short walk to a pair of wooden doors and the conference room beyond.

As was Orno's practice when spending time on alien planets, the Ramanthian was wearing contacts that consolidated what would have otherwise been multiple images into a single view as he entered the rectangular space. There was a table, six chairs, and a curtained window. A single human was waiting to greet him. A repulsive-looking creature who, judging from the way her clothes fit, had especially large lumps of fatty tissue hanging from her chest. Orno recognized the female as a low-ranking diplomatic functionary to whom he had once been introduced but had had no reason to contact since. Which explained why he couldn't remember her name. "This is a pleasure," Orno lied. "It's good to see you again."

It appeared that the Ramanthian diplomat remembered her, and Kay Wilmot felt a rush of pleasure as she hurried to reintroduce herself. "My name is Kay Wilmot. I am assistant undersecretary for foreign affairs reporting to Vice President Jakov. The pleasure is mutual."

"A promotion!" Orno said heartily. "And well deserved, too."

"Please have a seat," Wilmot said, as she gesturing toward a Ramanthian-style saddle chair. "I'm sorry I can't offer you any refreshments, but the Confederacy's embassy isn't aware of my presence, and while they have been helpful, the Thrakies feel it's necessary to maintain a certain distance."

"I understand," Orno said. "We live in complicated times."

Once both of them were seated, Wilmot took the first step in what promised to be some delicate negotiations by placing a portable scrambler on the surface of the table in front of her. It generated a humming noise, which was accompanied by a green light. Two doors down the hall a pair of Thraki intelligence agents swore as the feed they had been monitoring was reduced to a roar of static. But, effective though the device was, the scrambler had no effect on the photosensitive fabric from which the Ramanthian's loose-fitting robe had been made. Or the storage device woven into the garment's shimmery fabric. "No offense, Ambassador," Wilmot said. "But could I inquire as to the general nature of your present assignment?"

Orno couldn't tell the truth, not if the Wilmot creature was to take him seriously, so he lied. "At the moment I'm serving her majesty as a special envoy to the Thraki people. More than that I'm not allowed to say."

"Of course," the human responded understandingly. "I

hope you will forgive my directness, but there's a rather sensitive matter on which we could use your help, although it falls well outside the realm of your normal duties. And, were you to act on our behalf, we would require complete confidentiality."

The first emotion that Orno experienced was a crushing sense of disappointment. Rather than ask him to broker a peace deal, or something similar to that, the human was clearly paving the way for some sort of illicit business deal. Not what he had hoped for but well worth his consideration. Especially if he could use the funds to smuggle the Egg Orno off Hive. It wouldn't do to reveal the extent of his need however—so the ex-diplomat took a moment to posture. "My first loyalty is to the Queen," Orno said sternly. "Everything else is secondary."

"Of course," the human replied soothingly. "I know that. But what if it was possible to serve the Ramanthian empire *and* bank half a million Thraki credits at the same time? Wouldn't that be an attractive proposition?"

Orno pretended to consider the matter. "Well, yes," he said reluctantly. "If both things were possible, then yes, it would."

"That's what I thought," Wilmot said confidently. "So, I have your word? Whatever I tell you stays between us?"

"You have my word," the Ramanthian replied stoutly.

"Good," the official said importantly. "Because what I'm about to confide in you may change the course of history."

The Ramanthian was skeptical but careful to keep his doubts to himself. "To use one of your expressions, I'm all ears," the ex-diplomat said reassuringly.

"The situation is this," Wilmot explained. "While on his way to visit the Clone Hegemony, President Nankool was captured by Ramanthian military forces and sent to Jericho, where he and his companions will be used as slave labor."

"That's absurd!" Orno responded scornfully. "First, because my government would take Nankool to a planet other than Jericho, and second because his capture would have been announced by now."

"Not if the Ramanthians on Jericho were unaware of the president's true identity," Wilmot countered. "And we know they aren't aware of the fact that he's there, because we have an intelligence agent on Jericho, and he sent us pictures of Nankool trudging through the jungle. Images that arrived on Algeron five days ago."

Orno clicked his right pincer. "You came to the wrong person," he said sternly. "A rescue would be impossible, even if I were willing to assist such a scheme, which I am not." The statement wasn't entirely true, especially if he could raise the ante, and maximize the size of his reward.

"No, you misunderstood," Wilmot responded gently. "I'm not here to seek help with a rescue mission—I'm here to make sure that Nankool and his companions are buried on Jericho."

It took a moment for Orno to process what the human was saying. But then, as the full import of Wilmot's statement started to dawn on him, the fugitive's antennae tilted forward. "You report to Vice President Jakov?"

"Yes," Wilmot agreed soberly. "I do."

"Soon to be *President* Jakov?"

"With your help. . . . Yes."

"It is a clever plan," Orno admitted. "A very clever plan. But why contact me? My duties have nothing to do with Jericho."

"If you say so," Wilmot agreed politely. "But, according to the reports I've read, you *are* close friends with Commandant Yama Mutuu. Is that correct?"

Orno didn't have friends as such, but he did have a wide circle of cronies, some of whom remained loyal in spite of his disgrace. Was Mutuu among them? There was no way to be certain, but yes, Orno thought the odds were fairly good. And, given the old geezer's delusions of grandeur, he would be easy to manipulate. In fact, assuming Orno provided Mutuu with the right sort of story, the royal would kill Nankool for nothing! Which would allow the fugitive to pocket the entire fee. "It would take money," the Ramanthian lied. "One million for myself and half a million for Mutuu."

The price was steep, but well within the amount that Wilmot was authorized to spend, so the assistant undersecretary nodded. "I will give you half up front—and half on proof of death. And not just Nankool. The others must die as well."

The Ramanthian nodded. "You want all of the witnesses dead."

"Exactly. . . . And one more thing," Wilmot said coldly. "No action is to be taken against our intelligence agent. I want him to witness the executions and report the slaughter to Algeron. Understood?"

"Understood."

"Good," Wilmot said cheerfully as she reached out to reclaim her scrambler. "If you would be so kind as to wait in your vehicle, the first payment will arrive there within the next fifteen minutes. Proof of death should be delivered to the address that will be included along with the cash. The second payment will be forthcoming within one standard day. Do you have any questions? No? Well, it has been a pleasure doing business with you."

"And you," Orno replied, his heart filled with hope. Because here, in his hour of greatest need, was a way out. With the Egg Orno at his side, and a million-plus credits to grease the way, the two of them could disappear.

"One last question," Wilmot said coolly, as the Ramanthian rose to leave. "Our intelligence people believe you were the one who planted the bomb on the *Friendship*. Are they correct?"

There was a long moment of silence as the coconspirators

stared into each other's eyes. Finally, after what seemed like an eternity, Orno answered. "Yes," the Ramanthian replied. "It was my finest moment." And with that, the ex-ambassador left the room.

ABOARD THE *EPSILON INDI,* IN ORBIT AROUND THE PLANET ALGERON, THE CONFEDERACY OF SENTIENT BEINGS

The jungle foliage was thick. Too thick to see properly. But thanks to the fact that each member of Santana's platoon was represented by a symbol projected onto the inside surface of his visor, the cavalry officer knew exactly where they were relative to him and the Trooper II he was riding.

There wasn't anything subtle about the way that the ten-foot-tall cyborg plowed through the jungle, and there couldn't be given the war form's size. So Santana bent his knees and sought shelter behind the T-2's blocky head, as an army of branches and vines tried to rip him off the borg's back. Could the enemy hear them coming? Absolutely, assuming that the tricky green bastards were somewhere nearby.

But the alternative was to follow one of the already-well-established jungle trails north toward the objective. That would be quieter, not to mention faster, but such paths were almost certain to be booby-trapped and kept under constant surveillance by the enemy. So, cutting a new trail through the jungle was the better choice, or so it seemed to Santana.

Of course, the key to implementing that strategy was the use of the Integrated Tactical Command (ITC) system that allowed the aggressor team to "see" each other electronically, even though it was necessary for each cyborg to maintain an interval of at least a hundred yards between themselves and other units so that a single artillery mission wouldn't be sufficient to kill all of them.

So when the ITC suddenly went down, Santana's unit was not only too spread out to provide each other with line-of-sight fire support, but vulnerable in a number of other ways as well. . . . The officer felt something heavy land in the pit of his stomach, and he was just about to issue an order, when Corporal Gomez placed a hand on his shoulder. The unexpected contact caused Santana to jump as his mind was forced to break the connection with the virtual world and reintegrate itself with the real one. "Sorry to interrupt, sir," the noncom said. "But it looks like the brass hats want to noodle with you *now*. One of the *Indi*'s shuttles is waiting to take you dirtside."

"Don't ever do that again," Santana said, as he pulled the VR helmet up off of his head. "I nearly had a heart attack."

Gomez tried to look contrite but couldn't quite pull it off. "Yes, sir, that is no, sir. I won't do that again. Now, no offense, sir, but we need to board that shuttle."

Santana put the helmet down, removed the VR gauntlets, and stood. *"We?"*

"Yes, sir," Gomez answered evenly. "I took the liberty of having myself assigned to your command. I hope that's okay."

The cavalry officer frowned. His father had been an NCO, and he knew from experience that senior enlisted people could pull all sorts of strings if they chose to do so. But Gomez was too junior to have arranged such a posting on her own. "Was Major Lassiter a party to this arrangement by any chance?"

"Sir, yes, sir," Gomez said expressionlessly. "The major said that we deserve each other. Sir."

The comment could be taken in a lot of different ways, and Santana was forced to grin. "Okay, Corporal, but you may live to regret that decision. Let's get our T-1 bags and board that shuttle. I don't know why the brass are so eager to see us, but it can't be good."

* * *

It was dark when the shuttle emerged from a blinding snowstorm to hover over one of Fort Camerone's landing platforms. Nav lights glowed, and repellers screamed as the ship lowered itself into a cloud of billowing steam. Thanks to the fact that it was so cold, and the visibility was poor, the shuttle managed to touch down without taking sniper fire from the neighboring hills.

Only one person was present to meet the incoming ship—but the Hudathan was big enough to qualify as a reception party all by himself. His name was Drik Seeba-Ka. *Major* Drik Seeba-Ka, and he recognized Santana the moment the human emerged from the shuttle. What illumination there was came from one of the spaceship's wing lights as Santana approached the other officer. Coming as he did from one of the most hostile planets in known space, the Hudathan had no need for a parka. What might have been an expression of amusement flickered within his deep set eyes as the human dropped his T-1 bag and came to attention. "Captain Antonio Santana reporting as ordered, *sir!*"

"Stand easy," Seeba-Ka said as he returned the salute. "You're just as ugly as the last time I saw you."

"Look who's talking," Santana replied, and staggered as a massive hand slapped him on the back. The Hudathan made a grinding noise, which, based on previous experience, the human knew to be laughter.

"And who is *this*?" Seeba-Ka wanted to know, as Gomez arrived at the bottom of the ramp with her T-1 bag strapped to her back.

"Please allow me to introduce Corporal Gomez," Santana replied dryly. "But watch your step. . . . She doesn't like officers."

"I'll keep that in mind," the Hudathan growled. "Welcome to Algeron, Corporal. I'm sure the fort will be that much safer now that you're here to help guard it."

But Gomez didn't *want* to guard the fort—or anything else for that matter. She wanted to be with Santana. Partly because the noncom felt she owed the officer, partly because he appeared to be competent, and partly for reasons she wasn't ready to fully confront yet. So the noncom was about to object when Santana saw the look in her eye and hurried to intervene. "Report to the transient barracks, Corporal. I'll track you down."

Gomez heard the promise that was implicit in the officer's last sentence, took comfort from it, and managed a respectful, "Yes, sir."

Santana nodded, bent to retrieve his bag, and followed the Hudathan down into the fortress below. Gomez looked up into the thickly falling snow, felt a half dozen flakes kiss her face, and cursed her own stupidity. Joining the Legion had been stupid. Continually fighting the system was stupid. And falling in love with an officer was the stupidest thing of all.

The conference room was empty when Seeba-Ka and Santana entered. But it wasn't long before other people began to arrive, and the cavalry officer was introduced to Military Chief of Staff, General Bill Booly III, his chief of staff, Colonel Kitty Kirby, billionaire Admiral Sergi Chien-Chu, and Intelligence Chief Margaret Rutherford Xanith, plus a handful of trusted specialists. Missing from the meeting was Hudathan Triad Hiween Doma-Sa, who was off-planet.

Santana had never been in a room with so many VIPs and didn't want to be ever again. Especially since all of them were being deferential toward *him*, and he didn't know why. Finally, after the door was closed, it was Booly who brought the meeting to order. He chose to stand rather than sit and eyed those in front of him. "Most of you have seen the photos taken on Jericho, but Captain Santana hasn't. So bear with me as I bring the captain up to speed."

What followed was the most memorable briefing Santana was ever likely to receive. First came the news that an
entire battle group had been lost to the Ramanthians, followed by shocking holos of President Nankool being
marched through the jungle, with hundreds of POWs
strung out ahead of and behind him. Santana felt his heart
sink as he came to understand the true gravity of the situation, remembered all of the jungle-related VR scenarios
he'd been forced to complete on the *Indi*, and knew why.
Judging from the way in which he'd been treated, and the
way all the VIPs were staring at him, he'd been selected to
lead a rescue mission, the kind where a lot of people get
killed trying to accomplish the impossible.

Booly smiled grimly. "I can see from the expression on
the captain's face that he's asking himself why he was selected for what looks like a suicide mission. Well," the
general continued, "the answer to that question is quite
simple. The officer we're looking for needs to have some
unusual qualities. And when we ran the criteria through
the BUPERS computer, six names popped up. The first
was Antonio Santana's. And no wonder   because very few
of our officers have been awarded one Medal for Valor,
never mind *two*, and a Distinguished Service Cross to boot!

"But more important, from my perspective at least, is
that fact that Captain Santana has the right sort of personality and experience to land on Jericho and free the president from captivity. Some might disagree," Booly said
heavily, as his eyes swept the table. "They might point to
the fact that Captain Santana was court-martialed for dis-
obeying a direct order during a combat tour in the Clone
Hegemony. I would counter that the order that the captain
objected to was morally *wrong*, and point out that it takes
a lot more courage to disobey an illegal order than it does
to obey one. Add to that the experience gained on LaNor
under Major Seeba-Ka here, plus the nature of his service
on Savas, and you can see why I sent for him."

"However," Booly said, as his eyes returned to Santana, "there is a political component to this situation that could be even more dangerous than the mission itself. So, before you make up your mind, here's the rest of it."

Santana listened in near disbelief as the Military Chief of Staff provided a verbal time line of events, including the strategy to conceal Nankool's identity, and Vice President Jakov's failure to authorize a rescue mission.

Then, as the general completed his recitation, Chien-Chu stepped in. "I know this is a lot to absorb," the entrepreneur said kindly. "But seven days have passed since Jakov first saw the pictures of Nankool being marched through the jungle. And we can't wait much longer because each day brings the danger that one of the POWs will sell the president out. But if we send an unauthorized mission, then all of us could be charged with treason. And that includes *you*. So if you're about to say no, which any logical person would, say it now."

Seeba-Ka didn't consider himself to be an expert at reading human facial expressions. No Hudathan was. But the officer knew Santana pretty well. And, judging from what Seeba-Ka could see, the cavalry officer *was* preparing to say no. Not because of a lack of courage, but because he feared that an unauthorized rescue mission would be doomed to failure and result in unnecessary casualties.

But unbeknownst to the others in the room Seeba-Ka had a secret weapon at his disposal. Because he'd been on LaNor with Santana *and* Vanderveen and seen the two humans together. Not something he wanted to use—but something he *had* to use. The Hudathan reached out to capture a remote. "Before you answer that question," Seeba-Ka rumbled. "There's one additional thing to consider. The president is important, but hundreds of other prisoners are being held on Jericho as well."

Santana's eyes were drawn to a series of three-dimensional images as the holo blossomed in front of him.

He saw Nankool pass by the lens, followed by half a dozen other faces, and one that caused his heart to stand still. Christine Vanderveen was being held on Jericho along with the president!

Seeba-Ka saw the shock of it register on the human's face and felt a sense of guilt mixed with a large measure of satisfaction.

"That's a good point, sir," Santana said grimly. "Count me in."

7

Only one thing is required of prisoners—and that is absolute obedience.

—*Yama Mutuu Commandant*
Camp Enterprise
Standard year 2846

PLANET JERICHO, THE RAMANTHIAN EMPIRE

As the sun broke over the horizon and continued its journey into the sky, what looked like ectoplasm rose from the swampy ground to hover waist high around the ranks of prisoners lined up in front of the headquarters building. The POWs had been in what the Ramanthians liked to call "Camp Enterprise" for the better part of a week by then—and knew what to expect as they waited for Commandant Yama Mutuu to make his daily appearance. Outside of the jungle noises that emanated from the far side of the electrified fence and the hacking coughs that identified prisoners with walking pneumonia, the compound was eerily quiet. Because there were rules at Camp Enterprise, hundreds of them, one of which mandated a state of respectful silence prior to and during the commandant's morning pronouncements.

The whole thing was complete nonsense. That's what Overseer Tragg thought as he stood to one side and eyed the prisoners through his dark goggles. But, truth be told, he was subject to the same rules the POWs were. Because in spite of the weapons he wore and the robots positioned behind him, the mercenary was a prisoner, too. A prisoner to his fire-ravaged body, his gambling debts, and the fact that he couldn't leave Jericho without Mutuu's permission. All of which were things that he resented.

Christine Vanderveen stood in the second row not far from President Nankool. With help from Commander Peet Schell the LG (Leadership Group) was careful to keep reliable people around the chief executive at all times. Not to protect him from the Ramanthians, since that was impossible, but to shield Nankool from his fellow POWs. Because some of them had psychological problems and were unpredictable.

Worse yet was the possibility that short rations, poor health care, and miserable living conditions would cause one of the prisoners to reveal Nankool's true identity in exchange for more favorable treatment. A threat that was likely to intensify during the days, weeks, and months to come. Because short of an all-out victory by the Confederacy, Vanderveen couldn't see any hope of freedom.

The diplomat's thoughts were interrupted as a Ramanthian shuffled up a ramp onto the covered porch that fronted the long, low, prefab building, and took an intricately carved stick down from its pegs. Then, with all of the dignity of the Queen's chamberlain welcoming the monarch home from a long journey, the soldier struck the metal tube that hung next to the structure's front door. That produced the first of what were to be three melodic notes. As the last of them died away Commandant Mutuu emerged to address what he saw as his subjects.

Mutuu was related to the Queen, but permanently lost to his delusions of grandeur and other eccentricities. Which was why the functionary had been sent to Jericho, where his frequently embarrassing gaffes would be less visible to the Ramanthian public. One of his quirks was on full display as the elaborately dressed alien shuffled out onto the porch followed by a similarly costumed War Mutuu.

The twenty-five-foot-long strips of glittering cloth that had been ceremoniously wound around the Ramanthians' insectoid bodies were replicas of the war banners that the Queen's ancestors had carried into the Battle of Water-Deep, during which the pretenders had been slaughtered, thereby bringing all of the nest-clans under a single ruler. A proud moment and one that Yama Mutuu celebrated each morning by wearing the now-antiquated royal winding. No one knew whether the normally taciturn War Mutuu actively supported the practice or simply went along with it in order to please his mate.

Like most members of the royal court, Mutuu spoke standard but did so in short bursts, as if firing bullets from an air-cooled machine gun. "Greetings, loyal subjects," the royal began, as he looked out over what he momentarily perceived to be an army of brave Ramanthian warriors. "I have good news for you. The glorious enterprise is about to begin! Ships are dropping into orbit even as I speak. That means the supplies you need will arrive soon! Work will begin immediately thereafter. That will be all."

The Ramanthian soldier struck the gong as the commandant turned his back to the prisoners, and the War Mutuu followed him inside. Hooks, who was standing to Vanderveen's left, spoke out of the corner of his mouth. "What the hell was *that* all about?"

But there was no opportunity to discuss Mutuu's comments as Tragg strode out to stand in front of them. His voice was amplified by the sphere-shaped monitors that swept out to hover over the POWs. But the machines were slightly out of phase, which generated an echo when Tragg spoke. "That's right," the overseer said flatly. "The vacation is almost over. The Ramanthians are going to construct a space elevator about a mile from here. Once completed, it will be used to bring millions of tons of supplies and construction materials down from orbit."

The overseer paused to let the words sink in. "But working under zero-gee conditions requires experience, something the other slaves on Jericho lack. That's why the Ramanthians hired *me*. And that's why they permitted you to live. In order to work or to die. The choice is up to you."

A murmur of resentment ran through the ranks but stopped when Commander Schell shouted, "As you were!" And the first roll call of the day began.

After that it was off to chow, where the prisoners lined up to receive their share of the hot bubbling cereal that was served three times a day. All hoped to find two or three pieces of gray unidentifiable meat in their portions of the "boil," but that was rare unless they were friends with a "scoop." Meaning one of the prisoners assigned to scoop food out of the cauldron and deposit it on the metal plates.

And since Vanderveen was pretty, and most of the kitchen workers were male, it wasn't unusual for them to take her serving from the *bottom* of the cauldron, where the larger chunks of meat could typically be found. That wasn't right, and it made Vanderveen feel guilty, until she began to divide the chunks of meat into two portions. One serving for herself and the other for the increasing number of POWs housed in the dispensary—a structure consisting of a tin roof mounted on wooden poles, walls constructed from interwoven saplings, and a raised floor. A miserable place that the prisoners called "God's Waiting Room," since the majority of the people sent there died soon thereafter.

Then, having conveyed what scraps she could to one of the living skeletons who lay in the makeshift hammocks, Vanderveen typically returned to the hut where the LG was convened for its daily meeting. On that particular morning they were sitting around a small fire, eating the remains of their watery gruel, while Calisco turned a tiny corpse over the flames. Though numerous to begin with, and a welcome addition to the day's ration of protein, the little six-legged jungle rats were scarcer now. Two drops of fat sizzled as they landed in the fire, and President Nankool pointed his spoon at one of the upended five-gallon cans. "Pull up a chair, Christine—the commander is delivering a lecture on space elevators."

"That's right," the naval officer confirmed. "I've seen them used on a variety of planets but never one like this. Because even though you can move a great deal of cargo with an elevator, they cost a lot of money to construct. Which means they don't make a whole lot of sense on primitive planets."

"Not unless you're expecting a *huge* population explosion," Nankool said sourly. "Which the bugs are."

"Exactly," Schell agreed. "Which brings us to the way space elevators work. A space elevator is a bridge between the sky and the ground. The main components include an orbiting counterweight, a cable long enough to reach the ground, and a big anchor. Most of the bridge hangs from the counterweight, and the lowest tension occurs at the base. That means the center of mass, which is located just below the counterweight, will be in geosynchronous orbit.

"In order to climb the cable," Schell continued, "energy is typically beamed to the transfer vehicle from the ground or orbit. But in this case, given that the Ramanthians want to bring lots of stuff down in a hurry, they're going to get what amounts to a free ride. Because once the transfer vehicle is loaded, all the operator needs to do is apply the brakes in order to protect the module from overheating as it enters the planet's atmosphere. So, given the situation, the plan makes sense. For the bugs that is. . . . But the whole process of reeling out sections of cable and hooking them together, is going to be a bitch. Especially if our people are hungry, and in some cases sick, while they work. We can expect a lot of casualties."

There was a humming sound as one of the monitors floated into the hut and hovered over their heads. Everyone knew Tragg used the robots to intimidate prisoners and track their activities. Nankool pretended to ignore the robot as he licked the bottom of his metal bowl. Then, having removed every last calorie of cereal, he smacked his lips. "Damn! That stuff gets better every day!"

Tragg, who was watching a bank of monitors within the privacy of his well-guarded hut, smiled tightly. The guy with the bushy black beard had a sense of humor. You had to give him that. . . . The overseer continued to watch as the monitor made its rounds.

Nankool waited for the robot to leave, made a rude gesture, and turned back to the LG. "Where was I before the airborne turd entered the room? Oh, yeah . . . Peet makes a good point. But while we can't do much to improve their overall nutrition or health care, we *can* provide the troops with some refresher training. You know, lectures on zero-gee safety, that sort of thing. And we'd better get cracking because there isn't much time. Is that it? Or is there *more* bad news to discuss?"

"Sorry, boss," Hooks put in regretfully, "but it looks like Tragg is beginning to interview our people one at a time. It began yesterday, and appeared to be random at first, until we drew up a list and discovered that all their names began with the letter 'A.' "

"What sort of questions did he ask?" Vanderveen wanted to know.

"That's the weird part," Hooks replied. "As far as I can tell there wasn't any pattern to the questions. Some people were asked about their specialties, which might make sense when you're about to build a space elevator. But Tragg asked some of the others about their families, life in the camp, who's sleeping with whom and that sort of stuff. The bastard is crazy."

"Maybe," Vanderveen allowed thoughtfully. "But maybe not. . . . By asking all sorts of seemingly innocuous questions, he could get people to relax, build a matrix of information, and mine it for who knows what."

"And there's *another* possibility," Schell said darkly. "The whole process could be a cover for talking to people he has a particular interest in."

Nankool's eyebrows rose. "You think someone flipped?"

Schell shook his head. "I have no evidence of that, but I can't rule it out."

Then we've got to identify them, Vanderveen thought to herself. And the diplomat might have said something to that effect had it not been for a series of shouts that caused the entire LG to file out into the open. That was when Vanderveen heard someone yell, "He's making a run for it! Stop him!"

But it was too late by then as a human scarecrow dodged two of the men who were trying to capture him, spun like the athlete he had once been, and ran straight for the fence. A silvery monitor gave chase but wasn't close enough to fire its stun gun as the prisoner left the ground. He hit the wires with arms and legs spread to maximize the amount of contact and issued a long, lung-emptying scream as the electricity coursed through his body. The POW hung there and continued to cook long after he was dead. The air was heavy with the smell of burned flesh, and one of the prisoners threw up.

Oliver Batkin captured the whole thing from his heavily camouflaged nest in the forest, took some more pictures of the badly blackened corpse, and wondered if either one of his message torps had gotten through. Because if they hadn't, and help failed to arrive, *more* people would die on the fence. Many more . . . And Batkin didn't know how much he could stand.

PLANET ALGERON, THE CONFEDERACY OF SENTIENT BEINGS

The pit, which was the unofficial name for the military prison within Fort Camerone, was located more than ten stories below Algeron's storm-swept surface. The facility included two tiers of cells that looked down onto a common area or "pit." As Santana followed Command Sergeant Major Paul Bester out onto a platform that extended over the seventy-five-foot drop, the officer could feel the almost palpable mixture of anger, hatred, and hopelessness that surrounded those gathered below. All of them had been convicted of serious crimes prior to being sent to the pit where they were awaiting transportation to even-less-hospitable surroundings.

That was scary enough, but making the situation even worse was the knowledge that here, somewhere among all of those hostile beings, were the roughly twenty-four men, women, and cyborgs who would accompany him to Jericho. Because Booly and the other members of the sub-rosa group that Santana reported to knew any effort to recruit legionnaires from regular line units would be reported to Vice President Jakov.

Bester eyed the six pintle-mounted machine guns trained on the floor below and confirmed that all of them were properly manned before speaking into a wireless microphone. "Atten-hut!" The process of coming to attention took at least five seconds and could only be described as sloppy. But that was to be expected, and Bester was reasonably happy with the extent of their compliance as he eyed the inmates below. "The man standing next to me is Captain Antonio Santana. You will listen to what he says and keep your mouths shut until he is done. Is that understood?"

The response was automatic and something less than enthusiastic. "Sir! Yes, sir!"

Like the guards, Bester didn't rate the honorific "sir," outside of the pit, but he was god within it. "I can't *hear* you!"

"Sir! Yes, *sir*!" the crowd roared.

"That's better," the blocky noncom allowed grudgingly. "Because even though you might be scum, you're *Legion* scum, and therefore the best goddamned scum in the galaxy!"

Surprisingly, in spite of the fact that every single one of the people in the pit had been sentenced to prison by the organization to which they belonged, such was their overriding sense of pride that the response caused the railing under Santana's right hand to vibrate. *"Camerone!"*

It was amazing that an ancient battle in a small Mexican village could still evoke such passion. But it did, and Santana was moved by the strength of the response. Moved, and to some extent reassured, by the knowledge that the Legion had always been a refuge for criminals, who often fought valiantly in spite of their sordid backgrounds. Bester turned to Santana, assumed a brace, and saluted. "They're all yours, sir."

The legionnaire nodded gravely and returned the salute. "Thank you, Command Sergeant Major."

Santana raised his own microphone as he turned back toward the pit. "Stand easy. . . . I know you have important things to do—so I'll keep this session short."

That comment produced snorts of derision, some catcalls, and outright laughter from the assemblage below. Santana's eyes roamed the crowd as he waited for the noise to die down. Most of the inmates were bio bods, but scattered here and there among the beings who looked back up at him were the bland metal faces that belonged to the cyborgs. Twice-condemned creatures with nowhere left to run. "I'm here because I need to recruit some legionnaires for a very dangerous mission," Santana said honestly. "I can't divulge the exact nature of the mission, other than to say that it's very important to the Confederacy, and the chances of success are slim. That's the *bad* news," Santana concluded. "The good news is that any legionnaires who volunteer, and are selected for the team, will be pardoned. Regardless of their crimes."

There was a stir followed by the rumble of conversation as the prisoners reacted to the offer. "As you were!" Bester ordered sternly, and targeting lasers swept back and forth across the formation. The talk died away.

"But I won't take just anybody," Santana cautioned. "And there are only twenty-six slots. That means thirteen bio bods—and thirteen cyborgs. But if you want to see some action, and if you're interested the possibility of a pardon, then give your name to the guards. Interviews will begin later this afternoon. That will be all."

Bester said, "Atten-hut!" and there was a loud crash as the multitude came to attention. "Dismissed!"

Orders were shouted, and bodies swirled, as segments of the inmate population were sent back to their cells. Bester turned to Santana. The noncom's deeply seamed face bore a look of concern. "I don't know what you're up to, sir, but surely you can do better than this lot. . . . Whatever the mission is will be dangerous enough without having to watch your back all the time. Why half that bunch would slit your throat for the price of a beer!"

"I hear you, Sergeant Major," Santana replied. "But there's no other choice. The interviews will begin at 1400 hours assuming that we have some volunteers."

"Oh, you'll have them," the noncom allowed cynically. "The question is whether you'll want them!"

Maria Gomez had been laying on her rack, snatching some extra Z's, when the order arrived. And now, as the noncom followed the shock-baton-toting guard through a maze of passageways into the heart of the infamous pit, the legionnaire wondered what the hell she was doing there. Having cleared the last checkpoint the soldier led Gomez out into the open area beyond. "The captain is in room two," the private informed her, and pointed his club at a door on the other side of the hall.

Gomez thanked the guard, straightened her uniform, and approached the open door. She knocked three times, took two steps forward, and snapped to attention. "Corporal Maria Gomez, reporting as ordered, sir!"

Santana looked up from the printouts laid out in front of

him to the noncom who was framed by the doorway. The legionnaire's face was expressionless, and she was staring at a point about six inches above his head. He could use Gomez, that was for sure, but would that be fair? Sergeant Major Bester felt sure that at least some of the pit rats would volunteer. And, given the long sentences that many of them faced, would consider themselves lucky to escape the pit, no matter how dangerous the mission might be.

But, outside of a few run-ins with officers, Gomez had a clean record. Should he accept the noncom if she volunteered? Or find a reason to disqualify the legionnaire because he liked her? And would that be wrong? Such were the questions that swirled through Santana's mind as he said, "At ease, Corporal. Come in and take a load off. I have some interviews to conduct—but I wanted to speak with you first."

Gomez didn't know what to think as she entered the room and took the seat opposite Santana. That was when she became fully aware of the pistol, the cyborg zapper, and the shock baton that were laid out next to the officer's right hand. An interesting array of tools for a man who was about to conduct interviews. "Okay," Santana began, "here's the deal."

Gomez listened attentively as the officer glossed over what he described as ". . . a top secret mission," emphasized how dangerous it would be, and told her about the need to recruit prisoners. The enterprise was clearly hopeless. As was the way she felt about the serious-looking officer. But Santana was going to need someone to cover his six, so when he offered to find her a slot in another outfit, the noncom shook her head. "Thank you, sir, but no thanks. I like a good fight, you know that. So I'll go along for the ride."

Santana felt a surge of gratitude. Because he would have to sleep sometime, and without dependable noncoms to keep his team of cutthroats under control, he could wake up dead. He looked her in the eye. "You're sure?"

Gomez nodded. "I'm sure."

"Then welcome to Task Force Zebra, Sergeant. I can use the help."

Gomez was visibly surprised. "Sergeant?"

Santana nodded. "The team will be made up of two platoons—with two squads in each platoon. I'm putting you down to lead the first squad in the first platoon. Have you got any objections?"

It was a significant increase in responsibility, and to the noncom's surprise, she welcomed it. "No, sir. No objections."

"Good. Come around and sit on this side of the table. I want you to take notes as I conduct the interviews. Then later, when the process is complete, I'm going to ask for your input. Is that clear?"

"Yes, sir."

"Good," Santana replied. "I know you're going to like the first candidate. He's an insubordinate son of a bitch who was sent to the pit for punching an officer in the face."

It was dark when the forty-three heavily shackled prisoners were led up out of the pit to a landing platform, where they and the guards assigned to accompany them were loaded onto a couple of cybernetic fly-forms. Then, with a minimum of fuss, both aircraft lifted. According to their flight plans, both cyborgs were taking part in a special ops training exercise. Which, all things considered, they were. Because, after two days of intensive interviews, the first part of the recruiting process was over. Now all Santana had to do was sort the wheat from the chaff. Assuming there was wheat hidden in the chaff.

The flight lasted for about an hour and ended when the fly-forms put down in an abandoned village. The sun was up but wouldn't be for very long. Like many indigenous habitations, the village had been left to melt back into the countryside as the Naa who lived in it left to seek better lives in the city that was growing up around the fort. It was just one of many changes brought on by the war, the fact that the government had been relocated to Algeron, and Naa independence.

Once the prisoners and their guards were on the ground, repellers screamed and the fly-forms lifted off. Santana waited for the sound of the engines to die away before addressing the mob arrayed in front of him. The cyborgs had been slotted into unarmed T-2 bodies that towered above the bio bods.

"Welcome to Camp Bust Ass," the officer shouted, as the easterly wind tried to steal his words. "Congratulations on making the first cut. But since we have fifty volunteers, and only twenty-six slots, more than half of you will go back to the pit. So if you want to stay—show us what you can do. And I say 'us,' because Sergeants Norly Snyder and Pia Fox have joined the leadership team."

There were about twenty mounds, each signifying the location of an underground dwelling, and the prisoners whirled as two fully armed T-2s burst out into the open. A potent combination indeed, and a not-so-subtle message to any prisoner, or prisoners, who thought they might be able to overpower Santana and Gomez. "Sergeant Snyder served with me during the Claw uprising on LaNor," the officer continued. "And Sergeant Fox was part of the team that rescued the colonists on Hibo IV. So both of them know a thing or two about combat. You will follow their orders as you would follow mine."

The wind made a soft whining sound as it searched the village, found nothing of interest, and continued on its way. "Okay," Santana said, as he eyed the faces arrayed in front of him. "Beautiful though it is—there's an obvious shortage of amenities here at Camp Bust Ass. Conveniences like latrines, weatherproof huts, and a first-class obstacle course. Items that you will be privileged to dig, repair, and build, using supplies brought in yesterday. The noncoms will divide you into teams. Each team will have a goal, and each team member will have an opportunity to lead as well as follow. Those individuals who have the highest grades will get the opportunity to die glorious deaths. . . . And, all things considered, what more could any legionnaire want?"

"Beer!" someone shouted, and Santana grinned. "Only winners get to drink beer. So, prove yourselves worthy, and it will be on me!"

There was a loud cheer, followed by a volley of orders, and work got under way.

A long series of extremely short Algeron days passed as the village was gradually transformed from a collection of abandoned hovels into something that resembled a military encampment, complete with its own subterranean chow hall, underground barracks, and an extensive obstacle course.

But the process wasn't pretty. Santana was forced to bring one belligerent T-2 to her knees with a zapper, three bio bods were shot while trying to escape, and Gomez beat a fourth senseless when he made a grab for her. And there were less-dramatic washouts as well: soldiers who refused to work with people they didn't like, attempted to shirk their duties, or refused to obey orders. Every twelve hours the latest group of drops, plus an appropriate number of guards, were shipped back to Fort Camerone, where they were isolated from the rest of the prisoners so that word of what was taking place wouldn't reach Jakov.

Finally, once the original group had been winnowed down to the final twenty-four, Santana was ready to begin the next phase of training. But first, before additional gear was distributed, an evening of celebration was in order. It arrived in the form of two fly-forms. One was loaded with weapons, ammo, and other equipment. The other carried a keg of beer, two D-4020 Dream Machines that the borgs could to hook up to, and hot meals straight out of Fort Camerone's kitchens.

And, as Santana watched, two officers jumped down off the second fly-form and made their way over. Santana saluted General Bill Booly, who introduced First Lieutenant Alan Farnsworth, a man who was clearly too old for his rank. "The lieutenant just graduated from OCS (Officer Training School)," Booly shouted over the engine noise. "But don't let that fool you because he put in twelve years as a noncom before that! You need a platoon leader, and here he is. I would trust him with my life."

The comment implied a previous relationship, and some level of sponsorship as well, which was all right with Santana so long as Farnsworth could deliver the goods. And, as the two men shook hands, the officer liked what he saw. Farnsworth's face was a road map of sun-etched lines, his nose had clearly been broken more than once, and half of his left ear was missing. But the most important thing was the intelligence resident in the other man's gray eyes as he waited to see how his new CO would react.

"Welcome to Team Zebra," Santana said warmly. "I can sure as hell use someone with your experience. . . . And, if I trip over a rock, the team will be good hands."

Farnsworth grinned and seemed to relax slightly, as if he'd been unsure of how the academy graduate might react to getting saddled with a prior. "Thank you, sir. . . . I'm looking forward to the opportunity. Sort of."

All of three of them laughed as the fly-forms lifted off, snowflakes swirled, and darkness closed around them.

PLANET JERICHO, THE RAMANTHIAN EMPIRE

The rain began during the hours of darkness, continued as the dimly seen sun rose somewhere beyond the thick overcast, and turned the entire area around Camp Enterprise into a morass of thick, glutinous mud. The muck was so thick it formed clumps around the prisoners' boots and forced them to lift a couple of extra pounds each time they took a step. The result was a slow-motion parody of work that was unlikely to produce anything more than sick POWs, which would threaten Tragg's ability to stay on schedule, make money, and get off Jericho. That was why the overseer felt compelled to make the pilgrimage to the headquarters building, where the mercenary requested an audience with the commandant and was eventually shown into the richly decorated throne room. But only after removing his boots, washing both his hands and feet, and submitting to a pat-down. Then, careful to bow his head submissively, the overseer made his request. "Given the weather conditions, Excellency, and all of the mud, I recommend that we suspend operations until the rain stops."

The position of Mutuu's antennae signaled contempt. "So it's raining," the commandant replied scornfully. "Animals *need* rain! It keeps them clean. We have a schedule to maintain, human. So maintain it. Or, would you like to join the rest of your cowardly kind, as they live out their lives in the jungle?"

Tragg had been forced to leave his weapons at the front door, but it would have been easy to kill the commandant bare-handed, and the thought was very much on the overseer's mind as the dark goggles came up. But the War Mutuu was waiting with sword drawn. "Yes, human?" the alien grated. "Is *this* your day to die?"

So Tragg was forced to withdraw, and to do so without honor, which made him very angry. Because different though they were in most respects, the human and the War Mutuu had one thing in common, and that was their overweening pride.

The result was a silent fury that was visited upon the prisoners in the form of orders to draw their tools, march to the edge of the jungle, and resume the task of clearing more land for the airstrip. Meanwhile, on the other side of the electrified fence, Vanderveen could see a band of ragged civilians who were busy excavating one of the structures that the forerunners had left behind. The activity didn't make sense until Commander Schell pointed out that the ancient building would make an excellent anchor for the space elevator's cable. Never mind the fact that doing so might compromise or destroy what could be an extremely important archeological site. The Ramanthians had five billion new citizens to accommodate, and their needs had priority.

The all-pervasive mud sucked at the soles of Vanderveen's boots as the diplomat made her way over to the point where a team of "mules" were hauling loose debris out of the cutting zone and into the middle of the clearing. That was where Calisco was, so that was where Vanderveen wanted to be, since the FSO was determined to keep an eye on the shifty bastard. There were no objections as the diplomat grabbed on to a length of slippery rope and added her strength to that of the prisoners attempting to drag a heavily loaded sled across the water-soaked ground.

Calisco was pulling on the *other* length of rope, just six feet away from her, and as Vanderveen struggled to make some forward progress she watched him out of the corner of her eye. Was the official slacking? Just pretending to pull? It was difficult to tell, but yes, the diplomat thought that he was. Still, who *didn't* ease off at one time or another, especially if they were feeling ill?

Tragg was nowhere to be seen as the day progressed, but didn't need to be, since he could not only watch the work via the robotic monitors but comment on it as well. Which he did frequently. The clouds parted around midday, and the rain stopped.

A thick, undulating mist hung over the muddy field as Oliver Batkin watched the prisoners leave the work site to collect their ration of gruel. The spy had stationed himself high in a tree and had been there for some time. The cyborg was well aware of the space elevator by that point, having listened in on various conversations that pertained to it, and knew that the project was worth reporting to Algeron. Especially if the government was going to send a rescue mission. Unless neither one of his message torps had arrived that is. . . . Which was why the *third* vehicle would carry both the information sent earlier *and* everything he had been able to learn about the space elevator.

But before the message went out Batkin was determined to go for a bonus. Tragg had been interviewing five to ten prisoners per night. . . . The question was why? And what about the Ramanthians? What if anything could be learned from *them*?

All of this seemed to suggest the need for a dangerous but potentially profitable trip into the compound during the hours of darkness. Of course there would be the monitors to deal with, not to mention Tragg's Sheen robots. But, thanks to all the cloaking technology built into his body, the spy was confident that he could escape electronic detection. The more significant danger was that an especially alert guard would make visual contact with him and give the alarm.

So, cognizant of the fact that he might be caught, Batkin uploaded everything he had to one of his remaining message torps and programmed the device to depart in sixteen hours should no further instructions be forthcoming. With that accomplished, there was nothing to do but sit and wait while the POWs continued their work.

It was hot by then, and extremely humid, as the ragged bio bods struggled to enlarge the airfield. Meanwhile, even though it wasn't large enough to accommodate more than two aircraft at a time, the Ramanthians took advantage of the clear skies to bring in shuttle after fully loaded shuttle, each of which had to be unloaded. A process Vanderveen found to be very interesting indeed since she had followed Calisco over to the new task and was present when crates full of human space armor began to come off the shuttles. Once on the ground, each container had to be transported to the metal-roofed structures bordering one side of the strip. A task normally handled with machinery that was presently bogged down in the mud.

There was no way to know where the stuff was from without being able to read the bar codes printed on the crates, but it didn't take a genius to figure out that the material had been captured. It was still another indication of the extent to which the bugs were winning the war.

And it was while Vanderveen and eleven other prisoners were plodding across the well-churned mud that Tragg appeared. Everyone knew the overseer was pissed—but no one could say why. So most of the prisoners tried to fade into the background as Tragg and two of his robotic bodyguards wandered out onto the airstrip. "Uh-oh," the rating next to Vanderveen said, as the overseer appeared. "Here comes trouble." And the comment quickly proved to be prophetic as a none-too-bright sailor named Bren Hotkey chose that particular moment to step behind a crate and take a pee.

Tragg saw the movement, felt a welcome sense of outrage, and made a beeline for the crate. Work continued, albeit at a slower pace, as everyone who could watched to see what would happen next. Vanderveen was no exception. Her heart went out to the hapless rating, as Tragg disappeared from sight only to emerge dragging Hotkey behind him. The robots came into play at that point as they took control of the human and frog-marched the irate sailor toward one of the shuttles. "Let me go!" Hotkey protested loudly. "All I did was take a whiz. . . . What's wrong with that?"

But the machines made no reply as the sailor was positioned next to the shuttle and his wrists cuffed in front of him. Then there was a mutual moment of horror as Tragg dropped a noose over the young man's head, secured the other end of the rope to a landing skid, and walked out to the point where the Ramanthian pilots could see him. A single thumbs-up was sufficient to signal the all clear—and Commander Schell began to run as the shuttle wobbled off the ground.

Hotkey ran along below the aircraft as it began to move, but couldn't possibly keep up, and was soon snatched off his feet as the ship began to climb. The rating struggled to loosen the noose, but that was impossible, so there was little more that Hotkey could do than kick his legs as he was borne away to the east. The movement stopped moments later, and the body became little more than a dangling dot that was soon lost to sight.

There was nothing Commander Schell could do at that point but stop running and place his hands on his knees as Tragg brought a microphone up to his mouth. His voice boomed over the robotic PA system. "Pee in your pants if you have to. . . . But keep working. That will be all."

Commandant Mutuu, who had witnessed the entire episode via one of his pole-mounted security cams, nodded approvingly and ordered an attendant to pour even more hot sand into his daily bath. Jericho might be primitive by imperial standards, but there was no reason to suffer. The day wore on.

8

True excellence is to plan secretly, to move surreptitiously, to foil the enemy's intentions and balk his schemes. . . .

—*Sun Tzu*
The Art of War
Standard year circa 500 B.C.

PLANET JERICHO, THE RAMANTHIAN EMPIRE

As the orange-red disk slipped below the western horizon, and the already-long shadows cast by the buildings spread out to encompass the entire camp, the night creatures began a discordant symphony of screams, hoots, and grunts. And it was then, on the cusp between day and night, that the spy ball fired his repellers and emerged from his hiding place. Thanks to the cloaking technology built into his body, Oliver Batkin was fairly confident he could escape electronic detection. But that wouldn't render him invisible to the Ramanthian guards, or to the security cameras perched atop tall poles.

The moment Batkin crossed the fence, the cyborg dropped down so he was only a foot off the ground as he made his way toward the Ramanthian headquarters building. A journey that required the spy ball to hide in the shadows until the way was clear, speed across open ground, and then hide again. Each time Batkin did so, he expected to hear a shout, followed by the staccato *rattle* of gunfire, and a general alarm. But his movements went undetected, and the spy eventually found himself next to the building in which Commandant Mutuu lived and worked—an accomplishment that wouldn't mean much unless he could get inside.

Guards were stationed to either side of the front door, so that point of entry was blocked, as were the heavily barred windows. So Batkin fired his repellers, rose until he was even with the eaves, and followed the slanted roof upwards. Eventually the spy encountered a *second* pitched roof, which stood two feet above the first and sat atop its own supports. The vertical surfaces on both sides were covered with metal mesh intended to keep pests out while allowing hot humid air to escape from the rooms below.

But it was also a way in, or soon would be, as Batkin extended a small torch and cut a hole in the mesh. The opening was way too small to admit his rotund form. But that didn't matter because the cyborg had no need to enter personally. A small port irised open on the side of the agent's body, and a tiny sphere darted out into the humid air and bobbed up and down as an evening breeze tugged at it. Having taken control of the spy-eye, Batkin sent the device through the newly created hole into the structure beyond. Then, thanks to onboard sensors, the cyborg could "see" what the tiny robot saw and "hear" what it heard as the remote sank into the gloom below. Since the bugs were too cheap, or too lazy, to build something better, the interior walls rose only partway to the ceiling. That allowed Batkin's proxy to cruise the darkness while peering down into a succession of boxy spaces.

Batkin saw what looked like a shadowy office, and a throne room, followed by a space that caused his nonexistent heart jump. Because there, bathed in the light from a single glow cone, was a scale model of the space elevator! Complete with an orbital counterweight that dangled from a piece of string.

After checking to ensure that the conference area was

empty, Batkin sent the spy-eye down for a closer look and recorded everything the robot saw. Then, just as he was about to withdraw the proxy, additional lights came on as a pair of guards entered the room. There was just barely enough time to hide the spy-eye inside the miniature forerunner temple before the Ramanthian troopers sat down at the table and began to consume their dinners. Batkin cursed his luck but settled in to wait, knowing the bugs would leave the room when they were finished. And about thirty minutes later they did so. But not before making some rather derogatory remarks about the food, the sergeant of the guard's ancestry, and life in the army.

Thus freed, Batkin was able to propel the proxy out of the miniature temple, take a quick peek at Commandant Mutuu's private quarters, and retrieve the remote from inside the building. At that point it was tempting to ignore objective two, retreat to the jungle, and upload what information he had. And it made sense to do so since the data on the space elevator would be of considerable interest to Madame X regardless of any rescue attempt.

But having already risked so much to enter the compound, the spy was loath to leave without taking a crack at Tragg. The problem was that as the cyborg closed with the overseer, it was increasingly likely that one of the mercenary's robots would "see" through the electronic cloak that surrounded him and alert the renegade to his presence. Then, even if he managed to escape, the spy would *still* be in trouble because the Ramanthians would launch a full-scale search.

In the end it was a piece of good luck that helped Batkin reach a final decision. Klaxons began to sound as a shuttle roared overhead, and the pilot declared some sort of onboard emergency. That caused all eyes, including those that belonged to the guards, to swivel toward the adjoining airfield.

And it was then, as the shuttle settled into a nest of

flashing lights, that the spy flew a zigzag course over to the prefab structure that housed Tragg and his robotic servants. A Sheen robot stood guard outside the hut but didn't look up as Batkin passed over its head and came to rest on the crest of the peaked roof. The rather precarious perch required the cyborg to extend four stabilizers in order to keep his roly-poly body from rolling down the slope and off the edge below. The positioning was good, but not good enough, since the overseer's structure lacked the overroof the admin building had. So, being unable to penetrate the prefab from above, Batkin sent the proxy down the far side of the roof to attempt a ground-level entry.

The minibot was too small to carry cloaking technology, but it was also too small to generate a significant heat signature. That meant the robotic sentry experienced little more than a gentle buzzing sensation as its sensors were momentarily activated. The signal disappeared a couple of seconds later, however, which left the Sheen machine to conclude that the alert had been generated by a jungle rat, or a system anomaly. There was a persistent electronic overburden, however, as if something lay within detection range but wasn't registering the way it should. So, consistent with its programming, the robot triggered a routine systems check.

Meanwhile, having zipped in *under* the building, the tiny spy-eye cruised the length of a long supporting beam as Batkin peered up through cracks, gaps, and holes in the wood flooring. Finally, the agent found what he'd been searching for in the form of a small hole and sent his proxy up into the room above. It wasn't safe to fly, so the marble-sized invader began to roll along the base of a wall instead, a maneuver that made Batkin so dizzy he was forced to pause occasionally and let his "head" clear.

Eventually, having penetrated a well-lit room, Batkin brought the sphere-shaped spy-eye to a halt in the shadow cast by a centrally located table. A back could be seen above and opposite him. Tragg's head and shoulders were visible beyond. Even though it was dark outside, the overseer was still wearing his goggles. Because he needed them? Or to look menacing? If so, it was working, because judging from the POW's responses, he was clearly frightened.

But nothing came of the interview. Nothing Batkin could put a theoretical finger on anyway. Nor were the second, third, or fourth interviews any more productive than the first. Which was why Batkin was about to pull out and write the whole thing off to experience, when a fifth prisoner entered the room. Except rather than wait for an invitation to sit down as his predecessors had— this individual dropped into the guest chair as if reclaiming a piece of personal property. That alone was sufficient to stimulate Batkin's curiosity and cause the cyborg to leave the proxy in place.

"So you're back," Tragg said inflectionlessly.

"Yeah," the prisoner said. "And I'm risking my life to come here."

Tragg shrugged. "So tell me what you've got, and I'll take care of you. . . . It's as simple as that."

"No," the other man insisted. "It *isn't* as simple as that. Let's say I spill my guts. . . . How can I be sure that you'll uphold your end of the bargain?

"Because I said I would," the overseer answered coldly. "And there's something else to consider as well. . . . You're beginning to piss me off. And you've seen what can happen to someone who pisses me off. So quit screwing around, or I'll *whip* the information out of you!"

There was a pause, as if the prisoner was considering all of his options. Batkin wished he could see the expression on the man's face, but he was afraid, to move, lest he reveal the spy-eye's presence. "Okay," the prisoner replied. "How 'bout this? You make the arrangements to put me aboard a

Thraki supply ship, all expenses paid to Starfall, and I'll tell you what you need to know just before I step aboard."

"Why should I?" Tragg countered. "I can figure it out on my own. . . . Or torture it out of you."

The POW laughed harshly. "If you could figure it out on your own, you would have by now. That's why you interview prisoners every night—trying to figure out what if anything they're hiding. But it hasn't worked has it?

"As for torture. . . . Well, that's not very reliable is it? Because people will say *anything* to stop the pain. And I'm no exception. So why make things difficult? Schedule the flight, I'll give you what you want, and you can take credit for it. That should be worth something. Something *big*."

"Okay," the overseer agreed. "But remember this. . . . If what you tell me is false, the ship you leave on will be intercepted off Starfall, and you will be brought back to Jericho. And that, my friend, is when the *real* suffering will begin."

"You'll be satisfied," the prisoner promised confidently. "*Very* satisfied. Now, with your permission, I think it would be best if I left."

The chair made a scraping sound as the prisoner pushed it back and came to his feet. When he turned, the light illuminated the left side of his face, and Batkin was stunned by what he saw. Because the man who intended to betray not only President Marcott Nankool, but the entire Confederacy, was none other than Secretary for Foreign Affairs Roland Hooks! The same man with whom he had once shaken hands . . . A man who was posing as someone else, because had the mercenary been aware of the official's *true* identity, the rest would have been obvious.

That was important information, or would be, if the operative could pass it to the right people. That was when the Sheen robot sent a warning to the nearest guard tower, a Ramanthian guard swiveled a spotlight onto Tragg's roof, and Batkin was bathed in white light. A machine gun stuttered, the cyborg felt a slug rip through his electromechanical body, and alarms began to bleat.

PLANET ALGERON, THE CONFEDERACY OF SENTIENT BEINGS

A thin sheen of perspiration covered Kay Wilmot's naked back as she performed oral sex on Vice President Jakov while a Hobar Systems 7300 pleasure robot serviced the diplomat from behind. The androids were sold in a variety of configurations, but this particular unit was chrome-plated, sculpted to resemble a very athletic human male, and equipped with an extremely large, internally heated sex organ.

The diplomat had experienced two powerful orgasms by then. A fact not lost on the vice president, who delighted in watching the machine dominate the same woman *he* was dominating, because sex and power were very nearly the same thing where the politician was concerned.

The android placed both of its padded hands on Wilmot's generously proportioned buttocks and began to squeeze them. Just the sight of that was sufficient to bring Jakov to climax. His eyelids fluttered as wave after wave of pleasure surged through his body, and he uttered a grunt of satisfaction.

In spite of the physical pleasure she had experienced, Wilmot was quite conscious of other aspects of the situation, including the fact that the things her lover demanded of her had grown increasingly kinky since the beginning of their sexual relationship. And now, with the introduction of the 7300, she was beginning to worry about what might lie ahead. The robot, which could simulate an orgasm, timed its ejaculation to match the human's and withdrew as the bio bod did. Then, consistent with a signal from Jakov, the android returned to the closet, where it would remain until summoned again. The human lovers lay in each other's arms. "So," Jakov said lazily, "who performed best? The robot or me?"

"You did," Wilmot lied.

"I doubt it," the vice president countered contentedly. "But it doesn't matter so long as you had a good time."

"Which I did," Wilmot assured him.

"Good," the vice president said agreeably. "And you deserve it. Especially after engineering the brilliant deal with ex-ambassador Orno. Who knows? Nankool could be dead by now."

The sex-sweat had begun to evaporate off the diplomat's skin by then, and Wilmot shivered as she pulled a badly rumpled sheet up over her ample breasts. The photos taken on Jericho, and subsequently sent to Madame X, were entirely unambiguous. Nankool was alive. Or had been very recently. "Yes," she said cautiously. "He could be dead by now. . . . But I think it's too early to be sure. Especially since there has been no demand for payment from Orno."

"Which is why you want me to approve a rescue mission."

"Yes. Because later, after details of the prisoner massacre have been publicized, everyone will know you tried your best. And that will silence the Nankool loyalists."

"Who continue to plot against me," the vice president said darkly.

Wilmot frowned. If plots were afoot, why hadn't he told her earlier? Because she had yet to earn his full trust, that's why. "They're plotting against you?" she inquired gently. "In what way?"

"In *this* way," Jakov answered, as he lifted a remote. "I'm building my own organization within General Booly's staff one transfer at a time. . . . Eventually, after the massacre on Jericho, I'll force the bastard into retirement. In the meantime, I'm learning all sorts of interesting things about what the general and his cronies have been up to. Watch this."

As Wilmot looked on, a holo blossomed over the foot of

the bed and a legionnaire appeared. The soldier wore a hood to hide his face and his voice had been electronically altered to protect his identity. What light there was came from above. "Rather than wait for authorization from the vice president, officers acting on orders from a secret cabal of politicians, senior officials, and the Military Chief of Staff, are working to recruit and train a special ops team for the purpose of landing on Jericho," the informant reported. "Where, if the mission is successful, they plan to rescue President Nankool."

"Which supports what I've been saying," Wilmot put in, as the image exploded into a thousand motes of light. "Dozens of people including your informant *know* Nankool is alive. That will leak eventually. . . . Especially if the Nankool supporters become sufficiently frustrated. So let them send their mission, knowing it will most likely be intercepted by the Ramanthians or land only to discover that all the POWs have been killed. *Including* the president."

The suggestion made sense, a *lot* of sense, especially since there would be no need to reveal the extent to which the secret cabal had been compromised. "You are not only beautiful, but brilliant," Jakov said, as he pulled Wilmot close. "It shall be as you say."

Wilmot should have felt a sense of pleasure, because here was the power that she had sought for so long, even if her role was somewhat obscured. But for some reason the diplomat's skin was cold—and Jakov's embrace did nothing to warm it.

PLANET JERICHO, THE RAMANTHIAN EMPIRE

Oliver Batkin felt the bullet rip through his electro-mechanical body and knew he was injured as the beam of light washed across Tragg's metal roof. But the cyborg was far from defenseless. As the guards learned when the sphere burped blue light, and the tower they were firing from took a direct hit. One of the structure's four legs was severed, and even as their minds worked to assimilate that piece of information, a horrible *creaking* noise was heard. That was followed by a loud *crack* as a second support broke under the increased strain, and a chorus of Ramanthian screams, as the entire tower began to topple. It landed with a *crash*, broke into a dozen pieces, and sent splinters of dagger-sharp wood scything through the air. One of them took the sergeant of the guard's head off and sent gouts of blood shooting upwards before his body collapsed.

With no information to go on, the guards in the surviving towers quite naturally assumed that the prisoners were involved somehow, and aimed their searchlights at the electrified fence, where they expected to witness an escape attempt. Meanwhile, Batkin took advantage of the confusion to lift off, but hadn't flown more than a hundred feet when his main repeller failed. Fortunately, the cyborg wasn't very high at the time—and the mud cushioned his fall.

But the same Sheen robot that had alerted the guards to the cyborg's presence in the first place was closing in on Batkin. It fired as it came. Thankfully, the alien machine's armor was no match for the spy's energy cannon, and the robot flew apart as a blue bolt struck its chest. That was when two quick-thinking marines emerged from the surrounding darkness. "What the hell is it?" one of them wanted to know.

"I'm a Confederacy cyborg!" Batkin announced desperately. "And I have important information for your superiors. Can you hide me?"

"Holy shit," the first marine said uncertainly. "Let's find the sarge and ask him what to do."

"We ain't got time for that," the second jarhead replied pragmatically. "The bugs are going to be all over this area ten minutes from now! Let's put him in the supply locker."

Batkin didn't know what "the supply locker" was, but soon found out, as he was transported into a prefab barracks and placed on the floor. The rest of the grunts assigned to that particular building were outside trying to figure out what was going on, so the long, narrow room was empty.

Lights swept across the outside walls, and alarms continued to bleat, as the marines pried up a section of flooring and set it off to one side. Thirty seconds later the cyborg was lowered into a rectangular hole that was already half-full of stolen tools and other supplies that the marines had been able scrounge from the camp. A wooden lid was lowered into place after that, dirt was raked over the top, and the precut section of floorboards was lowered back into place.

With no exterior light, and nothing to hear other than the occasional indecipherable *thump*, Batkin was left to wait in what might be his grave. Especially were something to happen to the marines. But rather than focus on things like that, the cyborg triggered a diagnostic program. The results served to confirm his worst fears. His propulsion system had been severely damaged—and the nearest repair facility was more than a thousand light-years away.

Meanwhile, up on the surface, and outside the barracks, the entire camp was in an uproar as Commandant Mutuu, the War Mutuu, and Overseer Tragg all marched about shouting orders. There had been an escape attempt, or that's what they assumed, so the POWs were ordered to stand in formation for a head count.

Then, when it turned out that all of the prisoners were present, or accounted for, *another* head count was called for as Tragg and the surviving robots walked the perimeter and inspected the fence. But the second head count was consistent with the first, and there were no signs of an escape attempt.

That led the Mutuus to conclude that some sort of external force had been at work—a theory corroborated by the use of an energy weapon. Hastily convened combat teams were dispatched to sweep the surrounding jungle for any sign of an incursion, and the entire camp was subjected to a thorough search, even as the commandant continued to heap abuse on the prisoners.

The entire process lasted for more than eight hours, so that when the sun finally reemerged over the eastern horizon, all of the POWs were still on their feet. Those who were ill, or too exhausted to remain vertical without assistance, were held upright lest they attract the wrong sort of attention.

Like those around her, Vanderveen was exhausted—so tired that she found herself drifting off to sleep at times. Short periods during which the diplomat was magically transported to other planets, and during one especially pleasant interlude on LaNor, found herself wrapped in Antonio Santana's arms. But that brief moment of pleasure came to an end when President Nankool elbowed her ribs. "Christina!" the chief executive hissed. "Wake up!"

The foreign service officer brought her head up, forced her eyes to open, and soon wished she hadn't as the mass punishments began. Because in Commandant Mutuu's eyes the prisoners, those who had destroyed his guard tower, and the Confederacy of Sentient Beings were all part of the same evil organism.

This philosophy was explained to the assembled multitude by no less a personage than Mutuu himself, as his sword-wielding mate made his way through the ranks of ragged prisoners, and chose those who where were about to die according to criteria known only to him.

Vanderveen felt her stomach muscles tighten as the Ramanthian made his way down her row, ignored Nankool, and paused directly in front of her. *Was this it?* the diplomat wondered. *And, all things considered, would death come as a welcome relief?*

Perhaps that was why the human drew herself up and looked the War Mutuu right in one of his space black eyes as the bug's antennae turned this way and that. But, for reasons known only to the Ramanthian, it wasn't Vanderveen's day to die. Nor any other member of the LG, although Schell came close when the naval officer tried to intercede on behalf of his sailors and marines.

Nine out of the ten individuals selected for punishment made their way to the front of the formation under their own power, accepted the shovels that were handed to them, and began to dig. Only one man, a sick sailor, tried to resist. He screamed, flailed about, and was summarily shot. Then, with the same calm demeanor demonstrated earlier, the War Mutuu selected *another* victim, who was led up front to join the rest.

What made the moment especially poignant for Nankool was the fact that not one of those selected for execution attempted to obtain leniency by revealing the president's identity. Tears streamed down the chief executive's face, and at one point he made as if to go forward and join the men and women who were digging the communal grave, only to have Vanderveen and Calisco hold him back.

It took the better part of an hour for the ten prisoners to dig a hole large enough to contain all of their bodies. Then, having been lined up with their backs to the mass grave, the POWs came to attention, and remained in that position, as the War Mutuu shuffled past and shot each one of them in the head. The bodies fell backwards, dead eyes staring up at an alien sky, as they landed side by side. Vanderveen forced herself to look, to burn the moment into her memory, so that she would never forget.

Then it was over, the markerless grave was filled in, and the work day began. A seemingly endless stretch of time in which Vanderveen and her companions stumbled from one task to the next like slow-motion zombies. Finally, after what seemed like a day spent in hell, the POWs were released. All Vanderveen wanted to do was eat, fall face-down on her grubby pallet, and drop into a dreamless sleep.

But even that small pleasure was denied her because just as the diplomat joined the chow line, she was imme-diately called away. It seemed that the LG was about to hold what the word-walker called, "A special session," which left the foreign service officer with no choice but to attend.

As Vanderveen approached barracks nine, she saw that extra guards had been posted all around the structure. They didn't *look* like guards, since the marines were seem-ingly occupied by a variety of routine chores, but all of them were ready to intervene should a Ramanthian guard or an airborne monitor enter the area. Then, while the guards did whatever was necessary to stall, the LG would have time to break off their meeting and hide anything that might be incriminating.

But there were no signs of impending interference as the diplomat traded nods with the tough-looking noncom who sat cleaning his boots on the front steps and entered the building. Blankets had been hung over the windows, and the sun had started to set, so there wasn't much light inside. What there was emanated from a single glow cone and served to frost the top of the large sphere that rested on the table at the center of the room. The construct was about four feet in diameter and nearly identical to the re-con ball that Vanderveen had encountered during the final hours of the battle on LaNor.

All of which caused the diplomat's heart to leap since what she took to be a cyborg could be the first harbinger of help. Had one of the Confederacy's battle groups dropped into orbit around Jericho? *Yes!* Vanderveen thought excit-edly, and hurried to join the group gathered around the beat-up-looking sphere. Batkin was nearing the end of his narrative. ". . . At that point another prisoner entered, sat down, and began to talk. And it soon became obvious that he was ready to cut a deal with Tragg."

It wasn't what Vanderveen had been hoping for, and she was about to ask a question when Hooks beat her to it. "This is ridiculous," the official said contemptuously. "Why should we believe this nonsense? Assuming this individual is who he claims to be, then he's massively incompetent! Ten, no *eleven* people are dead, due to his negligence."

"Maybe," Nankool allowed cautiously, "and maybe not. Remember, Madame X works for *me*, and I know what she expects of her operatives. And she wouldn't be very happy if one of them were to spend all his time waiting for information to come his way. She would argue that it was Batkin's *duty* to enter the camp. Regardless of what might follow. Let's hear the rest of what he has to say before arriving at any conclusions."

Hooks didn't like the answer, but there wasn't much the secretary could do except fume, as Batkin prepared to resume his narrative. A rather tricky moment, because the spy not only knew who Hooks was, but *why* the official wanted to preempt the report. "Why listen to my second-hand account," Batkin inquired rhetorically, "when you can watch the *real* thing?"

That was when a holo blossomed over the cyborg and the entire LG was treated to a shot of a man's back with Tragg beyond. Hooks felt a moment of relief, but that emotion was short-lived as his voice was heard, and the rest of the group turned to stare at him. "I think the son-ofabitch is going to run," Batkin remarked mildly. However, Hooks was already in motion by then—and Vanderveen was the only person between the senior diplomat and the door.

But if Hooks thought he could run the blond over and make a dash for Tragg's prefab, he was sadly mistaken. Because rather than wait for the two-hundred-pound man to overpower her—the diplomat threw her body into the air and hit the official with what could only be described as a flying tackle. Vanderveen had the breath knocked out of her as both of them crashed to the floor.

Hooks struggled to extricate himself, and was just about to do so, when Schell and Nankool got ahold of him. The traitorous official attempted to call for help at that point, but took a blow to the jaw and was soon subdued. Ironically, it was Calisco, the very man Vanderveen had been so suspicious of, who helped her up off the floor.

Batkin would have smiled had he been able to do so. "Where was I? Ah yes, the holo!" The recording reappeared at that point, giving everyone present the opportunity to hear Hooks cut his deal and see the turncoat's face as he stood. Nankool was shocked. "Damn it, Roland . . . *Why?*"

"Because you're going to die anyway," Hooks said dispiritedly. "Can't you see that? Especially after today?"

"What I see is a traitor," Nankool answered coldly. "Yes, every single one of us may die here. . . . But who knows? Maybe one of Batkin's message torps got through. Perhaps help *will* come. But regardless of that, we have a war to fight—and we're going to fight it."

Schell frowned. "Sorry, sir. But I'm not sure I follow. We're prisoners, so how can we fight?"

"The space elevator," Nankool replied grimly. "The bugs need it— and we're going to destroy it. But not until they have invested lots of time, work, and money in it."

There was a moment of silence after that, followed by grim laughter, as half a dozen POWs nodded in unison. Unlikely though it might seem, the prisoners had declared war on their captors, and the first battle had been won.

It was about four hours later, when even Tragg was asleep, that something landed on the fence and the camp's alarms went off. More than a dozen Ramanthian guards were already busy trying to remove the badly charred body when the overseer arrived on the scene. Given the fact that the guards were under strict orders to keep the fence electrified at all times, it was necessary to pry the corpse loose with long wooden poles.

Only when that process was complete, and the corpse fell free, was it possible to make a positive identification. Tragg felt something cold trickle into his veins as he looked down into the traitor's staring eyes. *Why?* the overseer wanted to know. *Why would a man who was about to go free take a run at an electrified fence?*

But Hooks was dead, none of the guards could speak standard, and the people who knew the answer were elsewhere. Mutuu made a brief appearance, but being ignorant of the agreement between Hooks and Tragg, took the episode at face value and soon went back to bed. Finally, as the jungle creatures screamed and hooted, the long, bloody day came to an end.

9

A brave Captain is a root, out of which, as branches, the
courage of his soldiers doth spring.

—*Sir Philip Sidney*
Standard year 1580

PLANET ALGERON, THE CONFEDERACY OF SENTIENT BEINGS

Captain Antonio Santana lay belly-down on a layer of
ice-encrusted scree and stared through a pair of Legion-
issue binos. Each time the crosshairs passed over an object, its range and heat index appeared next to the image.
Santana knew that the long U-shaped valley below him
had been gouged out of Algeron's surface by a retreating
glacier roughly ten thousand standard years earlier.
Then, perhaps nine thousand years subsequent to that, a
tribe of nomads wandered into the basin and decided to
stay. And, thanks to the hand-dug well from which the
community took its name, the settlers eventually devel-
oped a dooth-powered, pump-driven water distribution
system.

It took hundreds of years of backbreaking work to clear
the fields of rock, build the stone walls that split the valley
into a patchwork quilt of family farms, and construct the
low one- and two-story homes that were so markedly different from the subsurface dwellings typical of most Naa
villages.

All of which explained why Deepwell had prospered, not only as a center of agriculture but as a bustling market town. Until two standard weeks earlier when a large contingent of bandits under the leadership of a Naa named Nofear Throatcut seized control of the town. Deepwell's warriors had given a good account of themselves according to Nostop Footfast—the Naa youth who lay to Santana's right. But given the element of surprise, and a force of 150 heavily armed fighters, the bandits won the battle with ease. And that was when the hellish rampage of murder, rape, and theft began.

It took Footfast the better part of seven standard days to reach the nearest village, where the elders passed word of the outrage along to Senator Nodoubt Truespeak, who brought the matter to General Booly. And it was then that Santana caught wind of the situation and requested permission to lead Team Zebra against the bandits. Not out of a sense of altruism but a very real need to test his newly formed company against an enemy that could shoot back. And who better to test a group of convicted criminals against than another group of criminals?

And the timing was perfect, because after weeks of waiting, a rescue mission had finally been authorized. And not a moment too soon. . . . Because having learned that Nankool was alive, the cabal had been about to load Team Zebra onto one of Chien-Chu's freighters and send them to Jericho *without* permission when the order came down. Some of the conspirators felt that the rescue force should depart immediately in spite of Santana's request for a combat mission, but General Booly counseled patience. He pointed out that if some part of Team Zebra was going to break, it would be far better to identify the flaw on Algeron than somewhere on the surface of Jericho.

Which was why Santana found himself about to lead his ragtag company against a gang of criminals. Clever criminals in this case, who, rather than pillage Deepwell and leave, had taken up temporary residence there. A low key presence intended to lure unsuspecting caravans into the village, where they could be slaughtered.

"What do you see?" Footfast wanted to know, as he thought about his family. His father had been killed during the initial attack. He knew that because he'd seen the body. But what about his mother? And his sister? The bandits did horrible things to females—and there was a profound emptiness at the pit of the youngster's stomach as he looked out over the valley.

"The village *looks* normal," Santana answered honestly, as he panned the binos from left to right. "Except for the fact that the streets are virtually empty, new stone walls have been constructed, and the holding pens are jam-packed with dooths."

"We must attack," Footfast said firmly. "Give me a weapon. . . . I will go first."

Santana lowered the binos as another two-hour-and-forty-two-minute day started to fade. "You are very brave," the legionnaire said soberly. "But it will take more than bravery to win. We must be smart as well."

The Naa had silvery fur with horizontal streaks of black on his cheeks. His pupils were yellow. "You have a plan?"

"Yes," Santana answered. "I have a plan."

The council room where the village chieftain and the elders met to resolve disputes, plan for the future, and bemoan the taxes that the new government had started to impose had been transformed into a chamber of horrors. The air stank of alcohol, vomit, and urine. Large sections of the wooden floor were sticky with congealed blood, and nit bugs were feeding on it.

The bandit leader was seated at the west end of the room, in the large almost thronelike wooden chair normally reserved for the village chief. A rather unfortunate old geezer, who along with the rest of his council, was suspended along the hall's northern wall. It was an excellent vantage point from which to watch the eight females who hung spread-eagled along the south wall, where they had been systematically gang-raped. Two of them were unconscious, and most had had been cut, burned, or beaten. Eventually, when his warriors began to complain, Throatcut would order up a new batch of playthings. But the dozen or so warriors who were currently pleasuring themselves with the females seemed happy enough, so there was no need to summon additional villagers as yet.

The thronelike chair, as well as its position on a raised platform, provided Throatcut with an unobstructed view of the head-high pile of loot stacked in front of him. Some of it wasn't all that valuable. The brass incense burners and copper cookware were good examples. *But there was plenty of silver, too,* the Naa thought to himself, as he took another swig of beer. Not to mention some gold, and lots of Legion-issued coinage, which could be exchanged for the new money that the government had promised to release. Much of the loot had been taken from unsuspecting caravans that continued to enter Throatcut's trap.

But nothing lasts forever. The bandit leader knew that and was already working on a new plan. His original gang of desperados had been so successful that entire bands of brigands had requested permission to join up, thereby swelling his overall force to about a 170 warriors. Approximately twenty of whom had been killed during the assault on Deepwell. That left Throatcut with a force of about 150, which seemed like a good thing at first, but was actually something of a two-edged sword. Because while the bigger force enabled Throatcut to tackle large settlements like Deepwell, it also meant a lot of mouths to feed, and it was bound to attract unwanted attention.

So, rather than keep the entire force together, the bandit was contemplating the possibility of splitting it into three fifty-warrior units when a breathless Salwa Obobwa passed through the door at the far end of the long rectangular room and hurried forward. "Hey, boss," the human said, as he stopped just short of the platform. "Doothman says a caravan is coming in from the north. We're talking six heavily loaded wagons, maybe fifty dooths, and a Legion-surplus RAV (Robotic All-terrain Vehicle).

Throatcut frowned. "What about guards?"

Obobwa shrugged. "The usual. About twelve warriors, all armed with rifles, plus half a dozen females."

The fact that the wagons were heavily loaded struck Throatcut as promising, but not as interesting as the wagons themselves, which were still something of a rarity on Algeron. Because it was only recently, during the last five years or so, that the main caravan routes been improved to the point where dooth-drawn conveyances were practical. And Throatcut could make use of the wagons to transport his loot to a safer location. As for the RAV, well, that would constitute something of a bonus, since the four-legged robot could handle rough terrain and transport up to four thousand pounds' worth of freight while doing so. *His* freight, since the notion of separating his share of the loot from all the rest appealed to Throatcut, who had very little reason to trust his subordinates.

"Okay," the bandit leader responded. "Assign someone to sort this pile of loot. The cheap stuff stays here. Everything else will go onto the wagons once we capture them. Confiscate all the booze. I want our people sober when the fighting starts. Check every warrior and every weapon. Fill their bellies with a hot meal and position them the same way you did last time. And tell Deaver to load Lindo's missiles. You never know when one of the Legion's fly-forms might happen by."

That was a lot to accomplish in a relatively short period of time, but Obobwa knew better than to complain. "Okay, boss," the human replied obediently. "I'm on it."

* * *

In spite of the fact that he was a cavalry officer, Santana had never ridden a dooth before and was extremely conscious of the fact that the big woolly beast was in charge as it carried him south. Fortunately, the animal was relatively docile and capable of navigating the road on its own. That left the heavily swathed human to rock back and forth in concert with the dooth's movements while he eyed the countryside ahead, terrain he had already seen and memorized thanks to the satellite imagery provided by Madame X. The first obstacles to overcome were a pair of stone fortresses located to either side of the road just north of the village. The "twins," as they were known, were three stories high, and served to anchor the thick stone walls that extended both east and west. The fortifications had originally been constructed to protect Deepwell's residents from neighbors to the north. But those days were largely over, which meant that the big iron-strapped gates remained open most of the time, allowing caravans to pass through. *Real* caravans, unlike the procession of six wagons and a single RAV that were strung out behind Santana.

There were no signs of activity on or around the blocky fortifications as the legionnaires drew closer. But the officer could *feel* the weight of bandit eyes as they scrutinized every detail of the approaching caravan. And even though Santana and his bio bods were bundled up Naa style, their faces being concealed by the long scarves that the locals typically wore, the legionnaire continued to worry that some detail of equipage would give his troops away. An assault weapon that was too new, the way the wagons were sprung, or any of a thousand other details.

Because even though Santana was confident that he and his troops could fight their way into Deepwell, he wanted to avoid that if at all possible. First, because the element of surprise was more likely to deliver a quick and decisive victory. Secondly, because the people of Deepwell had already suffered greatly, and the legionnaire hoped to retake their village without leveling the community in the process. And third, because the officer wanted Team Zebra to understand the importance of finesse. A quality that would be critical on Jericho.

And so it was that dooths snorted, wagons creaked, and RAV servos whined as the caravan passed between the twin towers and followed the gently curving road down the center of the valley toward the apparently peaceful village beyond. Except that it *wasn't* peaceful—as the scrambled transmission made clear. "X-Ray Two to Alpha Six," a female voice said casually. "I have you on IW-6 almost directly overhead. Hostiles five-five, repeat five-five, are assembled on the right side of the main road as it passes through the village. An unknown number of hostiles are hidden inside structures as well. The rest of bandit force Delta is located at the south end of the village facing north. Over."

Santana clicked his transmit button twice by way of an acknowledgment. By lining up along one side of the road, the bandits hoped to kill the incoming bio bods without firing on their own people. And, if he and his companions were lucky enough to survive *that* assault, another trap was waiting at the south end of the valley. *Throatcut is careful,* Santana thought to himself. *You have to give the bastard that.*

But Santana had no intention of leading the first platoon into a free-fire zone. So as his dooth drew level with the first east–west side street, the legionnaire issued orders. "Alpha Six to Alpha Two-Six, and Alpha Three-Six. Plan A. Streets left and right. Execute. Over."

There was a series of *clicks* as Sergeants Maria Gomez and Husulu Ibo-Da acknowledged the order. The first wagon followed Santana as he turned left. The second went right, and so forth, until the entire caravan had disappeared off Deepwell's main street. That was when *more* orders were issued, and the heavy tarpaulins were thrown aside as the T-2s rolled off the transports and activated their weapons.

There were seven cyborgs in all, three to a squad, plus Santana's mount. Her name was Norly Snyder. She had been a corporal back when the two first met on LaNor. Running into her at Fort Camerone had been the result of good luck. But removing the borg from the outfit to which she'd been assigned had taken pull. The kind of high-gee pull that only someone like General Bill Booly could exert.

So as Santana slid down off the big dooth and handed the reins to Footfast, the big Trooper II was ready and waiting. The officer was in a hurry as he took his place behind the cyborg's big blocky head and plugged into the T-2's com system. "Alpha Six to Alpha Two-Six and Alpha Three-Six," the officer said. "Let's stick to the plan. Over."

"Roger that," Gomez responded. "Two-Six out."

"I copy," Ibo-Da added. "Three-Six out."

And with that simple acknowledgment a unit that consisted of a crooked gambler, a convicted murderer, a sexual psychopath, a raving man-hater, a suicidal cyborg, and a woman who had tortured two Ramanthian prisoners to death swung into action. Meanwhile, a group of Naa volunteers gathered the first squad's dooths together and prepared to defend themselves if attacked.

Throatcut knew something was wrong by that time and had already begun to respond. "It's a trick!" the one-armed Naa shouted over his handheld com set. "Close with them! Kill them now!"

But the invading T-2s were already in motion by then. Santana led the first squad east, and Snyder had already turned the corner of the last building, when a group of bio bods boiled out of a side street. Rather than pause, as the hostiles might have expected her to, Snyder ran straight at them. The distance closed with surprising speed as the cyborg brought an arm up and began to fire her .50-caliber machine gun. The entire front rank went down like wheat to a thresher. That caused the second rank to break and scatter.

"Pull up," Santana ordered, as Snyder placed her right foot pod on a wounded Naa and crushed the life out of him. "Give the rest of the squad a chance to catch up with us." Then on the radio: "Three-Six? This is Alpha Six. . . . Give me a sitrep."

"We're in position," Ibo-Da replied laconically. "Over."

"Okay. . . . Let's squeeze them. Six out."

By prior agreement, the first squad turned toward the west, the second squad pivoted east, and they began to close on each other. The whole idea was to squeeze the bandits into an increasingly compact mass. Fifty-caliber machine guns thumped in the distance, assault weapons chattered, and Santana heard a metallic *ping* as an enemy slug flattened itself against Snyder's chest armor. "They're up on the roofs!" the cyborg warned. "Hold on!"

Santana felt Snyder start to sprint, and because the cavalry officer knew what to expect, he bent his knees to absorb some of the shock as the T-2 jumped fifteen feet into the air and landed on a flat roof. The sniper had begun to backpedal by then, but barely managed to fire a single shot before a bolt of blue energy burned a fist-sized hole through his chest.

That was the good news. The bad news was that a human holding a shoulder-launched missile (SLM) had just popped up out of a stairway and was preparing to fire his weapon. Snyder had started to turn, but knew she would never make it in time, which left Santana to deal with the threat. He stuck a hand into the bag that hung at his side, felt for a grenade, and pulled it free. What felt like an hour passed as the officer pulled the pin, threw the bomb, and ducked.

There was a loud *bang*, followed by an even louder secondary explosion, as the missile blew. Flying shrapnel made a rattling sound as it struck the T-2's armored body. "Good one, sir," Snyder commented mildly. "But you might want to warn me next time. . . . That stuff stings!"

"Sorry, Sergeant," Santana replied. "I'll try to do better. . . . How 'bout the next roof? Can you make it?"

"Let's find out," Snyder replied, as she took six giant strides and launched herself into the air. But rather than land on the roof as she had the time before, the big cyborg crashed *through* it, and into the room below.

Six bandits, all of whom were busy firing at Alpha Two-One through the store's slit-style windows, were caught by surprise as the T-2 and its rider fell through the roof and landed immediately behind them. Dust billowed, and loose debris continued to fall, as one of the bandits said, "Oh, shit," and tried to bring his weapon to bear.

What followed was a murderous frenzy of close-quarters mayhem as both Snyder and Santana opened fire, and the bandits fought back. But the bio bods couldn't see through the swirling dust, and the cyborg could, since the enemy heat signatures were plain as day. The entire exchange of gunfire was over within five seconds.

But short though the unexpected engagement was, Santana had been fighting rather than leading. It was a loss of situational awareness that could cost the company dearly. Especially when battling a numerically superior force armed with SLMs. "Get me out of here," Santana ordered, as he fired at a figure in the surrounding gloom.

"Your wish is my command," the cyborg replied cheerfully, as she kicked a hole in the stone wall. "Watch your head!"

Santana ducked as the T-2 stepped through the newly made door and out into the rubble-strewn street. Two bandits lay dead where they had fallen, their bodies surrounded by a halo of spent brass.

Without benefit of the usual helmet, and heads-up display (HUD), the company commander couldn't access an electronic display showing the way in which his troops were deployed. That meant Santana had to rely on what he could actually see, hear, and to some extent *feel* as the battle progressed. And not all of the news was good. Three explosions shook the ground as a voice spoke in Santana's ear. "Alpha Three-Six to Alpha Six. Over."

"This is Six," Santana replied. "Go."

"I have a problem," the Hudathan replied. "Alpha Three-Five committed suicide. Over."

Despite the fact that Husulu Ibo-Da had been court-martialed for killing a cowardly officer, Santana had put the big noncom in charge of the first platoon's second squad, knowing that if anyone could keep the convicts in line, Ibo-Da could. And now, assuming that the Hudathan was telling the truth, *his* T-2, a head case named Lazlo Kappa, was dead. Why was anybody's guess. Although it was common knowledge that the cyborg had been convicted of negligence where a friendly-fire incident was concerned. "What the hell happened? Over."

"I was forced to dismount in order to retrieve an enemy com set, and the minute my back was turned, Five took off down the main street. He was yelling, 'Shoot me!' and they did. Three times. The last SLM took his head off. Over."

Santana remembered the explosions he'd heard earlier and swore. Because as a result of Kappa's death he was one T-2 short, one of his squad leaders was on foot, and valuable time had been lost. "Okay, keep up as best you can. . . . First platoon, form on me, we're going to take this party downtown. Over."

Snyder turned left onto the main street, and units from both squads followed. The wreckage of Kappa's war form was scattered far and wide. "This is X-ray Two," the female voice said. "There are approximately three-zero, repeat three-zero, XL heat sigs moving north toward your position. Over."

Santana said, "Roger that," and was just about to issue orders when the ground began to shake, and a swirling mass of fear-crazed dooths appeared to the south. The stampeding animals filled the street from side to side as they sought to escape the spear-brandishing bandits who pursued them from behind. It was a clever strategy on Throatcut's part and a very real threat. Because if the dooths could knock the T-2s down, the bandits could attack the cyborgs with SLMs, grenades, and rifle fire. But there wasn't enough time to retreat. That left the cavalry officer with a single choice.

"Stand fast!" Santana ordered, as rifle shots were heard, and a wall of flesh and bone thundered toward them. "First rank, kneel! Prepare to fire! Fire! Second rank, prepare to fire. . . . Fire!"

Even though there hadn't been much time in which to prepare, the net effect was to focus the combined firepower of six Trooper IIs and seven bio bods on the charging animals. The results were horrendous. The front rank of dooths seemed to falter as the full weight of the fire swept across them. Their heads went down, and some of the big beasts completed full somersaults, as a blood mist rose to envelope the oncoming herd.

The second and third ranks continued to bawl loudly as the bandits prodded them from behind and drove the animals forward. It was difficult for the dooths to climb up and over the bodies heaped in front of them, and many beasts died trying, but some were successful. And, because the desperate animals could absorb up to twenty .50-caliber slugs before finally going down, each successive wave managed to advance.

Having dismounted, Santana felt his stomach fill with lead as he emptied clip after clip into the oncoming horde. Could the platoon stop the stampede? Or would the dooths roll right over them? The outcome was still very much in doubt. Meanwhile, the din around the officer continued to grow as the T-2s fired both their heavy machine guns and their energy cannons. Gunsmoke swirled, and the acrid stench of ozone filled the officer's nostrils as Maria Gomez appeared at Santana's side. The squad leader was armed with a grenade launcher, and each time one of her rounds landed among the dooths, the resulting explosion sent a gout of gore up into the air. A bloody mist blew back over the animals and dyed them red. Finally, just as Santana was beginning to wonder if the stampede would ever end, the remaining dooths began to falter. "Second rank, cease fire!" the cavalry officer ordered, as he took his place on Snyder's broad back. "First rank, *charge!*"

By happenstance, the first rank consisted of Gomez on Vantha, Sato on Prill, and Darby on Nacky. All of them fired their weapons as they made their way forward. "Ignore the dooths!" Santana shouted. "Kill the bandits!"

The order made sense since the bandits were driving the squealing beasts forward, but a price had to be paid. Nacky fired, attempted to sidestep an enraged bull, and felt the dooth slam into his side. The T-2 lost his balance and fell. Darby barely managed to jump clear and take refuge in a doorway. Nacky wasn't so lucky and took a terrible pounding as the last of the panicky animals trampled him.

But Santana and the rest of his platoon continued to advance, firing on targets of opportunity as they entered the small town square. Dead villagers dangled from the wooden lampposts that circled the plaza. Each corpse wore a mantle of crusty snow and the ropes creaked as the bodies swayed. "This is Alpha Six," Santana said, as Snyder paused to scan the area with her sensors. "That's the council building over on the right. . . . Alpha Two-Six will secure the area while Six-One and I take a peek inside. Over."

Gomez nodded. "Roger, that. Okay, people, spread out. And put those sensors on max. The party isn't over yet."

The council building's front door was open, which was

an ominous sign insofar as Santana was concerned because it suggested that at least some of the bandits had escaped. Possibly including Throatcut and his renegade Trooper II. "Let's keep a sharp eye out for booby traps," Santana suggested, as Snyder approached the door.

The cyborg paused to look for trip wires, pressure plates, or any other signs that an explosive device might be present. Then, having assured herself that the way was clear, the T-2 advanced.

Santana ducked his head as Snyder entered the high-ceilinged room, wrinkled his nose in disgust, and was struck by the horror of what surrounded him. Disemboweled bodies hung along both walls. Intestines dangled like ropes of obscene sausages each ending in a pool of blood. Cookware and other odds and ends rattled as Snyder kicked them out of the way on her way to the platform and the chair it supported.

Santana didn't know the village chief, but would have been willing to bet that the severed head that had been left on the thronelike piece of furniture was not only his, but a message of defiance from Nofear Throatcut. But where had the bandit gone? The officer could guess. "Alpha-Six to X-ray Two. . . . Please confirm movement of hostiles toward the south end of the valley. Over."

"Confirmed," came the almost immediate response. "Over."

"Copy that Bravo Six?" Santana inquired, knowing that Farnsworth and the second platoon were deployed south of the village.

"I not only copy, I can *see* the bastards coming," Farnsworth replied gruffly. "And one of them is riding a T-2. Over."

"That's *him*," Santana emphasized. "Don't let the bastard escape! And watch for friendlies. . . . We'll tackle the bastards from behind. Six out. Over."

"This is X-ray Two," the unseen woman said. "I have

two fly-forms chasing their tails at angels twenty. Would you like some help? Over."

"Thank you, but no," Santana replied grimly. "There won't be any air cover where we're going. Six out."

Dooths couldn't run, not in the true sense of the word, but they could achieve a clumsy canter. And the sight of two columns of heavily loaded animals, some carrying as many as three bandits each, was truly impressive. There was a thundering sound as clods of half-frozen muck were thrown high into the air, and scattered rifle shots were heard as some of the less-thoughtful fugitives celebrated what they assumed to be their imminent escape.

Behind the dooths, and running with a lot more grace, came a single T-2. Throatcut was determined to escape by following the main road south into the badlands, where he and what remained of his gang could hide in a maze of ravines and canyons while they regrouped. But as Lindo topped a rise, and Throatcut looked out over the T-2's left missile launcher, the Naa could see that the off-worlders had anticipated his move. Because there, half-hidden behind the crude stone wall the villagers had been forced to build across the road, stood *seven* T-2s. All ready to fire the moment the oncoming horde came within range.

Throatcut considered calling his warriors back, especially since they were carrying most of the loot, but concluded it was best to let them go. "Turn back," Throatcut ordered via the T-2's intercom. "The force behind has been weakened. Make both of your missiles count. Maybe we can break through."

Lindo had identified the Legion cyborgs before the bio bod had and knew he wouldn't stand a chance against them. Not even with twenty-five dooths and as many as sixty bio bods running interference for him. So the T-2 skidded to a halt, turned back toward the north, and began to run.

* * *

Neither Santana nor what remained of the first platoon was expecting a counterattack as the renegade Trooper II topped a rise and paused long enough to fire a pair of heat-seeking SLMs. The range was short, *very* short, which meant that outside of the electronic countermeasures triggered by the incoming weapons, there wasn't much that the Legion cyborgs could do except fire their energy weapons in a last-ditch attempt to intercept the missiles.

There was a loud explosion as one of the weapons detonated ten feet in front of Ichiyama, blew the cyborg's left leg off, and sent him spinning to the ground. A Naa deserter named Noaim Shootstraight had little choice but to ride the T-2 down and was fortunate to escape the fall without serious injury.

Meanwhile the second missile hit a second cyborg dead center, blew the T-2 in half, and killed his bio bod. Santana swore and shouted into the intercom. "Close with him, Sergeant! I want that one-armed bastard!"

With both cyborgs running at something like half speed they came together quickly. *Too* quickly to fire their weapons for more than a couple of seconds. There was a *crash* as their torsos collided, followed by the urgent whine of overworked servos, as both cyborgs battled to position their podlike feet.

Then, as the T-2s continued to grapple with each other, Santana and Throatcut were left to fight it out from atop their respective mounts. Both had pulled pistols by that time and fired at each other from point-blank range. But the movement of the battling cyborgs made it difficult to aim. And, although Gomez and the rest of the platoon had arrived on the scene by then, they couldn't fire without running the risk of hitting Santana or his cyborg. But the stalemate couldn't last forever, and didn't, as the legionnaire shouted into his headset. "Snyder! When I say 'break,' back away as fast you can. Understood?"

"I copy," the cyborg replied, and repositioned her feet.

Throatcut saw the legionnaire duck out from under a strap and wondered what the alien was up to as he dropped the newly freed loop over Lindo's head. Then the bandit leader spotted the bulging satchel and saw the human grin as he dropped a grenade into it. Throatcut shouted, *"No!"* But it was too late by then, as *all* of the grenades in the bag went off, and blew both the Naa and the cyborg to bits.

Even though she was backpedaling by then, Snyder was still blown off her feet. Fortunately, Santana was able to leap free as the T-2 went down. The impact knocked the air out of his lungs, but Sergeant Ibo-Da was there to help the human to his feet. The officer noticed that the Huduthan wasn't out of breath in spite of the fact that he'd been forced to run all the way from the village. "Congratulations, sir," the big noncom rumbled happily. "We slaughtered the bastards!"

"But we lost most of the first platoon," Santana countered, as he turned to look around.

"Not true, sir," Gomez put in from her position high atop Vautha. "We lost Kappa, Himby, and Imbo. But Nacky's going to be fine—and so is Ichiyama. Assuming you can requisition some new war forms, that is."

"And the second platoon is intact," Farnsworth added, as he and his cyborg arrived on the scene.

The engagement didn't *feel* successful, not from Santana's vantage point, but as the officer stood on the blast-blackened rise and looked around him, he decided that there were some things to feel pleased about. With the exception of Kappa, none of the criminals had mutinied, deserted, or turned on each other. And there was something new in the air. Something about the way both the bio bods and the cyborgs held themselves. Something called pride.

10

PLANET JERICHO, THE RAMANTHIAN EMPIRE

There were thousands of pieces of debris in orbit around Jericho, plus a number of spaceships, the most impressive of which was the Ramanthian dreadnaught *Imperator.* The warship was 262 standard years old, more than six standard miles long, and completely outmoded. All of which made her perfect for use as an orbital counterweight, which, once the space elevator was completed, would function to keep the long, thin cable aloft.

But that was in the future. When construction was complete. In the meantime the *Imperator* was slated to function as both the platform on which the crystalline graphite cable would be manufactured—and the habitat in which the slaves would live during the first phase of construction. That was why a team comprised of Vanderveen and five other prisoners were deep inside the once-proud dreadnaught making use of vacuum hoses to remove tons of graphite from a hold. And, because large sections of the ship's interior weren't pressurized, the POWs had to wear space armor as they worked.

The *Imperator*'s argrav generators were up and running, however, which made the process easier and contributed to productivity—the very thing Tragg and his Ramanthian employers were primarily interested in. Unfortunately, the graphite was so light that the artificial gravity wasn't sufficient to hold it down. The powdery material rose to swirl around Vanderveen and the others like a black blizzard.

The space suits were equipped with beacons, so the diplomat caught occasional glimpses of her coworkers through the gloom, but such sightings were rare. Most of the two-hour shift was spent in virtual darkness, feeding graphite to hungry machines that would mix the mineral with other substances to create long, thin fibers that were twenty times stronger than steel and four times less dense. Once a sufficient number of fiber strands had been produced, they would be braided into a cable long enough to reach the planet's surface and strong enough to carry heavy loads. Then the work would become even *more* dangerous as the POWs were sent out to connect the sections of cable.

In the meantime, all Vanderveen wanted to do was to make it through her shift and arrive at the blissful moment when the vacuum hoses were shut off and the graphite mist began to clear. That was when the replacement crew would arrive to begin their shift. Finally, after what seemed like an eternity, that moment came.

From the hold it was a long two-mile slog through dark, gloomy passageways to a lock that was soon pressurized, and powerful jets of water blasted the space suits clean. Once that process was complete, the prisoners were permitted to enter a large compartment where specially trained navy techs waited to help the POWs exit their armor. A moment Vanderveen looked forward to and dreaded. Because while it meant she could rest for a few hours, there were dues to be paid, which made the process unpleasant.

Normally, on a navy ship, for example, the diplomat would have been issued a pair of specially designed long johns to wear under her suit. But because the Ramanthians weren't willing to supply such niceties, she could wear overalls or nothing at all. The latter was the option most people chose because it was so hot within the suits. That meant exposing herself to both fellow team members and technicians, most of whom were male.

And, unbeknownst to the diplomat, there was someone else who liked to look at her naked body as well. Because Tragg made it a point to be in his private compartment whenever the POW came off duty so he could watch her strip via one of the security monitors located high on the bulkhead across from his desk. So as Vanderveen began to exit her suit the overseer sat at his desk and waited to be entertained. He particularly enjoyed the way the woman's breasts jiggled and the stark whiteness of her long-unshaven legs. The sight never failed to make him hard, and there was something about the prisoner that fascinated him, just as Marci had back before it became necessary to sacrifice her. But to think he could have another such relationship was foolish. Or was it?

Tragg's finger pressed the intercom button, and the words were barely out of his mouth, when he began to regret them. But it was too late by then—as his voice was heard in the compartment beyond. Having ordered the prisoners to surrender everything including their identification back on the *Gladiator*, the Ramanthians had subsequently been forced to assign numbers to each POW. So as the PA system clicked on, and Tragg ordered number 748 to report to his office, Vanderveen knew that the overseer meant her.

The diplomat was just about to enter the showers by then, and the people in the locker room glanced at the overhead speaker before turning to look at her. There was pity in their eyes, and Vanderveen felt something heavy land in the bottom of her stomach. Being ordered into Tragg's lair was bad enough, but being forced to enter nude made the situation ten times worse. Which was why the diplomat felt a sense of gratitude as one of the men tossed a pair of overalls her way.

Vanderveen nearly tripped on one of the long pant legs as she hurried to step into the foul-smelling garment. Then, once it was pulled up around her, the diplomat hurried over to the hatch, where a Sheen robot stood guard. The door slid to one side, and a gust of cool air touched the FSO's face as she stepped into a dark cavelike compartment.

The *Imperator* had been gutted and stripped of all nonessential items, so there was no furniture aboard. Not that Tragg would have been comfortable straddling a Ramanthian-style saddle chair anyway. Which was why he was seated on an empty cable spool in front of a makeshift desk. But if Tragg's quarters were something less than impressive, the man himself more than made up for it. A single glow cone lit the top of his hairless skull, the bridge of his nose, and the top of his cheekbones. The rest of his features fell into darkness. It took all of Vanderveen's strength to hold her head up and look directly into the Overseer's dark goggles. There was silence as the renegade allowed the tension to build. Finally, after what seemed like an eternity, Tragg spoke. "You interest me. . . . More than that, you remind me of someone. What's your name?"

"Trevane," Vanderveen lied. "Lieutenant Mary Trevane."

Tragg cocked his head and light played across the surface of his goggles. "And your specialty?"

"I'm a supply officer."

"You're very pretty."

Vanderveen remembered the tarmac, the sound of the

pistol shot, and Lieutenant Moya's crumpled body. "Pretty, but not pretty enough to kill?"

Even though she couldn't see his eyes Vanderveen could tell that Tragg was surprised. "You knew?"

"Yes," the diplomat replied stoically. "I knew."

Tragg removed the pistol from his lap and held it up along his cheek. The metal felt cool and reassuring. "So, if you know, then tell me *why*."

Vanderveen felt her heart start to pound. Some sort of weird psychological game was under way—but how to play it? An honest answer could earn her a bullet. . . . But then so could a lie. Eventually, the diplomat swallowed the lump in the back of her throat and took a chance. "You shot her to punish all of the women who wince when they look at your face."

Given the gun, and the nature of the situation, the last thing Tragg expected was honesty. The words went into him like an ice-cold dagger. His reply was little more than a growl. "I should kill you for that."

"Go ahead," Vanderveen replied insolently. "Why wait? You were planning to kill me anyway. But after you pull the trigger, the pain will remain the same."

Tragg knew it was true—and he knew something else as well. . . . If he killed Trevane, as logic dictated he should, the only person who understood him would be dead. Yet he couldn't let her go, not without imposing some sort of consequence, or the woman would have won. "Remove your clothing."

Tragg was going to rape her. Vanderveen felt sick to her stomach. Should she try to provoke him? In the hope that he would shoot her? Or submit and try to survive? A montage of images flashed through the diplomat's mind. Earth on a sunny day. Santana laughing at one of her jokes. Her mother waving good-bye. Reluctantly, Vanderveen brought her right hand up, and was just about to pull the zipper down, when Tragg intervened. "Remember this moment,

Lieutenant. . . . Remember what you were willing to do in order to live. And remember that if I want you—I can have you. . . . Now get out."

PLANET ALGERON, THE CONFEDERACY OF SENTIENT BEINGS

Having freed the village of Deepwell from Throatcut's bandits, and with all the necessary permissions in place, Santana was eager to load Team Zebra onto a shuttle and get under way. But any hopes of a speedy departure soon began to fade as a host of last-minute activities conspired to suck time out of the schedule. Before the team could depart the officer had to bring new members up from the pit, take delivery on new war forms, and account for T-2s lost in battle. A time-consuming affair that required the legionnaire to fill out forms and argue with obstinate supply officers.

But by working both himself and his direct reports day and night, Santana was able to cut what might have been a week's work down to a mere three days. As the parka clad officer watched the final load of supplies trundle up a metal ramp into the shuttle's brightly lit hold, a personnel hatch swung open, and General Bill Booly stepped out onto the icy steel. Santana tossed the senior officer a salute, and Booly returned the gesture. His breath fogged the air when he spoke. "You and your team did a good job in Deepwell. Congratulations."

Though seemingly genuine, the smile on Booly's lips didn't match the look in his eyes, a fact that made Santana uneasy. "Thank you, sir. . . . But Jericho will be more difficult."

"Yes," Booly agreed soberly. "It will. . . . Listen, Captain, I'm sorry to spring this on you at the last minute, but I was forced to accept a compromise in order to keep the mission on schedule."

Santana swallowed. "A compromise, sir? What sort of compromise?"

"A staffing compromise," Booly answered darkly. "Apparently Jakov, or one of this toadies, decided that it would be nice if the officer in command of the mission has political ties to the vice president. Something you lack."

Santana began to speak, but Booly held up a hand. "Believe me, I'm sorry, and if it were possible to intervene, I would. The people who backed this mission from the beginning might be able to force the issue, but that would take time, and time is something we don't have. The decision to attack Deepwell made sense and will no doubt pay off in the end, but further delay is out of the question."

Santana remembered the photos of Vanderveen being marched through the jungle and nodded. "Sir, yes, sir."

"Besides," the other officer continued fatalistically, "be it right or wrong, the fact is that we went around the vice president on this, and it's payback time. It isn't pretty—but that's how the process works. Fortunately, the man Jakov has in mind looks like a good candidate. His name is Major Hal DeCosta, and although I don't know him personally, he has a good record. DeCosta doesn't have any cavalry experience, I'm afraid, but he's known for his no-nonsense style of leadership and at least one member of my staff swears by him. You'll serve as Executive Officer. . . . Everything else will remain the same. Questions?"

Santana had questions. . . . Lots of them. Especially where the new CO's lack of cavalry experience was concerned—but knew the general wouldn't be able to answer them. He shook his head. "No, sir."

Booly nodded understandingly. "I know there are all sorts of things that the major will have to come to grips with before he can take over. But I'm counting on both you and Farnsworth to bring him up to speed during the trip out. He'll arrive in the next fifteen minutes or so—but I wanted you to hear the news from me."

"Thank you, sir," Santana said sincerely. "I appreciate that."

"It was the least I could do," Booly allowed, as he extended his hand. The grip was warm and firm. "Thank you, Captain, and good luck. Our prayers will be with you.

"Oh, and one more thing," the general said, as if by way of an afterthought. "I know you're busy, but a member of President Nankool's staff is here to see you off, and I would appreciate it if you could spend a couple of minutes with him."

Booly turned back toward the personnel hatch, and there, standing in a cone of soft buttery light, stood Charles Winther Vanderveen. He was a tall, patrician-looking man, with thick gray hair and eyes the same color as his daughter's. He was stationed on Algeron and had been ever since the government moved there. And, having completed his business on Earth, the diplomat had returned only to discover that the man he reported to had been captured by the Ramanthians.

The general saw the look recognition on Santana's face, and wondered what, if anything, the two men had in common. "I'll see you in a few weeks, Captain," Booly said. "Kill some bugs for me."

The officers exchanged salutes, and Booly nodded to Vanderveen as he reentered the fortress. Snow crunched under his shoes as the diplomat came out to greet Santana. "Tony, it's good to see you again."

"And you, sir," the officer replied, as they shook hands.

"I heard about DeCosta," Vanderveen said angrily. "I'm not supposed to take sides—but I can't help it. The vice president is an idiot."

Santana grinned broadly. "If you say so, sir."

"I do," the other man said fervently. "And I'm not alone. . . . But you know that."

There was a moment of silence as their eyes met, then drifted away. The diplomat spoke first. His pain was clear to see. "Christine is on Jericho you know."

Santana nodded. "Yes, sir. I know."

Vanderveen searched the younger man's face. "And that's why you agreed to go?"

"Partly, yes."

Vanderveen swallowed. "The mission isn't very likely to succeed, is it?"

"No," Santana replied soberly. "It isn't."

"Still, there's a chance," Vanderveen said hopefully. "Margaret and I will cling to that hope for as long as we can. But whatever happens, no matter which way it goes, we'll never forget what you did."

Or tried to do, Santana thought to himself. What was Christine's father telling him? That her family would grieve if he died? And accept him if he didn't? It seemed that way. "Thank you, sir. And please give my best to Margaret. And remind her that Christine is tough. . . . If anyone can survive on Jericho, she will."

There was a stir as the personnel door opened and a small wiry-looking major stepped out onto the steel platform closely followed by a sturdy-looking civilian. The officer wore jungle kit while his companion was nearly invisible inside a parka. Because Santana and Vanderveen were standing off to one side of the platform, they went unnoticed as the newly arrived legionnaire paused to sniff the cold air. "I *like* this planet, I really do," the officer announced to no one in particular. "But then I love *all* the Lord's creations. Except for the Ramanthians that is— because they chose to align themselves with the devil. Well, enough jibber-jabber. Come, Watkins. . . . It's time to inspect my flock." And with that, both men made their way up the ramp.

Santana watched the pair disappear with an expression of astonishment on his face. "Who the hell was *that*?"

"*That*," Vanderveen replied disgustedly, "was Major Hal 'The Preacher' DeCosta. Plus a civilian media specialist assigned to the mission by Assistant Undersecretary

Wilmot. It seems the vice president wants a full multimedia record of your mission."

"But *why?*" Santana wondered out loud.

"I don't know," the diplomat admitted. "But remember this. Watkins may *look* harmless, but he's a specially equipped cyborg, and a lot tougher than he appears to be. All of his news-gathering equipment is built into his body. So be careful what you do or say when he's around."

Santana nodded gratefully. "Thanks for the heads-up, sir. I will definitely keep that in mind."

"And one other thing," Vanderveen said soberly, as the wind ruffled his hair. "Good luck."

PLANET HIVE, THE RAMANTHIAN EMPIRE

Slowly, reverently, the Egg Orno took one last tour of her home. Looking, touching, and feeling each object so as to lock all of the sensations deep within, where they would forever be safe. Because finally, after weeks of careful planning, the fateful day had arrived. The process had begun with a pincer-written note from her mate that arrived on Hive sealed in a diplomatic pouch. Once on the planet's surface the message had been delivered by a fur-covered being, who, in addition to his responsibilities as a chauffeur, was also a member of the Thraki intelligence service.

The very sight of Always Orno's cramped writing had been sufficient to lift the Egg Orno's spirits, but it was what the letter said that filled her heart with joy. "I am alive, my dearest," the letter began. "Sustained only by my love for you. . . . Memorize what follows, burn this letter, and fly to my arms. There is no need to fear because our financial well-being is assured."

The rest of the letter had been dedicated to an exacting set of instructions by which the Egg Orno would be able to allay suspicions, escape from Hive without being intercepted by the government, and join her mate on Starfall. And the matron was in the process of following those instructions as she completed the tour of what had been her home. It pained the Egg Orno to leave all of her personal things behind. But the sacrifice was necessary if she was to escape—and material possessions were nothing when compared to being with her mate.

The deception had begun when her remaining servant had been given the day off. It was something the aristocrat had been forced to do more and more of lately as the last of her funds trickled away. Now, with no one present to witness the extent to which the Egg Orno was willing to shame herself, it was time to leave. Not via the front door, as she had thousands of times before, but through the nameless portal that no self-respecting member of her class would mention much less use. Because it was through that narrow opening that urns containing the family's waste products were passed each morning, so members of the lowly Skrum clan could carry them away, as was their birthright. And it was a *good* system, because rather than waste the night soil as so many societies did, the nutrient-rich waste matter was loaded onto trains and taken to the habitat's extensive subsurface gardens.

There were surface farms of course, which provided for the majority of the planet's dietary requirements, but the underground gardens continued to be important. Especially given the population explosion now under way. All of which accounted for the dark, dingy cloak that the Egg Orno pulled over herself, prior to securing a grip on a single bag. After that it was a simple matter to follow a ramp down into the servants' quarters and open the small door located toward the rear of the dwelling. A puff of incoming air brought the pungent odor of feces with it.

The Ramanthian's olfactory antennae began to writhe, and the aristocrat's breakfast threatened to rise as she forced herself to step through the opening into her own version of hell. A dark, shadowy place, where thousands of Skrum untouchables collected, processed, and distributed the filth generated by their social betters.

But once the door closed behind the Egg Orno it locked, which meant there was no going back. So, nauseated though she was, the Ramanthian had no choice but to pull the tattered cloak about her and follow a narrow ramp to the passageway below. There weren't very many lights, nor were they required, since the untouchables had far better night vision than the upper classes did.

However, thanks to what few glow cones there were, and the map the female had downloaded three days earlier, she was able to find her way. The paved sidewalk that the Egg Orno was on paralleled the train tracks one level below and continually split into narrow paths that led up to the domiciles and businesses above. She noticed that the specially designed wheelbarrows rattled as the untouchables pushed them uphill but were generally silent as they were brought back down, prior to being emptied into one of the open cars on the tracks below. By timing her movements carefully, the matron was able to avoid physical contact with the Skrum who passed to both sides of her. For to do so would be equivalent to touching what *they* touched, a possibility that filled her with horror.

It was warm under the city, way too humid for comfort, and noisome as electric-powered trains rattled past, and the incessant rattle of click-speech as the untouchables spoke to each other in their own semiliterate dialect. About *her*? Yes, the aristocrat thought so, because as she followed the main passageway south, the Egg Orno felt sure that her social inferiors had seen through her disguise to the being within. But there was no way to know if that was actually true as the matron made a sharp turn to the right, counted off a series of narrow access ways, and followed the fourth up toward the city above.

Once she arrived at the door, the Egg Orno knocked

three times. There was no response. So she tried again, and *again*, until the door finally swung open. A low-level functionary motioned for her to enter. If the male was surprised to see a visitor emerge from the city's depths, there was no sign of it as he led her up a ramp into what appeared to be a warehouse. Utility lights threw a harsh glare down onto the polished floor, brightly colored cargo containers had been stacked along one of the walls, and a loader was parked off to one side. There were no workers to be seen, as the aristocrat followed her guide across a large open space.

Though never privy to the details, the Egg Orno had always been aware that there was a dark side to her surviving mate's activities, as was to be expected of any functionary who rose to high office. Still, she was impressed by the extent to which Alway could influence events on Hive, as her guide stopped in front of an open shipping container. A well-padded nest had been created within, complete with a cell-powered light, and what looked like a cooler. "The module has its own oxygen supply," the functionary explained earnestly. "And will be fully pressurized during the journey into orbit. You'll find both food and water inside the cooler. The trip will last about twelve hours. Once aboard the Thraki vessel, you will be released. So now, if you would be so kind as to enter, I will seal you in."

The Egg Orno entered the module, took the only seat available, and strapped herself in. The functionary wished her "a safe journey," closed the door, and locked it. The fear the female felt as she eyed the dimly lit walls around her was mixed with excitement and a sense of anticipation. Because Alway was waiting, and every fiber of her being yearned to be with him.

Fifteen long minutes passed before some muffled sounds were heard, the cargo container shook as a pair of metal forks slid beneath it, and the entire box was plucked off the warehouse floor. And it was then, as the module was being transferred to a truck, that Chief Chancellor Itnor Ubatha shuffled out onto the warehouse floor. The head of the Queen's Intelligence Services appeared to join him. Because, rather than alienate someone with that much power, Ubatha had chosen to partner with the other official instead. That would mean less credit if their scheme proved successful but less blame if it didn't. Not to mention the beginning of what could be a profitable alliance. "Well, there she goes," Ubatha observed. "I trust your people are ready?"

"Very much so," came the confident reply. "My operatives will follow the Egg Orno every step of the way."

"It should be quite a reunion," Ubatha commented, as he imagined the moment when the Ornos met.

"It certainly will be," the intelligence chief agreed. "Once the Egg Orno draws the ex-ambassador out of hiding, the hunt will end."

"Her highness will be pleased," Ubatha said, as a big door rattled open and the truck passed through it.

"A most pleasant prospect indeed," the other official agreed. "Would you care to join me for breakfast?"

"Why yes," Ubatha replied contentedly. "I believe I would."

ABOARD THE *BARF BUCKET,* IN ORBIT AROUND THE PLANET JERICHO, THE RAMANTHIAN EMPIRE

Thousands of pieces of debris orbited Jericho, most of which were left over from battles fought back during the Hudathan wars, or had been jettisoned by vessels like those presently in orbit. The menagerie included five Thraki freighters, two Ramanthian destroyers, the massive *Imperator*, and four tugs brought in to serve her exacting needs. One of the tugs was currently outbound to the CE, or cable end. If that particular vessel had a name, none of the POWs knew what it was, which was why they called the ugly vehicle the *Barf Bucket*, in honor of the effect weightlessness had on some of them. Not *all* of them, though, since most of the naval personnel were used to zero-gee conditions.

Unfortunately, Vanderveen, wasn't very experienced in spite of the fact that Lieutenant Mary Trevane probably had been. So there was nothing the diplomat could do except ignore her rebellious stomach in hopes that she could complete the coming evolution without barfing in her helmet. A catastrophe that would not only force her to complete the mission with big globules of foul-smelling vomit free-floating all around her face—but would necessitate hours of painstaking cleanup back on the *Imperator*. Because while the techs were willing to repair the diplomat's suit, they were not required to clean up after what the navy people heartlessly called a "chucker." Meaning anyone stupid enough to hurl in their helmet.

Knowing that, Vanderveen struggled to focus all of her attention on the big cable reels that occupied the otherwise-open space directly in front of her. Like its sister ships the tug's U-shaped hull was built around a pressurized control room located at the center of the connecting bar. Powerful engines were mounted on each of two trailing pylons, both of which were capable of swiveling up, down, or sideways.

The POWs were required to ride in specially equipped slots located along the inside surface of the pylons just forward of the engines. The location put the slaves in close proximity to the twin cable reels that sat side by side on an axle stretched between the pylons. From that position the spools looked *huge*—large enough to blot out most of the stars—which made sense given that each reel carried a ten-mile-long section of cable. So, assuming that each team of POWs successfully "hung" *two* sections of fiber per trip, and each of the four available tugs completed eight missions per standard day, that meant the 23,560-mile-long elevator would be completed in approximately thirty-six days.

Except that wasn't going to happen, not if the prisoners could prevent it, which the LG was pretty sure they could. Various possibilities were currently under consideration, ranging from an attempt to hijack all four tugs to some sort of sabotage aboard the *Imperator*. But regardless of which method of sabotage they chose, the space elevator would be destroyed.

What no one wanted to discuss, however, was what would happen *next*. Because there wasn't much doubt regarding the way that Commandant Mutuu would react to the loss of his pet project. The POWs would be executed. *All* of them. And in some very unpleasant ways.

Vanderveen's thoughts were interrupted as the Ramanthian pilots fired the *Barf Bucket*'s bow thrusters, and the ungainly vessel began to slow. Tragg couldn't monitor what was taking place aboard all four tugs at the same time. But he could switch off between them, which he frequently did. "All right," Tragg said over the frequency that tied the team together, "it's party time."

From his position within the small, auxiliary spacecraft located just aft of the control compartment, the overseer had direct line-of-sight contact with both the cable reels and the POWs. Knowing Tragg could see her, Vanderveen hurried to release the clamps that held her vaguely chair-shaped utility vehicle (UV) against the starboard pylon and felt the unit float free.

That provided the FSO with a momentary view of Jericho, which caused her stomach to lurch and forced her to swallow some bile. The UV was controlled via a joystick located on the right arm of the chairlike framework. As the diplomat took in pure oxygen, she put out carbon dioxide that had to be scrubbed out of the air. Both of her heat exchangers were in the green, but it was still warm within the suit, and the temperature continued to climb as the UV floated up out of the *Barf Bucket*'s shadow and into full sunlight. The surface of Vanderveen's polycarbonate helmet automatically darkened to protect her vision as a locator beacon strobed in the distance.

The purpose of the flashing light was to identify the CE—and the point to which the next section of braided fiber would have to be attached. Vanderveen's job, as well as that of the man she was partnered with, was to latch on to the section of cable stored on reel one and pull it into place, where a couple of so-called hangers would secure it.

Her partner's name was Dent. And thanks to the fact that the bosun's mate was an old hand at zero-gee maneuvers, his UV was already in position and clamped on to the ten-mile-long section of fiber as the diplomat maneuvered her unit into place via a series of jerky movements. The petty officer understood the problem and wanted to offer some words of encouragement, but knew better than to do so. Because not only was Tragg *watching* the POWs, he was listening in on their radio transmissions as well, which made any sort of noncritical communication dangerous.

So Dent gave Vanderveen a thumbs-up as the FSO positioned her UV on the opposite side of the cable from his unit and made use of a C-shaped grasper to grab hold of the tightly braided fiber. Then, with both of them working in concert, it was possible to take the cable in tow. And what would have been difficult on Jericho's surface was relatively easy in space. The fiber came off the reel smoothly, and the UVs were closing with the beacon, when Tragg heard a buzzing sound. His eyes flicked to the screen on his right, and that was when he saw icon 2,436,271 emerge from behind the far side of the glowing planet, and shouted a warning. "Watch out! Incoming debris!"

But the fist-sized chunk of hull metal was traveling at roughly twenty-five-thousand miles per hour, which meant Dent was still processing the overseer's words when the piece of jagged steel passed through his armor, left biceps, chest cavity, and the right arm of his space suit. It missed Vanderveen by less than six inches before continuing on its way.

But the catastrophe wasn't over. The dead bosun's mate's body was still strapped in place, and his right hand continued to clutch the UV's joystick. Which, because it was jammed forward, caused Dent's unit to not only race out of control but drag both Vanderveen and the cable along with it.

And that was a significant problem since once all ten miles of fiber came off the reel, it would be a bitch to retrieve. It was something the Ramanthians might very well blame on Tragg if he failed to stop it. So the mercenary flipped a red cover up out of the way, grabbed hold of the Ramanthian-style squeeze bulb, and did his best to crush it. Gas jets blew the little spacecraft free of its mother ship, and the human had to react quickly in order to guide the pod up over the cable reels in front of him. "Hang on to that cable!" the renegade ordered grimly. "Or you'll wish you had."

Vanderveen heard the threat, knew she was pulling too much cable off the reel, and struggled to regain control. But that was impossible so long as Dent's unit continued to run amok. So the diplomat decided to free her suit from the UV, make her way over the top of the cable, and shut the other unit down. The problem was that if she were to lose her grip, both UV's would continue on their way, leaving her to drift. Would Tragg send someone to fetch her? No, that was unlikely, so any misstep could be her last.

Once free of the UV, the first step was to pull herself out over the cable toward what remained of Dent and his space suit. The gloves felt stiff and clumsy as the POW pulled herself across, secured a grip on the petty officer's right arm, and gave a tentative tug. Dent's hand came free of the joystick, his nearly severed arm doubled back on itself, and made a grisly bobbing motion in response to Vanderveen's movements.

The moment Dent's hand came off the joystick the UV's propulsion system shut itself down, causing the unit to coast. However, the crises wasn't over so long as cable continued to come off the reel. That meant the FSO had to pull herself back to her own UV and strap in before she could regain control. Something she had just managed to accomplish when Tragg's pod arrived on the scene. "Grab my tow point with your right grasper," the renegade instructed. "And I'll pull both you and the cable back to the beacon."

The FSO did as she was told. The ensuing ride gave Vanderveen a moment to grieve for Dent, marvel at the fact that she was still alive, and gaze at the planet below. Jericho was quite beautiful, which, given the likelihood that she would be buried on it, offered the diplomat a strange sense of comfort.

11

ABOARD THE FREIGHTER *SOLAR ECLIPSE,* IN HYPERSPACE

The *Solar Eclipse* hummed to herself as she passed through hyperspace and entered Ramanthian-held territory. Thanks to intelligence received from agent Oliver Batkin, General Booly and his staff knew Thraki merchant vessels were used to bring much needed supplies to Jericho, thereby freeing the Ramanthian navy to use its assets elsewhere. Which was why Chien-Chu Enterprises purchased a Thraki-built ship on behalf of the Confederacy and crewed it with Thraki mercenaries for the trip to Jericho. Where, if everything went as planned, Team Zebra would land undetected. Unfortunately, that meant living and working aboard a vessel designed for beings who averaged five feet in height, which explained why Santana's knees wouldn't fit under the fold-down desk.

But if there was a shortage of space, there was no shortage of work, a great deal of which had been generated by Major DeCosta. A man who, in addition to his overbearing religiosity, loved to produce plans for every possible contingency. All these plans had to be written, edited, and rewritten to the officer's often arbitrary standards before being electronically filed. And, because much of this work fell to the XO, Santana was cooped up in his tiny cabin, plowing through the latest iteration of crap, when someone rapped on the metal next to the open hatch. It was a welcome diversion—and the officer turned to see who it was. Maria Gomez came to attention, or was in the process of doing so, when Santana said, "At ease, Sergeant. Have a seat on my bunk, couch, and worktable."

The surface of the neatly made five-and-a-half-foot-long bunk was covered with printouts, aerial photos of Jericho, and pieces of standard-issue gear that Santana planned to modify prior to landing. The noncom made a space for herself and sat down. It was her opinion that Santana looked tired, which was troublesome, because if there was any hope for Team Zebra, it lay with him. Given her feelings for Santana, Gomez wanted to take the officer in her arms and comfort him. But that was impossible, and rather than make Santana's life easier as she wished to, the noncom knew she was about to make it more difficult. "So," Santana said facetiously. "I hope this isn't about the chow—because it isn't going to get any better."

"No, sir. It's not about the food," Gomez answered seriously.

The noncom was pretty in a no-frills sort of way. A fact Santana had been aware of all along but never allowed himself to think about. Because officers weren't allowed to fraternize with enlisted people, especially those in their own chain of command, no matter how pretty their big brown eyes might be. "Okay," Santana responded. "If it isn't about the chow, then what's up?"

Gomez looked him in the eye. "Permission to speak freely, sir?"

Santana felt a sudden sense of foreboding. "Permission granted."

"It's about the major, sir," Gomez said gravely. "I think he's crazy."

DeCosta was annoying, not to mention eccentric, but crazy? No, Santana hadn't seen any evidence of that. Even if he had, it wasn't a subject he could discuss with a non-com. No matter how good she was. Gomez saw the frown start to form and held up her hand. "Please hear me out, sir. I know that's a serious charge—but I can back it up. Hargo gave DeCosta some lip about an hour ago. The CO put Hargo on the shelf, and the team's pissed. The truth is that things are starting to get iffy down in the hold."

Santana knew that cyborg Jas Hargo was partnered with bio bod Nikko Zavala. Hargo was a convicted murderer, and Zavala was an inveterate gambler, but both had performed well during the fight in Deepwell. "A run-in?" the officer inquired. "What sort of run-in?"

"I wasn't there," the noncom confessed. "But the way I hear it, most of the team was in the hold, tweaking their gear, when the CO walked in."

Thanks to the fact that the *Eclipse* was a freighter, and had nothing to carry other than the team and its gear, the main hold was the natural place for everyone to congregate during the long, boring trip. Especially given how large the T-2s were—and how cramped the rest of the vessel was. So Santana could visualize the slightly chaotic scene as the hyperneat DeCosta made his unannounced appearance. His eyebrows rose. "Yeah? So, what happened?"

Gomez shrugged. "Nothing at first. . . . Not until the CO began to walk around and scope things out. That's when he noticed that Sato has a shotgun in addition to his table of organization (TO) weapon. Bozakov is packing *four* knives—and Tang was busy putting war paint on Hargo's face. His head looks like a human skull now—complete with bleeding eyeballs."

Santana sighed. "Don't tell me. . . . Let me guess. The CO went ballistic, ordered Tang to remove the war paint, and Hargo ran his mouth."

Gomez nodded. "Yes, sir. And that's when the major

ordered Zavala to pull Hargo's brain box and shelve it. Things began to get dicey at that point, but Sergeant Snyder was present, and she kept the lid on. But Hargo is a member of my squad, and *your* platoon. That's why I'm here."

But there was *another* reason, and both of them knew it. Because while common at one time, the practice of "shelving," as it was usually called, had officially been banned ten years earlier. And for good reason. Because without a war form or spider form to provide input to his senses, Hargo was effectively blind, deaf, and dumb while hooked to the high-tech life-support machine generally referred to as "the shelf." A punishment that was not only cruel, but patently unfair, since there was no equivalent penalty for bio bods.

And that made Santana angry, *very* angry, which Gomez could see in his eyes. Something that made the noncom proud but frightened, too, because she was afraid the XO would do something rash. It didn't make sense because Gomez hated officers—and had no reason to feel protective toward one. No *legitimate* reason anyway. But the cavalry officer was oblivious to such concerns as he stood and ducked his head. "Thanks for the sitrep, Sergeant. I'll have a word with the major. I'm sure we can straighten this out."

"Sir, yes, sir," Gomez replied obediently. "Can I make a suggestion?"

Santana paused. "Shoot."

"I think it would be a good idea to post an armed noncom in front of the ammo locker, sir."

Santana winced. "It's that bad?"

"The team is pretty pissed, sir. . . . And we have plenty of hotheads. So why take a chance?"

"Point taken, Sergeant. Lieutenant Farnsworth is catching some Z's—but it would be a good idea to roust him out. Tell him to arm Sergeants Snyder and Fox. Energy

weapons only. . . . That should give any would-be muti-
neers reason to pause."

"And Hargo, sir?"

"Leave him where he is for the moment," Santana
replied darkly. "I'll get back to you as soon as I can." Then
he was gone.

Having found the cabin assigned to him to be too small for
comfort, DeCosta had commandeered a larger compartment originally intended to serve as a lounge for Thraki
merchants. As Santana entered the compartment, the half-
naked major was seated at one end of the long, narrow table
that split the space in two, with his legs folded under him.
DeCosta had short black hair, a single eyebrow, and a
beard so heavy it would sprout stubble within an hour of
being shaved. Though not a big man, the infantry officer
had broad shoulders, a well-developed chest, and a pair of
powerful arms. Judging from the way the major held himself, and the fact that his eyes were closed, it seemed that
he was meditating.

Karl Watkins was present as well. And given the fact
that his right leg was laid out on the table in front of him,
it appeared that the cyborg was performing maintenance
on it. The civilian looked up as Santana entered, nodded
politely, and returned to his work. A servo whined as his
stylus touched a relay, and the waxy-looking foot flexed.

Santana was just about to speak when DeCosta pre-
empted him. "That's a very distinctive cologne, Captain. . . . Perhaps it has escaped your attention, but God
gave the Ramanthian race a very acute sense of smell. The
average trooper could detect your presence from fifty feet
away. . . . Something to think about, eh?" At that point
DeCosta's eyes snapped open as if to witness the other officer's reaction.

"That's a good point, sir," Santana allowed patiently.
"Although the average Ramanthian trooper could smell

my sweat, too. . . . So I'm not sure it would make much difference. But it's a moot point since I never wear cologne in the field."

"I'm pleased to hear it," DeCosta said self-righteously. "Now, how is the latest edit coming along?"

"Most of the changes have been made," Santana replied. "But that isn't why I'm here. . . . Sergeant Gomez tells me that Lance Corporal Hargo stepped out of line."

"Yes, he did," DeCosta replied gravely, as he methodically cracked his knuckles. "I took issue with the nonreg paint job that was being applied to his head. Then, after he told me to take the Legion's regulations and shove them up my ass, I ordered one of your ruffians to shelve him. There's nothing like a little time-out to teach these criminals a lesson. And it appears some lessons are in order, because during the short time I spent in the hold, I noticed at least half a dozen infractions. Some of which are quite serious. The possession of unauthorized weapons being an excellent example."

Santana clenched his fists to prevent his hands from shaking. Watkins was watching by then, and the cavalry officer knew that the cyborg could, and probably would, record the interchange. *"Sir,"* the cavalry officer began carefully. "Before you assumed command of Team Zebra, I authorized war paint for any cyborg rated completely satisfactory by his noncom, and gave my permission for bio bods to carry nonspec weapons so long as they carry a full load-out for their TO weapons. I neglected to check those exceptions with you, and I won't make that mistake again. So, given that the fault was mine, I request permission to remove Hargo from the shelf."

"That was quite a speech," DeCosta said, as his bare feet slapped the deck. "And you're right. . . . You were at fault. For flouting regulations, contributing to an overall lack of discipline, and ignoring your responsibilities as an officer. All of which will be noted on your fitness report."

"Assuming he lives long enough to receive a fitness report," Watkins put in dryly, as his leg rotated and locked itself into place.

The comment took Santana by surprise—and earned Watkins a nasty look from DeCosta. "This conversation is between the captain and myself," the major said primly. "And, as for Hargo, another hour on the shelf will do him a world of good. The fact that you gave him permission to wear war paint is no excuse for gross insubordination."

"No, it isn't," Santana agreed tightly. "But I would remind the major that unlike the use of war paint, or carrying a nonspec weapon, shelving constitutes a crime under the provisions of the Uniform Code of Military Justice. And I refuse to comply with what I believe to be an illegal order."

DeCosta placed both fists on his hips. His eyes were dark with anger. "I read your P-1 file," the major responded thickly. "The last time you disobeyed a direct order, you were court-martialed! And, by God, I'll see that you are again!"

"Those orders were issued by a bug," Santana responded contemptuously. "A Ramanthian who ordered me to fire on innocent civilians. Now, sir, if you'll excuse me, I'm going to remove Hargo from the shelf."

"But *why?*" DeCosta demanded, as bluster gave way to genuine befuddlement. "God hates an abomination, which is to say anything unnatural, and what could be more unnatural than a cross between a man and a machine? We need the borgs right now, I realize that, but why coddle the creatures? Eventually, after the bugs have been eradicated, every one of their evil breed should be destroyed!"

Santana looked at Watkins. "Are you recording?"

The civilian made a face. "I am."

"Good," the cavalry officer replied. "Save that stuff. . . . Assuming any of us survive, I look forward to playing that footage for General Booly." And with that Santana turned to go.

"Wait a sec," the cyborg said. "If it's all the same to you, Captain, I think I'll move into the hold."

"No problem," Santana answered. "You'll be welcome there."

DeCosta fell to his knees after the heretics left and called upon God to strike the evil ones down. But if DeCosta's God was listening, he, she, or it chose not to respond.

THE THRAKI PLANET STARFALL (PREVIOUSLY ZYNIG-47)

The alien sky was so dark that it was almost black. The rain fell in sheets, and rattled on the top of the chauffeur-driven car, as it carried ex-ambassador Alway Orno along a highway of fused glass toward the dimly seen high-rise spaceport in the distance. Lightning stabbed a nearby hilltop, as if probing the planet for weak spots, but the Ramanthian was happy. No, *joyous*, because within minutes, an hour at most, he and his sole-surviving mate would be reunited.

Then he would take her home to the rental house in the country, a mostly comfortable place where she could rest while he went to Jericho. Yes, Mutuu could be and generally was a cantankerous old coot. But Orno remained confident that he could successfully manipulate the deluded royal into slaughtering the POWs and for free, too! That would allow Orno to keep Mutuu's share of the fee.

Once that task was complete, it would be time to return to Starfall, take delivery on the second payment, and book passage on a Thraki liner. There were colonies of Ramanthian expatriates out on the rim—some of which were said to be quite pleasant. Places where the residents were much more interested in how much money one had than the vagaries of imperial politics.

In fact, based on what he'd heard, some of the settlements had chosen democratic forms of government. *Who knows?* Orno thought to himself. *Maybe I'll run for office, use my experience to good effect, and wind up better off than I was!* Such were the Ramanthian's thoughts as the car was forced to pause at a rain-drenched checkpoint before being allowed to enter the spaceport.

An air car hovered above, and a multiplicity of eyes watched as the limo snaked its way across the shiny black tarmac toward the hangar beyond. But Orno was oblivious to such matters because his thoughts were focused on the future and the good times that lay ahead.

The nearly empty office was part of a hangar, and while a bit colder than the Egg Orno might have wished, a lot more private than the main terminal would have been. And the aristocrat took comfort from the fact that her long voyage through space was finally at an end. As soon as the shuttle cleared Hive, and the cargo module had been transferred to the Thraki freighter, the Egg Orno had been released. But it wasn't until the ship was in hyperspace, where the Queen couldn't possibly touch her, that the aristocrat had been able to relax.

What the Egg Orno *didn't* realize, however, not at first anyway, was the fact that the merchant vessel was scheduled to make stops in two Ramanthian-held systems prior to the much-anticipated arrival off Starfall. Each stop raised the possibility that government agents would storm aboard and take her into custody. But they didn't, and the freighter completed its journey without incident.

And now, having been brought down to the surface of the planet, the Egg Orno was in an agony of suspense. Had her mate aged? Had *she* aged? Would they be happy? *Could* they be happy? Would she have servants? And what if she didn't?

All of those thoughts and many more swirled through the aristocrat's mind as she stood in front of the Thraki-sized window and stared out across the tarmac at the rain-smeared lights beyond. *True* happiness was impossible without the War Orno, but at least she still had one mate, and that gave her life purpose.

That was when the door opened, the Egg Orno turned, and felt an explosion of warmth in her chest. Because there, coming through the entranceway, was her beloved Alway! And, judging from the finery that he wore, things were going well indeed.

The female hurried forward to stand inside the circle of intimacy where only mates could linger for more than a few seconds and allowed her antennae to absorb the wonderful cocktail of pheromones produced by her mate.

And that's where they were, wrapped in the chemical equivalent of an embrace, when two Ramanthian agents entered the room. They had been outside, waiting for Orno to enter, and water continued to drain off their poncho-style raincoats as they shuffled into the room. Both held silenced pistols. Alway turned to confront the assassins, but it was too late. "So," Ifna Bamik said contemptuously. "Look what crawled out from under a rock. . . . All that was required to catch this vermin was the right kind of bait."

Orno felt his heart sink as he stepped sideways to shield the Egg Orno's body with his own. He should have known. It had been too easy to get his mate off Hive. The whole thing was part of a plot to lure him out of hiding so government agents could kill him! But what about the Egg Orno? Did the assassins have orders to terminate her, too? Or could he buy her life? *Both* of their lives? It was worth a try. "Please," the ex-diplomat said imploringly. "Don't fire until you hear what I have to say. . . . I have information, extremely *valuable* information, that pertains to Marcott Nankool."

The War Bamik had heard it all before. The extravagant lies, the heartfelt pleas, and the shameless attempts at bribery. Yet none of those strategies had been successful because he was just as much a soldier as anyone in uniform and a patriot besides. A patriot who was in love with the godlike power that went with his profession. "Stop that," the assassin said disgustedly. "Don't embarrass yourself. . . . Not after such a long and colorful career. Yes, it would have been nice to die while taking a nice warm sand bath, but very few of us are granted *that* privilege. You'll be happy to hear that both of us are excellent shots—so the whole thing will be over before you know it."

"Kill me if you must," Orno replied earnestly. "But spare my mate. Her only crime is loyalty to me. Besides, what I said was true, I really *do* have information about President Nankool. Information that would be extremely valuable to the Ramanthian government!"

Bamik glanced at his partner. "Did you hear that, Nondo? Some people simply refuse to listen." That was when the agent fired. There was a *pop* as the bullet entered the ex-diplomat's chest, exited through his back, and struck the Egg Orno. Both collapsed without a sound and lay motionless in a steadily expanding pool of blood.

"Nice work, boss," Nondo said admiringly. "The idiot never saw it coming. . . . Not to mention the fact that you took care of both targets with one bullet!"

Bamik looked down at the bodies and nodded. "We're on a budget," the assassin said coldly. "And bullets cost money."

Nondo thought that was funny, and was still clacking his left pincer in approval, as Bamik took a series of photos plus two tissue samples, all of which would be sent to Hive to prove that the hit had been completed. Then, having accomplished their mission, the agents left. But, unbeknownst to the assassins, *one* of their victims was still alive.

PLANET JERICHO, THE RAMANTHIAN EMPIRE

There was a solid *thump* as the shuttle's skids touched the tarmac, followed by a steadily diminishing *scream* as the engines spooled down, and the troopers at the front of the cargo compartment rose and went to work. Because the POWs had been divided into multiple work groups Tragg was no longer able to oversee all of the prisoners personally. So to enhance security the slaves had been chained to their seats and couldn't leave the spacecraft until released. A good five minutes passed before Vanderveen and her companions were freed, ordered to stand, and herded out into the bright sunshine.

The sky, the humid air, and the feel of solid ground under the diplomat's feet all came as something of a shock after weeks in orbit and made her head swim. There were gasps of astonishment as the POWs paused to look up at the long slivery thread that hung suspended above them. The origins of the space elevator were too high to be seen, and the cable end wasn't low enough to touch the ground as yet, but the results of their efforts were plain to see.

Like those around her, Vanderveen couldn't help but feel a moment of pride as she looked up into the achingly blue sky, saw the crosshatched contrails created by the hardworking tugs, and knew that more sections of cable were being hung even as she watched. And soon, as more and more of the elevator became subject to Jericho's gravity, both the POWs and the tugs would move down to the surface. It was a moment Vanderveen and the other members of the LG were looking forward to because Nankool was still in orbit, and it was difficult to protect him there.

The POWs might have gawked a bit longer had they been allowed to, but the Ramanthian everyone referred to as "gimpy" behind his back was in a hurry to get rid of his charges and eat dinner. "You move!" the guard insisted, as he jabbed a marine with his rifle. "Or I shoot you good!"

So with the Ramanthian limping ahead, and more guards following along behind, the slaves made their way across the hot tarmac. Vanderveen noticed that a lot of things had changed during her absence. More shuttles were parked along the edge of the field. And in spite of the fact that the furballs claimed to be neutral, some of the ships belonged to the Thrakies.

And given the number of spacecraft on the ground, it wasn't surprising to see ragged looking POWs loading cargo modules onto a train of driverless flatbed carriers that whined loudly as they followed a lead unit off the apron and into the jungle.

Farther out, beyond the airfield's perimeter, Vanderveen could see that the newly excavated forerunner ruins were being prepped to receive the cable end. Which, if the scuttlebutt was correct, was what she and her companions were slated to work on next.

Tower-mounted automatic weapons tracked the prisoners as the gate swung open to admit them, and the line of emaciated scarecrows who sat with their backs resting on the wall of the so-called dispensary sent up a reedy cheer as their newly returned comrades entered the camp. But Vanderveen was saddened to see that very few of the patients were able to stand, much less come forward to greet their friends, as they might have four or five weeks earlier. And they were the healthier specimens, the ones judged fit to go outside, while those who were dying lay within.

But other than the handful of people sitting outside the dispensary, the rest of the camp was practically deserted. Partly because the able-bodied personnel were outside the fence on work details, but also because hundreds of prisoners were still working in space, where they would remain until phase two began.

So Vanderveen had every reason to expect that she her comrades would immediately be put to work. And maybe they would have if Tragg had been present. But in the absence of orders from the Ramanthians, most of the POWs withdrew to the huts, where they took much-needed naps. And the diplomat was no exception. Within moments of going facedown on a sour-smelling pallet, Vanderveen was unconscious, and remained that way, until a few hours later when the noise generated by the returning work crews woke her.

Vanderveen was hungry by then, *very* hungry, and followed the others to the chow line where the so-called scoops were serving the same gray gruel they had been ladling out when she left. Except that after weeks of cold MSMREs eaten aboard the *Imperator*, the hot mush actually tasted *good*! A sad state of affairs indeed. There wasn't enough of the brew, however, and Vanderveen was busy licking the bottom of her bowl, when Calisco plopped down next her.

Some people, no make that *most* people, had been systematically weakened since the surrender. But Calisco was a notable exception. Because by some form of alchemy the diplomat couldn't quite fathom, the sly, often-leering sycophant she had known aboard the *Gladiator* had been transformed into a person Vanderveen could almost like. Because he was a man who had been through a terrible experience and somehow been purified by it. Even if Calisco still had a tendency to look at the FSO as if she were naked.

Calisco had been on the ground while Vanderveen worked on the *Imperator*—so the next fifteen minutes were spent exchanging information until both were up-to-date. "So," the bearded official concluded, having checked to ensure that no one was listening, "tonight's the night."

Vanderveen raised an eyebrow. "Tonight's the night for what?"

"For Batkin," Calisco said conspiratorially. "As luck would have it, Tragg left a navy robo tech here on the ground when he took the rest of you up into orbit. We scavenged bits of wire here and there and stole parts from incoming cargo modules. The tech took what we gave her, cobbled it all together, and got Batkin up and running again. He can fly!"

"Damn!" Vanderveen enthused. "That's wonderful. . . . Congratulations."

"Yes, it *is* good news isn't it?" Calisco commented contentedly. "With Batkin on the other side of the fence, who knows what we can accomplish? But first we need to get him out of here, and that's where the suicide comes in."

Vanderveen's eyes widened. "Someone's going to commit suicide?"

Calisco nodded. "Yeah. . . . Petty Officer Kirko is still up and around—but the doc says he has a terminal disease. So just after sundown, Kirko's going to attack one of the guards at the east end of the camp. Then, while the Ramanthians are busy killing him, Batkin will cross the fence. Slick, huh?"

The way Calisco explained it sounded so matter-of-fact, so devoid of emotion, that had someone from off-planet been able to hear the conversation, they might have concluded that the official with the bright eyes and the deeply tanned face was a cold-blooded monster.

But Vanderveen knew better. The prisoners had to fight with whatever weapons they could lay their hands on, and if that meant taking advantage of Kirko's inevitable death, then so be it. Because if they could put Batkin on the other side of the electrified fence, where the cyborg would be free to roam, then an important battle would have been won. But there was a potential problem. A serious one. "What about reprisals?" the FSO wanted to know.

Calisco shrugged. "We're hoping there won't be any. . . . Not if Kirko can get himself killed without harming one of the guards. But if there are reprisals, it will *still* be worth it."

Vanderveen looked away. "Is Batkin aware of all this?"

Calisco shook his head. "Hell no. . . . He knows there's going to be a diversion but nothing more."

The diplomat nodded understandingly. "That makes sense. He might refuse if he knew. So, what now?"

"It's time to say good-bye to Kirko," the official announced solemnly. "And wish him God's speed."

No matter how long she lived, Vanderveen knew she would never forget the on-again, off-again line of POWs that straggled through Kirko's barracks. Each paused to offer the petty officer a few words of prayer or a gruff joke as they said their good-byes.

Vanderveen didn't want to cry, promised herself that she *wouldn't* cry, but the tears came anyway. Kirko was obviously in pain but managed a smile nonetheless and offered words of comfort. Which, coming from the man who was about to die, were backwards somehow. "Don't worry, ma'am," Kirko said kindly. "I know my messmates are waiting for me—and they'll show me the ropes."

By the time the good-byes were over, darkness was beginning to fall, and Batkin was nervous. And there was plenty to be nervous about since there hadn't been any opportunity to test the makeshift repairs outside the four walls of the barracks. But the alternative, which was to hide under the floorboards until his power ran out, wasn't that attractive. Besides, the spy had a job to do, and remained determined to do it.

So Batkin remained where he was, with two marines to keep him company, until a very brave petty officer picked up a rock and threw it at one of the Ramanthian guards. The ensuing burst of gunfire, followed by the urgent bleat of a Klaxon, and a whole lot of yelling was Batkin's cue to fire his repellers, ease his way out into the cool night air, and make straight for the fence.

The spy waited for the cry of alarm, and *another* burst of gunfire, but nothing happened as he cleared the top of the electrified barrier and sped toward the jungle. The trees welcomed the cyborg back, the darkness took him in, and Batkin was free.

12

There is no way to know what archeological treasures lie hidden beneath the surface of planets like Jericho—or what knowledge will be lost if the planet falls into the wrong hands.

—Hibeth Norroki
Turr academic
Standard year 2743

PLANET JERICHO, THE RAMANTHIAN EMPIRE

Within seconds of exiting hyperspace the *Solar Eclipse* was challenged by a Ramanthian traffic control officer and two Sting Class patrol vessels were dispatched to intercept her. But thanks to information provided by agent Oliver Batkin, the ship's Thraki pilots were not only familiar with in-system arrival protocols, they had the latest recognition codes as well—meaning anything less than six months old. That vulnerability would be eliminated once all ships were equipped with hypercom sets, but that day was off in the future.

So that, plus the reassuring sight of some Thraki faces, put all Ramanthian fears to rest as the patrol boats turned away, and the *Solar Eclipse* entered orbit. Meanwhile, down in the main hold, twenty-one specially modified drop pods were loaded and ready to be ejected once the ship was in position. Sixteen of the capsules contained one cyborg and one bio bod each, plus a thousand pounds of food, ammo, and other gear required to support them on the ground. The remaining pods carried RAVs, each of which was loaded with additional supplies.

The problem was that unlike military drop ships, which were equipped to jettison up to thirty-six pods at once, the *Solar Eclipse* didn't have drop tubes, which meant that Thraki crew members would have to push Team Zebra's containers off the stern ramp two at a time. And no matter how quickly the mercenaries completed the task, the pods were going to hit Jericho's surface miles apart, thereby forcing the legionnaires to waste precious time coming back together.

But there was no way around it, so as a team of four space-suited crew members waited to propel the pods down the roller-equipped ramp, the beings sealed inside the entry vehicles continued to communicate with each other on a low-power, short-range com channel. Each egg-shaped container was pressurized and divided in half. That meant that as Santana stood on a compartment packed with supplies he was effectively face-to-face with his ten-foot-tall T-2, even though a well-padded partition served to separate them. The idea was to make sure that each two-person fire team hit the dirt together, thereby enhancing their chances of survival as well as their ability to engage the enemy within minutes of touchdown.

But it was claustrophobic inside the module, and Santana was extremely conscious of the way the hull pressed in around him, so much so that DeCosta's prayer came as a welcome distraction. And even though the platoon leader wasn't a religious man there was no denying the beauty and power of the ancient words.

> "Yea, though I walk through the valley of the
> shadow of death,
> I will fear no evil: For thou art with me;
> Thy rod and thy staff, they comfort me. . . ."

And as the words went on, Santana's thoughts turned to Vanderveen, and the very real possibility that he would see her soon. But what if he didn't? What if it turned out that she was dead? That possibility brought a lump to the legionnaire's throat as the prayer came to a close.

"Surely goodness and mercy shall follow me all the days of my life,
and I will dwell in the House of the Lord forever."

"*After* I kill every frigging bug on this planet," squad leader Husulu Ibo-Da put in, his words serving to drown out DeCosta's "Amen."

There was a chorus of laughter, and Santana couldn't help but smile knowing that the response would drive DeCosta crazy, assuming the little bastard was sane to begin with. The major started to speak but was cut off for a *second* time as the Thraki pilot overrode him. And the words were familiar since Santana had been required to write them at DeCosta's behest. "All personnel stand by for launch. . . . Check onboard nav functions and reset if necessary. . . . The ship is now in orbit. . . . Stand by for launch in thirty seconds. . . ."

And so it went until Santana felt the pod start to move, followed by a sudden bout of nausea as the module fell clear of the argrav field, and the steering jets fired. Because there were thousands of pieces of space junk circling Jericho, the officer was fairly confident that the pods would be lost in among them. But if the Ramanthians took issue with the sudden appearance of twenty-one additional blips on their tracking screens, then the *Solar Eclipse*'s pilot would admit to dumping garbage and accept the inevitable tongue-lashing. Then, having delivered a cargo of delicacies that the Ramanthian command structure hadn't ordered but was unlikely to refuse, the freighter would depart.

In the meantime the computer-guided drop pods were following trajectories calculated to reinforce the impression that they, like the hundreds of other objects that entered the atmosphere each day, were about to burn up. Santana felt the pod began to vibrate, and even though he couldn't *see* the three-thousand-degree envelope of plasma flowing around him, he knew it was trying to find a way in through the capsule's thermal protection system. And the officer could feel the heat start to build up inside the pod as the vehicle shook violently. The legionnaire chinned the intercom. "Snyder? How are you doing?"

"I *was* taking a nap," the cyborg lied. "Until you woke me up that is."

Santana laughed. "Sorry about that. . . . Go back to sleep."

And, had such a thing been possible, the next few minutes would have been the time to try. Because once the pod lost a sufficient amount of altitude, parachutes were deployed, and Santana felt a distinct jerk as the vehicle slowed. That was followed by a gentle swaying motion— and the sure knowledge that they would be on the ground soon.

However, pod Bravo Two-Four, which carried bio bod Jamie Ott, and cyborg Bindi Jasper was in trouble. Both legionnaires felt a jerk, followed by continued free fall, as a buzzer began to sound. The NAVCOMP triggered the reserve chute, which turned into a streamer, as the capsule continued its plunge toward the jungle below. Ott took over at that point, fired all of the drop pod's retros, and was still punching buttons as the vehicle hit the ground. There was no explosion, but the impact crater was fifty feet across, and at least fifteen feet deep.

But the jungle had covered other secrets over the ages, thousands of them, and the force of the impact brought long dormant seeds to the surface, where the sunlight could find them. And even before the wreckage could cool, vines had already begun their slow-motion advance in from the margins of the newly created clearing to reclaim what was rightfully theirs.

The sudden loss of Ott and Jasper was immediately visible to the entire team as the Integrated Tactical Command (ITC) system threw a revised TO chart up for the legionnaires to see. But there was no time to mourn for lost comrades as their pods hit the jungle's topmost canopy of vegetation, where they paused for a fraction of a second before crashing through a second layer of foliage to land on whatever lay below. Which in Santana's case was soft loam.

The capsule bounced once, landed at something of an angle, and blew itself apart. Santana fell free, rolled into the shelter offered by a fallen tree, and brought his assault rifle up. Snyder broke out of what remained of the shell, shook off some loose pieces, and began to scan. If there was some sort of threat in the immediate area, the cyborg would find it.

A variety of jungle smells filled the legionnaire's nostrils as he came to his feet and eyeballed the data provided by the ITC. The good news was that there was no sign that a Ramanthian reaction force was on the way to intercept them, and all of the surviving pods had landed safely. The bad news was that Team Zebra was spread out along a twenty-mile-long axis. But DeCosta had a plan—which the impatient officer was quick to implement. "This is Zebra Six. . . . All team members will form on Bravo Six and myself. And let's find those RAVs. . . . We're going to need them. Over and out."

DeCosta's reasoning was sound as Santana could see on his HUD. Because Bravo Six, which was to say Farnsworth, was closest to the coordinates where the POWs were being held. So it made sense for both the platoon leader and those fire teams closest to him to remain stationary, while the rest of the team hurried to catch up. The mission clock was running, and there was no way to shut it off.

Now that Santana had a clear mental picture of how the company was deployed, it was time to look at the needs of his own platoon, and figure out how to link up with his legionnaires. Since Gomez and the rest of the first squad were *north* of his position, and therefore closer to the final objective, the platoon leader decided to remain stationary while he waited for Sergeant Ibo-Da and his squad to arrive from the south.

A decision that was further justified by the fact that according to the topo map projected on the inside surface of the officer's face shield, one of the RAVs was located only a half mile away. Which meant that he and Snyder could secure the robot while the second squad caught up. Having dragged the debris into the jungle and concealed it as best he could, Santana helped Snyder clamp the auxiliary supply module to her chest. With that accomplished, Santana sent two succinct radio messages. One to DeCosta, letting the major know what he planned to do, and the other to his squad leaders.

Then it was time to climb up onto Snyder's back and strap in. The T-2 could "see" the RAV on the topo map superimposed over her electronic vision, so there was no need for the bio bod to do anything other than duck branches and become more familiar with his environment as the cyborg carried him through the jungle.

By that time the local residents had recovered from the violent manner in which the alien invaders had crashed through the upper regions of their largely green universe and were busy screeching, howling, and chittering at the ten-foot-tall, two-headed monster lumbering through their forest.

Santana leaned backwards and let the harness accept his weight as he looked up through the sun-dappled foliage to patches of blue sky. Every once in a while it was possible to catch a glimpse of sleek bodies as they jumped from branch to branch and gibbered at each other.

Water splashed up and away from Snyder's blocky feet as she forded a shallow stream, made her way up the opposite bank, and followed a game trail into the forest. The RAV was right where it was supposed to be, standing near the remains of its pod, when the T-2 and bio bod entered the newly created clearing. The robot consisted of two eight-foot-long sections linked by an accordion-style joint and supported by four articulated legs. Though not intended for offensive purposes, each RAV was equipped with two forward-facing machine guns and a grenade launcher. Which, when integrated into a defensive perimeter, could be quite useful in repelling ground attacks.

Having dismounted, and with the T-2 there to provide security, Santana gathered the pieces of the RAV's specially designed pod together and carried them over to a natural depression, where he did what he could to hide them without killing any of the vegetation. And that was when the officer came across an empty meal pak with Ramanthian script on it, plus more than two dozen pieces of broken shell, which suggested that whatever had once been inside the egg had hatched. That was interesting because the legionnaire had read all of Batkin's reports at least three times, and therefore knew that thousands, if not millions of Ramanthian tricentennial eggs, had been transported to Jericho and "planted" by specially trained teams of civilians.

A first, insofar as the experts knew, since it was believed that all of the previous megahatchings had taken place on Hive, where they had been responsible for social upheaval, prolonged warfare, and extended famines. Problems the Queen and her advisors were trying to avoid this time around. Santana put both the empty meal pak and a fragment of eggshell in his backpack and made a mental note to share both the artifacts and his conclusions with De-Costa.

Sergeant Ibo-Da and the rest of his squad arrived shortly

thereafter. Good-natured insults flew back and forth between the cyborgs, and Snyder gave as good as she got as the combined force left the clearing. Darby and Nacky had the point, followed by Santana on Snyder, the RAV, Shoot-straight on Ichiyama, and Ibo-Da on Kappa. The last two had the drag position, which meant Kappa had to walk backwards much of the time in an effort to protect the column's six.

But there were no threats in the area. None the T-2s could detect anyway—as the huge cyborgs made their way north. There was something about the rhythmic motion of Snyder's body, the comforting *click, whine, thud* of her gigantic footsteps, and the now-familiar scenery that made Santana sleepy. But it wasn't until Darby's voice came over the radio that the officer realized he'd been dozing. "This is Alpha Three-Four. . . . There's a clearing up ahead—with a large corpse at the center of it. Six or seven dog-sized things were gnawing on the body but took off once we arrived. Over."

"This is Alpha Six. . . . Hold your position," Santana instructed. "We're coming up behind you. How 'bout it Alpha Three-Three? Have you got video for me? Over."

Santana eyed his HUD, saw a box appear, and watched video roll inside of it. The first thing he saw was foliage, an opening, and the clearing beyond. The badly ravaged carcass was clear to see. But the predators, or scavengers as the case might be, were little more than a blur as they took off in a half dozen directions.

Santana chose one of the images by focusing on it and blinking twice. The fugitive froze, grew larger, and began to rotate as the ITC system took the visual data and made an educated guess as to what the rest of the creature would look like. And the result looked very familiar indeed. Because like their human counterparts juvenile Ramanthians were known to follow what the xenobiologists called, ". . . a simple development pattern." Meaning that nymphs looked like adults, except that they were smaller, and, judging from the video, a helluva lot faster.

All of which served to confirm Santana's hypothesis that the tricentennials were not only hatching out, but well into the equivalent of early adolescence, a stage of development the Confederacy's scientists knew very little about. Especially in the wild since what little information they had pertained to nymphs hatched in civilized settings.

Snyder paused next to Nacky, which allowed Santana to nod at Darby before directing his T-2 out into the clearing. The carcass was surrounded by a cloud of voracious insects, and big gaping wounds made it difficult to tell what the creature looked like *before* the nymphs tore into it, other than to say that it had a relatively small head, a highly specialized claw-tipped tentacle that extended from what would otherwise have been described as its nose, and four short legs. Judging from appearances, the Ramanthians had swarmed the beast, opened its belly with their parrotlike nose hooks, and ripped its guts out. Not a pleasant way to die, but interesting, because it implied some sort of group cohesion.

"Alpha Six to all units," Santana said as he looked down at what remained of the jungle animal. "Be advised that a large number of Ramanthian nymphs have hatched out and are on the loose. They could be dangerous, especially if encountered in large numbers, so keep your eyes peeled. Over and out."

What followed came so quickly it was as if DeCosta had been waiting to punch the "transmit" button. And rather than utilize the command push, so his comments would be heard by Santana alone, he chose to broadcast them to the entire company. "*I* will be the judge of what does and does not constitute a threat to this team," DeCosta grated. "Which means your role is to submit what you consider to be relevant data to *me*. At which time *I* will analyze it and notify the team if that's appropriate. Understood? Over."

Ibo-Da and the rest of his squad didn't approve of the rebuke and directed disbelieving looks at each other, but there was nothing they could do but glower and look uncomfortable as Santana gave the only response he could. "Yes, sir. Over."

"Good," DeCosta concluded stiffly. "Zebra Six, out."

Had the bio bods been on foot, the next three hours of travel would have been exhausting, as Santana and half his platoon fought their way through vegetation so thick that whichever T-2 was in the lead had to use his or her energy cannon to clear a path. And on one occasion, the cyborgs were forced to ford a river so deep that the bio bods had to stand up straight in order to keep their heads above water.

So thanks to the cyborgs, the bio bods were able to not only conserve their energy, but enjoy moments like the one when the legionnaires marched through a cathedral-like open space where shafts of dusty sunlight fed pools of gold, and jewel-like insects flitted through the air. But such moments were all too rare as the temperature increased, the bio bods' hot, sweaty uniforms began to chafe, and time seemed to slow.

Finally, as darkness began to fall, the second squad found itself within five miles of Sergeant Gomez. Santana was tempted to proceed, confident that the T-2s could find their way through the dead of night if necessary, but DeCosta refused, insisting that each group camp and create its own defensive perimeter. That was stupid to Santana's way of thinking, since a unified platoon could mount a better defense than two isolated squads, but it was not for him to decide.

So the platoon leader chose a rise, where attackers if any would be forced to advance uphill, and ordered the cyborgs to clear a 360-degree free-fire zone. Though far from happy about it, the bio bods dug defensive positions *before* they sat down to eat. Then, once the T-2s were finished constructing a barrier made out of fallen logs and sharpened stakes, it was time to settle in for the night. A scary business for any bio bod not accompanied by four battle-ready war forms. Especially given the strange sounds and continual rustlings that issued from the jungle.

The hours of darkness were divided into four two-hour watches, and Santana had just completed his shift when DeCosta spoke over the command push. "This is Zebra Six. . . . Do you read me? Over."

The major sounded strange, or so it seemed to Santana, although the officer knew he might be mistaken. "This is Alpha Six. . . . I read you. Over."

"How are things at your location? Over?"

Santana frowned. The answer was obvious, or should have been, given the fact that DeCosta could access the ITC. It was as if the other officer was simply nervous and wanted to chat. "No problems so far, sir," the platoon leader answered. "What's the situation there?"

"We lost Frayley," DeCosta replied harshly. "She went outside the perimeter to take a leak, fired three shots, and was gone by the time her T-2 arrived on the scene. Smith saw more than a dozen heat signatures but withheld fire out of fear of hitting her. Over."

Santana wasn't wearing his helmet at that point, so he hadn't seen Frayley's name and status pop up on the ITC, but he remembered the legionnaire well. A fresh-faced young woman with reddish hair and a scattering of freckles across the bridge of her nose. One of the few team members with a clean record, who, if rumors were correct, had volunteered in order to be with Sergeant Jan Obama. "Damn," Santana said sadly. "How is Bravo Two-Six taking the news? Over."

"Obama went nuts, if that's what you mean," DeCosta answered clinically. "We had to restrain her. Over."

There was a long, uncomfortable silence, as if DeCosta was hoping that Santana would make sense of the incident somehow and thereby make him feel better. But the cavalry officer didn't have anything to say, other than it was stupid to pee outside the perimeter. A lesson Frayley learned the hard way. Eventually, when it was clear that the conversation was over, DeCosta broke the contact. "Zebra Six, out."

It was difficult to sleep after that, but Santana finally managed an hour or so and woke just before dawn, when standing orders required that all units serving in the field stand to arms. It was a tradition that went back hundreds of years and was based on the fact that predawn attacks were and always would be common.

But no attack was forthcoming, which left the second squad free to brew hot drinks and eat their MSMREs before taking fifteen minutes to erase the more obvious signs of their presence. Then it was up and off, as the legionnaires made their way through a long, narrow gorge before climbing up over a thinly forested ridge and descending into the jungle below. And that was where Sergeant Maria Gomez and the first squad were waiting for them. There were the usual catcalls, insults, and other greetings, but the only person Gomez truly cared about was her platoon leader.

Santana took note of the fact that the noncom had chosen to spend the night with her back to a cliff and a good field of fire. The pits had been filled in, however, and the barricade had been removed, which meant the first squad was ready to move. The platoon leader nodded approvingly. "Nice job, Sergeant. Any excitement last night?"

But before Gomez could answer, DeCosta was on the team freq, his voice tight with anger. "Zebra Six to Alpha Six. . . . The clock is running! Or have you forgotten? Please bring your platoon forward as quickly as possible. Over and out."

It was the sort of thing that Gomez expected from officers, and her anger was clear to see. She opened her mouth to speak, but Santana frowned and shook his head. Then, having made no response, he ordered Snyder forward.

Meanwhile, as Santana took to the trail, the platoon seethed. None of the legionnaires approved of the way De-Costa was harassing the XO, and Hargo least of all. The serial murderer was still angry about the manner in which DeCosta had shelved him. "Who the hell does the little shit think he is?" the cyborg wanted to know. "One of these days I'm going to grab the bastard and twist his pointy head off!"

"That will be enough of that," Gomez said sternly. "Stow the bullshit, or I'll put you on point for the next five days."

With the shrewdness of enlisted people everywhere, Hargo had taken advantage of the disagreement between Santana and DeCosta to keep the war paint on in spite of the major's order to get rid of it. Which meant that, as the T-2's big blocky head turned her way, Gomez found herself looking into a pair of bleeding eyes. Hargo was pissed, the noncom knew that, but couldn't be allowed to run his mouth. Slowly, so as to emphasize what she was doing, the squad leader pulled the zapper out if its holster and held it up for him to see. "You want to dance, big boy?" she inquired. "If so, then bring it on!"

There was a pause, followed by a synthesized rumble. "I got no beef with you, Sarge. You know that."

Gomez made the zapper disappear. "Yeah, I know that," she replied casually. "I was checking, that's all. Come on, you slackers. Let's get our asses in gear before the major goes crazy on the captain *again*."

The next few hours were largely uneventful as Santana led his platoon north. The column bushwhacked where necessary, but followed game trails whenever possible, to save time. But the legionnaire knew there was something even more important than speed, and that was the need to maintain the element of surprise. Because the moment the Ramanthians became aware of the team, they would bring an overwhelming amount of firepower to bear, and the mission would be over. Worse yet, the bugs might figure out what the legionnaires had been planning to do and identify Nankool.

So when the fire team at the front of the column announced a clearing ahead, plus some sort of structure, the platoon leader was quick to order both squads off the trail. Once all of them were hidden, Santana directed Snyder to keep an eye on the back door while he followed Private Noaim Shootstraight forward. The brindled Naa was a crack shot, a skilled scout, and had been court-martialed for desertion. Not once but *twice*. However, in spite of the fact that there weren't any jungles on Algeron, and the way his sweat-matted fur caused him to pant, the Naa seemed to slide between the leaves and branches as if raised on Jericho. Santana, by contrast, made twice as much noise, and was hard-pressed to keep up.

Ten minutes later the twosome arrived at the edge of a blackened clearing that had obviously been created with energy weapons or something very similar. And there, sitting at the very center of the open space, was a cylindrical structure. The construct was about twenty feet tall, shaped like a grain silo, and had evenly spaced holes all around its circumference. Ramanthian script had been spray-painted onto whatever the object was along with a six-digit number. None of it made any sense to Santana—but was seemingly obvious to Shootstraight. "It looks like a feeder, sir," the private whispered. "Like the ones we have for dooths back home."

What the Naa said made sense. But the Ramanthians didn't have any dooths. Then the officer had it. . . . The food was for their tricentennial nymphs! The same ones who were out hunting. He was about to say as much when DeCosta spoke in his ear. "Zebra Six to Alpha Six. . . . What are you waiting for? Get a move on. Over."

There were no Ramanthians in sight, young or old, which meant that the way was clear. Or that's how it seemed. But the area around the silo was littered with the remains of dead animals. Bones mostly, since it looked as though scavengers had been at them, but some half-eaten corpses as well. Had foraging nymphs killed them? Or had the slaughter resulted from something else?

"Answer me, damn it!" DeCosta demanded shrilly. "I know you can hear me!"

DeCosta was distracting, so Santana killed the input, as he brought his binos up and inched them from left to right. There was nothing to see at first, other than corrugated metal, but then he spotted them. Half-hidden within the shadow cast by the feeder's conical roof was an array of spotlights, vid cams, and some sort of weapons! Which made sense if the bugs wanted to observe what the nymphs were up to and keep indigenous animals from getting their food. The platoon leader reactivated his radio to discover that DeCosta was in mid-rant. ". . . or I will know the reason *why*! Over."

"This is Alpha Six," Santana said softly. "We ran into a Ramanthian feeding station—complete with cameras and a computer-controlled weapons system. That means we've got to backtrack and go around it. Out."

Even DeCosta could understand that, so there was no reply, which the platoon leader chose to interpret as a win. But Hargo wasn't so easily satisfied. He took each of DeCosta's diatribes *personally*—and continued to fume.

Having backtracked more than a mile and successfully circled around the Ramanthian feeding station, the first platoon continued toward the north and a reunion with the rest of Team Zebra. The much-awaited linkup took place at about 1500 hours, which left them about five hours of daylight.

DeCosta, who was clearly eager to get going, chose to position himself near the head of the column just behind the team on point. The decision spoke to his personal courage since both he and his T-2 would almost certainly be in the thick of things were the company to be ambushed.

In the meantime Santana found himself in the drag position, which made tactical sense, but might be by way of a punishment as well. But whatever the reason for the assignment, the platoon leader took his duties seriously, which meant Snyder had to as well, even if that required extra effort. Because rather than simply walk backwards every once in a while, and scan the back trail with her sensors, the officer ordered the T-2 to leave the trail periodically, hunker down, and wait to see if anyone was following. And not just following, but lagging so far back, as to initially fall outside of sensor range. Which seemed unlikely at best—and forced Snyder to jog in order to catch up with column.

Consistent with Snyder's expectations the first five attempts produced negative results. But then, just as the legionnaire was beginning to resent the process, something registered on the cyborg's sensors. And not just *one* something, but a parade of heat signatures, all coming up the trail. The targets weren't large enough to qualify as Ramanthian troopers, plus they had a tendency to advance in a series of fits and starts, but the presence of so many unidentified life-forms was unsettling, nevertheless. Especially if the targets were Ramanthian nymphs.

So Snyder told Santana, who ordered her back onto the trail, and relayed the information to DeCosta. And rather than pooh-pooh the report the way the platoon leader half expected him to, the major even went so far as to offer up a grudging, "Well done." Followed by a brusque, "Keep an eye on the buggers." Which Santana did.

Darkness fell earlier on the forest floor than up above the canopy. So, when the column came across some vine-covered ruins, DeCosta called a halt while there was still enough light to work by. Lieutenant Farnsworth's platoon was ordered to establish a defensive perimeter around the stone structure. That left the first platoon to set up camp, which required them to clear obstructing vegetation, establish firing positions, and seal off the steep stairwell that led underground.

Santana monitored the work by walking around. He paused every now and then to offer words of encouragement, but generally let his noncoms make decisions, knowing it was important to build confidence in their leadership.

Eventually the work was done. And just in time, too, as the sun sank in the west, and six small fires were lit inside the embrace of the ancient walls. They threw shadows onto the carefully fitted stones, but none were positioned to silhouette the legionnaires or reveal too much to prying eyes.

DeCosta was sitting in a corner, reading a holy book by means of the lights built into his helmet, and Farnsworth had the first watch. That meant Santana had the small fire all to himself as he consumed his rations. "So," a voice said, as servos *whined*. "We meet again."

The officer turned to find that Watkins was standing next to him. Having been ejected from the ship immediately after DeCosta, the civilian and his T-2 landed within half a mile of the major, and had been with the officer ever since. Santana gestured to the space next to him. "Pull up a chair. . . ."

"I'm sorry about all of DeCosta's bullshit," the media specialist said, as he lowered himself to the ground and crossed his legs. "You've been very patient."

Santana was surprised by both the tone of the comment and its source. "Really? No offense, sir. . . . But it was my impression that two of you were pretty tight."

Even though his plastiflesh face was less responsive to

emotion than skin-covered muscle would have been—there was no denying the look of disgust on the cyborg's face. "I can certainly understand how you came to that conclusion," the civilian allowed. "But no, the truth is that I met DeCosta just two hours prior to boarding, and have come to like the man less with each passing day. His attitude toward cyborgs is nothing less than appalling."

Rather than agree with Watkins, which would have been disloyal, the cavalry officer chose a less risky path as he bit into a fruit bar. "If you don't mind my asking, why *did* you come along?"

Watkins smiled thinly. "Well, that depends on whom you ask. . . . Assistant Undersecretary Wilmot would tell you that I'm here to document the mission. Because if you and your legionnaires succeed, then she wants the credit to accrue to Jakov. And, if you fail, she wants evidence that an attempt was made."

The fruit bar was woefully dry, and Santana chased the first bite with a mouthful of water from his canteen before wiping his mouth with a sleeve. "No offense, sir. . . . But if we fail, the odds are that you're going to wind up dead, along with the rest of us."

The cyborg chuckled. "That's true. Which is why the *Solar Eclipse* dropped some message torps into orbit before she left. I upload everything I have twice a day. And if I fail to do so, the torps will return to Algeron on their own."

"So," Santana said, as flames began to lick around his empty MSMRE box. "That's how the assistant undersecretary would account for your presence here. . . . But how would *you* explain it?"

Watkins gave the officer a sidelong look. "You don't miss much, do you? No wonder General Booly chose you to command the mission. Well, as it happens, I *do* have a personal reason for coming along. One I hope you will keep to yourself."

Santana shrugged. "Sure. . . . So long as it won't compromise the mission or endanger my troops."

"It won't," the cyborg assured him. "It's a family matter actually. . . . One that goes back about five years. It all started when my sister Marci fell in love with a total bastard named Maximillian Tragg, then ran off with him. He was a Confederacy marshal back then—and charged with enforcing the law.

"But, marshals don't make much money," Watkins continued harshly. "Or not enough to satisfy a man like Tragg. Especially given the fact that he liked to gamble. First he lost *his* money, then Marci's, and finally the house my parents gave them.

"My sister begged him to quit," the cyborg said wearily, "but he wouldn't or couldn't. So Marci went to work in an effort to make ends meet. Meanwhile, Tragg continued to gamble—and wound up owing a lot of money to the combine.

"But the mob was understanding, *very* understanding, so long as my brother-in-law was a marshal. But that came to an end when he was arrested for a long list of crimes and placed in jail. But not for long because Marci put up the money required to bail him out in the naïve belief that he would change his ways.

"Well, the combine came a-calling shortly after that," Watkins added sadly. "Looking for the money Tragg owed them."

The civilian paused at that point, as if finding it difficult to continue, and Santana was about to break the conversation off when the other man raised a hand. "No, I want you to hear this. With no money to give them, and no badge to protect him, Tragg gave the mob the only asset he had left. My sister. Marci was pretty you see," Watkins said bitterly, as he stared into the fire. "*Very* pretty. And there are people who will pay large sums of money to use, abuse, and destroy beautiful women.

"So my brother-in-law listened to Marci's screams as they took her away, packed a suitcase, and ran. I followed. It took six standard months, and all the money I had, but I found the bastard on Long Jump.

Watkins shook his head sorrowfully. "It was foolish, I know that now, but I wanted to kill Tragg with my own hands. However, I was a journalist, and he was an ex–law enforcement officer, which put me at something of a disadvantage. All of which is a long-winded way of saying that Tragg won the fight and left what remained of my body in an alley. Which, in case you wondered, is how I wound up as a cyborg.

"But he didn't escape untouched. . . . Oh, no he didn't!" Watkins said with obvious satisfaction. "The fight took place in the repair shop where he was working at the time. And having otherwise been disarmed, I grabbed a blowtorch. The flames burned his face so deeply that no amount of reconstructive surgery is going to make the bastard look normal again. And that's why I'm here," the cyborg added, as he turned toward Santana. "Because Tragg's face was among those that Oliver Batkin recorded and sent to Algeron. Except he isn't one of the prisoners. He's guarding them! For the bugs! If you can believe that. The fact that I was working for the government, and in a position to hear about the mission was providence, or random chance. It makes no difference."

Santana looked into the other man's eyes. They weren't real, not like flesh and blood, yet the pain was clear to see. "So, you came here to kill him?"

"Exactly," Watkins confirmed grimly. "Only this time I plan to do the job right."

"And your sister?"

"Never heard from again."

"I'm sorry," Santana responded sincerely. "I really am. But why tell me about all of this?"

The cyborg looked down into the fire and back up

again. "Because," he said finally, "none of us know how things will turn out. Maybe I'll survive—and maybe I won't. But if I die, and *you* make it through, promise me you'll kill him."

It was a bizarre request, and all things considered, one that Santana knew he should refuse. But such was the other man's passion, and the extent of his pain, that the officer relented. "You have my word."

13

Blood is the price of victory.

—Carl von Clausewitz
On War
Standard year 1832

PLANET JERICHO, THE RAMANTHIAN EMPIRE

It was raining, and had been on and off for two days, as a succession of weak storm fronts crossed over Camp Enterprise. President Marcott Nankool and FSO Christine Vanderveen sat side by side as they ate their noon meal and looked out over the muddy compound. "So," the chief executive said listlessly, "what's *your* guess as to what that thing it is?"

Vanderveen knew the "thing" Nankool referred to was the raised platform and thatched roof that was gradually taking shape under Tragg's watchful eye. Because now that phase one of the space elevator project had been completed, the renegade was living dirtside again. Like everyone else in the camp, the diplomat had considered Nankool's question before but had been unable to come up with a believable answer. Still, thinking about "the thing" was better than thinking about the metallic taste she couldn't seem to get rid of, the persistent ringing in her ears, or the fact that she hadn't had a period in more than a month. Symptoms that troubled her, but were nothing compared to what some of her fellow prisoners suffered, as a persistent lack of vitamin B caused their limbs to swell up. They were easy to spot because of the way they shuffled along. Which, since it was similar to way the Ramanthians moved, had become known as "bug walking." "It beats me," Vanderveen answered finally. "But whatever that thing is, I doubt we're going to like it."

The words proved to be prophetic the next morning when the rain stopped, the sun reappeared, and Vanderveen left her barracks for breakfast. The monitor hummed ominously as it swept in to hover in front of her. The computer-generated voice was flat and inflectionless. "Are you prisoner Trevane?"

The diplomat had been using the dead officer's name for so long by that time that she didn't have to think before answering. "Yes, I am."

"Please follow me," the robot said, as it turned and began to move away.

Vanderveen frowned. "Please?" She couldn't remember an occasion when the word had been spoken by either Tragg or one of his mechanical minions. A dozen POWs watched sympathetically as the young woman was forced to follow the monitor out toward the center of the gently steaming compound. Because they knew that attention, *any* kind of attention, was almost always bad.

Meanwhile, Vanderveen felt something cold gather in the pit of her stomach as she was led toward the mysterious platform. It was finished now, or that's the way it appeared, and a table plus two chairs had been placed under the pitched roof. Maximillian Tragg was seated off to the right, and judging from the smirk on the mercenary's badly scarred face, he was pleased with himself. "Come on up," Tragg said conversationally, as the diplomat paused in front of a short flight of stairs. "I've been waiting for you."

An invitation from Tragg was equivalent to an order— so the FSO had no choice but to make her way up onto the platform. Once there, Vanderveen realized that the table was covered with white linen and set with silver. If she hadn't known better, the diplomat might have thought she was about to join her parents for a meal on the veranda. "Please," Tragg said, as he gestured toward the empty chair. "Have a seat."

Since there hadn't been any direct one-on-one contact with the overseer since the day Dent had been killed, Vanderveen assumed Tragg had lost interest in her. Now he was using the P-word and inviting her to sit down. There had to be a reason. . . . But what was it?

"Please. . . ." Tragg reiterated. "Have a seat. Breakfast will be along in a moment."

So being unsure of what was taking place, and hoping to forestall one of the murderous episodes Tragg was famous for, Vanderveen sat down, an act witnessed by POWs far and wide. Many of whom continued to spoon their morning mush into their mouths as they watched the tableau unfold. "Good," Tragg said approvingly, as Vanderveen took the chair across from him. "It's been a while since that chunk of metal nearly took your head off. A lot has been accomplished since then."

That was true. Because by turning her head only slightly Vanderveen could see the lower end of the silvery comma that hung over the camp. "Yes," she said levelly. "And a lot of people have died."

"That's one of the things I like about you," Tragg replied indulgently. "Besides your tits that is. You have the guts to speak your mind. Even if that is somewhat stupid at times."

The largely one-sided conversation was interrupted as a pair of heavily burdened POWs arrived carrying trays. Both were so starved they looked like walking skeletons as they placed heaping plates of hot food in front of the diners. The sight and smell of the feast caused Vanderveen's stomach to growl. Even though she knew one of the men, he refused to meet her eyes.

"There," Tragg said, as the servers left. "All of it was frozen, I admit that, but it beats the hell out of the crap that *you* eat every morning! Dig in!"

Vanderveen swallowed the flood of saliva that had entered her mouth and kept her hands in her lap. "No."

One of Tragg's nonexistent eyebrows rose a notch. "Why not?"

"Forcing me to have breakfast with you is a trick," the diplomat stated. "A device that's intended to drive a wedge between me and the rest of the prisoners."

"That's very astute," Tragg observed. "But it's more than that. Have you seen yourself lately? No, I don't suppose you have. Take a look in the mirror."

For the first time Vanderveen realized that a small mirror lay on the table next to her place setting. Eating the food was wrong, but looking at herself in a mirror seemed harmless enough, so she did so. And what the diplomat saw came as a shock. Her previously blonde hair was almost white having been bleached by weeks of tropical sun. Her eyes were still blue but stared back at her from cavernlike sockets.

Tragg saw the horror in her eyes and nodded. "That's right. You look like hell. Not quite as bad as I do, but close enough! Which brings me back to what I was saying before. Eat the food, drink the juice, and take the vitamins on your plate. You'll feel better within a week. Especially since I plan to have you over for breakfast, lunch, and dinner. Then, in a month or so, you'll be worth looking at again."

There was a *clatter* as the mirror fell, and Vanderveen stood. "No!" she said angrily. "I won't do it!"

"Oh, but I think you will," Tragg responded grimly, as he reached for the rifle that was leaning against the rail.

"Go ahead," Vanderveen said defiantly. "Shoot me! It's what you wanted to do from the very start."

"Thanks, but no thanks," the overseer replied dryly, as he worked a shell into the weapon's chamber. At that point

Tragg brought the long gun up in one swift motion, tucked the butt in against his shoulder, and selected a target.

Vanderveen shouted, "No!" but the sound of her voice was lost in the flat *crack* of the rifle, and the echoes that followed. The bullet flew straight and true, plucked a marine off his rag-wrapped feet, and dumped him on his face. Everyone saw it, and given the way Vanderveen was standing there, it looked as though she was spotting for Tragg. Even Nankool sat stunned as the diplomat took her seat at what was already rumored to be a feast.

But, strangely enough, it was Calisco who came to Vanderveen's defense. "I know what you're thinking," the skinny little official put in. "But that's bullshit. She's stronger than either one of us." Nankool wanted to believe that, he really did, but found it difficult to do.

PLANET ALGERON, THE CONFEDERACY OF SENTIENT BEINGS

There were only two sentries posted outside of General Booly's quarters, and because it was their job to protect the Military Chief of Staff from deranged soldiers and the possibility of Naa assassins, they had no reason to expect trouble from a squad of marines. Especially given the fact that the jarheads were not only under the command of a hard-faced captain, but marched up the corridor as if on parade and came to a crashing halt. The fact that one of the marines was armed with a sledgehammer should have triggered suspicions, but it wasn't until the soldiers leveled their weapons at the legionnaires that the sentries understood the true nature of the situation.

One of the legionnaires opened his mouth, as if to speak into his lip mike, and took a rifle butt to the head. A marine caught the unconscious body before it could hit the floor. The second sentry surrendered his weapon without protest.

Booly was asleep when the sledgehammer hit the front

door and a resounding *boom* echoed through his dreams. But, having no reason to expect a break-in, it wasn't until the *third* blow that the officer sat up and started to turn toward the pistol on the nightstand. But it was too late because the marines had entered the apartment by then. "Drop it," the marine officer said, as Booly's fingers closed around the grip. "Or die in bed."

Booly took note of both the command and the officer's failure to use the honorific "sir," and knew what was taking place. Maylo was sitting up by then with a sheet clutched to her otherwise-naked breasts. "Bill? What's going on?" Her voice was tight but level.

"I think it's called a coup d'etat," the legionnaire replied, as he put the weapon down. "Isn't that right, Captain?"

But the marine wasn't about to be drawn into a conversation. A corporal confiscated the general's weapon as the officer pointed his pistol at Maylo. "Get up. . . . And keep your hands where I can see them."

Booly struggled to control his temper. "There's a closet over there. . . . Perhaps one of your men would be kind enough to get my wife's robe."

The marine's eyes narrowed as the pistol came back to Booly. "Shut up! I won't tell you again. Now, both of you, get off that bed. Or die right there. . . . It makes no difference to me."

Both Maylo and Booly could see that the officer wasn't bluffing, which forced them to stand, something the male marines thoroughly enjoyed. Because although Booly was clad in a pair of boxer shorts, Maylo was completely naked. Her breasts were small, but firm, with brown nipples. Creamy skin led down to a narrow waist, flared hips, and long shapely legs. And rather than attempt to hide her private parts, the business executive held her hands out away from her body. "So, Captain," she said. "Are you looking for weapons? Or just *looking*?"

The captain blushed, ordered a female marine to help

Maylo get dressed, and turned his attention back to Booly. "Clasp your hands behind your head and turn around."

Booly had no choice but to comply. The marine gave a snort of disgust when he saw the ridge of silvery fur that ran down the senior officer's spine. Evidence of a coupling that some saw as unnatural but many scientists pointed to as evidence that humans and Naa had common forerunner ancestors. "So what they say is true," the marine said disgustedly. "You *are* a half-breed freak. And in command of our armed forces, too. Well, President Jakov will soon put a stop to that! Let's find some civilian clothes for you to wear—since you have no right to a uniform."

A feeling of anticipation pervaded the executive dining room as a mix of civilians and military officers stood waiting for the moment that all of them knew was coming. The long dining table had been pushed over against one wall—and a single chair stood on the riser at the south end of the room as the crowd awaited Vice President Leo Jakov.

Assistant Undersecretary for Foreign Affairs, soon to be Secretary of Foreign Affairs Kay Wilmot, was extremely tired. And she had every right to be since the vast majority of the administrative work associated with what she preferred to call "the succession" had fallen to her. But as Jakov entered the room and took his place on the throne-like chair, it was worth it. Because even though ex-ambassador Alway Orno had been assassinated *before* he could arrange for Nankool to be killed, she felt confident that the new strategy would not only work, but work brilliantly. Especially given the fact that a rescue mission *had* been sent to Jericho, thereby proving Jakov's sincerity, even though he was about to assume the presidency.

Yes, there was the possibility that the rescue mission would find Nankool alive, but the battle group that was supposed to extract Team Zebra had been "diverted" to help with a very real threat elsewhere. Which meant no one would arrive to pick them up! So the succession plan was secure. Or would be once certain troublemakers had been dealt with.

There was a stir at the back of the room as more than two dozen hooded figures were escorted into the room. All wore cuffs and leg shackles, which in the case of the Hudathan prisoners, had been *doubled* to make sure they couldn't break free. And, judging from the black eyes, cut lips, and swollen faces that were revealed as the hoods were removed, it quickly became apparent that many of the former officials and officers had put up a fight. The purpose of the hoods was to prevent people in the halls and corridors from recognizing the prisoners. Especially General Booly, who, because of his popularity with the troops, was especially dangerous. Later, after a carefully worded indictment had been released, officers recruited by Jakov would take over.

Among those being herded into the room were General Bill Booly, his wife Maylo Chien-Chu, Colonel Kitty Kirby, Major Drik Seeba-Ka, Intelligence Chief Margaret Xanith, Ramanthian expert Yuro Osavi, diplomat Charles Vanderveen and a dozen more Nankool loyalists. All of whom looked grim and defiant. One individual was missing, however, and given his history, was a cause for concern. But even though Sergi Chien-Chu was still on the loose, Wilmot felt certain the marines would find the industrialist and bring him in.

Fortunately, from Wilmot's point of view, Triad Hiween Doma-Sa was off-planet. Because the Hudathan was not only a close ally of Nankool's, but a head of state as well, he couldn't be neutralized in the same fashion as the others could.

So it was a special moment. One that Jakov had been looking forward to and was determined to enjoy. That was why the group had been brought before him. Not because there was any real need to do so—but to revel in his newly acquired power. "Good morning," the vice president said, as the last of the prisoners was revealed.

The greeting elicited snickers and even outright laughter from the sycophants, toadies, and other self-serving individuals who supported Jakov. All of them fell silent as the executive raised his hand. His eyes glittered as they roamed the room. "The Confederacy is at war, the president has been missing for months, and our citizens deserve strong leadership. With those factors in mind, and consistent with my responsibilities under the constitution, I will take over as interim Chief Executive as of 1300 hours this afternoon. The Senate has been notified to expect an announcement, as have the press, and I have every reason to expect a quick confirmation. Once that process has been completed my administration will take immediate steps to resolve the unfortunate conflict with the Ramanthians."

"The president is *alive*," Booly said grimly, as his eyes roamed the faces in front of him. "And all of you know it. . . . You're traitors, nothing more, and you'll never get away with it."

"*Really?*" Jakov inquired sarcastically. "Rather than attack the legally constituted government, I suggest that you, your wife, and the cadre of scum you've been plotting with begin to think about how to defend yourselves against charges of criminal conspiracy and treason. Who knows?" the politician asked rhetorically. "Perhaps some of the criminals in the pit can offer you some advice. Especially the ones *you* sent there!"

That elicited another round of jeers and laughter as the hoods were replaced for the long roundabout journey down to the pit. But as Booly waited for the cloth to come down over his eyes, he made a mental photograph of each face in front of him and sealed the images away. Because somehow, someday, they were going to pay.

* * *

The normally raucous prison, also known as "the pit," was extremely quiet. And for good reason. Because while the prisoners weren't in the political loop, they were hypersensitive to even the smallest change in prison routine. So when all their normal guards were suddenly "reassigned," and replaced by marines brought in from off-planet, they knew something important was afoot—something very important indeed. So when orders were shouted, gates *clanged* open, and a new contingent of hooded prisoners shuffled into the space between the clifflike cellblocks they paid attention. The females were separated out and led away as the men were freed from their restraints.

Chains rattled as shackles were removed, and cuffs clanged as they were tossed into a cleaning bucket before the heavily armed guards backed out of the pit. That was when the newly inducted prison rats were free to remove their hoods and look around. There was a long moment of silence while both groups regarded the other followed by a loud comment from one of the lowest tiers. "Well, I'll be damned," a grizzled legionnaire commented loudly. "If it isn't General Bill Booly. . . . Come to lead us on the march into hell!"

What happened next left the newly appointed warden dumbfounded. Because rather than turn on the general, as she had been led to believe they would, the prisoners shouted a greeting instead. It consisted of a single word. A word so loud it made the windows in her office rattle as she looked down into the concrete canyon.

"CAMERONE!"

PLANET JERICHO, THE RAMANTHIAN EMPIRE

Stars glittered above, but down on the jungle floor it was as black as the inside of a combat boot, and the cyborgs were the only ones who could truly "see" the growing host of nymphs as they generated an almost deafening chittering noise, caused the foliage to rustle as if in response to a windstorm, and filled the air with the acrid scent of their urine. The resulting tension was sufficient to make even the most-combat-hardened veteran sweat.

Like all the rest of the bio bods, Santana was wearing his helmet, which not only served to protect his head, but provided access to the ITC and served to amplify the ambient light. But there wasn't much light to amplify, which meant the legionnaire saw little more than green streaks as the adolescent Ramanthians dashed back and forth outside the stone walls. The team had flares, of course, but their effectiveness was limited by the forest canopy, which meant the company would have to use jury-rigged spotlights once the fighting began.

Which was why every single legionnaire was at his or her post as Major DeCosta made his rounds. And, except for the senior officer's tendency to reinforce his orders with scriptural references, Santana had to admit that DeCosta had done a good job of preparing the company for combat. Each corner of the roughly rectangular space was protected by a well-entrenched RAV and a T-2. The rest of the cyborgs were evenly spaced along the perimeter, and interspersed with bio bods, who stood on improvised firing steps so they could fire over the walls. All of which should make for an impenetrable curtain of fire once the nymphs attacked.

That was DeCosta's plan, anyway, and it would have worked if the nymphs hadn't found their way into the labyrinth of passageways below Team Zebra and boiled up out of the ground *inside* the defensive perimeter. The stairway had been blocked, but not well enough, as the madly chittering mob managed to force its way through the opening. Watkins, who hadn't been given a place on the firing line, was the first to notice the incursion. "Watch out!" the civilian shouted, as the first bugs appeared. "They're inside the wall!"

But the warning generated a smaller response than the media specialist expected, because the aliens located *outside* of the enclosure chose that moment to attack as well, thereby forcing the defenders to respond to them at the same time. Flares shot upwards, collided with the canopy, and went off. Some of them remained there, trapped in the foliage, and others drifted down under tiny parachutes. Battle lights came on, and the fifties began to *thump* as what looked like a tidal wave of sharp beaks, chitinous bodies, and fluttering wings surged toward the walls. Each slug killed at least half a dozen Ramanthians as bolts of coherent energy plowed bloody furrows through the oncoming horde. The chatter of assault weapons and submachine guns was interspersed with the occasional *crack* of a grenade as hundreds of attackers fell.

A legionnaire yelled, "Take that, you bastards!" as he emptied a clip into the mob and fumbled for another. But even as the oncoming wave faltered, the defenders were attacked from within. Sergeant Jan Obama screamed as two nymphs landed on her back. Body armor protected her from the first few bites, but a third found her throat and ripped it out. Blood sprayed the surrounding area as Private Dimitri Bozakov turned to spray both the dead legionnaire *and* the Ramanthians with steel-jacketed bullets.

But before the troopers on the wall had time to fully engage the enemies behind them, *another* wave of nymphs surged out of the jungle and into the harsh light. DeCosta was busy. So that left Watkins, Santana, and Farnsworth to deal with the steady stream of Ramanthians that continued to pour up out of the passageways below. Not an easy task since a poorly aimed shot could kill one of the legionnaires beyond. "Put your backs to the walls and keep them contained!" Santana shouted, as he fired a burst from his CA-10. The tricentennials seemed to fly apart as the bullets shattered their exoskeletons and threw sheets of viscous goo in every direction.

Watkins had armed himself with a pump-style shotgun that turned out to be an effective weapon for the situation at hand. Because every time the civilian pulled the trigger at least one bug exploded. Until the media specialist ran out of shells that is—and was forced to back away as he fumbled more into the receiver.

Fortunately, Farnsworth was there to take up the slack with an ugly-looking submachine gun. Having come up through the ranks, the officer had seen just about everything during his years in the Legion and wasn't about to be intimidated by a thousand baby bugs. He fired his weapon in carefully modulated three-round bursts, a pace calculated to keep the barrel cool and conserve ammunition. The Ramanthians chittered as they charged the veteran, driven by hunger, and a wild inarticulate hatred of everything not them.

But the well-aimed bursts cut the attackers down, and continued to do so, until Santana managed to toss a couple of grenades into the stairwell. The platoon leader yelled, "Fire in the hole!" and went facedown, as twin explosions strobed the night. The blast decimated the bugs fighting their way up through the narrow passageway as Watkins began to fire his newly reloaded shotgun at the invaders still on the surface.

Snyder had been detached to assist them by that time and Santana was quick to call upon the cyborg's enormous strength. "Grab some rocks!" the officer ordered. "And toss them in the hole!" The rocks that Santana referred to had once been part of the structure itself, but the combined forces of heat and cold had loosened them over time, and caused one of the internal wing-walls to fail. So as the bio bods began to fire into the blood-splattered stairwell, Snyder threw blocks of stone into the opening, thereby crushing some of the nymphs and blocking others. It took more than five minutes of hard work, but once the exit was sealed, Santana felt satisfied that the bugs wouldn't be able to break through. But just to make sure, the platoon leader ordered Watkins to guard the exit before heading for the wall and the battle beyond.

A hellish sight greeted his eyes as Santana stepped up onto an ammo container and looked out onto the south side of the body-strewn clearing. As one flare burned out, and thereby allowed darkness to claim the outermost reaches of the killing field, another was launched. There was a soft *pop* as it went off and threw a garish glow over the scene below. The battle lamps added their own cold white glare to the nightmarish scene as still *another* wave of alien flesh swept in toward the walled compound. It wasn't so easy to advance now that the Ramanthians had to climb up and over piles of their dead and wounded comrades. But each succeeding wave went a little farther—until they began to break only yards from the walls.

And as Santana added his fire to all the rest, the officer wondered what drove the nymphs. Was it hunger? Yes, that much seemed clear, based on the evidence observed earlier. But the mindless, suicidal rush, seemed indicative of something else as well. It was as if the tricentennial bodies had grown faster than the minds they housed and were under the influence of some very primitive instincts. A wilding intended to sweep everything that could compete with them away—thereby creating conditions in which the survivors could flourish. It was a violent process that had no doubt devastated Hive during past birthings and clearly accounted for the Ramanthian desire to acquire more real estate. Later, within a month or two, Santana suspected that the locustlike behavior would end, thereby giving the adult bugs an opportunity to round up their feral progeny and install them in crèche-style facilities where they could be raised.

But all such considerations were driven out of Santana's mind as Corporal Diachi Sato screamed, and a nymph tore his throat out. "It came from above!" DeCosta shouted into his mike. "First platoon, maintain fire. . . . Second platoon, switch to air defense. . . . Execute!"

Because the platoons had been integrated, the order made sense, as roughly half of Team Zebra's considerable fire-power was directed upwards. And none too soon. Because as Santana released an empty clip and seated another one in the CA-10, at least a hundred tricentennials dropped onto the legionnaires from above! *All* Ramanthians had wings, the officer knew that, but rarely flew. Of course that applied to adults, and judging from the ominous *whir*, the nymphs were under no such constraints.

Why the nymphs had waited to take to the air was a mystery, but one that the legionnaire had no time to contemplate as he shot an incoming bug and turned just in time to pull another off Darby's back. The nymph struggled in an attempt to free itself, and snapped at Santana's face, as the soldier threw the juvenile down. There was a horrible *cracking* sound, followed by a squeal of pain as the officer stomped the Ramanthian.

"Well done," DeCosta said matter-of-factly as he strolled past, pistol in hand. "Smite them down, for you are the hammer of God!"

The senior officer paused at that point, raised his pistol, and shot the nymph that was trying to find a way into Nacky's armored head.

But Santana was back in the battle by that time and felt a wave of heat wash across the left side of his face as a T-2 named Prill fired the flamethrower that that been installed in place of his energy cannon. The weapon sent a flare of light across the compound, and the tongue of fire caught two bugs in midair. They screeched piteously as their wings caught fire but were soon put out of their misery by well-aimed bursts of fire from Farnsworth's SMG.

All of the T-2s were out of machine-gun ammo by that time. As were the RAVs, because even though more ammo was available, the bio bods didn't have time to load it.

That meant the cyborgs had to rely on their energy cannons and in some cases flamethrowers to defend the compound. But the jets of liquid fire, combined with accurate shooting on the part of the bio bods, proved to be an effective combination. So effective, that after twenty minutes of sustained fighting, the nymphs' assault began to falter. Sensing victory, DeCosta was quick to follow up. "Send the Godless heathens to hell!" he shouted hoarsely. "Loose the Lord's fury upon them! For thou art the angels of heaven sent to cleanse this polluted planet!"

Though surprised to hear that they had been elevated to the status of angels, the criminals under DeCosta's command understood what the officer wanted, and increased their rate of fire. Muzzle flashes stabbed the darkness, grenades sent gouts of jungle loam and body parts high into the air, and there was an occasional *whir* of wings as Santana patrolled the perimeter. The air was thick with the stench of nitrocellulose, ozone, and burned flesh. The combined odor caught in the back of the officer's throat and caused him to gag as he paused to deal with a wounded nymph. The nameless tricentennial was pinned under the legionnaire's helmet light, desperately trying to drag itself forward, when Santana pointed the CA-10 at the creature's head. And it was then, in the fraction of a second between the order he sent to his index finger, and the recoil of the weapon, that something jumped the gap between them.

Because while the hatchling wasn't truly sentient yet, the potential was there, and in that brief moment prior to the nymph's death Santana thought he had a glimpse into the Ramanthian's soul. A place so unfathomable that the human knew he would never understand it. But then the nymph was dead, the moment was over, and what had been a hellish symphony of chittering bugs, madly whirring wings, and rattling machine guns began to die down until there was little more than an occasional rifle shot to punctuate the end of the bloody conflict. "They're leaving," one of the T-2s said out loud, as her sensors started to clear.

"Thank God for that," DeCosta put in gratefully. And no one chose to contradict him.

Hot metal pinged, a breeze ruffled the jungle foliage, and it began to rain. The battle was over.

Raindrops drummed against his alloy casing, and his jury-rigged propulsion system had a tendency to cut out every once in a while, but Oliver Batkin was happy for the first time in months. Partly due to his recent escape from Camp Enterprise, but mostly because his reports had been received, and a rescue party was on the ground!

The good news had arrived a few days earlier when the same freighter that dropped Team Zebra into the atmosphere sent out a millisecond-long blip of code. It hit Batkin like a bolt out of the blue and elicited a whoop of joy so loud that it scared a flock of blue flits out of an adjacent tree.

Now, having traveled day and night ever since, the cyborg had entered the area where the rescue party should be. An exciting prospect, but a dangerous one, given the fact that the legionnaires would be understandably paranoid and therefore likely to shoot anything that moved, including spherical cyborgs should one appear without warning.

So Batkin ran a full-spectrum sweep as he weaved his way through the treetops and was eventually rewarded by a burst of scrambled conversation on a frequency often used by the Legion for short-range communications. That was sufficient to bring the spy ball to a temporary halt while he sought to make contact. "Jericho One to Team Zebra. Do you read me? Over."

There was a long pause, as if the legionnaires hadn't

heard him, or were busy deciding how to respond. Then, after about twenty seconds, there was a challenge. "This is Zebra Six. . . . We read you, Jericho One. Please authenticate."

So Batkin rattled off a nine-digit code, which was soon answered in kind, thereby satisfying both parties that security was intact. With that out of the way, the spy was able to make visual contact with the rescue team within a matter of minutes. And the much-contested battlefield was a sight to see. Due to the effects of sustained gunfire, energy weapons, and flamethrowers the partially blackened clearing was larger than it originally had been. And there, within the eye of what had obviously been a storm, was a walled enclosure. Which, judging from the way that waves of dead nymphs lapped up against it, had been extremely hard-pressed. Thanks largely to the fact that he didn't smell or look like food, the spy ball had been able to avoid the roaming packs of tricentennials thus far, but it had seen what they could do to native species. And it wasn't pretty.

All of the legionnaires who weren't standing sentry duty around the clearing looked upwards as the cyborg swept in to hover at the center of an excited crowd. There were cheers from the troops, but rather than the warm welcome the cyborg expected to receive, the officer who came forward to meet him was cold and matter-of-fact. The way he always was where cyborgs were concerned. "So," DeCosta began, "what can you tell me about President Nankool? Is he alive?"

Though taken aback by the way the bio bod had addressed him, Batkin managed to maintain his composure. "And you are?"

"DeCosta," the officer answered impatiently. "*Major* DeCosta. I'm in command here."

"And my name is Batkin," the agent replied calmly.

"Welcome to Jericho. I'm glad you're here. The answer to your question is yes. President Nankool *is* alive. Or was when I escaped from Camp Enterprise."

The next few minutes were spent bringing DeCosta and his officers up to speed regarding Nankool, the POWs generally, and the camp itself. "I have pictures of everything," Batkin finished proudly. "Plus detailed information regarding defenses, Ramanthian troop strength, and daily work routines."

"That's wonderful!" Santana commented enthusiastically. "What you managed to accomplish is nothing short of amazing."

"Yes. . . . Well done," DeCosta added tepidly. "Tonight we will go over that material in detail. In the meantime, we have a schedule to keep. . . . So, if Captain Santana, and Lieutenant Farnsworth would be so kind as to pull the pickets in, we'll get under way. And, if you would be willing to serve as scout, then so much the better. There's nothing like a bird's-eye view of the terrain ahead to keep one out of trouble."

Santana waited until the other officers were out of earshot before addressing the cyborg. "I'm sorry about the reception. Believe me. . . . We are *extremely* happy to see you! And, should I be fortunate enough to survive this mission, I will do everything in my power to ensure that you are recognized for what you accomplished here."

Batkin would have shrugged had he been able to. "That isn't necessary. . . . But thank you."

"Can I ask a question?" Santana wanted to know. "About one of the prisoners?"

"Of course," the spy responded cautiously. "Remembering that I had contact with only a small number of the POWs."

"Yes, I understand," Santana agreed. "The person I have in mind is female, about the same age I am, and blond. Her name is Christine Vanderveen—and she's a diplomat.

She was a member of Nankool's staff when the *Gladiator* was captured. So, if the *president* survived, then she might have as well."

Santana felt a sense of dread as the cyborg reviewed the faces and the names of the POWs with whom he was familiar. The answer, when it finally came, was more than a little disappointing. "I met a blond," the cyborg allowed. "But her last name was Trevane, and she was a naval officer rather than a diplomat. A lieutenant if I remember correctly. I'm sorry."

Santana nodded mutely and turned away. Only years of military discipline, plus a strong will, were sufficient to keep what the officer felt inside as he took his place on Snyder's back and the march began. As the column made its way out of the body-strewn clearing and topped the rise beyond, they passed three graves. Obvious now, but soon to be lost, as had thousands of others over the years. Santana offered the legionnaires a salute as he passed, wondered where Vanderveen was buried, and gave thanks for the face shield that hid his tears.

14

PLANET HIVE, THE RAMANTHIAN EMPIRE

The Queen was dying. *She* knew it, her courtiers knew it, and all but the most ignorant of Ramanthian citizens knew it. Because, ironically enough, death was the price each tricentennial queen had to pay for the creation of so many new lives. It was a bittersweet process that systematically destroyed their much-abused bodies and a reality the current monarch had accepted years earlier. Not only accepted, but *planned* for, by doing everything possible to prepare her successor for the throne.

And now, being only weeks away from the day when the last egg would be ceremoniously laid, the Queen was still in the process of imparting all of the knowledge gained during an active lifetime to the female generally known as "the chosen," a seemingly low-ranking servant who had been brought in from off-planet and integrated into the royal staff many months earlier. A position that provided the chosen with an intimate knowledge of the way the royal household worked and gave her access to the lies, plots, and counterplots that continuously swirled around the Queen. Something that was going to come as a shock to individuals who had been rude to the chosen. "So," the monarch said solicitously, as she looked down at her successor. "Are you ready?"

"Yes, Highness," the chosen replied humbly. And she *was* ready. Unlike her five billion newborn cousins, the Queen-to-be had come into the world twenty years earlier the same way most Ramanthians did. Then, having been selected at the age of five, she and six other candidates had been raised to fill a position only one of them could actually hold.

"Good," the monarch said soberly. "Give me your opinion of Chief Chancellor Itnor Ubatha."

The younger female looked up. Her eyes were like obsidian. "He's very proactive," the chosen observed thoughtfully. "Which is good. But he's extremely ambitious as well, and would turn the monarch into little more than a megaphone through which to speak, if allowed to do so."

"I can see that I chose well," the Queen replied contentedly. "So, knowing Ubatha as you do, make use of him but be careful. Because when a tool works, and works well, there is a natural tendency to reach for it first regardless of the circumstances. And that is Ubatha's strategy. So identify other advisors, place them in powerful positions, and thereby balance him out. Am I clear?"

"You are, Majesty," the younger female replied as her eyes returned to the floor.

"Then enter the cloister and continue to learn."

The chosen bent a knee, backed away, and shuffled over to a corner where a curtained enclosure allowed her to observe all that took place *without* revealing her identity. It was a tradition that went back thousands of years and signaled the upcoming transition.

Meanwhile, in a waiting room normally reserved for those of lesser rank, Ubatha shuffled back and forth across the chamber while deep in thought. Because while any royal audience was stressful, he knew this one would be even more so, due to the fact that the chosen would be present. There was no way to know which of the seven eligible females had been selected, but the Chancellor hoped that the Queen had chosen well. Not only for his well-being but that of the Ramanthian people as well. Because even though the war was going well, it would take a strong pincer to guide the empire through the next few years. The Ramanthian's contemplations were interrupted as a midlevel functionary entered the room. "Chancellor Ubatha? The Queen will receive you now."

The official clacked his right pincer by way of an acknowledgment, checked to ensure that both his antenna and wings were positioned just so, and left the waiting area for the ramp that led up to the royal platform. All manner of courtiers, officials, and military officers had emerged from their various lairs to take up positions on the platforms adjacent to the walkway. Ubatha exchanged greetings with the more-senior members of the royal entourage as the rich amalgamation of odors associated with the Queen and the egg-laying process came into contact with his olfactory antennae and triggered the usual chemical changes.

Having gained the top level, Ubatha saw the brand-new enclosure off to his right, and decided to risk the Queen's displeasure by nodding in that direction. A gesture intended to convey acceptance and respect. Then, having turned toward the monarch, he bent a knee. "I'm not dead *yet*," the Queen said tartly.

"Nor will you ever be," Ubatha replied smoothly. "Since you live within our hearts."

That elicited the Ramanthian equivalent of laughter, since the royal didn't believe a word of it, but admired the way it had been done. "You are absolutely shameless," the Queen observed indulgently. "But useful nevertheless."

Ubatha bowed. "Majesty."

"So," the monarch said, "it seems that congratulations are in order. . . . I understand you located ex-ambassador Orno and put him to death."

"Thank you, Majesty," Ubatha replied humbly. "But the credit for the execution belongs to your chief of intelligence rather than myself."

Meanwhile, still hidden within her fabric-draped enclosure, the chosen took note. Another one of the things that made Ubatha different from so many of the empire's officials was his willingness to form alliances and then honor them. It was a strategy cunningly devised to make him more effective *and* reduce the amount of blame that would otherwise come his way when an initiative went awry. All of which would be taken into consideration when the Chancellor went to work for *her*.

"Yes," the Queen replied. "My intelligence service deserves both credit for terminating the ambassador—and some of the blame for allowing the Egg Orno to live. The agent responsible for that failure has been assigned to a research station on an ice planet."

"As he should be," Ubatha replied sanctimoniously. What was the chosen thinking, he wondered? And would she be as challenging to deal with as her predecessor? *Yes,* he decided. *The royal clan breeds true.*

"But that's a minor detail," the monarch continued dismissively. "My intelligence chief offered to take care of the oversight personally, but I told him no. Having lost both mates and narrowly escaped death herself, the Egg Orno has suffered enough."

"You are known for your mercifulness," Ubatha intoned, and momentarily wondered if he had pushed it too far. But because the Queen truly *believed* she was merciful, the flattery slid past *her* if not the chosen one.

"But you didn't come here to discuss the Ornos," the monarch said, as she gave birth to another fifty citizens.

"No, Highness. I didn't," Ubatha agreed. The Confederacy put out an announcement, a rather interesting announcement, that was relayed to me by the Thraki ambassador."

"An ugly breed," the Queen observed distastefully. "But I digress. What is that pack of degenerates up to now?" Both the monarch and the chosen listened intently as Ubatha relayed the news regarding Nankool's disappearance and Jakov's elevation to the presidency.

"What do we know about this Jakov person?" the Queen wanted to know, as the narrative came to a close.

"We know he's ruthless," Ubatha observed. "Since he made the announcement in spite of the possibility that Nankool is alive. Details regarding Jakov's background will be included in your mid-morning intelligence briefing."

"Good," the monarch replied. "Perhaps *this* human will prove to be more reasonable than his predecessor was."

That was a given insofar as the chosen was concerned. Because she had been careful to memorize *all* the information available regarding Nankool's staff—and was pretty sure that Jakov would make significant concessions for a peace that left him in charge of the Confederacy. A promising development indeed.

"And Nankool?" the Queen inquired. "*Is* he among the prisoners?"

"I don't know yet, Majesty," Ubatha replied honestly. "But I will certainly find out."

PLANET JERICHO, THE RAMANTHIAN EMPIRE

Thanks to the repellers that kept it aloft, the Ramanthian scout car could travel more slowly than a conventional aircraft could, giving the insectoid troopers plenty of time in which to inspect the verdant jungle below. And that was what they were doing as the air car drifted over the treetops.

Thanks to advance notice from both Batkin and the T-2s, Team Zebra had been given plenty of warning before the scout car arrived. Enough to hide themselves under a thick layer of foliage, activate all of their countermeasures, and suspend use of their radios. That strategy that had proven effective *three* times over the last few days.

As the insistent thrumming noise generated by the scout car increased, and the downdraft from the Ramanthian repellers caused the treetops to thrash about, Santana and the rest of the legionnaires peered upwards. They hoped to escape notice one more time but feared they wouldn't. And for good reason since it was clear from Batkin's electronic intercepts that the bugs knew some sort of incursion had taken place.

How didn't really matter, although there was the distinct possibility that the battle with the nymphs had been visible from space or that one of their patrols had stumbled across the body-strewn clearing. And, had the Ramanthian military presence on Jericho been larger, it was almost certain the team would have been interdicted by that time. But since there weren't all that many soldiers on the ground, and those present had their pincers full guarding both civilian *and* military POWs, the aliens had been unable to bring a sufficient amount of bug-power to bear on the problem. Up until that point anyway.

As if working in concert with Santana's thoughts, the scout car paused almost directly above the hidden legionnaires and hovered, as if the Ramanthian troopers had seen something suspicious. If they had, and tried to report it, Batkin would "hear" and order the T-2s to fire. The scout car and its occupants would almost certainly be destroyed. But, rather than improve, conditions would almost certainly become worse. Because when the scout car failed to return, even *more* units would be sent to the area, and the team would soon be located. So everything was at stake as the enemy vehicle hung like a sword over the legionnaires' heads.

But just when Santana feared that discovery was imminent, the engine noise increased, and the vehicle slid toward the north. No one moved. . . . And it was a good thing, too. Because the Ramanthians returned four minutes later. The scout car thrummed softly as it passed over them a hundred feet higher than before. *They're looking to see if anyone or anything went into motion after they left,* Santana thought to himself. *The bastards.*

The team was forced to remain where it was for another hour before DeCosta felt it was safe to proceed. Precious time was lost, but the team had gone undetected. Fortunately, the rest of the afternoon was relatively uneventful. The company was able to make fairly good time since they had Batkin to scout the area ahead and guide them around obstacles.

Finally, as the sun started to set, Batkin led the team out into a shallow lake. It was the *same* lake the Confederacy POWs had been forced to cross on their way to Camp Enterprise. And it was then, as they passed through a grove of frothy-topped trees and entered the oily-looking water, that everyone got a good look at the space elevator hanging above them. The structure was very nearly pink at the moment, and incredibly beautiful, as it hung suspended halfway between day and night.

A line of poles led them out to the island at the center of the lake. It was the same spot where the POWs had camped for the night—and Cassidy had subsequently been roasted over a fire. Camping on a trail utilized by the Ramanthians clearly entailed some risk, but Batkin theorized that the marauding nymphs wouldn't want to get wet, and DeCosta was willing to try it.

But rather than camp outside, as the POWs had, the major insisted that the entire team spend the night *inside* the half-buried building, where they were less likely to be detected from the air. The mazelike interior was a mess— so work was required to make a section habitable. It was dark by the time carefully screened fires were lit, battle lamps came on, and the evening routine began.

The second squad of the second platoon had guard duty. That left the rest of the legionnaires free to choose a section of floor to sleep on and prepare a communal meal, a brew made more flavorful by the addition of nonissue sauces and spicy condiments.

Then, once the meal had been eaten, and the legionnaires' mess kits had been washed in the lake, it was time for the so-called foot patrol, which was when Kia Darby, who doubled as a medic, went from person to person and inspected their feet. A none-too-pleasant chore, but an important one for any group of soldiers, including those who rode war forms all day. Because in spite of that advantage, the bio bods *still* had blisters caused by the continuous up-and-down movement natural to riding a T-2. And most of them had a fungus known as J-rot (Jericho rot), which was resistant to every medication Darby could bring to bear— except for the strange goo that Sergeant Ibo-Da conjured up from his Hudathan-style med kit.

It was different for the cyborgs however, who had no need for sleep sacks, improvised meals, *or* Darby's rough-and-ready medical care. They *did* require maintenance, however, and lots of it, which meant that once cybertechs Toolman and Bozakov had been checked by Darby, they went to work making whatever adjustments and repairs they could. The process normally consumed at least a couple of hours. Then, once *that* task was done, it was time for the weary technicians to work on the RAVs. Which was why neither legionnaire had to stand guard duty.

Meanwhile, as the troops took care of routine matters, DeCosta was holding an impromptu strategy session in one of the boxlike rooms. The ostensible purpose of the get-together was to formulate a plan that would carry them from their present location to Camp Enterprise. But the truth was that DeCosta already knew how he wanted to proceed, and was primarily interested in getting the other officers to concur, a pro forma agreement that would help cover his ass if anything went wrong. "The crux of the matter is *this*," the little officer said earnestly, as the light from a small fire lit his dark jowls from below. "The T-2s have been valuable up to this point, I concede that, but the tactical situation is about to change. The cyborgs generate heat, which in spite of their shielding, can be detected by Class III scanners like the ones we can expect to encounter at Camp Enterprise."

Meanwhile, what none of the officers knew was that legionnaire Jas Hargo was standing on the other side of the wall, listening to every word through a small crack. Listening, and becoming increasingly angry, as the strategy session continued.

"It's a possibility," Santana allowed politely. "But if Class III scanners were present, you would think the bugs would have nailed Batkin *before* he crossed the fence. Or later when he was inside the camp. Maybe we should ask him to join us."

"You can't be serious," DeCosta replied incredulously. "I mean think about what you're saying man. . . . He's one of *them*."

"By which you mean cyborgs," Farnsworth put in.

"Yes, or course I do!" the major replied irritably. "Don't be thick, Lieutenant. Now, where was I? Oh, yes, the final approach. . . . Stealth will be everything, surely you can see that, which means that ten-foot-tall electromechanical freaks will be a liability."

Upon hearing himself described as a "freak," it was all Hargo could do to prevent himself from putting an enormous shoulder to the wall and knocking it down on top of DeCosta. But that would be stupid because the serial killer had no desire to return to the pit.

"Stealth *will* be important," Santana allowed, as he met the other officer's eyes. "But so will firepower. And that's where the T-2s come in. Once we close with the camp, we'll be up against a well-dug-in, numerically superior force. You've seen the pictures Batkin took. Without the cyborgs, we'll never penetrate the fence."

DeCosta was angry by then, and it showed. "You have a negative attitude, Captain. A *very* negative attitude. Something I will make clear in my after-action report."

"You do that," Santana replied grimly. "And be sure to include the following. . . . I formally protest your plan as being both unprofessional *and* contrary to the traditions of the Legion, since it's clear that you intend to abandon part of your command on an enemy-held planet."

"That's absurd!" DeCosta responded hotly. "Once we enter the camp, and I assure you we will, the cyborgs will come forward to join us."

"Maybe," Farnsworth allowed cautiously. "But what if there isn't enough time for that to occur? Or the bugs pin them down? The pickup ships aren't likely to wait."

"All of us are expendable," DeCosta replied darkly. "Even your precious freaks. And that brings this meeting to a close. Good evening, gentlemen. I'll see you tomorrow."

Servos whined, and a gigantic fist opened and closed in the room next door, as Santana and Farnsworth got up to leave. The ancient building was quiet after that, until morning came, and it was time for muster. The plan was to cross the rest of the lake *before* sunrise. That would take a while, especially since the bio bods were not only going to travel on foot but carry heavy packs as well.

There was a sizable entry hall on the west side of the building, and that's where Santana was, adjusting the straps on his pack, when Farnsworth entered from outside. What light there was came from their helmets. "Excuse me, sir," the veteran platoon leader said. "But we have a problem."

Santana frowned. "A problem? What sort of problem?"

"It's Major DeCosta, sir," the other officer answered deliberately. "We can't find him."

Santana stood. "You searched the island?"

"Twice, sir. The last person to see the major was Sergeant Gomez. That was about two in the morning when the major made his rounds."

Santana was silent for a moment. When he spoke, his voice was bleak. "Was Private Hargo on sentry duty at that time?"

Farnsworth nodded slowly. "Yes, sir. He reports to Gomez. So, you think Hargo had something to do with the major's disappearance?"

"It's a possibility," Santana said thoughtfully. "But I wouldn't want to put the theory forward without proof. Jericho is a dangerous place. All sorts of things could have happened. Let's search the island one more time—and send Batkin up for a look-see. Even though it's dark, the major's heat signature should be visible assuming he's alive."

"Sir, yes, sir," Farnsworth replied hesitantly. "And if he isn't? Or we can't find him? Are the cyborgs going to remain here or come with us?"

"They're coming with us," Santana said grimly. "We're going to need them. And there's no way I'm leaving anybody behind."

"Yes, sir!" Farnsworth replied cheerfully, and did a neat about-face.

Santana heard the whine of servos and turned to find Snyder looming over him. His helmet light wobbled up to her immobile face. "Is what they say true, sir? Does the major plan to leave us here?"

"I believe that was the major's intent," the platoon leader replied honestly. "But he's missing. So, unless he turns up soon, I will be in command."

"And you wouldn't leave us, would you, sir?" the cyborg asked uncertainly.

"Are you kidding?" Santana demanded. "I'd have to walk! And you know how I feel about infantry regiments."

Snyder made a deep rumbling sound that Santana

knew to be laughter. And, because all of the T-2s could communicate with each other by radio, the rest of the cyborgs were aware of the XO's comments within a matter of minutes.

Jas Hargo couldn't smile. The cyborg simply wasn't capable of doing so. But he felt a tremendous sense of satisfaction when the final word came down ten minutes later. DeCosta was missing, Santana had assumed command, and the bio bods were going to mount up.

The entire outfit was under way ten minutes later, minus Major Hal DeCosta that is, who lay about fifteen feet offshore with a 150-pound block of stone on his chest. His head, which had been torn off, rested fifty feet farther out. There were witnesses, of course, but none of them were sentient, or could ever be called upon to testify. They *were* hungry however—and eager to eat their fill.

PLANET ALGERON, THE CONFEDERACY OF SENTIENT BEINGS

Winter was almost over, so half of the underground storeroom was empty and would remain so until more bags of flour arrived in the fall. That meant there was plenty of space in which to have a meeting one level below the floor where the bakery's ancient ovens continued to produce bread for the citizens of Naa town.

With a single exception, all of those present in the room were Naa, and therefore uniformly suspicious of the blond man who sat below a dangling glow rod, his hands on his knees. His name was Sergi Chien-Chu, and while decidedly male, didn't really think of himself as human anymore. Not since his brain had been removed from his dying body and installed in the first of what would eventually become a succession of cybernetic vehicles. The latest of which had been fashioned to resemble that of a twenty-five-year-old human male. "So, human," the baker growled. "The entire council is here. Just as you requested.

Now tell me why we shouldn't remove your head—and turn it in for the one-million-credit reward that the government is offering?"

"Because doing so would be messy," Chien-Chu replied calmly. "Not to mention the fact that I'm still using it."

Though town dwellers now, most of the council had been warriors once, and chuckled appreciatively. Although he was alone, and unarmed, the human wasn't afraid. Or, if he was, had the ability to hide it. A truly Naa-like quality and one they admired. "But, more to the point," the businessman continued, "I'm here because the *Confederacy* needs your help. President Nankool is alive, but being held by the Ramanthians, who don't know they have him. By announcing that fact, Jakov may cause the president's death, or provide the bugs with leverage they wouldn't otherwise have, thereby threatening the Confederacy. And I believe that *you* have the power to stop it."

"Surely you jest," the local undertaker put in cynically. He had craggy features and black fur interspersed with streaks of white. His clothes were dark—and his boots were caked with mud. "President Nankool . . . President Jakov . . . It hardly matters to us. Back before the Confederacy came into existence, we were oppressed by the human empire. Now that the Confederacy exists, we are *still* oppressed. Nothing has changed."

"That isn't true," Chien-Chu responded simply, and pointed up toward the glow rod that dangled above him. "Where does the power for that light come from? What about the medical care the townspeople receive? And the money in your pockets? All of them flow from the Confederacy. Is it perfect? Hell no, and I should know, because I helped create it."

There was a buzz of conversation as the dozen or so council members consulted with each other before a candlemaker named Nightwork Waxman stood. He had tan fur with white tips, and a pair of bifocals were perched on the end of his nose. "You are *President* Chien-Chu?"

"I *was* president," the businessman admitted. "But that was a long time ago."

"I met you once," the candlemaker said. "We shook hands. But you look different now."

"My brain is the same," Chien-Chu responded. "But the body is new. You could think of it as the civilian equivalent of a T-2."

"All of which amounts to nothing," the undertaker grumbled. "Who cares what was? It's what *is* that counts."

"And I couldn't agree more," Chien-Chu said as he eyed the faces around him. "So let's talk about what *is*. The Naa people have their own government now, with Senator Nodoubt Truespeak to speak for them, and a future that looks bright. But only if people like Jakov can be prevented from hijacking the duly elected government. And that's what he's trying to do."

"But *how*?" the butcher wanted to know. He was a burly male still clad in the bloodstained apron he'd been wearing when summoned. "We were told that there were checks and balances to prevent anyone from taking over."

"And there are," the cyborg agreed patiently. "And the system would have worked, except that Jakov had all of the people who might oppose him arrested and placed in the pit. General Bill Booly among them."

That announcement caused quite a stir, because every one of them knew that General Booly's grandmother had been Naa, and that he had always been sympathetic to their people. Furthermore, the locals knew Booly was married to Chien-Chu's niece, the female credited with saving Senator Truespeak's life not long before. All of which played into the complicated system of clan ties, blood debts, and deed-bonds that held Naa society together. So, now that Booly was in the mix, the already lively discussion grew even *more* heated, which forced Chien-Chu to sit and wait.

But the billionaire was a patient man and, because of the many capabilities built into his electromechanical body, could pursue other activities while the debate raged. One of which was to monitor the squad-level radio traffic generated by the off-planet marines assigned to track him down. The jarheads who weren't familiar with Algeron, or the Naa people, which was why no one other than a few juveniles would agree to speak with them. Not that Jakov and Wilmot had much choice where troops were concerned, since Booly was popular with his legionnaires, who were already starting to grow restive.

Chien-Chu's thoughts were interrupted as the baker spoke. "The council agrees that there is truth in what you say. But what would you have us do? The fort has withstood countless attacks."

"I agree," the cyborg answered. "An attack on Fort Camerone *would* be pointless. "No, the *real* opportunity is to recruit some ex-legionnaires and smuggle them inside. Once within the walls, they will go down to the pit and free General Booly. It's my opinion that both the prisoners *and* the Legion will support him. Jakov will be forced to plead his case in the Senate, and once all of the facts are made known to them, I believe the senators will make the right decision."

"But *how*?" the baker asked for the second time. "How will we get the ex-legionnaires inside the fort?"

"That's a good question," Chien-Chu answered, as he transferred his gaze from the baker to the undertaker. "Tell me, Citizen Deepdig, how many bodies do you remove from the fort each day?"

The Naa frowned. "Three or four on average . . . Mostly from the hospital."

"And once the bodies have been buried, what happens next?"

"My number two son takes replacement coffins back inside," Deepdig answered. "They are custom-made to Legion specifications and . . ."

The undertaker paused at that point, his face lit up with understanding, and the council member smiled. "You are clever human—I'll say that for you."

The rest of the council chuckled, food was summoned, and the *real* work began.

15

THE THRAKI PLANET STARFALL (PREVIOUSLY ZYNIG-47)

The Thrakies were an industrious people, and during the relatively short period of time they had been in control of Starfall, entire cities had been constructed. Cities in which most Thrakies chose to live after spending generations on tightly packed ark ships. But some of the more adventurous citizens had begun to construct vacation homes in the surrounding countryside. A trend Ex-ambassador Alway Orno had taken advantage of by renting a small house, which subsequent to his death, the Egg Orno was forced to live in.

Though pleasant by Thraki standards, it was terribly isolated, located mostly above ground, and uncomfortable. Everywhere the Egg Orno looked she saw angles instead of curves, stairs where ramps should have been, and ceilings that were far too low. In fact it was only in the basement, where Alway's presence could still be felt, that the female felt halfway comfortable.

It was a large room, which the ex-ambassador had apparently prepared with her comfort in mind and clearly preferred himself. As the Ramanthian prepared to sort through her mate's belongings, she was still in the process of recovering from the gunshot wound and ensuing surgery. The fact that she had survived the process was something of a miracle given the fact that the Thraki surgeons weren't all that familiar with Ramanthian physiology. But, thanks to self-programming nano injected into the wound, she continued to recover.

Of course, Alway deserved most of the credit for saving her life. By placing his body in front of hers, the functionary had absorbed most of the bullet's force. The female remembered the shock of the impact, a moment of free fall, and a profound darkness that rose to wrap her in its arms. All of which led the assassins to believe that she was dead.

But the Egg Orno *wasn't* dead, even though at first she wished she was and contemplated suicide immediately after the operation. But as time passed, her mood changed. It had been stupid to believe that she could escape Hive undetected. The aristocrat knew that now. Both Chancellor Ubatha and the Queen had been determined to find Alway and kill him. With that realization came a deep and abiding anger. And a desire for revenge.

But *how*? The Egg Orno was not only ill, but without friends and vulnerable to a second assassination attempt. Because even though Alway was dead, there was no way to know how vindictive the Queen would be. That didn't matter, though, not anymore, which was why the female was determined to go through her mate's belongings no matter how painful the process might be. Because if the ex-diplomat had left anything useful behind, it was likely to be there among his personal effects.

The next couple of hours were spent going through Alway's computer files plus piles of printed documents. It seemed like a meaningless mishmash of material at first, until the Egg Orno came across a handwritten note that referred to ". . . the first payment from the Confederacy," plus a Thraki bank statement dated the next day, and a variety of other documents related to a rim world occupied by Ramanthian expatriates. Was that where Alway planned to take her? Yes, it seemed likely.

But the discoveries raised as many questions as they answered. Why would the Confederacy give money to her mate, the same individual who had caused them such grief? There had to be a reason. A good reason. And, if "the first payment" had been received, then where was the second? Or the third? Those questions and more plagued the Ramanthian as she worked to knit all of the available facts into a coherent pattern. Unfortunately, she had very little to show for it once the process was over. So the Egg Orno went back and reviewed all the files for a *second* time just in case something important had escaped her. But to no avail.

That left the aristocrat with nothing to do but rummage through her mate's clothes in case something of value had been left in one of his voluminous pockets. But *that* search came up empty as well. So the female was busy refolding the garments when one of them caught her interest. The robe consisted of a rich shimmery cloth, which if she remembered correctly, was actually a photosensitive fabric. The ex-ambassador was not only proud of the device—but had demonstrated it for her on more than occasion.

The Egg Orno felt a tingle of anticipation as she searched for the ribbonlike connector. What images, if any, were stored in the robe she wondered? A boring meeting most likely. But even if she couldn't see Alway, she'd be able to *hear* him.

Once the Egg Orno located the lead, she plugged it into the computer and pinched a series of budlike keys. Dozens of images appeared, but that was normal for anyone with compound eyes, and the Ramanthian found herself looking at a human being. A female, if she wasn't mistaken—and an ugly one at that. Though not as fluent as her mate had been, the Egg Orno spoke serviceable standard, which enabled her to follow the conversation without difficulty. "My name is Kay Wilmot," the alien said. "I am the assistant undersecretary for foreign affairs reporting to Vice President Jakov. The pleasure is mutual."

The Ramanthian felt a sudden surge of excitement. Alway had met with a high-ranking Confederacy official! Could this be *it*? What she'd been looking for? The aristocrat watched intently as the alien revealed that President Nankool had been captured and was being held on Jericho. It was valuable information. Or so it seemed to the Egg Orno. But what to do with it? Alway would have known what to do. She felt sure of that. But he was gone.

However, rather than sit and worry at the problem, there was something more pressing the female had to take care of. And that was her mate's funeral, a sad affair scheduled for the following morning. Where, if the Queen's assassins wanted to finish her, they would have the perfect opportunity.

But when the next day dawned clear and bright, and two of Alway's Thraki friends joined the Egg Orno in front of the funeral pyre she had commissioned, she was the only Ramanthian present. So as the flames rose to enfold the carefully wrapped body, there was no one other than her to extol the dead diplomat's virtues or list his many accomplishments. A sudden wind took hold of the smoke along with her words and carried them east. A good omen according to Ramanthian traditions—but of no comfort to the bereaved widow.

Once the ceremony was over, and the fire had burned itself out, the Egg Orno shuffled down the gentle slope toward the car she had hired. A Thraki was present to see her off. He had light brown fur, beady eyes, and prominent ears. "The ambassador didn't receive much mail," the official explained, as he offered her an envelope. "But what there was came through me. That's an invitation to a reception at the Drac embassy. I know because I received one, too. Rumor has it that Triad Hiween Doma-Sa will attend."

The Egg Orno felt something clutch at her stomach. "The Hudathan?"

"Why, yes," the Thraki replied mildly. "Do you know him?"

"We never met," the Ramanthian replied bleakly. "But I know *of* him. . . . He fought a duel with my *other* mate and killed him."

The official looked crestfallen. "I'm terribly sorry," he mumbled contritely. "I was unaware of the connection, and I—"

"There's no need to apologize," the Egg Orno interrupted. "I would like to meet Triad Hiween Doma-Sa. Can I attend in Alway's place?"

The Thraki swallowed uncomfortably. "Er, yes, I guess so. . . ."

"Good," the Ramanthian replied. "I'll see you there."

PLANET JERICHO, THE RAMANTHIAN EMPIRE

Thousands of eyes peered up into the azure blue sky as the specially equipped air car towed the free end of the space elevator south, toward the point where it would be captured by the ground crew and reeled into the forerunner ruins. Then, if all went well, the superstrong cable would be secured to the huge shackle-style fitting that had been installed there. And if things *didn't* go well, then there would be hell to pay since both Commandant Mutuu and the War Mutuu had turned out to witness the historic moment from the comfort of a shaded pavilion and were unlikely to be very forgiving.

That added to the pressure Tragg felt as he and his slaves waited for the tubby air car to tow the 23,560-mile-long cable into position. From where the renegade stood, the whole thing looked like some sort of magic trick because of the way the space elevator hung seemingly unsupported under the vast canopy of blue sky.

But it *was* supported by the dreadnaught *Imperator*, which orbited high above. So the only problem was a variable wind, which presently sought to push the cable to the east, even as the air car fought to pull the shiny thread south.

And it should have worked, *would* have worked, except for one thing: The air car was not designed to function as a tug. So as the wind blew, and the operator began to use more power, the engine started to overheat, something the pilot became aware of as an audible alarm went off and a wisp of black smoke issued from the vehicle. Given all of the countervailing stresses involved, the Ramanthian knew that he had a minute, maybe less, in which to complete his mission.

"Drop the dragline!" the operator ordered, and felt a sense of relief as the troopers directly behind him wrestled a huge coil of rope up and over the side. The car bobbed in response, but because it was connected to the space elevator, couldn't go far.

Tragg shaded his eyes as he looked upwards. A steady stream of smoke was pouring out of the air car by then, and the overseer felt a sudden stab of fear as the dragline fell toward the ground. Because the POWs were supposed to grab on to the line, and gain control of it *before* the space tether was released, but none of them were close enough to do so.

Meanwhile, as the engine began to cut in and out, the wind disappeared. That caused the air car to veer toward the west and the air strip. The pilot tried to compensate, but couldn't overcome the tug's inertia and gave the only order he could. "Release the cable!"

One of the crew members had been waiting for that

very order and jerked a lever. The effect was to let the long, thin cable fall free of the air car. Because the dragline was connected to the free-swinging space elevator, it flew across the surface of the airstrip like a three-hundred-foot-long whip.

Tragg screamed, "Catch it!" But the words came too late, as the dragline cut two Ramanthian troopers in half and went straight for the pavilion where Mutuu and his mate were up on their feet. The regally attired commandant hurled an invective at the pilot as the War Mutuu threw him down. And just in time, too, as the whiplike rope severed the pavilion's roof supports and brought the entire structure crashing down around them.

Thanks to the fact that most of the dragline's kinetic energy had been expended, it was transformed from a whip into an elusive snake that slithered back and forth across the tarmac as if determined to escape into the jungle. The POWs, led by an infuriated Tragg, were in hot pursuit by then. But most of the prisoners were in such poor condition that they couldn't run fast enough to catch up. Christine Vanderveen was one of the few exceptions. Not because the FSO was inherently stronger than the rest—but because of the extra food Tragg had forced her to eat.

But none of that was on Vanderveen's mind as she led the chase across the airstrip in an effort to capture the rope as quickly as possible and prevent reprisals. However, some of the other prisoners saw the situation differently, like the sailor who intentionally tripped the diplomat in hopes that the runaway space elevator would destroy itself.

Nankool and the rest of the LG knew better, however, because in spite of the fact that the drag-rope was elusive, it was only a matter of time before the Ramanthians brought it under control with or without help from the prisoners. So as a bruised Vanderveen picked herself up, Commander Schell yelled at the POWs to "secure that goddamned line!"

And, when the wind in the upper atmosphere shifted slightly, they were finally able to do so as a couple of POWs pounced on it. Then, as more bodies piled on, the rope gradually came under control.

But the task wouldn't be over until the errant cable was safely shackled deep inside the forerunner ruins. Vanderveen was among those who began to pull the dragline across the tarmac toward a similar length of rope that led down into the ruins where it was attached to a winch. So once the two lengths of rope were joined, it was possible for the POWs to let go, while Tragg issued orders via a handheld radio.

Vanderveen saw the dragline jerk as the winch came on, and Tragg gave the POWs new orders. "It will take some time to remove all the slack," the overseer informed them. "That's when the cable eye will come down—and the winch crew will need your help to secure it. So haul your asses over there and get to work. And that includes *you*, sweet cheeks."

The last was directed at Vanderveen, and when combined with a conspiratorial wink, was sufficient to reinforce the notion that the two of them had a special relationship. The tactic had proven to be wickedly effective at driving a wedge between the diplomat and her peers in spite of efforts by people like Calisco to counter Tragg's manipulations.

The result was a series of supposedly accidental bumps, guttural insults, and thinly veiled threats as the group of six raggedy POWs jogged toward the ruins. There was nothing Vanderveen could do but ignore the comments and keep her distance from the other prisoners as they entered the passageway that led back into what had originally been a steep pyramid. The top had been removed so that the space elevator could be anchored deep within—a laborious process that required weeks of hard labor and cost more than a dozen lives.

The cable eye was already in sight by the time Vanderveen and her companions entered the anchor chamber. There was a loud whining noise as the last fifty feet of dragline wound itself onto the drum, accompanied by a nearly deafening *clatter*, as a dozen metal pawls passed over the huge ratchet wheel positioned to secure the space cable once the correct amount of tension was applied. A decision that would be made by the Ramanthian engineer assigned to supervise the process. And, lest the prisoners attempt to interfere, five heavily armed troopers were present as well.

"You!" the Ramanthian said, as he pointed at Vanderveen and her companions. "Lift the pin and prepare to push it home."

The "pin" was about six feet long and a half foot in diameter. And, thanks to the fact that the cylinder was made out of solid metal, it was heavy. So four prisoners were required to hoist the pin up off the floor and position one end next to the enormous shackle.

"Here it comes!" someone shouted, as the winch pulled the cable eye down through the hole above. That was the signal for a second team of POWs to rush forward and grab the fitting. But there was still plenty of slack in the space cable, so when a strong gust of wind hit the line two thousand feet above them, the eye jerked upwards and took two marines with it.

There was a horrible scream, followed by a bloody rain, as one of the men was crushed against the edge of the overhead opening. "Hold!" the Ramanthian ordered sternly, as the winch pulled the cable eye down into the anchor chamber for the second time. Vanderveen held her breath as the loop entered the open shackle and waited for the Ramanthian to say, "Now!" The diplomat helped her fellow POWs lift the heavy pin and push it through the holes. The metal cylinder slid smoothly through the holes on both sides of the shackle, thereby locking the space tether in place. Metal rattled as the cable tested the strength of its mooring, the POWs fell back, and the most important part of the space elevator was complete.

What the Ramanthian engineer *didn't* know was that the structure holding the shackle in place had been systematically weakened during the construction process, and while strong enough to do the job under normal circumstances, would come apart if subjected to excessive stress. Or that's what the POWs *hoped* would happen. But there was a lot of guesswork involved, so no one could be sure.

It was late afternoon by that time, so the prisoners were marched along the edge of the airstrip past the Ramanthian who had been in charge of the overheated air car. He was dead by then, having been hanged from a light standard as an example to the rest of the troops. One of Tragg's robotic monitors was waiting for Vanderveen as she entered the camp. The machine spoke loudly enough for everyone to hear. "Your dinner will be served in ten minutes, Lieutenant Trevane. . . . Master Tragg is waiting."

That was sufficient to earn the diplomat another barrage of verbal abuse from the rest of the prisoners. But to refuse would have been to sentence one of them to death. That left Vanderveen with no choice but to trudge across the compound to the gazebo, where the renegade sat waiting. "You're covered with blood," Tragg observed, as the young woman took her seat.

"Yes," Vanderveen said matter-of-factly, as she examined the brown blotches on her upper chest and her arms. "And so are you."

Tragg didn't like that, and his right hand strayed to a pistol. Vanderveen smiled thinly. "Go ahead," she suggested. "Pull that gun and shoot me."

The blond had said similar things before, and Tragg knew she meant it. The problem was that the naval officer had been pushed so far, and for so long, that she no longer feared death. In fact, judging from the look in Trevane's eyes, the young woman *wanted* to die. She still cared about those around her, however, and that provided the mercenary with the leverage he required. "Eat your food," the overseer said coldly. "Or would you like to see someone else die?"

So Vanderveen ate her food. And it tasted good, and her body wanted it, and that made her feel guilty. Tears had begun to flow, and were carving tracks through the grime on her cheeks, when a strange chittering sound was heard. The noise wasn't that noticeable at first, but soon grew louder, as the foliage beyond the electrified fence began to rustle.

Tragg was on his feet by then and reaching for his rifle, as the first nymphs emerged from the jungle. They were fairly large by that time, about the size of the average ten-year-old boy, and *very* hungry. Their cognitive functions had increased, too—as evidenced by the way some of them probed the fence with long sticks. That produced a shower of sparks, which sent most of the juveniles scurrying back into the jungle. But they returned a couple of minutes later—and more appeared with each passing second.

The chittering sound was *much* louder by then, loud enough to bring both Mutuus out of the headquarters building, as the acrid scent of nymph urine filled the air. The Ramanthians up in the towers aimed their machine guns down at the juveniles but were clearly reluctant to fire. Vanderveen had left the gazebo by then and noticed something that should have been obvious before. The top of the electrified fence angled *outwards*, meaning the Ramanthians were more concerned about external attacks than prisoner escapes! Which meant they *knew* the nymphs could be hostile.

No sooner had the thought occurred to the POW than a spear fell from the quickly darkening sky, struck a sergeant in the upper thorax, and shattered his chitin. The soldier fell without making a sound, and the chittering increased. That was enough for Commandant Mutuu, who screamed, "Fire!"

But even as the machine guns began to *chug*, and the *rattle* of automatic rifle fire was added to mix, a loud *cracking* sound was heard. The tree that the nymphs had chosen to fall was well back in the jungle. But it soon became evident that the very top of the forest giant was within range of the fence as the mass of foliage descended on the camp. There was a *crash*, accompanied by an explosion of sparks, as the tree trunk flattened a section of fence. Within a matter of seconds the nymphs had swarmed up onto the newly created bridge and were following it in toward the center of the compound. Grenades went off, and body parts were hurled high into the air, as the guns continued to cut the invaders down. But there were plenty more—and all of them were hungry for protein.

The prisoners had evacuated their barracks by then and were beginning to congregate at the center of the camp, when a flight of fifty well-thrown spears rained down on them. A sailor screamed as one of the incoming missiles drove her to the ground. Vanderveen went to the rating's aid but found there was nothing she or anyone else could do.

Within a matter of seconds *more* trees were falling, at least *half* of which missed the mark, but the result was to divide the Ramanthian machine-gun fire, which allowed dozens of nymphs to successfully enter the compound. Tragg and his Sheen robots were there to meet the *chittering* invaders. There was no way to know if the overseer was trying to defend himself or his Ramanthian employers, not that it made any difference.

But the nymphs could *fly*. And it wasn't long before dozens of airborne attackers landed on the towers, which forced the Ramanthians on the ground to fire up at them or risk having their machines guns turned on *themselves*.

Though not a military man, Nankool believed he knew

what would happen next as he appeared at Vanderveen's side. The president's heavily bearded face was gaunt, and his voice was urgent. "Mutuu is going to call in an airstrike on the camp! Tell everyone to take cover! Do it now!"

So Vanderveen, along with other members of the LG, did the best they could to urge those prisoners still out in the open to roll under buildings, take shelter in latrines, or hide in any other place that might provide protection from both the flying nymphs and the planes that were most likely on the way.

As the POWs scattered, each searching for his or her personal hole, the War Mutuu had taken to the field. Backed by two troopers armed with rifles, the warrior was standing in front of the main building, seemingly oblivious to the spears that fell around him. Light glinted off steel as his razor-sharp blade rose and fell. There was an audible *ka-ching* each time a head rolled, interspersed by rifle shots, as the soldiers kept flying nymphs at a distance.

But there was no further opportunity to observe the War Mutuu or anything else as a brace of ground-based aerospace fighters roared overhead and began their bloody work. Not with bombs, which would have destroyed *every-thing*, but with rockets and guns. Not just around the perimeter of Camp Enterprise alone, but along the edges of the airfield, where dozens of nymphs threatened to over-run the space elevator's anchor point.

Vanderveen went facedown in the dirt as one of the fighters made a gun run parallel to the south fence, and felt someone grab hold of her ankles. It wasn't until after the diplomat had been pulled in under the dubious protection of the admin building that she turned to discover that her rescuer was none other than Undersecretary of Defense Corley Calisco. He grinned. "Fancy meeting you here! You gotta give the bugs credit. . . . They certainly know how to keep the kids in line." The comment was punctuated by a series of explosions as one of the low-flying planes made a rocket run to the north, and the ground trembled in response.

The fight continued for another ten minutes, but came to its inevitable conclusion soon after that, as the surviving nymphs were driven back into the surrounding jungle. The fighters made one last pass, and upon getting the all clear, turned back toward the north. A heavy silence hung over the camp as the smoke started to clear. Then, as the POWs began to emerge from their various hiding places, the Ramanthians went out to gather their dead. And not just the adult soldiers but the juveniles as well. A *huge* task, given that the casualties lay in drifts, but one they carried out themselves, in spite of the fact that slave labor was available. Adding to the horror of the situation was the fact that while some of the nymphs were wounded, none showed any inclination to surrender, and snapped at anyone who attempted to aid them. Shots rang out as they were put down.

The Ramanthians didn't have tear ducts, so they couldn't cry, but there was no mistaking the feeling of intense sorrow that hung over the camp as the sun dipped below the western horizon, and huge funeral pyres began to take shape. Because nameless though the attackers were, each nymph was born of the Queen, and a citizen of the empire. So when morning came the fires would be lit, the half-grown bodies would be purified, and the smoke would carry more than a thousand spirits away.

But no matter how moving the process might be, Vanderveen knew she could never forgive the atrocities that the bugs had committed and watched clear-eyed as the Ramanthians harvested their dead. *You think that's bad?* the POW thought to herself. *Well, just wait. . . . I may not live to see it. . . . But there's more to come.*

Having completed the hike from the shallow lake to a point only two miles shy of Camp Enterprise, Santana and his company had gone into hiding. No easy thing to do where the ten-foot-tall cyborgs were concerned—and a task made even more difficult by the heat that radiated from their bodies.

But unlike his dead predecessor, Santana was a cavalry officer and therefore more knowledgeable regarding what the borgs could and couldn't do. He knew the T-2s could not only operate underwater, where their heat signatures would be concealed, but do so for days if necessary. So rather than hide them in the jungle, Santana followed a river down to a series of stair-stepped pools, where the cyborgs were ordered to submerge themselves. The officer knew that would be boring, but it would also be safe, and that had priority.

Having hidden the most formidable part of the team where aerial patrols were very unlikely to find it, Santana was free to turn his attention to Camp Enterprise. Thanks to what Oliver Batkin had accomplished earlier, the cavalry officer already had an excellent idea of how the compound was laid out. But time had passed since the cyborg's escape from the POW camp, which meant things could have changed. Not to mention the fact that Santana was hungry for the sort of tactical minutiae the government spy had no reason to collect. Like the location of drainage ditches, the exact disposition of the POWs, how many could walk, the precise number of Ramanthian troops inside the wire, the size of the quick-reaction force stationed at the airstrip, how many shuttles were parked on the tarmac, where the power core was located, the status of the space elevator project, and much, much more. All of which would have a bearing on the plan of attack.

In order to gather the necessary intelligence, Santana planned to send Batkin forward during the cover of darkness in the hope that the cyborg would be able to penetrate the camp's perimeter and collect useful information. Meanwhile, Noaim Shootstraight, Dimitri Bozakov, and Santana himself were to infiltrate the area with an eye to finding the best avenues of attack.

Farnsworth took exception to *that* part of the plan, suggesting it was foolish for the commanding officer take such risks, but his objections fell on deaf ears. Santana wanted to see the lay of the land with his own eyes, not just hear about it, so Farnsworth was left in command as the officer and his scouts disappeared into the jungle. All three were lightly dressed, carried a minimum amount of equipment, and wore green-and-black face paint.

It was midafternoon when they left the riverbank and entered the sun-dappled world of the forest. The first thing Santana noticed was the almost complete absence of the raucous jungle sounds he had grown used to. In their place was the sound of his own breathing, the steady *swish-swish* of his pant legs as they rubbed against each other, and the occasional *snap* of a dry twig. Was their presence responsible for the change? Or was something else at hand? Unfortunately, there was no way to tell as the scouting party continued to weave its way between spindly vine-wrapped tree trunks.

But as the threesome continued to advance, and paused every now and then to look and listen, Shootstraight became increasingly concerned. Because the legionnaire had an extremely acute sense of smell, and as a light breeze pushed its way in from the west, it brought something with it. A scent so faint the Naa wasn't sure what it was, until the *chittering* sound began. "Nymphs!" Shootstraight said urgently. "Quick! Climb that tree. . . . It's our only chance!"

In spite of the fact that nothing had registered on *his* senses Santana had a great deal of faith in the Naa and reacted accordingly. Though not an experienced tree-climber, the officer was in good shape, and there were plenty of footholds. Not to mention vines to pull on, which made the ascent easier and helped the legionnaires make their way up to the point where five branches shot out like spokes in a wheel. That created a natural place to stop as the first wave of nymphs passed below.

The officer half expected the juveniles to pause and look upwards. But judging from the way they moved, the juveniles had a specific destination in mind. Which, given the way they were headed, was the camp itself. That hypothesis proved accurate fifteen minutes later, when gunfire was heard, aerospace fighters roared over the treetops, and a series of ground attacks began. "Holy shit," Bozakov said feelingly. "The little buggers are attacking their own kind!"

"And being killed by them," Santana observed.

"What about the POWs?" Shootstraight wanted to know. "How will *they* fare?"

"They're inside the fence," the officer replied optimistically. "So that should offer some protection."

The Naa wasn't so sure, especially given the fact that the bugs could fly, but decided to keep his doubts to himself.

The sounds of battle died away eventually, the sun went down, and there was a loud rustling as hundreds of nymphs retreated through the forest below chittering as they went. That was very frightening, especially since the bio bods couldn't *see* and were so lightly armed. But while the juveniles were aware that protein things lived in the branches high above them, they also knew how elusive such creatures could be and made no attempt to scale the tree.

Once the rustling noise died away, and usual night sounds began to reassert themselves, the scouts returned to the ground. Then, with Shootstraight in the lead, they continued the journey north. It was impossible to get lost because the swath of destruction created by the nymph army was like a superhighway that led straight to Camp Enterprise. Which, understandably enough, was very well lit.

The lights were their cue to climb another tree and

scope the compound from above, which Santana did with assistance from a pair of powerful light-gathering binos. That was when the officer saw the way the fence had been breached, the crews working feverishly to repair it, and the less obvious activity beyond. But even with the illumination provided by the pole-mounted floodlights it was difficult to make out the fine details of what was going on, so there was very little Santana and the other scouts could do but get some rest before the sun rose.

It wasn't easy, but having tied himself in place with some light cord, the officer eventually fell asleep. There were dreams, lots of them, and one face haunted them all. But Vanderveen was dead, as were his hopes, and all of the futures that might have been.

Bozakov heard the officer mutter in his sleep and understood, because he had nightmares of his own, dreams so bad his squad mates had to wake him at times. But the bio bod knew it was important to let the officer rest. Because the entire team agreed that if there was any one individual who could get them off Jericho, that man was Captain Antonio Santana.

16

Wars are fought in many ways—and in many places.

—*Clone Ambassador Ishimoto-Seven*
Standard year 2840

THE THRAKI PLANET STARFALL (PREVIOUSLY ZYNIG-47)

The Drac embassy consisted of a ten-story-tall block of windowless concrete that seemed to crouch between the high-rise buildings that rose all around it. But though not especially interesting to look at, the structure's flat roof was the perfect place for VIPs to land and take off. And, given that Triad Hiween Doma-Sa qualified as such a person, his air car was immediately cleared for landing. There was a solid *thump* as Runwa Molo-Sa put the Hudathan-made vehicle down on the well-illuminated pad.

Heavily armed Drac security officers hurried forward to meet the Hudathan dignitary and his aide as they stepped out onto the surface of the flat roof. The Dracs wore head-to-toe black pressure suits. And, because their faces were obscured by breathing masks, it was almost impossible to tell them apart. Not that Doma-Sa wanted to become better acquainted with the treacherous breed. Though officially neutral, it was well-known that the Drac Axis was at least psychologically aligned with the Ramanthians, which put them in the same lowly category as the Thrakies insofar as Doma-Sa was concerned.

But the methane breathers had a navy, and therefore the ability to project power, so it would be foolish to ignore them. Especially given the fact that Doma-Sa's race had been forced to forgo having ships of their own in order to gain membership in the Confederacy and thereby escape their dying planet. Which had everything to do with Doma-Sa's presence. Because if the triad could do or say anything that would help prevent the Dracs from actively entering the war on the Ramanthian side, then the pain-filled evening would be worth the sacrifice.

Having confirmed that the Hudathans were invited guests, the seemingly interchangeable Dracs led the giants into a featureless elevator that fell so fast the 350-pound triad wondered if his feet would come up off the floor. The platform slowed quickly and coasted to a stop. The door opened onto a public area already crowded with partygoers. Most of the guests were Thrakies, which made sense, given that Starfall belonged to them. The rest of the crowd consisted of humans, a couple of Finthians, four exoskeleton-equipped Dwellers, and a handful of other aliens. They all stood around and pretended to like each other as they sipped, snorted, and siphoned intoxicating liquids into their bodies.

Like the building's exterior, the interior had a utilitarian feel, and because Dracs were color-blind, there was nothing to brighten the atmosphere. The human partygoers were sure to notice, but it was of little interest to Doma-Sa, who could perceive color but wasn't especially interested in it.

Being a head of state, as well as the Hudathan representative to the Confederacy, Doma-Sa was one of the highest-ranking individuals present and therefore in great demand. But rather than circulate, the way most diplomats did, the Hudathan put his back to a wall and allowed the ass-kissers, lie tellers, and social sycophants to come to him, which they quickly lined up to do. And, predictably

enough, the topic everyone wanted to talk about was Marcott Nankool. Was the chief executive dead? Would Vice
President Jakov assume the presidency? And if he did, how
would that impact the war?

The answers to such questions were obvious—or so it
seemed to Doma-Sa. Yes, Nankool was probably dead.
Yes, Jakov would assume the presidency. And yes, that
would have an impact on the war. Because as with so many
squats, the human politician was a spineless piece of dra,
who would rush to cut a deal with the bugs so that
dreamy-eyed elites on Earth could sleep better at night.

But the triad knew there wasn't anyplace for the truth
in a roomful of liars, so he told everyone who asked that
there was a very good chance that Nankool was still alive
and might very well be rescued. Not because Doma-Sa was
in love with what he often thought of as the Confederation
of Stupid Beings, but because the Hudathan people would
be vulnerable without a strong star-spanning government,
and his first duty was to *them*.

And that's what the Hudathan was doing when his
conversation with the Finthian ambassador came to a
close, and the brightly plumed diplomat stepped away.
The noise level in the room suddenly decreased as a female Ramanthian appeared in front of him. "This is the
Egg Orno," Molo-Sa said by way of introduction. "Mate
to ex-ambassador Alway Orno—who was assassinated a
few weeks ago."

The mention of the name, plus the relationship, took
Doma-Sa back to the day when he and the Egg Orno's *other*
mate had faced off on the surface of Arballa. It had been
hot that day, with high, puffy clouds that seemed to sail
across a violet sky.

There were rules against dueling aboard the orbiting
Friendship—so the fight had been scheduled to take place
on the arid planet below. No one lived on the surface of

Arballa, least of all the wormlike Arballazanies, who dwelt deep underground.

But everyone wanted to see the fight, so all manner of shuttles had been employed to ferry dozens of diplomats, politicians, and senior officials down to Arballa, where the would-be spectators were forced to don a variety of exotic breathing devices in order to move around on the planet's inhospitable surface.

By mutual agreement, a bowl-like depression had been chosen as the site of the contest. Horgo Orno entered the natural arena first. Doma-Sa remembered feeling the first stirrings of fear as the Ramanthian stood there with his well-oiled chitin gleaming in the sun. And now, as the enormous Hudathan looked down into the Egg Orno's shiny eyes, he suspected that the female was frightened but still had the courage to face him. The question was *why*.

The Egg Orno had been on Hive the day that her beloved Horgo fought the big ugly Hudathan. So this was the first time she had seen him. The alien had a large humanoid head, a low-lying dorsal fin that ran front to back along the top of his skull, and funnel-shaped ears. His skin was gray, but would turn white if the temperature were to drop, and black were it to rise. "It's an honor to meet you," Doma-Sa said gravely. "However, I would be lying if I told you that I regret the ex-ambassador's death. Or that of your other mate, although he fought bravely and died a warrior's death. Of that you can be proud."

The Hudathan had been truthful, and the Egg Orno was strangely grateful for that. "Thank you, Excellency," the Ramanthian replied gravely. "Both for your honesty *and* the words of respect for Horgo. But I'm not here to discuss the way my mates died but to avenge them."

Those words were enough to bring Molo-Sa forward to shield Doma-Sa's body with his own. But the triad put out a hand to restrain him. "Thank you," the Hudathan said gratefully. "But I don't believe the Egg Orno will attack me."

"No," the Ramanthian agreed. "I won't. . . . Although I would if I could. I'm here to discuss the relationship between the late ambassador and the Jakov administration. Which, if I'm not mistaken, will be of considerable interest to you."

That alone was sufficient to start a buzz of conversation, and Doma-Sa knew better than to hold what could be a sensitive discussion in a public place. "That sounds interesting," the triad responded noncommittally. "Would you be available to talk about it in an hour or so? Or would you like to make an appointment for another day?"

"This evening would be fine," the Egg Orno replied gratefully. "Please let me know when you're ready to leave."

"We will," Doma-Sa assured her. "And one more thing . . ."

The Egg Orno looked up at him. "Yes?"

"I meant what I said about the War Orno, but I had no desire to hurt you, and I'm sorry that I did."

There was a long moment of silence during which the beginning of a strange bond began to form. And after they left the party, and spent more than two hours talking within the security of the Hudathan embassy, the bond grew even stronger. That was something that might well have been of interest to both Vice President Leo Jakov *and* the Ramanthian Queen. Had either been aware of it.

PLANET JERICHO, THE RAMANTHIAN EMPIRE

The funeral pyres crackled as the orange-red flames rose to enfold the dead nymphs, and the rich, fatty odor of cooked meat filled the air, as six columns of black smoke rose to stain an otherwise-pristine blue sky. Efforts to repair the security fence were still under way, and Ramanthian outposts all around the camp remained on high alert, as Maximillian Tragg crossed the compound to the administration building. There was no way to know exactly why he had been summoned, but the overseer assumed the Mutuus were going to assign more of the reconstruction work to the POWs. That was fine with the renegade because the prisoners were easier to control when they were busy.

As Tragg approached the headquarters building, he noticed that *four* Ramanthian troopers had been posted outside the front door rather than two as in the past—one of many changes resulting from the nymph attack. The human had to surrender his weapons and remove his boots before being allowed to enter the richly decorated throne room. It was a ritual the renegade had performed dozens of times before. Except this time there was something different in the air, a tension that could be seen in the way that the impeccably dressed commandant held himself, the fact that the War Mutuu's sword was symbolically unsheathed, and the presence of six heavily armed soldiers. All because of the nymphs? Or was there another reason as well? The mercenary felt cold lead trickle into his stomach. Tragg lowered his eyes and bowed respectfully. "Greetings, Excellencies—"

That was as far as the renegade got when a baton struck him across the kidneys. The pain was excruciating, and he went down hard. "Don't strike the animal's head, and don't break any of his bones," the War Mutuu instructed as the blows continued to fall. Tragg had curled up into a ball by that time, with his arms around his head, as the troopers continued to beat him. It hurt, but the renegade knew more about pain than they did and had a tolerance for it. So he took comfort from the orders that the War Mutuu had given and waited for the assault to end.

"That's enough," the commandant said, after what felt like an hour but was actually no more than fifteen seconds. "Help him up."

It felt as if every bone in his body had been broken as the Ramanthians lifted Tragg up off the floor. But that wasn't the case, and even though the renegade's knees were a bit weak, his legs were strong enough to support his weight.

"Now, having been punished, the animal wants to know *why*," Commandant Mutuu said coldly. "The answer is simple. . . . Thanks to our brilliant scientists, a faster-than-light communications device has come into being, which means officials on Hive can communicate with planets like Jericho in real time. Such calls are rare, however. . . . So, imagine our surprise when Chancellor Ubatha called to inform us that a very special guest is staying here at Camp Enterprise. A person *you* chose to protect or, even worse, were so negligent as to overlook. Which is why you were punished."

A moment of silence ensued, which Tragg chose to interpret as permission to speak. Clearly, assuming that he understood the Ramanthian correctly, a VIP of some sort was hiding among the prisoners. But *who*? The informer might have told him, but he was dead. "Thank you for the clarification, Excellencies," the renegade said humbly. "Please be assured that had I known such a person was present I would have notified you immediately. . . . Am I permitted to know the identity of this individual?"

"Yes," the commandant allowed loftily. "You are. More than that, it's our expectation that you will find this person and bring him to us."

Tragg nodded. "If he's here, then I'll find him. Who is he?"

"His name is Marcott Nankool," Mutuu replied. "And, until recently, he was president of the Confederacy."

Tragg didn't have eyebrows. Not anymore. But the scar tissue over his eyes rose. Nankool! A very big fish indeed. Who was pretending to be someone else. A deception of that sort should have been impossible, *would* have been impossible, had it not been for the unforgivably sloppy way in which the POWs had been processed immediately after the surrender. That meant the POWs had been laughing at him all this time, because with the single exception of the informer, he'd been unable to get any of the others to flip. The realization made the renegade angry—and brought blood to his badly scarred face. "Don't worry," Tragg said grimly. "Now that I know Nankool is here, I'll find him."

"I hope so," the War Mutuu put in, as he joined the conversation. "But there's another possibility isn't there? The possibility that you killed him? Or allowed him to die? That would be very unfortunate indeed. Especially for *you*."

Tragg tried to visualize the faces of the people he had shot in hopes of eliminating that possibility, but their features were lost to him, along with whatever impulse had led to their deaths. A lump filled the back of his throat, and he was barely able to swallow it. But what about all the prisoners that *you* and *your* troops killed? He wanted to ask. But such a question would have been suicidal, so the renegade maintained his silence.

"You have until sunset," Commandant Mutuu said sternly. "Find Nankool or die."

It was uncomfortable in the tree, *very* uncomfortable, especially having spent the previous night in it. However, it did provide the scouts with an excellent vantage point from which to observe the layout and daily routines within the POW camp. Starting with the funeral pyres that were lit just after sunup and continuing with the routines that followed. Information was being recorded and continuously edited for playback to the rest of the legionnaires when Team Zebra regrouped that evening.

But there was only so much that one could learn from staring at the compound. And the process was somewhat depressing given what poor condition the prisoners were in. So Santana, Shootstraight, and Bozakov took turns staring through the powerful binos. And, as luck would have it, the Naa was on duty when the commotion started. "There's some sort of ruckus going on inside the wire," the legionnaire observed as he panned the glasses from left to right.

Santana paused with a spoonful of mixed fruit halfway to his mouth. He was seated on one branch with his boots resting on another. The only thing he lacked was some sort of backrest. "Yeah? What's up?"

"I'm not sure," Shootstraight replied as he turned to pass the binos to the officer.

Santana ate the fruit that was sitting on the spoon, tipped the contents of the can into his mouth, and savored the last dollop of juice. Once the can had been deposited in a dangling garbage bag, the legionnaire wiped his fingers on his thighs before reaching out to take the binos. Interestingly enough, not a single patrol had ventured into the surrounding jungle since the nymph attack the day before. Probably out of fear that a sortie could trigger another attack. The hesitancy could work in Team Zebra's favor so long as the nymphs left the off-worlders alone.

Being so far up in the air, the officer found it difficult to look through the binos without becoming disoriented and had to grab a branch in order to steady himself as he eyed the compound. Shootstraight was correct. It appeared that all the POWs, including those who were sick, were being herded toward the center of the compound where the human with the dark goggles was waiting.

A man Santana had first seen back on Algeron, when General Booly and the others showed him the video of POWs being marched through the jungle, including shots of Christine Vanderveen. And more recently he had learned even more about the man named Tragg from media specialist Watkins, including the nature of their private feud.

The cyborg would be overjoyed to learn that his nemesis was still present on the planet—but the company commander had other concerns. Why were the prisoners being mustered he wondered? And more than that, who was the person sitting behind Tragg, in the gazebo-like structure?

The binos were powerful, but the target was a long ways off, and no amount of fiddling with the zoom control was sufficient to bring the fuzzy image into focus. That was the moment when Tragg pulled a pistol and shot one of the POWs in the face.

Vanderveen had just finished her breakfast, and was about to leave the gazebo, when Tragg returned from the HQ building. The overseer was limping, and judging from his expression, extremely angry. "Stay here," he ordered curtly. "We're going to have some fun when this is all over. Or, at least, *I'm* going to have some fun. You'll be sorry you were ever born." And with that he was gone.

The threat was frightening enough, but when *all* of the POWs were ordered to assemble at the center of the compound, the diplomat knew something bad was about to happen. What she didn't anticipate was just how bad it would be. That became clear once the prisoners were assembled and Tragg stood in front of them. The ever-present monitors amplified his voice and produced a slight echo. There were no preliminaries. Just a straightforward demand that left no doubt as to how much the overseer knew. "One of you is President Marcott Nankool. . . . You will step forward now."

After months of confinement, the POWs were far too sophisticated to respond to a statement like that one. But they stiffened, as if waiting to receive a blow, and it came as Tragg shot Corporal Karol Gormley in the face. The right side of her skull exploded outwards, showering those beyond with blood and brain matter as her rail-thin body collapsed.

"Marcott Nankool is *male*," Tragg emphasized, as he tilted the gun upwards and a wisp of smoke trickled out of the barrel. "That means I can shoot every single female present without any fear of making a mistake. So, I'll say it again. One of you is President Marcott Nankool. You *will* step forward now."

There was a pause, followed by a mutual gasp of consternation, as a heavily bearded man took one step forward. "My name is Marcott Nankool," he said in a loud clear voice. "Please holster your weapon."

FORT CAMERONE, PLANET ALGERON, THE CONFEDERACY OF SENTIENT BEINGS

In spite of his hard-won reputation for fistfighting, and his undeniable strength, Quickblow Hammerhand was afraid of the dark. And the ex-legionnaire wasn't all that fond of enclosed spaces, either. Which was why the trip from Naa Town into Fort Camerone required every bit of the courage and self-discipline the warrior possessed.

The journey had begun in the local funeral home, where Hammerhand and three other volunteers had been required to lower themselves into MilSpec coffins that had been preloaded with weapons and ammunition. "I always figured I'd wind up in one of these," Fastspeak Storytell said cheerfully. "But I assumed I'd be dead!"

The comment was worthy of a chuckle and got one from the other veterans, but something blocked Hammerhand's throat as one of the undertaker's sons closed the coffin's metal lid and began to fasten the latches. The ex-legionnaire wanted to scream but wasn't about to reveal the weakness he had worked so hard to conceal for more than forty years, and thereby run the risk that they would leave him behind. A fate even worse than dying inside a pitch-black coffin. So the Naa bit his upper lip and focused on the pain.

Hammerhand could hear the sound of muffled conversation as the supposedly empty coffins were loaded onto a wagon—followed by a period of extended silence as a hardworking dooth pulled the heavily loaded conveyance up toward the fort. That delay was bad enough. But, unfortunately for Hammerhand and his companions, *other* vendors were already lined up in front of the open gate. The result was a long, and for Hammerhand torturous, wait.

Eventually, after what seemed like a week, the wagon drew level with the guard station. Although many of what Vice President Jakov and his staff considered to be critical security functions were presently being handled by marines, the fort was still being run by the Legion. A necessity given the fact that they outnumbered the jarheads a hundred to one. So the Sergeant of the Guard knew the undertaker's number two son, and having seen him at least a couple of times a week for many months, nodded politely. "Good morning, Citizen Bodytake. What have you got for us?"

"Four coffins," the Naa replied, as his breath fogged the air. "And a horrendous hangover."

The sergeant knew a thing or two about hangovers and smiled sympathetically. "I know what you mean. . . . If you would be so kind as to eyeball the scanner, and place your thumb on the sensor pad, we'll process you in."

Bodytake removed a glove, thumbed the pole-mounted pad, and knew that his retinas were being scanned as he did so. It took less than a second for the fort's computer to compare the incoming biometric data to the undertaker's file and approve it. "All right," the sergeant said, as he waved the wagon through. "As for the hangover . . . Drop a pain tab into a cup of hot caf, add a half teaspoon of gunpowder, and chase it with a beer. It works for me!"

Bodytake thanked the legionnaire for the advice and held his breath as the wagon rattled through an ice-encrusted framework. The purpose of the device was to detect common explosives, radioactive materials, and large quantities of metal. And that raised an important question. Would the small arms stored in the coffins trigger the detector? But no alarms went off as the wagon rolled through, so the undertaker felt free to take a deep breath as he neared the gate.

Meanwhile, less than two feet away, Hammerhand was at war with himself. He uttered a whimper as the wagon began to move—and took comfort from the gun in his hand.

Though never a pleasant place to be, the pit had gradually been transformed from a reasonably well-run military detention facility into a badly crowded prison where murderers, thieves, and deserters rubbed shoulders with noncoms, officers, and government officials who had been arrested on trumped-up charges and jailed so that Vice President Jakov and his toadies could consolidate their power without fear of opposition. That meant the political prisoners were vulnerable to all sorts of predation, or would have been, except for the presence of Legion General Bill Booly. Because, contrary to what seemed like common sense, the vast majority of the criminals interred in the pit were still willing to take orders. So long as the orders came from someone they respected.

Realizing that, Booly and the other officers who had been arrested for purely political reasons quickly went to work reorganizing the prisoners into squads, platoons, and companies, and thereby restored them to a system of discipline they were familiar with. And most of the legionnaires not only welcomed the newly imposed sense of order but the feeling of purpose that accompanied it, because even the least sophisticated prisoners could see that the vice president was abusing his power. There were exceptions, of course. Psychopaths and the like, who were soon confined to a prison-within-a-prison, where the other convicts kept them under lock and key. The new warden didn't approve of the arrangement—but was powerless to stop without triggering a full-scale riot.

So as the days passed, the prisoners were systematically reintegrated into the Legion as the marines looked on. Which was a step in the right direction but brought Booly very little peace because he knew that with each passing day, Jakov's grip on the bureaucracy, and therefore the government, grew tighter and tighter. And with the vote to confirm him being held in a couple of weeks—rumor had it that many senators were ready to accept what they saw as inevitable.

But there was nothing that he or the other officials could do but formulate some contingency plans and try to stay in shape as time continued to pass. So, in an effort to keep the legionnaires both fit and occupied a round of kickboxing tournaments had been organized. And that's where Booly was, judging a fight between two spider forms, when a long, hollow scream was heard.

It came from above and echoed between the tiers, as a marine fell toward the bottom of the pit. He was a machine gunner. Or had been back before Quickblow Hammerhand threw the unfortunate jarhead over the rail. His body made a sickening *thud* as it hit the duracrete floor.

That was when the Naa commando took control of the unmanned weapon, lifted the gun up off the pintle-style mount, and opened fire on the warden's office located on the opposite side of the canyonlike abyss. Glass shattered, empty casings fell like a brass rain, and Booly came to his feet. "This is what we've been waiting for!" the officer bellowed. "You know what to do!"

Though not really expecting a rescue attempt, Booly and his staff had formulated plans for that eventuality, along with several others. So even though a third of the inmates were a bit slow on the uptake, two-thirds responded appropriately, as Hammerhand and his companions engaged the guards.

There were only two ways to enter or exit the pit, and both came under immediate pressure as the marine guards were forced to cower beneath a hail of airborne shoes, toothbrushes, and even an artificial limb or two. All intended to keep them occupied while the would-be rescuers cut their way through layers of security.

Having been freed inside the storeroom where the normally empty coffins were kept, the lightly armed Naa straightened their uniforms and stepped out into the hall. Then, having assumed an air of grim authority, the invaders headed for the pit. The stratagem couldn't last forever, though, and their luck ran out when they tried to bluff their way into the prison and were forced to knife three guards. The challenge was to release enough prisoners quickly enough to hold the facility against the reinforcements that would soon arrive from elsewhere. Which was why Hammerhand followed the walkway he was on halfway around and opened fire on the second checkpoint.

Because the facility had been designed to keep people *in*, rather than keep them *out*, the marines found themselves caught between a rock and a hard place. So when Hammerhand let up on the trigger, a white rag appeared, followed by six inches of the rifle barrel it was attached to.

Two minutes later, the marines were facedown on the duracrete floor while prisoners streamed past the control station and were formed into companies. Shots could still be heard elsewhere in the facility. But rather than send a mob to deal with marine holdouts, Booly ordered Major Drik Seeba-Ka to arm a single platoon of handpicked prisoners and secure the rest of the prison.

That move was met with considerable resentment on the part of the hard-core inmates, who not only wanted a chance to run amok but had scores to settle with the guards. But thanks to the manner in which they had been integrated into units controlled by strong no-nonsense NCOs, discipline was maintained. "We need to push our way out of the pit," Booly told Colonel Kitty Kirby. "Or they'll seal us inside. That's what I would do."

Kirby nodded grimly. "Sir, yes, sir."

"And, Colonel . . ."

"Sir?"

"Do everything you can to minimize casualties. The marines are on our side, or will be, if we can put things right."

Kirby came to attention and offered a salute. "Yes, sir! Camerone!"

Booly returned the gesture, and because some of the troops had witnessed Kirby's comments, the familiar shout went up. "CAMERONE!"

In spite of the fact that he had not been confirmed as president, Jakov had nevertheless taken over Nankool's office, and was seated behind the missing man's desk. And though not given to physical demonstrations of emotion, it was clear to everyone, including Assistant Undersecretary Kay Wilmot, that the vice president was extremely angry. "So, let me see if I understand," the politician said coldly. "While you sat on your hands, a group of Naa terrorists were allowed to enter the fort and free hundreds of prisoners. Is that correct?"

"*No,*" a voice from the back of the room said. "That isn't true. . . . There were only four of them, which hardly qualifies as a 'group,' and they aren't terrorists."

The crowd seemed to part of its own accord to reveal someone none of them recognized. A short, rather plump man, with black hair and Eurasian features. Just one of the bodies billionaire Admiral Sergi Chien-Chu could "wear" when he chose to do so. And *not* the one that Jakov's security forces had been looking for.

The stranger smiled woodenly. "What they are," the businessman added reasonably, "is patriots. A title to which none of *you* can lay claim."

Jakov was about to order his security detachment to arrest the intruder when there was a disturbance in the corridor. There was a shout, followed by a scuffle, and the sound of a single pistol shot. Then, before any of the officials could react, General Bill Booly entered the room. The fighting had been brisk, but was short-lived, as word of the prison break began to spread. Because the vast majority of the Legion continued to be loyal to Booly, as were many of the senior marine officers, who resented the way in which they had been used. Now, with the exception of a few diehards, the battle to retake Fort Camerone was all but over.

The general, still clad in his prison-issue sweats, looked Jakov in the eye. His voice was hard and as cold as the outside air. "Good afternoon, Mr. Vice President. Unlike you and your cronies—we believe in the rule of law. So, consistent with the constitution, you will remain in office until President Nankool returns or you are confirmed. In the meantime, orders to the military will have to be cleared with the Senate's leadership before my staff or I will be willing to act on them. Is that clear?"

Jakov felt a sudden surge of hope. And why not? Nankool was almost certainly dead. And since each and every one of the senators was subject to political pressure of one sort or another, all he needed to do was squeeze, bully, or bribe them. So, if Booly and his band of starry-eyed dreamers were stupid enough to grant him the gift of time, then who was he to refuse it? And later, once the presidency was his, each and every one of the bastards would be taken out and shot. "Yes," Vice President Jakov said thoughtfully. "The situation is very clear indeed."

17

There are times when men have to die.

—United States Secretary of War Henry Stimson
Standard year 1941

PLANET JERICHO, THE RAMANTHIAN EMPIRE

The sun rose slowly, as if reluctant to give birth to another day, and was nearly invisible above a layer of gauzy clouds. Bit by bit the heat penetrated the planet's surface and began to tease moisture up out of the ground. The resulting mist shivered whenever a breeze came along to tug at it— but seemed reluctant to part company with the row of crosses that appeared to float over it. Twelve of the POWs had been crucified. Not because of anything they had done, but because of something they *hadn't* done, which was to reveal Nankool's presence to the Ramanthians.

That was Maximillian Tragg's claim anyway. But as Vanderveen stood on one of the two crosspieces that were fastened to the centermost pole, she knew it was more than that. Especially in *her* case. Because to the renegade's psychotic way of thinking, she had betrayed his trust. And made him look ridiculous, which was more than the mercenary's fragile ego could handle.

There was something else, too. . . . Because once the newly constructed cross was laid out on the ground, and the diplomat had been forced to take her place on it, Tragg began to refer to her as "Marci," a woman the renegade hated so much he insisted on driving the nails through Vanderveen's wrists personally. The diplomat didn't want to scream, and was determined not to, but the pain proved to be too much. So Vanderveen emptied her lungs as the spikes went in and saw how much pleasure that gave Tragg just before she fainted.

When Vanderveen awoke her cross was upright and firmly planted in the ground. The center of what Tragg called his "garden." Fortunately, most of the diplomat's weight was supported by the crosspiece under her feet. The innovation was intended to extend both her life and her suffering. Which, without water, would probably last another five or six days. Or more if it rained. Not that it mattered because Vanderveen was in an altered state of consciousness when a shoulder-launched missile hit the watchtower located at the southeast corner of the compound. There was an explosion, followed by a loud *boom*, as hundreds of pieces of debris fell slowly toward the ground. That was followed by more explosions as the T-2s fired missiles at carefully selected targets, and large gaps began to appear in the fence.

"Well, I'll be goddamned," Corley Calisco said, as the bombardment began. "The cavalry has arrived."

Having fired their missiles, the ten-foot-tall war forms left the protection of the jungle, crossed the free-fire zone, and poured through newly created gaps in the security fence. There they were met by stiff resistance from the Ramanthian defenders, who, having been reinforced in the wake of the nymph attack, responded with a hail of gunfire from assault weapons, crew-served machine guns, and rocket-propelled grenades.

Jas Hargo, the cyborg responsible for Major Hal DeCosta's murder, placed one of his big podlike feet on a subsurface mine. There was a loud *crump* as the shaped charge went off and sent a jet of white-hot plasma upwards. The resulting explosion killed the bio bod who was strapped to the cyborg's back and blew the T-2's head off. It fell, rolled for a few feet, and came to rest looking upwards. That was when Hargo saw Snyder coming his way, and shouted "No!" as a big metal pod descended on his face.

Like his mount, Santana was completely oblivious to the manner of Hargo's death as the cyborg's brain box was crushed under him. Because just about all of the officer's attention was focused on the camp and the situation around him. Resistance was stiff, but that was to be expected, and the first objective had been achieved. The security fence had been breached—and Team Zebra had entered the compound! But where was Nankool? Batkin was in charge of finding the chief executive but had yet to report in.

Snyder's body began to jerk rhythmically as she opened fire with her .50-caliber machine gun. The big slugs tore into a file of recently arrived Ramanthian troopers and ripped them apart. That was when the company commander spotted the row of crosses and knew the POWs must have been crucified after his departure the day before. One more group of people to remember once the extraction phase of the operation began.

It was a subject Santana continued to worry about because the pickup ships should have been in contact with him by then. Had the task force been intercepted? And, if so, what if anything could he do about it? But those thoughts were interrupted as Snyder spoke over the intercom. "Look at the cross in the middle, sir. Is that Miss Vanderveen?"

"No," Santana responded automatically. "It can't be because . . ." But then, as the officer turned his head, he caught sight of some blond hair and made a grab for his binos. Snyder knew Vanderveen, having met the diplomat on LaNor, and could zoom in on any object she chose to.

So if the cyborg said that the person on the cross was Christine, then it might be true. And when the officer brought the binos up he knew it was! More importantly, judging from a slight movement of her head, Vanderveen was alive!

That realization drove everything else out of Santana's mind. Fearful that Vanderveen might be killed by a stray bullet, Santana hurried to pull the plug on the intercom and hit the harness release. Snyder started to object as the officer hit the ground, but spotted a Ramanthian with a rocket-propelled grenade launcher, and had to respond.

Gomez was about a hundred feet away and watched in horror as Santana began to run. "Alpha Two-Six to Alpha Six," the noncom said desperately, but received no reply as bullets whispered around the legionnaire. Meanwhile the gazebo-like structure at the center of the compound exploded into a thousand fiery pieces, and a series of explosions marched across the camp. The assault, which had been so focused to start with, was beginning to falter.

Gomez was about to urge her cyborg forward, in hopes of reestablishing contact with Santana, when an RPG hit her T-2's chest. The noncom felt the resulting explosion, knew both of them were falling, and hit the harness release. Gomez felt herself fall free, but took an unintended blow from one of Vantha's outflung arms, and the lights went out.

The attack on Camp Enterprise made the War Mutuu angry rather than frightened, which was why the Ramanthian took his sword and exited the administration building through the front door. He should have been killed immediately, as were two of his bodyguards, but it was as if nothing could touch the haughty warrior.

Those POWs still strong enough to do so had joined the battle by then, some with weapons acquired from dead Ramanthians and others with little more than improvised spears. Two of them ran straight at the War Mutuu, hoping to impale the Ramanthian on their sharpened sticks, but the warrior twisted away. Steel flashed, and blood sprayed the ground as the first human went down.

The second screamed something the War Mutuu couldn't understand, took a cut at the Ramanthian's retrograde legs, and made contact. The warrior stumbled and regained his balance, just as an SLM made violent contact with a Ramanthian air car. There was a primary explosion, quickly followed by a secondary, as the vehicle crashed into the dispensary. Most of the patients were killed.

But there was no time to consider such developments as the War Mutuu deployed his wings, jumped into the air, and cut the second POW down. The human produced an ear-piercing scream as the blade sank into his shoulder, but the sound was abruptly cut off, as the warrior's sole surviving bodyguard shot the wounded prisoner.

That was when the stern-faced aristocrat saw that one of the invading animals had abandoned the protection of his cyborg and was in the process of running toward the crosses. The War Mutuu had no particular interest in the POWs Tragg had chosen to crucify but wasn't about to allow an attacker to give them aid. A bullet hummed past the Ramanthian's head, and a chunk of shrapnel missed him by inches as the warrior turned toward the crosses and began to advance. Finally, after years of patient waiting, his moment of glory had come.

Because of his status as a civilian, Watkins was the last member of Team Zebra to enter the compound, albeit on a lumbering RAV rather than a T-2, since all of the war forms were required for combat. That made for a slower ride but provided the media specialist with a relatively steady platform from which to record everything he saw and heard. But as the robot paused to fire a burst from its nose gun, Watkins was only marginally aware of the battle he'd been sent to cover. Because the only thing the civilian *really* cared about was finding Maximillian Tragg and killing him. The problem was *how?* Reinforcements had arrived by then, and a T-2 exploded as it took a direct hit from an RPG.

Meanwhile, *another* guard tower fell and crushed a file of bugs under its weight, as the battle continued to ebb and flow. All this seemed to suggest that it would be impossible to find Tragg, until Watkins noticed that a flight of three silvery remotes were headed toward the airfield and remembered the pictures of Tragg walking through the jungle accompanied by a coterie of robots, including the type now headed north. The bastard was trying to escape!

Excited now, Watkins slid down off the RAV and began to run. And, thanks to the capabilities of his electro-mechanical body, the cyborg was *fast*. The media specialist had a rocket launcher slung across his back along with a reload. The weapons bounced painfully as he ran. A Ra-manthian machine gunner had noticed the interloper by then and turned his weapon in that direction. Geysers of dirt flew up all around Watkins as he zigzagged across what had been the camp's assembly area and made for the fence beyond. "Don't worry, Marci," the cyborg said. "I'll get the bastard this time. . . . And he's going to pay!"

Vanderveen could *see* giants striding through the lazy ground mist, *hear* the sporadic rattle of automatic fire, and *smell* the acrid smoke. And *there*, standing right in front of her, was Antonio Santana! That was impossible, of course, so it *must* be a dream. A wonderful dream in which he had come to rescue her. The legionnaire's visor was up, and his face was filled with concern. "Christine? Can you hear me? Don't worry. . . . We'll have you down in a minute."

It seemed so real that Vanderveen tried to respond. But try as she might nothing came out of her mouth until she saw the War Mutuu appear out of the billowing smoke.

That was when the words finally took form. "Tony! Behind you!"

Santana whirled to find that a Ramanthian was ready to strike. And because the warrior's sword was already up in the air, poised to split the officer in two, there was no time in which to do anything other than push the assault weapon up with both hands. But the War Mutuu's monomolecular blade sliced through the CA-10's steel receiver as if was warm butter and would have gone on to bury itself in the legionnaire's skull had the soldier been even a fraction of a second slower to react.

The Ramanthian jerked his weapon loose, raised it over his head, and brought it back down again. Fortunately, Santana was in the process of throwing himself backwards by then. He landed on his back as the superthin blade sliced through empty air.

That was the War Mutuu's cue to raise his sword for what should have been an easy kill, and what *would* have been an easy kill, had it not been for Maria Gomez. Because as a horrified Vanderveen looked on, a much-bloodied legionnaire lurched out of the smoke and threw herself forward.

Santana felt Gomez land on top of him, and as he looked up into a pair of pain-filled eyes, the officer saw something he would never forget. A look of longing the likes of which he'd never seen before. Then it was gone as the War Mutuu's blade sliced through the noncom's body armor and into her spine.

The Ramanthian withdrew his sword, and was about to take another cut, when he heard the telltale whine of servos. Though delayed, Snyder arrived in time to see Gomez die, and that made the T-2 angry. So when the War Mutuu turned to confront the cyborg she chose to fire her flamethrower rather than the .50-caliber machine gun. There was a *whoosh*, as the liquid fuel hit the Ramanthian, followed by a solid *whump* as the warrior was enveloped by a cocoon of orange-yellow flames. That was followed by a series of bloodcurdling screams as the aristocrat began a horrible dance of death.

The end came when Santana managed to roll out from under Gomez, scrambled to his feet, and drew his pistol. It took three shots to put the War Mutuu down. But even as the Ramanthian's chitin crackled, and his internal organs began to sizzle, the sword clutched in his charred pincer continued to shine.

Meanwhile, Santana forced himself to concentrate on his command. It wasn't easy, not with Vanderveen still standing on the cross above him, but the legionnaire knew the entire team was counting on him to provide direction. Fortunately, the data on his HUD, plus what the officer could see with his own eyes, suggested that Team Zebra was well on its way to controlling the camp. But they hadn't found Nankool yet, more Ramanthian reinforcements were probably on the way, and there was no sign of the goddamned navy. "This is Alpha Six," the company commander said. "We're going to need some tools and a couple of medics to get the people down off those crosses. And has anyone seen Batkin? We need to grab the target and get the hell out of here."

Vanderveen's throat was bone dry—and her voice was hoarse. "Look in the administration building. The commandant has him."

Santana was going to thank her when what sounded like a runaway train *rumbled* overhead. That was followed by an earsplitting *crack* as a large crater materialized at the center of the compound. A windmilling T-2 fell out of the air, landed with a sickening *crunch*, and was half-buried by falling dirt. Even though they ran the risk of hitting their own troops, the Ramanthians had decided to fire energy cannons from orbit rather than allow the compound to be overrun. "Damn it," Santana said, as what sounded like another freight train *rattled* through the atmosphere. "Where *are* those ships?" There was no reply other than a loud explosion, the continued *clatter* of a machine gun, and the sound of another scream.

The administration building shook as something struck the ground outside. A blizzard of dust particles came loose from the rafters to drift down through a momentary shaft of sunlight even as a burst of machine-gun bullets passed within a foot of Marcott Nankool and ripped holes in the wall beyond.

But if those things bothered Commandant Mutuu, the impeccably dressed Ramanthian showed no sign of it as he poured hot water through a strainer filled with gold-colored leaves. "There," the aristocrat said contentedly, as he reached over to remove a cup of amber liquid from under the filter. "Please be so good as to tell me what you think. Is the Oburo Gold superior to the Zecco Red? Or is it the other way around?"

The bizarre tête-à-tête between Nankool and the effete commandant had been triggered by the human's obvious knowledge of Ramanthian etiquette. A capacity which, to Mutuu's mind at least, signaled the presence of someone who, if not an equal, had a profound understanding of Ramanthian culture. And that, combined with the prisoner's rank, made the human worth interacting with.

Having accepted the tumbler of hot liquid, Nankool sucked some of the tea into his mouth and swirled it around. It was a noisy process, and intentionally so, because that signaled enjoyment. The brew tasted like battery acid, or what Nankool imagined battery acid might taste like, and it was all he could do to get the bitter stuff down. And no sooner had the chief executive swallowed than an errant rocket-propelled grenade smashed through a window and lodged itself in the opposite wall. The human gritted his teeth and waited for the weapon to explode. It didn't.

"Come now, don't be reticent," the Ramanthian insisted. "What do you think?"

"The Zecco Red was superior," Nankool said decisively. "But just barely."

"Exactly!" Mutuu agreed eagerly. "The difference between the two is slight, almost indistinguishable to all but the most discerning of palates, yet sufficient to set one above the other. It's so pleasant to have a visitor who appreciates the finer things in life."

"Thank you, Excellency," Nankool replied humbly. "You're too kind. Now, having refreshed ourselves, I wonder if we should seek cover? The battle seems to be heating up."

"There's no need to worry about that," the commandant said dismissively. "The War Mutuu will soon put things right."

"I wouldn't count on that if I were you," Oliver Batkin said, as he coasted into the throne room. "Not unless your mate has the capacity to return from the dead."

It had taken the spy a while to locate Nankool, cut a hole large enough to pass through, and enter the building. Now, as the cyborg hovered at the center of the room, the Ramanthian produced a small weapon. An energy gun from the look of it—which he brought to bear on President Nankool. Or *tried* to bring to bear as Batkin fired a single .50-caliber round. The impact threw the aristocrat backwards and brought a delicately painted panel crashing to the floor along with him.

"Nice shot," Nankool said appreciatively, as he came to his feet. "And you are?"

"Resident Agent Oliver Batkin," the cyborg replied formally. "Presently attached to the team sent to bring you out."

Nankool felt his spirits soar as an assault weapon rattled outside. "That's wonderful!"

"It's good," Batkin allowed cautiously, "but something short of wonderful."

The president frowned. "Why's that?"

"It's a long story, Mr. President," the spy replied wearily. "But suffice it to say that the naval units that were supposed to pick us up are nowhere to be seen. Perhaps they were intercepted—or maybe the mission was canceled. We're screwed either way. Still, the officer in command of the mission knows his stuff, so let's get you out of here. . . . Please keep your head down. It would be a shame to lose it at this point."

The long, silvery space elevator pointed at Maximillian Tragg as the renegade ran for his life. The overcast had begun to burn away by then, revealing white streaks left by high-flying Ramanthian fighters and the blue sky beyond. The aircraft had been on standby thus far but would go into action the moment that the Confederacy Navy appeared. It was just one of many factors Tragg would be forced to take into account as he sought a way off Jericho.

That was why the overseer was jogging toward the airstrip, in hopes of finding a way off the planet's surface, when a shoulder-launched missile struck a Sheen robot. The resulting shock wave was powerful enough to knock Tragg off his feet. Which was just as well, because a second rocket was already on its way, and blew the remaining android to smithereens. Sharp pieces of shrapnel flew in every direction and might have killed the human had he been standing.

Watkins felt a sense of satisfaction as he dropped the launcher and began to advance on his intended victim. Two of the silvery remotes continued to hover above and behind Tragg, but the Ramanthian-made machines were a lot less formidable than the Sheen robots had been, and one of them went down as the cyborg fired the assault weapon he carried. "Stand up, you bastard!" the media specialist ordered, "So I can look into your eyes while I shoot you down!"

Tragg was confused as he came to his feet. Not only had he never seen his assailant before, but the man wasn't wearing a uniform, so who the hell was he? That didn't prevent the renegade from firing one of his pistols at the stranger however.

Watkins staggered as the slugs slammed into his body armor, laughed out loud, and continued to advance as Tragg tried for a head shot and missed. "You don't know who I am, do you?" the media specialist demanded, as a shuttle lifted from the airstrip to the north. "I'm the one who burned my signature into your ugly face!"

Tragg looked at the man and looked again. Marci's brother? No, that was impossible! Yet who else would say something like that? The renegade lowered the pistol. *"Watkins?"* he inquired unbelievingly. "Is that you?"

"It sure as hell is," the cyborg replied grimly. "So get ready to die."

"Let me see if I understand," the overseer said as he began to stall for time. "You survived the fight on Long Jump and followed me here, all because of Marci? You *are* a fool. But I'm glad you came, because that will give me the opportunity to kill you all over again, and do it right this time!"

Watkins raised the assault weapon, placed his finger on the trigger, and was just about to fire when the remaining monitor came within range. The robot had very little in the way of armament but a single shot from the machine's stun gun was sufficient to paralyze what remained of the cyborg's nervous system. And without instructions to the contrary—his electromechanical joints buckled and he dropped to his knees. The assault weapon clattered as it hit the ground, and Watkins collapsed facedown in the dirt.

Meanwhile there was a *roar* of sound as a Ramanthian aerospace fighter came in low over the camp, released a stick of bombs, and screamed away. The ground shook as a series of overlapping explosions merged into a single uninterrupted *CARRRUUUMP*. Geysers of dirt shot up into the air, took half a dozen bodies along with them, and fell back down again. It was impossible for Tragg to know which side was winning, but it didn't matter. What *did* matter was the passage of time. So when the renegade went to flip the cyborg over, he was in a hurry.

Watkins "felt" a boot hook under his body and roll it over. A halo of blue sky surrounded his brother-in-law's head. The cyborg ordered his body to respond, to do something, but there was no reaction. "So, shithead," Tragg said contemptuously, as he pointed the pistol downwards. "I assume Marci's dead by now—so say hello to the silly bitch for me,'"

Watkins saw a flash of light, felt a sense of release, and knew he had failed.

With both of the Mutuus dead, along with most of the camp's defenders, Team Zebra owned the cratered landscape. But without a way to escape, and under continual attack from above, it was a pyrrhic victory. Which was why Santana, Nankool, and a few others were huddled at the bottom of a bomb crater trying to come up with a plan as the airstrikes continued. "It doesn't matter *why* the navy isn't here," Santana said pragmatically. "What we need to do is find a way off this planet. How about the shuttles at the airfield?" he inquired hopefully.

Technically, Commander Peet Schell outranked the legionnaire, but lacked the skills to fight a ground action and knew it. He was an expert on spaceships, however, and was quick to weigh in as another fighter began its run. "I'm sorry, Captain, but we wouldn't get far. Not without some sort of hyperdrive."

"Maybe we could use the shuttles to hijack one of the ships in orbit," Lieutenant Farnsworth suggested. "They have hyperdrives."

"Yes, they do," the heavily bearded naval officer agreed. "But a successful hijack attempt would require the element of surprise. And once we steal a couple of shuttles, the Ramanthians would be expecting us to attack the orbiting ships."

"That's true," Nankool said, as he spoke for the first time. "But what about the *Imperator*?"

Schell frowned. "She has a hyperdrive," he said thoughtfully. "That's true. . . . But what about the space elevator? It's like a twenty-three-thousand-mile-long anchor chain."

"Could we cut it?" Santana wanted to know. "Because the bugs wouldn't expect something like that."

"No," Schell replied, as a steadily growing sense of excitement began to grip him. "They sure as hell wouldn't! And yes, assuming you have some explosives, we can cut it. Which I would enjoy a great deal."

"Can we ride the space elevator *up*?" Farnsworth wanted to know. "Why steal shuttles if we don't have to?"

"No, the elevator was designed to bring a whole lot of tonnage down to the surface in a short period of time," the naval officer answered. "But that's okay. My people can fly *anything*. . . . And that includes Ramanthian shuttles. So, let's go!"

It was a crazy plan, an *insane* plan, but anything was better than sitting in the ruins of Camp Enterprise waiting to die. So Santana sent Farnsworth plus a squad of war forms off to the airfield. Two pilots were assigned to go with them—and help secure two Ramanthian shuttles.

Once they were gone, the legionnaire worked with the surviving noncoms to organize an evacuation. Most of the sickest POWs had been killed when the dispensary was destroyed, but even the so-called healthy prisoners were weak, and some had been wounded. So the most critical patients were put aboard the RAVs, which could handle two people each, while those like Vanderveen were loaded onto makeshift stretchers. The rest were forced to walk. That meant that the entire column was vulnerable to air attack as the POWs and their would-be rescuers emerged from hiding to walk, limp, and in some cases hop toward the airfield.

It didn't matter where Santana was. Not at that particular moment, so the officer chose to stay with Vanderveen as a pair of fighters circled the camp and prepared to attack the POWs. So when the diplomat opened her eyes, it was the legionnaire she saw, walking at her side. Santana turned to look down at her, saw that her eyes were open, and took hold of her right hand. That hurt, but Vanderveen didn't care, as the Ramanthian planes strafed the slowly twisting column.

But there was a price to be paid for attacking the war forms, as one of the Ramanthian pilots found out when a heat-seeking missile entered his port air intake and exploded. The fighter came apart in midair, was consumed by an orange-red fireball, and transformed into metal confetti.

Santana saw spurts of dust shoot up as pieces of debris landed around them and gave silent thanks as the badly mauled column made its way out onto the tarmac. "Pick up the pace!" he shouted. "Get in among those shuttles before the fighters make another run!" There were four atmosphere-scarred shuttles parked next to the airstrip, and it was the legionnaire's hope that the Ramanthian pilots would be reluctant to fire on them. The POWs responded as best they could, and the occasional *rattle* of gunfire was heard as Farnsworth and his detachment continued to mop up what remained of the airfield's security detail.

It wasn't long before the cavalry officer spotted Watkins and went over to kneel beside the body. The cyborg was lying on his back, staring sightlessly up at the sun, with a blue-edged hole between his eyes. *Tragg,* Santana thought to himself. *The bastard is alive.*

And as if to prove the officer's conclusion, there was a sudden burst of gunfire as one of the previously quiescent shuttles suddenly came to life and lifted off its skids. The copilot's saddle-style seat was too uncomfortable to sit on, so Tragg had been forced to crouch next to the Raman-thian pilot. He aimed the gun at the bug's head as a hail of bullets flattened themselves against the fuselage. "If I die, then *you* die, asshole. So get me out of here."

Having seen his copilot gunned down in cold blood, the alien took the threat seriously and applied additional power. Thrusters roared as the shuttle gained speed and took to the air. The hard part was over, or so it seemed to Tragg, as Jericho's surface fell away. Thraki ships were in orbit, or so he assumed, and the furballs would do just about anything for money. And, thanks to the heavy money belt strapped around the renegade's waist, he could afford to pay. It was chancy, but Tragg was a gambler and always willing to place a bet. Especially on himself.

18

Never give up hope! Because when all seems lost, a hero will appear, and lead the way.

—*Looklong Spiritsee*
A Book of Visions
Standard year 1967

PLANET JERICHO, THE RAMANTHIAN EMPIRE

Dark gray smoke billowed up from what had been Camp Enterprise, a muffled explosion was heard as flames found their way into the armory, and engines screamed as a shuttle clawed its way into the sky. Santana had no way to know who was aboard, but assumed some of the Ramanthians were making a run for it, and he swore bitterly. Because the combined force of rescuers and POWs were going to require *two* shuttles, and only two remained. "Speak to me, Bravo Six," the officer said into his lip mike. "And tell me that the rest of those ships are secure. Over."

"Roger that," Lieutenant Farnsworth replied. "We weren't able to capture any Ramanthian pilots—but the swabbies claim they can fly these things. Over."

"I sure hope they're right," Santana responded, as the tail end of the column passed by. "It's my guess that the fighters will receive permission to fire on the shuttles any moment now, so load them quickly. Over."

"I'm on it," Farnsworth replied. "My platoon will provide security until all of the POWs have boarded. Out."

Conscious of how precious each passing second was, Santana threw himself into the process of getting the POWs onto the shuttles. For a while it seemed as if the officer was everywhere, shouting encouragement and lending a hand whenever one was needed. Vanderveen could hear him even though she was strapped to a stretcher and took pleasure in the sound of his voice. Then Santana was there kneeling beside her and checking the straps that would hold the diplomat in place once the ship was airborne. The officer smiled. "I went to your home, but you stood me up."

Vanderveen looked up into his eyes. "I know I did—and I'm very sorry. Did you get my note?"

Santana nodded soberly. "Your mother gave it to me."

"Were you angry?"

"No," the officer replied honestly. "But I was disappointed. You owe me."

"Yes," Vanderveen agreed, as tears began to well up in her eyes. "I do. We *all* do."

She would have said more, *wanted* to say more, but that was when Commander Schell came into view. If he thought the tête-à-tête was strange, he kept his opinions to himself. "We're ready, Captain. . . . Or as ready as we're likely to be."

That was when Santana felt the vibration beneath his boots and realized the shuttle's engines were running. "I'm glad to hear it, sir. Let's load the rest of my team and get the hell out of here."

Schell grinned. "My thoughts exactly."

An additional five minutes were required to get Farnsworth and his people aboard the other shuttle and strap everyone in. Santana stood at the top of the ramp as the last T-2 lumbered aboard Ship 1. And, when he lowered his visor to get a look at the heads-up display, the officer was shocked by what he saw. More than half of his thirty-person team had been killed on the surface of Jericho. The knowledge was sufficient to dampen any sense of jubilation the legionnaire might otherwise have felt as the ramp came up, and the shuttle wobbled into the air. It wasn't easy for the navy pilot to manipulate the strange knob-style controls at first, but she soon caught on, and it wasn't long before the ship began to gain altitude.

"Well done!" President Nankool said heartily as he appeared at Santana's elbow.

"Thank you, sir," the legionnaire replied as he reached up to grab a support. "I'm sorry it took so long—and I'll be damned if I know where the pickup ships are."

"Batkin filled me in on the political aspect of this," Nankool said bleakly. "And it's my guess that the mission was canceled. But that's for later. We have a battleship to steal first!"

There was something infectious about the chief executive's cheerful optimism, and it gave Santana an insight into how Nankool had been so successful in the past and why Vanderveen believed in him. Before the cavalry officer could agree, however, both men were thrown to the deck as the pilot put the shuttle into a tight right-hand turn. "Sorry about that!" a female voice said tightly. "But the bugs want to play. . . . So, hang on to your hats!"

Santana didn't have a hat, but he had a helmet, which he clutched under one arm as he helped Nankool crawl over to a bulkhead where one of the more able-bodied POWs helped strap the chief executive down. And just in time, too, as the shuttle banked the opposite way and shook as it passed through the turbulence created by a Ramanthian fighter. And so began an airborne game of cat and mouse as the Ramanthians attempted to shoot the hijacked shuttles down while the humans sought to clear the atmosphere, knowing that the conventional aircraft wouldn't be able to follow. Of course space-going fighters might very well attack the moment they entered space, but that couldn't be helped, and the pilots could only cope with one problem at a time.

And it wasn't easy, especially for Lieutenant Jerry Woda, who was flying Ship 2. Partly because of the unfamiliar controls but mostly because of a bad engine, which explained why crude staging had been positioned next to the ship when the legionnaires took possession of it. And that pissed the pilot off because both he and the other POWs had been through a lot and didn't deserve to die. But deserving or not it soon became clear that they *were* going to die as a fighter locked on to the ship's tail and began to fire its energy cannons. "Okay," Woda said, as blips of blue energy tore past the control compartment. "You wanna dance? Let's dance."

There was only one way the uneven contest could end. That's what all three of the Ramanthian fighter pilots believed as they took turns shooting at the severely underpowered shuttle. And they were correct, or mostly correct, as Woda put Ship 2 into an extremely tight turn. Suddenly two of the enemy pilots found themselves rushing straight at the unarmed shuttle at a combined speed of eight hundred miles per hour. There was time, but not very much, as Woda steered Ship 2 straight at one of his pursuers. "I'm sorry," the pilot said over the intercom. "But at least we're going to take one of the ugly bastards with us!"

There was no opportunity for the POWs and the legionnaires to react as both aircraft merged into a communal ball of fire. But they would have approved, especially as a *second* fighter ran into the fiery debris and sucked a chunk of metal into its engine. The resulting explosion was visible from many miles away but didn't mean much to the nymphs who witnessed it from below. Because all they felt was an abiding hunger—and the momentary roll of thunder was soon forgotten.

Everyone aboard Ship 1 had experienced weightlessness before, and welcomed it, because they knew that conventional aircraft couldn't follow them into the vacuum of space. Not that they were safe given the fact that any warship larger than a patrol boat was sure to carry fighters designed for combat outside planetary atmospheres. But how would such units be deployed? Santana wondered. Would they be ordered to attack the stolen shuttles? Or kept close in order to protect whatever ship they belonged to? Because the bugs had every reason to expect a Confederacy task force to drop hyper. The legionnaire's thoughts were interrupted by the pilot's voice.

"This is Lieutenant Tanaka," she said somberly. "I'm sorry to announce the loss of Ship 2 and all those aboard. They took two fighters with them, however—and allowed us to clear the atmosphere. Our ETA aboard the *Imperator* is fifteen minutes. There are no fighters on the way as yet. . . . More when I have it."

Farnsworth and fully half of the company's surviving team members had been aboard the other shuttle, so the announcement hit Santana like a blow to the gut. But it was important to try and neutralize the emotional impact associated with the loss and get ready for what lay ahead. The legionnaire freed himself from the tie-downs and made his way out to the center of the cargo compartment. The running dialogue was intended to distract the mixed force of sailors and legionnaires from the loss of Ship 2 and focus their minds on the task ahead. "Okay," Santana said. "If you don't have a weapon, and you're healthy enough to fight, then draw one from Sergeant Ibo-Da. And remember . . . There are some very good reasons why boarding parties rarely use projectile weapons. Like the possibility that you might destroy the very thing that you're trying to capture. So be careful with those slug throwers.

"Once we put down inside the landing bay, the T-2s will exit first," Santana continued. "Sergeant Fox and Private Urulu will neutralize whatever kind of reception party the bugs have waiting for us. Commander Schell, if you would be so kind as to supply some qualified people to blow that space elevator, you can count on Sergeant Snyder and Private Ichiyama to get them there."

"No problem," the naval officer said approvingly. "However, I suggest that the demolition team avoid firefights, and go straight to the space elevator."

"Roger that," Santana agreed. "Once the landing bay is secured, the rest of us will head for the control room. And it would be a good idea to keep our pilots out of the fighting unless you'd like to walk home. Does anyone have questions?"

"Yes, sir," Shootstraight put in. "How are we going to get off this tub without pressure suits?"

It was an obvious problem, or should have been, except that the legionnaire hadn't thought of it. Fortunately, Schell was there to field the question. "Rather than blast-proof doors, the *Imperator*'s launch bay is protected by a permeable force field. So the landing area will be pressurized. Unless they have the means to bring the ship's overshields back online that is. . . . In which case we *are* in deep trouble."

"Aren't you glad you asked?" Bozakov inquired, as he slapped a fully loaded mag into his assault rifle. That produced some very welcome laughter, for which Santana was grateful, as the shuttle began to close with the ancient dreadnaught.

Confident that preparations were under way, the cavalry officer went back to check on Vanderveen. All of the naval personnel were better at zero-gee maneuvers than the soldier was, but by being careful never to release one knob-style pincer-hold before securing the next, Santana managed to pull himself back toward the stern without coming adrift.

Having received some pain tabs and antibiotics from the legionnaires, not to mention plenty of water to wash them down with, Vanderveen was feeling better by then. So when Santana arrived, he found the diplomat working side by side with a navy med tech to prepare for the likelihood of additional casualties. One of the RAVs had been taken aboard, and with some help from the diplomat, the supply-starved corpsman was in the process of looting it. "Isn't this the same woman I found nailed to a cross?" the cavalry officer wanted to know.

"It is," Vanderveen admitted. "But that was then—and this is now. One of the navy docs looked me over and says I'll be fine. . . . Assuming nobody shoots me."

"I want you to stay on the shuttle until the fighting is over," Santana said sternly.

"Or *what?*" the diplomat wanted to know.

Santana recognized the same defiant look he had first seen on the planet LaNor. He smiled sweetly. "Or I'll tell your mother and let *her* deal with you."

Vanderveen laughed, the shuttle slowed, and Tanaka's voice came over the intercom. "We're sixty seconds out—prepare for landing. And remember, there's a good chance that the *Imperator*'s argrav generators are still running, so prepare for the sudden restoration of gravity."

"Be careful," Vanderveen said softly, as she looked up into Santana's eyes. "We have some unfinished business to take care of."

"Yes," Santana agreed solemnly. "We certainly do."

ABOARD THE RAMANTHIAN DREADNAUGHT *IMPERATOR*

As seen from the *Imperator*'s enormous flight deck, the permeable force field looked like a blue whirlpool. It rotated from left to right and crackled as it spun. The movement could have a mesmerizing effect if viewed for too long. Which was why File Leader Sith Howar was careful to look away from time to time in spite of the fact that a shuttle-load of alien escapees might arrive at any moment.

The whole affair had been handled badly. That was Howar's opinion. First, his superiors mistakenly assumed that the animals would attempt a rendezvous with a Confederacy relief force. Then, when the enemy ships failed to materialize, the higher-ups assumed the escapees would attempt to board one of the merchant vessels and positioned all of the available fighters to block such an effort. Finally, when it became clear that the humans were headed for the *Imperator*, the eggless incompetents dumped the whole mess on *him*. "You will defend the space elevator to the very last trooper." Those were his orders—and there was no mention of reinforcements.

Still, having become acquainted with the slaves during the time they'd been aboard the warship, Howar was confident of his ability to eradicate the aliens. The accomplishment would hasten both his promotion and the point at which he could transfer to a more civilized world.

Such were the Ramanthian's thoughts as the incoming shuttle nosed its way in through the center of the whirling force field and immediately put down on the durasteel deck. The boxy vessel was already taking small-arms fire by then, but nothing *too* powerful, lest the defenders inadvertently damage the dreadnaught's hull.

Still, one of the crew-served energy projectors was able to score a direct hit on a landing skid. That caused the vessel to slump sideways but in no way impeded the ramp, which was in the process of being lowered when four T-2s jumped down onto the blast-scarred deck.

File Leader Howar had heard about human cyborgs, and even fought some of them via virtual-reality training scenarios, but never actually confronted one. So when four of the exotic creatures appeared, and opened fire with their arm-mounted weapons, the officer was shocked by the sheer violence of the attack. The fire from more than two dozen assault weapons served to slow the cyborgs but in no way damaged them, as the legionnaires began to advance. Howar finally found his voice as bolts of coherent energy scored direct hits on the same crew-served energy weapon the Ramanthian was counting on to stop the alien monstrosities. "Take cover!" he shouted unnecessarily, and hurried to obey his own order.

Meanwhile, confident that the other cyborgs had the situation under control, Snyder and Ichiyama took off at a trot. Each T-2 carried a gunner's mate plus enough explosives to sever the twenty-three-thousand-mile-long space elevator. Something they needed to accomplish quickly before bug reinforcements arrived on the *Imperator*. A possibility that, though not apparent to Howar, was crystal clear to his most senior noncom, an irascible veteran who had taken the liberty of stationing himself aboard the traveling chain-hoist positioned high overhead.

So while one of his troopers activated the machine, which put the boxy control module into motion, the oldster was standing on the observation platform ready to drop grenades on the cyborgs as they passed below. And the initiative would have been successful, too, had it not been for Oliver Batkin, and the agent's ability to fly. "Sorry to disappoint you," the cyborg said as he rose directly in front of the surprised noncom. "But it isn't nice to drop things on people."

A single shot from the spy ball's .50-caliber gun was sufficient to kill the Ramanthian as the unsuspecting T-2s passed beneath him. That brought the second Ramanthian outside to be dispatched in a similar fashion. With that accomplished, Batkin departed. Taking control of a battleship was no easy task—and there were plenty of things for the spy to do.

Although two of the hulking cyborgs had departed the launch bay, two of the fearsome machine-things remained, so Howar was careful to keep his head down as his troops sought firing positions among a mountain of cargo modules. Having concealed themselves, the Ramanthians were free to fire on both the T-2s *and* the shuttle, an effort intended to pin the POWs down until help arrived. That was the theory anyway, until the shuttle wobbled into the air and began to advance!

Santana, Shootstraight, and Bozakov were standing on the partially extended ramp as the shuttle lifted off. It was hard to maintain their footing given how unsteady the ship was, but each man was secured to the Ramanthian vessel by a cargo strap, which allowed him to lean forward without falling off.

Within moments of taking to the air, Tanaka began to rotate the shuttle so that the stern pointed at the stack of cargo modules. That gave Santana a good look at the enemy's position, as well as the rest of the bay and the shuttles parked there. There were no signs of activity around the other ships, for which the officer was grateful.

Bullets began to *ping* around the legionnaires as Tanaka backed the shuttle toward the Ramanthian stronghold, and energy bolts splashed the hull as the bio bods returned fire. And a devastating fusillade it was as the ship passed *over* the pile of cargo modules, thereby allowing the threesome to fire down on the bugs below. That sent the Ramanthians shuffling every which way as the bio bods pursued them with short bursts of fire.

Santana suspended firing just long enough to throw three well-aimed grenades before bringing his assault weapon back up again. The resulting explosions threw body parts and chunks of debris high into the air as Shootstraight fired shot after well-aimed shot into the maze below. Each bullet brought one of the enemy soldiers down as the shuttle slid back and forth above their exposed heads.

Howar *wanted* to surrender at that point, but knew he couldn't, as the shadow cast by the shuttle slid across his face. So he struggled to remain upright in spite of the downward pressure caused by the roaring repellers, said a mental good-bye to both of his mates, and looked death in the eye. The human with the black hair fired, and Howar fell. It wasn't the way things were supposed to end.

The fighting continued for another two or three minutes, but with no leadership, and having lost the high ground, it wasn't long before the last of the enemy troopers went down. The shuttle landed shortly thereafter, which gave Santana an opportunity to inspect the battlefield, but the sight of so many broken bodies brought him no pleasure, only a moment of relief, followed by a vast weariness and the knowledge that more work remained.

Having been alerted to the invasion by File Leader Howar, a group of Ramanthian naval personnel were quick to open fire on the cyborgs and their riders as they left the lift and turned into a corridor. And, like their peers in the launch bay, they were completely unprepared for what ensued. The barricade they had thrown across the passageway outside the cargo-handling facility did very little to stop the large-caliber bullets or the bolts of coherent energy that Snyder and Ichiyama fired at them. So it was only a matter of seconds before the ten-foot-tall invaders marched the length of the hall and killed the last defender.

Though not fully operational yet, the space elevator was secured to a specially designed framework located just beyond the air lock the Ramanthians had attempted to defend. And having worked aboard the ship, the ex-POWs knew they wouldn't be able to enter the airless space without pressure suits.

So it was agreed that the sailors would prepare the explosive charges, and the cyborgs would place them. Then, once everything was ready, the charge would be triggered from the hallway.

Having won the battle in the corridor, and with one of the demo packs dangling from her massive neck, Snyder felt confident as she followed Ichiyama into the lock. Both cyborgs had to bend over in order to enter and were forced to remain in that position as the air was pumped out of the chamber.

The T-2s half expected to run into an ambush once the hatch cycled open, but nothing happened. That allowed them to enter the cavernous hold and look around. Roughly half the space was taken up by color-coded cargo modules. Various pieces of half-lit cargo-handling equipment were parked in the surrounding murk, and while some of them continued to radiate heat, there were no signs of Ramanthian personnel in the area. "It looks like we've got the place to ourselves," Snyder said approvingly. "Let's get this over with."

The head end of the space elevator was directly in front of them. It consisted of a massive framework that had been tied into the ship's steel skeleton and supported a computer-controlled winch, which was there to keep the cable from becoming too taut or too loose. A system of guides kept the cable centered and prevented it from making contact with the surrounding hull.

Lower down, just below the crosspiece that supported the winch, Snyder could see the platform from which the specially designed self-braking cargo modules could be loaded onto the elevator. Ichiyama saw it, too, and immediately made his way out onto the ramp so he could place his charge. Knowing that one demo pack would be more than sufficient to sever the cable, Snyder was content to merely watch.

Such were the legionnaire's thoughts as a giant pincer plucked the cyborg off the deck and lifted her up into the air. The loader was at least ten times larger than the T-2, and controlled from a compartment located in the machine's blocky head, which was where a technician and inveterate slacker named Gontho was taking a nap until a series of radio messages woke him up. But rather than rush into battle, and potentially get himself killed, Gontho was content to remain where he was until the enemy cyborgs appeared below. At that point it was a simple matter to take the loader off standby and grab hold of the nearest war form. It was a feat the Ramanthian could accomplish with minimal risk to himself. Now, confident that he could destroy the Confederacy cyborg, Gontho began to squeeze.

Snyder "felt" the huge metal pincers start to close and struggled to free herself. But the legionnaire soon discovered that she was going to die. Not like the last time, when the medics pulled her back from the brink, but for *real*. "Blow charge two," Snyder ordered over the radio. "And do it *now*!"

"*What?*" one of the gunner's mates wanted to know. "I thought Ichiyama was going to plant the charge."

The cyborg knew the bio bod couldn't see them and was understandably confused. "He is," Snyder confirmed, as her torso shattered under the unrelenting pressure. "But I want you to trigger charge two, and I outrank your swabbie ass. So, blow the pack *now*!"

The bio bod did as he was told, and the demolition charge attached to Snyder's chest exploded. It destroyed the Trooper II *and* blew a large hole through the loader's torso. Gontho swore as his controls went dead, the machine staggered, and tried to right itself. The Ramanthian hit his hatch release, but nothing happened, as Ichiyama called on the gunner's mates to trigger *his* charge. That produced a flash of light, but no sound to go with it, as the space elevator fell through the hole and into space.

The significance of that registered on Gontho's brain just as the technician felt the badly damaged loader topple forward. He screamed, "No!" but there was no one to hear as both the operator and his machine fell through the hatch and entered space. However, rather than follow the cable down as the tech feared he would, the War Gontho soon found himself in orbit. He screamed over a radio that no longer worked, watched his air supply continue to dwindle, and cursed his rotten luck. Gontho had an excellent view of Jericho, however, even if he couldn't find the serenity to enjoy it, and was soon consumed by the surrounding darkness.

The space elevator didn't fall at first because roughly half of it was still weightless. But without the dreadnaught to serve as a counterweight, it wasn't long before the bottom half of the twenty-three-thousand-mile-long cable began to pull the top half down. And once that process began, the rest was inevitable.

The first hint that something was wrong came when the free-falling superstrong cable began to tug at its anchor point. Which, unbeknownst to the Ramanthians stationed around it, had been systematically weakened during the installation process. Metal clanged on metal, and the cable jerked spasmodically, thereby alerting the ground crew to the fact that something was wrong.

However, it wasn't until an upper-level jet stream took hold of the errant space elevator, and pulled the free end toward the east, that the Ramanthians realized the full extent of the danger they were in. But it was too late by then, as the cable plucked the anchor assembly out of the pyramid it had been secured to and converted the heavy-duty hardware into a massive flail!

A variety of competing forces caused the superstrong cable to whip back and forth across the adjoining airstrip. It leveled the terminal building with a single blow, made a loud *cracking* sound as it cleared fifty acres of jungle, and erased what remained of Camp Enterprise. Then, as Jericho's gravity continued to pull more of the line down, the ground shook as if in response to an earthquake.

The cable was falling in five- and ten-mile-wide coils by that time. Each loop scoured portions of the planets clean as they were pulled sideways and sent clouds of dust thousands of feet up into the air. And it all happened so quickly that Vice Admiral Tutha had no more than felt a tremor and looked up to see hundreds of flyers burst out of the Hu-Hu tree in front of his headquarters building than the free end of the cable destroyed 80 percent of his command. Including the prefab structure he was standing in.

But by some stroke of luck, Tutha emerged from the debris almost entirely unscathed, to wander aimlessly through the wreckage of what had been the largest military base on Jericho. Later, after all of the damage assessments were completed, it would turn out that 7,621 Ramanthians had been killed by the collapsing space elevator.

Of course that wasn't the worst of it. Somewhere, out in the jungle, tens of thousands of nymphs were about to emerge from the wilding stage. Which was the moment when teams of specially trained civilians were supposed to gather the youngsters in and begin the process of socializing them. Except that wouldn't happen now. Which meant thousands of the Queen's offspring were going to die, or worse yet, live like savages in the primordial jungle.

The horror of that was too much to bear, and the officer was busy searching the debris for a weapon with which to take his own life, when the energy stored inside a coil of cable located three miles to the north was suddenly released. The whiplike space elevator lashed out, erased a major river, and sent a tidal wave of soil flowing over the spot where Tutha had been standing. Meanwhile, many miles above the devastation, the *Imperator* floated free.

19

Where law ends, tyranny begins.

—*William Pitt, First Earl of Chatham*
Speech in the House of Lords
Standard year 1770

ABOARD THE RAMANTHIAN DREADNAUGHT *IMPERATOR*

The *Imperator*'s spacious control room was located deep within the ship's hull, where it was safe from missiles, torpedoes, and cannon fire. Everything except the least likely threat of all: a single alien armed with two pistols. But there Maximillian Tragg was, with a blood-splattered officer lying dead at his feet, and a gun clutched in each fist. Ten Ramanthians of various ranks and specialties stood arrayed before him. Some were frightened, but most were angry, and ready to attack the human if given the chance. Also witness to the tableau, but invisible in the glare produced by the overhead lights, was a tiny sphere. It bobbed slightly as air from a nearby ventilation duct flowed around the device.

"Okay," Tragg said levelly. "Now that I have your attention, listen up. In case you haven't heard, a group of POWs murdered Commandant Mutuu, stole two of your shuttles, and landed one of them on this ship. Now, having cut the space elevator loose, they're going to come here in hopes of taking control. A plan which, if successful, will land you in a Confederacy POW camp. Or," the renegade continued, "you can take me where *I* want to go and return home safely. The choice is yours."

None of the Ramanthians found either option to be very appealing as the ensuing silence made clear. "Let's try it again," Tragg insisted, as he shot a junior officer in the head. "Either you will do what I say, or you will die!"

"All right," one of the officers said, as the reverberations from the gunshot died away. "We'll do as you say."

Batkin had been "watching" the scene unfold via the tiny marble-sized remote, which had threaded its way through the ship's ventilation system and into the control room. "He just murdered another member of the bridge crew," the cyborg said, as he swiveled his globe-shaped body toward Santana. "And the bugs are beginning to cooperate. That will allow Tragg to take the ship wherever he wants."

The two of them, along with a combined force of legionnaires and ex-POWs, had arrived outside the control room, only to find that the access hatch was locked from within. Not by the Ramanthians, as they initially supposed, but by Tragg. Who, having been refused passage aboard a Thraki ship, had taken refuge on the *Imperator*. "We have to get in there," Santana said grimly. "Can your remote open the hatch?"

"Maybe," the cyborg allowed doubtfully. "I could take a run at the door switch. But the remote is so small, it might not pack enough mass to close the circuit. And Tragg isn't likely to give me any second chances."

"But what if we could distract him?" Santana wanted to know. "So you could take two, or even three tries if that was necessary?"

"That would be wonderful," the spy ball agreed. "What have you got in mind?"

"I will need access to the ship's PA system," the officer answered. "So we can talk to Tragg. . . . As for the rest, well, we'll see. Maybe the sonofabitch believes in ghosts and maybe he doesn't."

Meanwhile, knowing that the POWs had cut the space elevator loose, the Ramanthians threw everything they had at the *Imperator*. And, because it was going to take at least half an hour to bring her drives back online, the dreadnaught was an easy target for all of the fighters, patrol boats, and destroyers that came after her.

But at Tragg's urging the bridge crew had been able to restore the battleship's overshields—which meant none of the weapons thrown at her were actually hitting the hull. Not yet anyway, although that could change because the systems involved hadn't been maintained in a long time. And the much-stressed force field could fail at any moment. That possibility was very much on Tragg's mind as the renegade sat with his back to a corner and felt the hull shake as a torpedo struck the ship. The Ramanthians were forced to grab pincer-holds as one of the lights went out and particles of decades-old dust avalanched down from above. *I won't be able to keep all of them under control,* the fugitive thought to himself. *Not for two or three weeks in hyperspace. So it would make sense to kill four of five of the bastards the moment we get under way. But which ones?* Such were Tragg's thoughts as a female voice came over the intercom. "Max? Can you hear me? This is Marci."

Tragg felt ice water trickle into his veins. Did the voice belong to Marci? Who had returned from the dead? No! It was a trick! "You're not Marci," the renegade objected, as his eyes began to dart around the room. "Your name is Mary Trevane."

Tragg wasn't using the intercom system, but Vanderveen could hear him, thanks to an audio relay from Batkin's remote. "No," the diplomat replied. "Trevane is dead. *You* crucified her."

The Ramanthian bridge crew looked on in alarm as the human stood and began to turn circles with both weapons at the ready. "You can hear me," Tragg said suspiciously. "But that's impossible."

"I listen to you all the time," Vanderveen replied. "It gives me something to do while I wait for you to die. I'm looking forward to that. . . . Aren't you?"

The hatch was locked from the inside, but by using the remote to strike the slightly concave pressure-style switch, Batkin could theoretically trigger the door. So while Vanderveen sought to keep Tragg occupied, Batkin sent the tiny device racing toward the switch. There was a loud clacking sound as the sphere made contact with the pressure switch, but the hatch remained stubbornly closed, and the spy ball knew it would be necessary to try again. "What was *that*?" the renegade demanded suspiciously, as he turned toward the sound.

At least two of the Ramanthians had seen the tiny sphere hit the switch, bounce off, and sail away. But they weren't about to say anything as the pistol-wielding madman flew into a rage. "What are you staring at?" Tragg screamed at them. "Get this ship under way, or I'll kill every damned one of you!"

Vanderveen chose that moment to switch personas. "This is Mary Trevane," the diplomat said over the PA system. "You can kill them—but you can't kill *me*. Because I'm already dead!"

Batkin took advantage of the distraction to trigger the remote again. And because the robotic device was part of him, the cyborg went along for a virtual ride as the sphere sped through the air and smashed into the concave surface of the switch, a process that resulted in the electronic equivalent of pain.

But the results were worth it as the contacts closed, power flowed, and the hatch hissed open. Tragg heard the sound and whirled. But Santana had entered the control room by that time. Both men fired, but it was the soldier's bullet that flew true. It hit the renegade over the sternum, and while unable to penetrate Tragg's body armor, packed enough of a whallop to throw the renegade down.

Tragg fired both weapons as he hit the deck, but his bullets went wide as he slid backwards. A series of shots, all fired by Santana, struck various parts of the renegade's body. One bullet creased the side of Tragg's skull, two struck his right arm, and one smashed into his left. The mercenary's pistols clattered as they hit the deck.

That was the moment when a shadow fell across Tragg's scarred face, and Vanderveen stared down at him along the barrel of a borrowed weapon. "My real name is Christine Vanderveen," the diplomat said coldly. "This is for Marci, her brother, and me. More than that, it's for *all* of those you murdered on Jericho."

Tragg tried to fend off the bullets with his badly broken arms, but the projectiles went right through and pulped his face. The *Imperator* shuddered as if in sympathy as another missile exploded against her screens. That was when the president of the Confederacy of Sentient Beings arrived on the bridge. "Now that was a nice piece of diplomacy," Nankool remarked approvingly as he looked down at Tragg. "Good work, Christine. Let's go home."

PLANET ALGERON, THE CONFEDERACY OF SENTIENT BEINGS

Gradually, over a period of months, what had been President Nankool's dining room had been converted into a chamber where Vice President Leo Jakov could receive official guests. Or, as was the case on that particular morning, sit on his thronelike chair and brood. And there was plenty to brood about because, ever since the prison break, General Booly, his wife, and the rest of the Nankool loyalists had been hard at work trying to prevent his confirmation. And with some success, too—if the rumors could be believed. Which was why Jakov felt mixed emotions as Kay Wilmot entered the room. *What kind of news will she have for me?* the vice president wondered as he eyed the diplomat's face.

Wilmot looked tired, and therefore older, which was just one of the reasons Jakov had begun to have sex with potential replacements. And there were other issues, too, such as the fact that the plump official had become far too knowledgeable about both him and his supporters, some of whom placed a high value on their privacy. That was why Wilmot wasn't going to survive much longer regardless of how the upcoming vote turned out. "You look beautiful this morning," Jakov lied, and waited to see her face light up.

"Thank you," the diplomat replied. "I'm pleased to say that I have some good news for you! There are some fence sitters of course, senators who will wait until the very last second before committing themselves, but even without their support it looks like you will be confirmed."

One of Jakov's eyebrows rose slightly. "By how many votes?"

"Two," Wilmot answered. "But," the assistant undersecretary hastened to add, "that hardly matters does it? A win is a win."

That wasn't entirely true, since a narrow victory would inevitably be seen as a sign of weakness, but Jakov forced a smile. "Yes, of course. A win is a win."

The conference room adjacent to General Bill Booly's office was full to overflowing. Maylo was there, as were Colonel Kitty Kirby, Major Drik Seeba-Ka, Margaret Xanith, and Charles Vanderveen. The crowd stirred as Sergi Chien-Chu arrived and people made room for him. "Okay, Sergi," Booly said hopefully. "What have you got for us?"

"Nothing good," the cyborg answered dejectedly. "Based on my polling, it looks like Jakov will be confirmed by a narrow margin."

Faces fell, and there was a chorus of groans as the group absorbed the news. "There is another option," Seeba-Ka said ominously. "The Legion's loyalty belongs to *you*—not Vice President Jakov."

"No," Booly replied wearily. "I know that's the way such matters are settled on Hudatha, but Triad Doma-Sa is working to change that. We have a constitution, plus the body of law that supports it, that we're all sworn to obey. To violate that oath is to become the very thing we despise."

"In spite of the fact that Jakov broke the law," Vanderveen agreed reluctantly.

"Unfortunately, we have no proof of that," the legionnaire put in. "Just suspicions. So, given the political realities, I suggest that everyone prepare for the worst. You should expect to lose your jobs at a minimum. . . . And some of us may face trumped-up charges intended to put us on the defensive while Jakov and his toadies settle in. I'm sorry. I wish things were different."

It was a sobering assessment, and one that left Booly's allies with no choice but to shake hands glumly and go their separate ways. Booly, Maylo, and Chien-Chu remained where they were. "Don't be alarmed if I disappear for a while, the industrialist said as he prepared to leave. "If Jakov attempts to prosecute one or both of you—I'll be back with the best legal team money can buy. And I'll do everything in my power to find out what happened to Nankool as well."

Booly said, "Thanks," as his wife went over to plant a kiss on her uncle's cheek. Then, once the two of them were alone, the legionnaire took Maylo into his arms. The kiss lasted for a while. Finally, when they broke contact, Booly looked down into his wife's beautiful face. "I don't suppose you would be willing to leave Algeron prior to the vote."

"Sure I would," Maylo replied cheerfully. "So long as you come with me."

Booly laughed. "Have I mentioned how annoying you are?"

"Frequently," the woman in his arms replied. "Does that mean you're going to divorce me?"

"Yes," Booly replied. "As soon as I find the time. The problem is that I'm so busy."

"Too busy for *this?*" Maylo inquired innocently, as she put her hand where it would do the most good.

"Hey! We're in a conference room," the general objected.

"So, close the door," Maylo responded huskily. "And let's hold a conference."

And they did.

The space that had once served as Fort Camerone's theater had since been converted into chambers for the Senate. The huge room contained five hundred seats. They slanted down to a flat area and a raised stage. The words, "*Legio Patria Nostra,*" "The Legion Is Our Country," had once been inscribed above the platform in letters six feet tall. And, in spite of the fact that they had been painted over, a keen eye could still make them out.

The first five rows of seats were reserved for senators, who with very few exceptions, were present. Partly because activists representing both sides of the upcoming vote had been working to ensure a good turnout, but also because the confirmation process made for excellent theater, and there was a woeful lack of entertainment on Algeron.

Most of the people present already knew how the vote was going to turn out, or believed they did, but it was common knowledge that the outcome would be close. So close that even a couple of defections could deny Jakov the presidency. That served to keep the level of tension high, and rather than posture the way they often did, the vice president's supporters were maintaining a low-key demeanor.

There were formalities to attend to, including the usual roll call, which preceded a long, rather dry description of the events leading up to Nankool's disappearance and the need to replace him. That was followed by an equally boring recitation of applicable law and a review of the voting process.

Finally, with all of that out of the way, the moment everyone had been waiting for was at hand. That was when Jakov, Wilmot, and a handful of other senior advisors slipped into the chamber and stood at the back of the room. Half a dozen airborne news cams swarmed around the politician to get tight shots as breathless reporters provided voice-over narrations of the historical moment for viewers throughout the Confederacy. Because later, once the outcome was known, the resulting reports would be sent out via the new hypercom technology—a development that was bound to revolutionize both journalism *and* politics.

Then, as the senator representing Earth stepped up to the podium, the cameras darted away from Jakov each seemingly intent on reaching the front of the room first. Booly and Maylo had seats behind the senators, in a row reserved for senior officials, and knew the networks would go to them for reaction shots.

"The voice vote is about to begin," the senator from Earth intoned. "Please provide your name, followed by the political entity you represent and your vote. A 'yes' vote is a vote to confirm—and a 'no' vote is a vote to deny confirmation. Now, unless there are questions, we will proceed."

And that was the moment when Triad Hiween Doma-Sa, who had been visibly absent from the proceedings until that point, entered the chamber via a side door. There was a *thump* as it closed behind him and a considerable stir as the big Hudathan made his way up onto the stage. "Good morning," Doma-Sa said, as he turned to face the audience. "As most of you know I represent Hudatha, and I hereby invoke the provisions of paragraph 3, of page 372, of the Senate Rules and Procedures, which allow any senator who wishes to do so to make a final statement prior to a voice vote."

The Hudathan's unexpected arrival, plus the nature of his demand, triggered an uproar as Jakov's supporters voiced their objections, and the vice president's opponents attempted to shout them down. Because like Booly's, Doma-Sa's loyalties were well-known. And if the triad wanted an opportunity to speak, then it would clearly be in opposition to Jakov.

So the senator from Earth called for order, the master-at-arms thumped his ceremonial staff, and the chief clerk was called upon to check paragraph 3 of page 372, to see if Doma-Sa's assertion was correct. It soon turned out that the paragraph in question was a rather obscure section of verbiage originally intended to allow last-minute posturing by senators who were trolling for publicity. But it was rarely invoked because voice votes were rare.

So after considerable grumbling from the vice president's supporters, it was agreed that Doma-Sa could speak, although it immediately became apparent that a pro-Jakov politician would rise to counter whatever the triad put forward. The Hudathan's voice rolled like thunder as he spoke. "As many of you know, I have been off-planet for the last month or so, having returned only hours ago. And it was while on Starfall, attending a diplomatic function, that I met the Egg Orno, mate to the late *Senator* Orno, and *Ambassador* Orno, who was known to many of you."

That statement was punctuated by a loud *clatter*, as Runwa Molo-Sa opened the same side door through which Doma-Sa had previously entered, thereby enabling the Egg Orno to enter the room. Because of the war, the female was the *only* Ramanthian present. That, plus the shimmering robe she wore, caused everyone to stare at the aristocrat as she shuffled up a ramp and onto the stage. "What's going on here?" one of Jakov's supporters demanded angrily as he came to his feet. "Triad Doma-Sa has the right to speak—not stage a parade!"

That stimulated a chorus of comments both pro and con, as Booly looked at Maylo, and both of them wondered what the Hudathan was up to.

"The rules place no limitations on *how* I choose to speak,"

Doma-Sa rumbled. "So, shut up and listen. The robe that the Egg Orno is wearing once belonged to Ambassador Orno, who wore it when he met with Assistant Undersecretary for Foreign Affairs Kay Wilmot, on the planet Starfall. However, unbeknownst to her the garment you're looking at consists of a photosensitive fabric which recorded everything that passed between them. Let's watch and listen."

There was a loud rustling noise as at least half the people in the room turned to look at Wilmot, and the flying cameras jockeyed for position. The foreign service officer felt a sinking sensation at that point and turned to look at Jakov. It appeared as though all of the blood had drained out of the politician's face, and his jaw tightened as Molo-Sa connected the robe the Egg Orno was wearing to the room's AV system. Seconds later a life-sized holo of Wilmot appeared behind Doma-Sa and began to speak.

"The situation is this," Wilmot explained. "While on his way to visit the Clone Hegemony, President Nankool was captured by Ramanthian military forces and sent to Jericho, where both he and his companions are going to be used as slave labor."

"That's absurd!" Orno was heard to say. "First, because my government would take Nankool to a planet other than Jericho, and second because his capture would have been announced by now."

"Not if the Ramanthians on Jericho were unaware of the president's true identity," Wilmot countered. "And we know they aren't aware of the fact that he's there, because we have an intelligence agent on Jericho, and he sent us pictures of Nankool trudging through the jungle. Images that arrived on Algeron five days ago."

"You came to the wrong person," Orno replied sternly. "A rescue would be impossible, even if I were willing to assist such a scheme, which I am not."

"No, you misunderstood," Wilmot responded. "I'm

not here to seek help with a rescue mission—I'm here to make sure that Nankool and his companions are buried on Jericho."

There was a pause followed by a question. "You report to Vice President Jakov?"

"Yes," Wilmot agreed soberly. "I do."

"Soon to be *President* Jakov?"

"With your help. . . . Yes."

There was more, but the sudden uproar made it impossible to hear, as outraged senators from both camps vied with each other to condemn Wilmot and distance themselves from Jakov. Meanwhile, conscious of the fact that the spotlight would soon shift to *him*, Jakov turned to leave via the back door. But Booly was waiting for the politician—as were a full squad of armed legionnaires. "None of it's true," Jakov said stoutly. "The holo was faked. . . . As *you* well know!"

"Save it for your trial," the legionnaire replied unsympathetically. "And while you're sitting in prison think about this. . . . The penalty for treason is death."

PLANET EARTH, THE CONFEDERACY OF SENTIENT BEINGS

Captain Antonio Santana lay on his back and stared up at the sky. It was light blue, crisscrossed here and there by contrails, but entirely empty until a hawk arrived to turn graceful circles above him. More than a month had passed since the much-abused *Imperator* had dropped into orbit around Algeron, and Nankool had been restored to the presidency. But it seemed longer, since both the officer and every other person aboard the old dreadnaught had been subjected to seemingly endless debriefings as prosecutors worked to amass evidence against Vice President Jakov and his codefendants, even as defense teams sought to counter it, and the news networks fought over scraps of conflicting information. So viewed from the perspective of Earth, the conflict raging out beyond the local solar system seemed to be more about political skullduggery than a battle for survival.

Meanwhile, based on what little information was available, the Confederacy was losing what the legionnaire considered to be the *real* war. The Ramanthians hadn't overrun any major systems as yet, but a number of planets out along the edge of the Confederacy's territory had fallen to the bugs, and the aliens were more aggressive of late. Some analysts attributed that development to a new and more energetic queen. Others pointed to the enormous number of Sheen ships that had been added to the Ramanthian fleet. But the result was the same. The bugs were coming, but the citizens of Napa Valley were oblivious to the fact as they continued to enjoy their privileged lives.

But then the sky was gone as Christine Vanderveen stepped in to straddle the legionnaire and sit on his abdomen. Her hair hung like a blonde curtain around her face, and her skin looked healthy again, as did the rest of her. She was dressed in formal riding clothes. The long-sleeved white blouse served to hide the scars on her wrists. "It's time for lunch," the diplomat announced. "So mount up."

Santana groaned. "Can we walk instead?"

Vanderveen laughed. It was a lovely sound—and one he couldn't get enough of. "Walk?" she inquired. "Why would we want to do that? Especially when we have two perfectly good horses waiting not ten feet away."

"Because it would be less painful," the legionnaire said, as he reached up to pull her down.

"I thought you were a cavalry officer," Vanderveen replied. "A proud member of the 1st REC . . . A man of . . ."

The rest of her words were lost as their lips made contact. Santana was consumed by a vast feeling of tenderness, and everything else fell away. Part of him knew that the war was waiting. . . . But there, on a sunlit hill, the soldier was at peace.

AUTHOR'S NOTE

On January 28, 1945, 121 men led by the pipe-smoking Lieutenant Colonel Henry Mucci of the 6th Ranger Battalion penetrated enemy lines in the Philippines and marched cross-country to rescue 513 survivors of the Bataan Death March being held by the Japanese. Though not based on that rescue, this book was certainly inspired by it and by the unbelievable bravery of both the rescuers and the POWs. For anyone who would like to read a full account of that amazing mission I highly recommend the book *Ghost Soldiers* by Hampton Sides.